Deeper in Sin

By Sharon Page

DEEPER IN SIN

DEEPLY IN YOU

BLOOD CURSE

BLOOD FIRE

BLOOD SECRET

"Wicked for Christmas" in
SILENT NIGHT, SINFUL NIGHT

BLOOD WICKED

BLOOD DEEP

BLOOD RED

BLOOD ROSE

BLACK SILK

HOT SILK

SIN

"Midnight Man" in WILD NIGHTS

Deeper in Sin

THE WICKED DUKES

SHARON PAGE

KENSINGTON BOOKS
www.kensingtonbooks.com

KENSINGTON BOOKS are published by

Kensington Publishing Corp.
119 West 40th Street
New York, NY 10018

All Kensington titles, imprints, and distributed lines are available at special quantity discounts for bulk purchases for sales promotion, premiums, fund-raising, educational, or institutional use.

Special book excerpts or customized printings can also be created to fit specific needs. For details, write or phone the office of the Kensington Sales Manager: Kensington Publishing Corp., 119 West 40th Street, New York, NY 10018. Attn. Sales Department. Phone: 1-800-221-2647

Kensington and the K logo Reg. U.S. Pat. & TM Off.

eISBN-13: 978-1-61773-095-5
eISBN-10: 1-61773-095-5
First Kensington Electronic Edition: September 2015

ISBN-13: 978-1-61773-094-8
ISBN-10: 1-61773-094-7
First Kensington Trade Paperback Printing: September 2015

10 9 8 7 6 5 4 3 2 1

Printed in the United States of America

ACKNOWLEDGMENTS

Writing a book always involves one or two false starts, a few incidences of banging one's head on the kitchen counter, and a crisis of faith—the point at which the book just feels like an illogical mess. Thankfully, that is also always followed by the magical moment where a problem is solved and the story comes together. But even then, the author fears that euphoria might just be wishful thinking. So she turns over the book to her editor.

So once again I have to say thank you to my intrepid and terrifically knowledgeable editor, Esi Sogah, for ensuring this story became the very best it could be.

Thank you also to Kensington for packaging this story so beautifully.

Thank you to my agent, Jessica Faust, who is always prompt and wise.

Thanks have to go to my author friends, who understand all the ups and downs, and who are there to share laughs, tears, and glasses of wine along the way.

But my greatest gratitude, as always, is for you—the reader. I wouldn't be here without you, and I hope you fall in love with Sophie and Cary's story as much as I did.

1

At the tender age of sixteen, I became quite familiar with the expression "From the frying pan into the fire" when I left my severe and overbearing father and ran off to Brighton, where I became the mistress of the severe and overbearing Viscount Mullon. He wore a threadbare nightshirt and a yellowed nightcap, and he snored loud enough to wake the horses in the stables. I decided that my future career as a courtesan would be severely impaired if I did not move up in the world—from viscount to earl, then on to a marquis, to be followed by a duke, then a royal duke (except none are handsome), and thus on to a prince, for the Continent was packed with those, even if England was not.

Besides, if I was to learn the sensual arts, I needed a gentleman capable of teaching them. Poor old Mullon believed fifteen minutes of feeble poking was adequate.

So off I went to London because, as every aspiring courtesan knows, London is filled to the brim with gentlemen.

—From an unfinished manuscript entitled _A Courtesan Confesses_ by Anonymous

London—March, 1820

Gentlemen were *everywhere*.

The ballroom was packed with them. Tall, handsome ones in the first stare of fashion; young, shy-looking ones; balding, middle-aged ones with large stomachs that strained at their waistcoats.

Standing at the entry of the assembly room, Sophie Ashley took a deep breath. Thank heaven for the manuscript left to her by her mother—the mother she had never known. In that unpublished book was everything she needed to know about being a courtesan.

Except for one thing, Sophie noticed, that her mother had not mentioned.

Cyprians—those elegant courtesans who looked like proper ladies—did not choose men for their appearance. The oldest men had the loveliest women in their arms—cooing, caressing women in low-cut, glittering gowns.

Apparently, they were the wealthiest men.

There were perhaps a hundred gentlemen in the room, and only about a dozen or so women. The group of celebrated courtesans who held these balls gave out few invitations to other women. In fact, they tried very hard to keep other women away.

Sophie took a deep breath.

Her best friend, Belle, had been horrified by Sophie's plan. Belle hadn't wanted her to go through with this.

But Sophie had to do this. She *could* do this. She had come to London to become a sought-after courtesan because she had no other choice. She and Belle and the children were all going to starve unless she found work. And any respectable work wouldn't pay her enough to support three young children and two grown women.

She and Belle had pooled their money—enough to buy Sophie a pretty gown, a fancy bonnet, fine gloves, and new slippers. With sufficient left over for two things: a stage fare to London and a fortnight's rent on a room. She had evaded the pickpockets and lecherous men. She'd managed to flee from crafty, wicked madams who tried to lure—or grab—young women off the streets. From her mother's manuscript, she'd learned there were balls and parties and risqué salons held before the regular Season. Gentlemen wanted to pick their paramours before they were caught up in the social whirl of London.

She had taken more of her money, had gone to Drury Lane, and had asked around until she found an opera dancer named Kate willing to tell her all about London's famous Cyprians—for a small bribe. Following Kate's instructions, she had found her way here, to the first lavish Cyprian ball of the year.

Kate had warned Sophie that the events were invitation only—and the invites came from the courtesans. When Sophie had asked how to get an invitation, Kate had laughed rather loudly. Most of the courtesans would not invite a young, pretty interloper onto their turf, Kate pointed out. There was one who would, but only if she were well bribed, and Sophie knew she didn't have enough money left for a substantial bribe.

So Sophie had devised a plan to get in.

She'd slipped in through the kitchen entrance wearing her plain brown wool cloak. Then she'd used the servants' stairs and doors to get to the ballroom. There she'd stripped off her cloak and boots and dull bonnet, and hidden those in a room beside that stair.

But since she had sneaked in, she had to keep out of the sights of the hostesses of the ball. So she remained along the outskirts of the ballroom—in the shadows along the wall, on the fringe of the glittering, beautiful crowd.

She looked toward the center of the room. There, in gowns of the gauziest silks and muslins, wearing glittering jewels and décolleté necklines that showed jiggling breasts, were the courtesans. The rulers of the London's ladybirds.

Sophie swallowed hard. It felt like months, not days, since she'd sat with Belle and plotted out how she would do this. The planning she'd done with matter-of-fact courage.

That courage faltered now.

She hadn't exactly *forgotten* that being a courtesan meant she had to entice a man to be her lover. She wasn't exactly *innocent* after all. She had made love with Samuel, her intended, before he'd gone to war.

She had ended up pregnant, had borne a baby out of wedlock, and now she was ruined.

"But I don't regret it!" Sophie whispered defiantly to herself. She'd *loved* Samuel and he was going away to *war* and she'd wanted . . . she'd wanted to show how much she loved him. She'd wanted a night of passion to treasure! And while he'd been gone, she'd borne him a son—a son he'd never seen. Of course, having a baby had marked her as a fallen woman and had meant everyone had turned their backs on her, but she hadn't cared. Not then.

But now, looking at all these men, some handsome and some not, she didn't know if she could do it. Could she make love to one of these men without being in love?

She must. She absolutely, positively *must*.

The last thing Fitzwilliam Montcleif, the Duke of Caradon—known to friends as Cary—needed was advice on how to find a bride.

But his friend Grey, the Duke of Greybrooke, was now happily married, and he and his wife were expecting their first child. Grey was determined to push the rest of the so-called "Wicked Dukes" into the same state.

"I know your past has affected you, Cary," Grey said quietly. "But what you need to do is find a mistress. Go to one of the Cyprian balls, find a woman, make love to her. Put the past behind you. It can be done—I'm proof of it."

Cary set his brandy down, untouched. He faced Grey across the polished expanse of the desk in Grey's study. He sat in a wing chair, along with Grey and Sax—the Duke of Saxonby. "That's not going to work."

Grey looked serious. "It will. You told me you haven't been able to be with a woman since you were kept a prisoner of war in Ceylon. You need to prove you can forget the memories that haunt you, and make love to a bride. The only way to find out is to take a woman to bed. I'd drag you there and find you a pretty female myself, but I'm now a happily married man. I have no interest in being anywhere near courtesans . . . and Helena would kill me if she found out."

"Your wife wouldn't kill you. She knows you would never stray." Cary leaned back, trying to appear normal and relaxed. His friends did not know the real reason why his time as a prisoner of war had left him unable to take a lover. "I am glad Helena tamed you, Grey. You were damned unhappy before."

"Haunted by my hellish past. And because of that, I understand what you are going through." Grey hesitated. "I had problems. . . . The memories, the suspicions, the fears almost prevented me from loving Helena as she deserved. Those burdens made it hard for to me to accept her touch or—" He broke off, blushing faintly. Amazing, since his friend used to be a rogue and a scoundrel with women, notorious for his plentiful, wicked sexual exploits—that often involved ropes, whips, and shackles.

"I have to try to get over it," Cary admitted. At the questioning looks in his friends' eyes, he continued, "I received a letter from my mother today. She's worried about me, and since she is in delicate health, it is hurting her to fret about me. It's killing her, damn it. She told me bluntly that anticipating my marriage—and the chance to see grandchildren—would give her the will to live. So if I don't want to kill her, I have to find a bride."

"Your mother was always blunt."

"Good with guilt." Cary sighed. "But in this, she is right."

Cary's mother had stayed at the country estate while he had gone to London. For the last few months, the duchess had been constantly tended to by his younger sisters, as well as companions and nurses. Her heart was weak, and she became exhausted easily. But she had given him her ultimatum.

If he didn't want to kill her, he had to get married and have a child.

Cary knew it was blatant blackmail. But she was ill—and she was right. It was his duty to marry and have children.

His father, when he was alive, was enraged by Cary's reluctance to marry a wealthy, landed young woman and expand the family's power and influence.

Brusquely, coldly, his father would remind him that a duke was merely a stepping-stone to the next generation—a studhorse with a house. But when his father talked of the time Cary would inherit, he could see the revulsion in his father's face.

"So you have to go to the Cyprian ball and get over these damnable memories of yours," Grey continued. "Prove you can take a woman to bed without the war horrors getting the better of you. Sax will go with you. I want to make sure you leave the place with an enticing lover," he said magnanimously.

"I don't need an escort to a Cyprian ball," Cary protested. "I'm thirty, damn it."

"If I don't send Sax with you, you won't go, Cary. I damn well know it."

Sax had been drinking his brandy, relaxing in one of Grey's wing chairs. He looked up. Grinned. "I'll ensure he finds a ladybird tonight. You have to get back in the saddle, Cary."

"It's not that bloody simple," Cary muttered.

But his friends ignored him. And hell, he would not tell

them what had happened to him when he'd been a boy of five. That secret would die with him.

Sax stood. "Come on, Cary. Time to unleash the Cyprians on you."

Cyprians, Sophie had discovered, were not particularly kind. They competed for gentlemen like wildcats. Claws were being bared around the room.

And she was holding her breath right now—as was everyone else around her—because two of the women were fighting. It was a real fight, where they tore dresses and slapped each other and pulled hair.

And it was all over a tall, broad-shouldered man with golden blond hair and stunning pale blue eyes.

A quarter-hour before, when the clock had struck twelve, the blond gentleman had entered the ballroom. He was accompanied by another gentleman who possessed unusual silver hair paired with dark brows and lashes. Both men were handsome, but the blond man with the light blue eyes was utterly stunning, in Sophie's opinion.

She had been near the door, so she'd watched them come in. The friend had to push the tall blond man through the door.

But the moment the blond man passed the threshold, every gaze riveted on him. Voices rose in murmurs. She caught fragments of what they said.

"He is here!"

"He rarely leaves his house—except to go to his club."

"They say his imprisonment left him half mad. That he has never smiled since he returned."

Imprisonment? Surely, a gentleman could not have gone to prison, gotten out, and come to a Cyprian ball. For such a man to go to the gaol, it would have been for something terribly serious.

Sophie was curious, so she kept watching.

With his golden hair, which fell in careless waves, the tall man looked like a knight from a fairy tale. He didn't look like someone who had been in a prison cell. And though both he and his friend were stunningly handsome, the gentleman with the golden hair captured most of the attention.

Sophie had been driven to find out who he was.

So she could overhear, Sophie had sidled close to a dark-haired courtesan who wore a bright pink gown and garish jewels. "The Duke of Caradon," the woman said, almost licking her lips, "has ignored every invitation to draw him out. Ever since he was held as a prisoner of war in Ceylon. As a war hero, he would be adored everywhere, but he leaves his home only to ride in the Park and go to his club. So now that he is here, I am going to snare him before those other harridans get their claws into him."

A prisoner of war. A hero. Sophie swallowed hard and suddenly realized *she* wanted to snare him.

He was so beautiful. And obviously noble.

He would be the perfect protector.

And she ached deep inside. And she felt all warm. And rather anxious.

She knew what that meant—she desired this man.

Though a little voice warned she should know more about him before she bluntly told him she wanted him to take her to his bed.

The other woman, who had henna-dyed red hair, chuckled. "You are too late already. Another woman has already pounced."

Sophie whirled around to look. She'd waited too long!

A woman had hold of the duke's right arm and clung to him like an octopus. She was a Cyprian with hair so pale it was almost silver-white. She wore a white gown, white gloves, and pale white diamonds. She was pressed so tight against his side that his arm was almost trapped in the cleavage of her breasts, which were served up like two mounds of jelly, jiggling over her low-necked bodice.

"Ha! You are old enough to be His Grace's mother!" A young girl launched forward, saucily thrusting her chest out. A young woman with jet-black hair and a lovely face, pink cheeks, huge violet eyes, and a Cupid's bow mouth. She wore a pale pink dress.

"How did you get in here?" the pale-haired woman demanded with the ice of a duchess. "You were hardly invited. You are so fresh off the farm, you still smell of it, Sally."

"I do not," Sally declared. "You smell like me grandmamma, Angelique. And ye're as old as she. I'm sure His Grace is not interested in having a mistress who's so old."

The girl stalked over to his side and gave the white-haired courtesan a shove. "Tell her, Yer Grace. Which of us would ye like on yer arm?"

The poor gentleman gave a desperate glance back toward the door. His friend laughed gently. "I think poor Caradon would enjoy a waltz."

The black-haired farmer's daughter rushed forward and clasped his free hand. "Will ye dance with me first, Your Grace? I should be ever so thrilled if ye would."

The girl tried to pull him with her and jerked him away from the courtesan called Angelique. Sally gave a laugh of triumph, which was quickly smothered by the sound of fabric tearing.

Her gauzy skirt lay half on the floor, and her white petticoats were exposed.

And her skirt was captured under Angelique's slipper.

The girl's face screwed up, turning purple with rage, and she screeched, "Ye did that on purpose! Ye wicked cat! Ye frumpy old hag!"

"You are a stupid little brat," the woman hissed.

Sophie shivered. Angelique looked elegant and placid, but her voice exuded sheer fury. She snapped her fingers and, suddenly, footmen appeared. She pointed regally at the younger girl. "This young woman has no invitation. She is to be removed."

"I do too have an invitation."

"Bribed your way inside, I presume."

"Well, what if I did?"

"Angelique, my dear, do not be so hard on the young woman," said the duke's friend.

But the footman approached the girl, obviously ready to toss her out.

The girl let out a screech of fury and jumped at the older courtesan. She tore at the woman's hair, pulling it from its pins. She pulled at Angelique's necklace and tore it free, sending it clattering. Which got her a sudden, vicious slap. The young woman slapped back.

"Ladies! Ladies, please!" shouted the friend.

The golden-haired duke had not said a word. Never had she seen a man with a more wooden expression. He looked terribly uncomfortable.

In front of him, the two women tore at each other like lionesses fighting over a lion. The Duke of Caradon stepped forward and picked up the torn dress and the broken necklace. Then he pushed his way in between the two women. Without saying a word. A few blows rained on him by accident.

Angelique drew back as he handed her the necklace. Her chest rose with fast breaths. Her eyes blazed. "Your Grace, I apologize."

The duke said nothing.

The black-haired girl pulled her ruined skirt fabric from his hand and flashed a considering look at him. Then she burst into noisy tears and ran.

"Damnation," the duke muttered. Then he followed.

"Wretched girl," Angelique snapped. "Those tears were as false as her bosom—she puts padding in her bodice."

If the duke's friend was shocked, he didn't look it. Instead, an amused smile twitched his lips. Indeed, he was handsome, but the golden-haired Duke of Caradon was the most gorgeous gentleman Sophie had ever seen.

"You played a foolish game, Angelique," the duke's friend stated. "He's always the knight errant. Though I should thank you—pursuing a tearful damsel in distress will be good for him."

Angelique began to sputter, but then she smiled. Smugly. "I'm afraid, Your Grace, you are wrong."

His friend was a duke too? Sophie hadn't expected that. And the golden-haired duke was returning.

"Where's the girl?" his friend asked.

The duke looked as if his cravat were squeezing him tight. "This was a mistake, Saxonby," he muttered. "The girl flung herself on me and then, when I agreed to make her my mistress on the spot, got in a fury at me, jumped in a carriage, and galloped away."

He possessed a deep voice, slightly hoarse, as if it were a labor for him to speak. Perhaps that was why he'd let his friend talk instead.

"Viscount Willington's carriage," Angelique pointed out. "The girl already has a protector and obviously hoped to replace him with you. She's a bold, ambitious little vixen. Not the type for you at all, Your Grace. But I do apologize for that scene. Her dress was torn by accident, but she came at me like a wildcat."

"After all, Angelique, it is not as if you are legendary for your intense passion and your even more intense temper." The duke's friend Saxonby grinned.

"I shall endeavor to make your evening more pleasant, Your Grace."

"Sure she will, Caradon." A man standing in the crowd near them leered openly at Angelique's figure.

Sophie realized men had gathered around, drawn by the women's fight. While they all looked as if they'd enjoyed it, the duke looked as if he had sat on a hedgehog—downright un-comfortable.

"It is fine, Angelique," the blond duke said. "It's been a long time since I've gone anywhere but my club. I hope your neck-lace can be repaired."

"I heard of your terrible experiences in Ceylon. Perhaps I could give you some comfort."

"I'm afraid I'm not ready for comfort yet." He bowed, then walked away, followed by his friend Saxonby.

"Let us get you a drink, Caradon," the friend said.

Sophie was intrigued. The Duke of Caradon was simply gorgeous.

It had been a long time since Samuel had died at Waterloo—almost five years. For the first time in a long time, Sophie was looking at a man and her heart was pounding hard and she was thinking: *I would want him to kiss me.*

Then she saw Angelique's expression, and Sophie gasped. The courtesan watched the duke leave with pure venom in her eyes.

Angelique turned and glared at her. "Who in heaven's name are you?" she snapped.

Damn! Sophie didn't answer. She whirled around and raced after the two dukes, trying to vanish into the crowd and also, hopefully, meet the dukes.

She almost caught up to the men. Then she overheard Sax-onby say, "Don't give up hope—you'll find a female yet. Re-member your obligation to your nursery."

Now Sophie was mixed up. Nurseries were for babies. Was the duke looking for a wife? *Here?*

Even from behind, the Duke of Caradon was obviously hand-some. His golden hair shone in the candlelight. He had impressive shoulders and a narrow waist. Neither he nor Saxonby were be-having like the other men here—no pawing, loud laughter, silly remarks.

The thing was—her mother had been a courtesan. She hadn't known, not until she had fallen pregnant with Samuel's child. Then she had been told the truth. But she didn't know her mother's name. Her mother had left her a letter, signed only "Your Mother." And her mother had left the unfinished manuscript. The story of her life as a courtesan. In it, her mother insisted that sometimes protectors fell in love with their mistresses.

But a gentleman of the aristocracy wouldn't be so eccentric as to look for a wife at a courtesan's party, would he—?

A hand grasped her arm and roughly jerked her back. "Don't run away from me," snapped a hard female voice. "How did you get in?"

A hand in a white satin glove clutched her arm. Hard enough to make bruises.

It was Angelique.

Sophie knew she must be honest. She had seen this woman cattily rip another woman's skirt, but surely, Angelique would understand how desperate she was. Surely, that would touch her heart.

"I've just come to London," she explained. She spilled out her story as fast as she could. In her fancy corset, designed to make her look fashionable, she quickly became breathless. But she managed to get out every detail—about how she had been turned out of her house, how her husband was dead (it wasn't exactly a lie; though Samuel wasn't really her husband, they had *planned* to marry), and how there were three children who needed food.

Angelique looked at her coldly. "So you saw fit to come without an invitation. Admittance is granted only by me or by the other five hostesses."

"I know it was wrong, but you must understand, I have to support my family," Sophie pleaded. "I have to ensure the children have enough to eat. They have the best natures and have endured everything so far very stoically. We've had to sleep in barns. And scrounge for food. Though we've never stolen anything. We would never—"

"Do please stop," Angelique demanded. The woman put her gloved hand to her head as if Sophie's hurried words had given her a headache. Angelique's eyes narrowed—she had huge eyes, and though her hair was pale blond, her lashes were dark and her eyes were rimmed carefully in black. "You are following the Duke of Caradon. I want to know why."

When Sophie didn't answer, Angelique tightened her grip. "You will tell me now."

Sophie remembered how Angelique was draped over him. He must be her favorite. Which meant Sophie definitely could not have him. And she could not get thrown out. Not now. "I wasn't following him. I just walked this way. And I guess so did he."

"Do not be smart with me," the woman snapped. "I saw you watching him. You want him." Angelique's dark eyes peered at her. The woman's gaze roamed over her. "Are you acquainted with the duke?"

"Oh no."

"But you want him."

"Oh, I—" She thought quickly. "I only came because I must support the children. I must find a protector, but I wouldn't dream of trying for a duke. And I could see he knows you. And he wouldn't be interested in me, if he already knows you." She feared she was laying it on a bit too thick, but what else could she do?

"What is your name?"

"Sophie, ma'am."

Angelique's brow lifted again. Then a slow smile touched her lips. "Well, Sophie, I have just the gentleman for you. He is a marquis—which is only one step below a duke. Fabulously wealthy."

Next thing Sophie knew, she had been hauled to the side of

the ballroom and introduced to a short, pot-bellied man with gray hair. A marquis.

She tried to smile politely as Angelique almost shoved her at the man and walked away. Angelique was offering her a rich man, but she could *not* become this man's mistress.

An excuse hovered on her lips—

The marquis grasped her forearm and spun her so her backside faced him. He stared at her bottom. And smacked his lips.

"What a marvel is Angelique. A discreet payment, and she exceeds herself. You are perfect, my fair Callipygian. They speak of the Venus Callipyga, but your buttocks are far more shapely, generous, and beautiful."

His hand grabbed and squeezed as if to test his point.

Good heavens.

"Please, my lord, you're hurting me."

"Nonsense!" he barked. "You've got a lovely fat arse. It's made to be squeezed."

"I'm afraid it is not." Sophie tried to shove his hand away, to no avail. He might be gray-haired, but he possessed a solid, bulky build, and he had strength. He kneaded her bottom so painfully, she whimpered.

"If this is meant to entice me, it does not—you are hurting me, sirrah." The courtesan book may have spoken about satisfying a peer's unusual tastes, but she could not do this.

"Nonsense. You're all tougher bits of horseflesh than you pretend to be. Nothing wrong with a bit of rough play, my dear. I pay well for it."

"Whatever rough play you have in mind, I have no intention of taking part."

"I'll make it well worth your while to play my games. Shall we start with giving those lush globes of yours a good spanking?"

Her skirt came up—yanked by his hand. While she recoiled in shock, he slapped her bottom—hard—with his open palm.

"Ow!" she cried. She stomped. On his foot. He wore polished boots and she wore slippers, but he jerked back in shock. His face went red with fury—

His gloved hand closed in a fist, and she tried to run, knowing he meant to hit her. But his reflexes were too quick. He grasped hold of her skirt and pulled her back, slamming her hard against the wall.

She lost her breath and fought for it. Tears burned. "Don't hit me. I don't want to be spanked or hurt. Please!" she cried desperately.

His fleshy lips curved in a smug leer. "A little resistance makes it all the more delightful—"

He broke off as he was pulled back abruptly. Sophie was yanked away from the wall and found she was suddenly planted behind a large male body. Stunned, she drank in broad shoulders, a jacket of dark blue, and hair of burnished gold.

It was the Duke of Caradon.

"Back off, Halwell," he said. "The girl is mine."

2

At first I took to the stage, for I had a fine singing voice and I looked very fine in breeches. Gentlemen flocked to Drury Lane to see my most stirring performances.

Gentlemen were so bold as to assume that a bouquet of roses or perhaps a sparkly bracelet could buy my favors. But I was not to be swayed—until, finally, I succumbed to the ardent pursuit of a most gloriously handsome man.

Having found the perfect earl—he was thirty, unmarried, and in possession of a vast fortune. He was of course the Earl of R—— (as you see, if you are a reader of a male persuasion and of exalted position, a lady can select her moments to be discreet if she is motivated to take such action). Every feminine wile I bestowed upon him seemed to leave him inexplicably cold.

So frustrated was I that I visited his bedchamber one night. Aroused to a fit of feminine pique, I wandered about his bedchamber while he slept, slapping my legs with a riding crop. The thwack of the leather both awakened and aroused him. With glowing eyes, he shyly suggested that he roll upon his stomach and I playfully punish him accordingly.

At that moment, my eyes were opened to the odd and out-landish tastes of gentlemen.

—From an unfinished manuscript entitled *A Courtesan Confesses* by Anonymous

"Caradon, goddamn it, I could call you out!" the marquis sputtered.

For the first time, Sophie saw the Duke of Caradon smile. Watching the sun rise would prove pedestrian after this. His smile was not a wicked grin like his friend Saxonby's, but something so beautiful, she would have been tempted to launch a thousand ships to get him.

"Not wise, Halwell. I spent years soldiering, and I am a very good shot."

They were going to shoot each other? Shock, as well as sheer fury, gripped her. Sophie exploded out from behind the duke. "You can't be serious, both of you! You can't shoot at each other over this! What if you kill each other—?" She thought of Samuel. He had gone to battle to serve his king. He had been young, with everything to live for, and a bullet had stolen his life from him. "How can you want to shoot another man over something like this? Dear God, after there has been war. What an utterly stupid—" She broke off.

Caradon stared at her with startled pale blue eyes.

"My dear—"

"No!" she cried. Samuel would have much preferred to have lived. He gave his life for his country, and she had shed tears every day for two years after he had died, wishing he could have survived. How could these men throw away their lives so casually?

"It's senseless and horrible, and I won't let you do it," she declared.

"Keep out of this, you daft, idiotic girl," Halwell snapped.

She glared at the marquis. "You behaved in a most ungentlemanly manner, my lord. You assaulted my person. You have absolutely no right to be insulted, and you should apologize."

"Apologize? To a tart?" Halwell laughed. "I think not."

"I would be careful," Caradon spoke smoothly, but his tone made Sophie shudder. There was something about it . . . something strong, threatening, something that made her feel she would most definitely obey and be careful.

"You assaulted my new mistress, Halwell, so I am the wronged man here. Should I call *you* out? I will do it right now if you push me further. Then you'll face me over a pistol whether you are willing or not."

The bulky marquis withered before her eyes. Light revealed beads of sweat on his brow. "I didn't see you with the lass, Caradon. I had no idea she had been spoken for. Angelique presented her to me. The fault lies with that manipulative whore, not with me."

"Begone." Caradon's voice, though raspy, was like ice.

The marquis, who had been so bullying with her, scurried away.

The duke turned to her. "Are you all right, Miss—"

"Sophie." Her voice came out breathless. "Sophie Ashley."

"The Duke of Caradon. At your service."

In this circumstance, any woman would gawk in blatant admiration at her handsome rescuer. Sophie did just that. Staring at his dark-lashed, blue eyes—light blue like a wintery morning sky—she observed, "He's a bully. He fell apart when you called his bluff. You certainly didn't have to do much to scare him away. Why is he afraid of you?"

The duke's brows lifted in surprise. She thought he wouldn't answer, then he said, "Because I actually am a good shot." He said it in a self-deprecating way. "So Angelique threw you into his clutches?"

Sophie nodded, then shuddered. "She couldn't have known what kind of a gentleman he is."

The Duke of Caradon shook his head. "She did, I am sure. She was his lover once."

Sophie squirmed. "Why did she do such a cruel thing? If Angelique wanted rid of me, why not just send me packing?"

"To Angelique, it was probably a humorous joke."

"But I explained why I came here without an invitation. I told her why I must be here. I have to find a protector, or my family will starve. And she thought the marquis would be perfect for me. I thought—I thought she seemed sympathetic."

The intensity of his gaze made her cheeks heat. It wasn't a lustful stare though. Still, she took swift breaths—something about the way he was looking at her made her short of breath.

"Women like that are not sympathetic to young, pretty competition." His eyes searched hers. "You have a starving family, you said. The truth?"

Tears stung her eyes. She couldn't cry—she didn't look pretty when she cried. So she nodded. "It is true. Three children." Her voice was wobbly and strained as she battled those wretched tears.

"Yours? You look so young." He wore a troubled expression.

Oh goodness. He definitely did not appear happy at the idea of children. And one was indeed hers. "My—my friend's . . ." she began. Then she stopped. Maybe it was easier just to stop at that. At a not-exactly-a-lie moment. "My friend and I had both lost our homes, so we have been trying to survive together."

He didn't say anything for several minutes. She was not sure what to do. In her mother's manuscript, it was advised that mistresses had contracts—legal papers that laid out exactly what they could expect and what they could keep after the affair. When would he mention that? Talk about the house, the carriages, the jewels—the things she desperately needed.

And she hated herself for thinking so avariciously.

She'd never cared about this kind of thing. She would have been content to have been as poor as church mice with Samuel. But having a child changed everything.

She could starve. She couldn't let children starve.

When he didn't say anything, her stomach began to gnaw with worry. "You called me your new mistress, Your Grace," she reminded him. "I am very thrilled to begin my—uh, my new position."

He had been studying her with a frown. Now he started. "I beg your pardon?"

"I am your new mistress?" She said it hesitantly. Why didn't he either make her the offer he was supposed to, or at least try to kiss her or something?

"Oh, that," he said carelessly. "I wanted to scare off Halwell. Of course you are not my mistress. We have barely met."

Disappointment crashed in on her. It was true. She knew nothing about him. But he'd come to her rescue. He was honorable. And—

And so gorgeous, she felt breathless around him.

"You would be quite fine to be my protector," she assured him. "I would be happy with you as my choice."

His brows shot up again. "My dear—"

A sharp, grating sound interrupted them. She knew what it was—the first draw of a bow over strings. The strains of a waltz filled the ballroom.

"A waltz!" She jumped up and down with excitement. Now that Halwell was gone, she was in no danger, and she had met a dazzling duke who was perfect to be her protector, she remembered where she was.

In a *ballroom*.

Where there was music.

And waltzing!

No one in Newton-Upon-Avery, where she grew up, had

ever waltzed. But she had seen drawings of the elegant dance. It was so close. So shocking. The woman rested her hand on the man's shoulder and clasped his other hand. The gentleman—

His free hand pressed to the woman's low back. Right over her bottom.

A shiver ran through Sophie at the idea of Caradon's hand there. A delicious shiver.

She had wanted to try waltzing with Samuel, but he'd thought her mad. He'd preferred kissing and groping, which, truth be told, had been very hot and exciting.

"We must waltz." She grasped his hand. "Could we? Please?"

"You are amazing," he said.

"Thank you! Now quickly, before we run out of music. I have no idea how to do it, and I might be dreadful, but it would be so wonderful to try!"

The duke shook his head. "Sweetheart, you obviously do not belong here."

"Of course I do! I wasn't actually invited, but I do want to be here. I need to be here."

He did the worst thing in the world. He chuckled.

She was new to the business of being a courtesan, but her mother's manuscript talked of men being besotted, being mad with desire.

Chuckling was not good.

The duke stood his ground and, with one tug on her hand, brought her back to him.

"I mean, you are sweet and innocent, and this world will corrupt you and ruin you," he said. "What you need to do, love, is go back home. This world"—he encompassed the packed ballroom of eager gentlemen and brazen women with a careless nod—"is filled with vice and sin. Some I suspect you can't name. Some you don't even know exist."

She lifted her chin defiantly. "I am worldly."

"I doubt it." Softly, he said, "Do you have the fare for a coach to take you back home?"

"I can't go home. If I go home with empty hands, three innocent children starve."

Home! What a horrible word that was for her now. She had no home. She had been thrown out. She belonged nowhere. And as their money had dwindled, she and Belle had been forced to take shelter in worse and worse places. For a while, they had taken refuge in an old barn.

Home for her was anywhere they could keep rain off their heads.

She couldn't go back without the hope of money to support her family. Not when the revolting Earl of Devars was waiting to get her into his clutches. He wanted her to be his mistress, but he was even worse than the Marquis of Halwell.

Devars made Halwell look a perfect gentleman, he was so awful.

"There must be another way for you to save your family other than shatter your innocence and give your body to a gentleman in exchange for money," Caradon said. "What of marriage? You are a sweet and beautiful young woman."

With an illegitimate child. She couldn't marry. Making love to Samuel before he had gone to war had destroyed any chance she had of a proper marriage. "There are reasons I can't marry," she hedged. "Anyway, there is more to being a mistress than just going to a man's bed in exchange for money. A courtesan is *so* much more than that."

"Is she?" A smile played around his lips again. "How is a courtesan more?"

She wished he would stop smiling as if he found her immensely amusing. It didn't bode well. He should be panting with desire for her, promising her the world. That was what a protector was supposed to do, according to her mother's memoirs.

"Well, we would have stimulating conversations," Sophie said. "I would be a very gracious companion. I would make him very happy and please him. And perhaps there might be love between us."

"Love," he repeated. The duke looked at her as if she had just told him the sky was green and had always been that color. Then he shook his head. "I can't let you do this. It's not right."

He looked like Dr. and Mrs. Tucker had when she'd had to admit she was expecting a babe. So disapproving.

But he was a duke. Wealthy beyond imagination. He had no idea! "It is easy for you to say. You have no idea what it is like to watch children sob quietly because their tummies are empty and they know there is no point in asking for more food because there isn't any!" Frustration crackled inside her. "And if you think it is so wrong for a woman to be a courtesan, why are you here?"

"I didn't say it's wrong for a female to be a ladybird. It's wrong for you to be one."

His light blue eyes and his long dark lashes dazzled her. How gorgeous he was. But this was hopeless. Utterly hopeless.

"I do thank you for your advice," she said stiffly. "Since you are so obviously experienced with my type of situation—I'm sure you've spent many days penniless, with an entire family dependent on you—I will most assuredly take your advice to heart."

She began to walk away.

His hand clamped on her wrist, stopping her. "Walking away from me to find another charming protector like Halwell? You will get on a coach and go home if I have to plant you on the seat myself."

She could not go home! Lord Devars knew what she had done to save her family—the terrible thing she'd had to do. He could have her arrested and transported.

He had offered her a bargain. He would not turn her in to

the magistrate if she became his lover. He'd given her a fort-night to make her decision.

But if she had a lot of money, she could move Belle and the children somewhere Devars would never find them. And if he came after her, she could use her wealth to make them all disap-pear.

She could not go back just as impoverished as when she'd left.

"I can't go home with empty hands. I can't look at all their faces and see the disappointment and the fear. I don't care what the price is for them to be fed and safe and happy."

"You do not even understand the price," he said softly. "Come with me."

"To dance?"

"No. I have something to show you."

Cary had planned to find a mistress here tonight so he could prove to himself he could take a bride and have a normal mar-ried life with her. A married life that would include children—the duty of every English peer.

Instead, he was leading a pretty dark-haired young woman down a quiet corridor to show her the truth about life as a courtesan.

At every turn in their conversation, Sophie Ashley had star-tled him. She had argued with him. She had disdained him for being here, looking for a mistress when she was looking for a protector. She'd accused him of being clueless when it came to poverty. Then, when she'd decided she'd wanted to waltz, she'd guilelessly tried to drag him onto the dance floor. She'd sparkled like a jewel, her lovely green eyes wide and full of hope and ex-citement. Her innocence had shone like a candle's glow.

She had sweetness. And spirit.

She was an absolute beauty with her lush black hair and massive green eyes.

And she had no bloody clue what she was doing.

He led her out of the ballroom and down one of the corridors of the assembly rooms. He took her farther from the crowd, where the hall was darker. For all appearances, it was deserted, but he knew differently. At these events, a Cyprian usually lured a lover away to ensure she sealed the deal.

He heard a soft, saucy giggle. A guttural male moan.

Cary led Miss Ashley to the door, which was partly open. A low fire burned in the grate, giving enough light so she could see into the room.

He pushed the door open farther.

And stood back, expecting to see poor Miss Ashley freeze, go chalk white with shock, then back away in haste.

Seconds later, he realized she was still watching. And she was not pale.

Her cheeks had gone sweetly pink. Her eyes were wide. Her tongue swept over her lips in a way that was like a sharp slap to his cock, telling it to wake up.

He watched her tongue sweep, tap, lick, and make her full, lush lips shiny and moist.

"Look what she's doing to him." She gasped breathily. "Goodness, look at his face. He's transported by pleasure. He loves every minute of it." She turned to him and dabbed her full lips again. "Do you like to have that done to you?"

What was she talking about? Cary realized he had better look. . . .

The duke had pushed the door open so stealthily, so gently, there had been no sound. Sophie had heard giggles and groans and, when she'd looked, she had seen a naked woman get down upon her knees in front of a man who wore only a white linen shirt.

The Duke of Caradon stood right behind her. She couldn't see him, but her whole body was aware of him. She was quivering, waiting to feel him touch her somewhere.

Then he leaned closer, and his warm breath washed over her ear. She let out a moan. She couldn't help it. Her whole body went tense and wobbly at the same time.

He sucked in a sharp breath.

At the same moment, in the room, the woman's head moved between the man's legs. She took hold of his thick staff with both hands and pointed it to her mouth.

Was she going to kiss it?

Not quite. The woman parted her lips and ran her tongue along the veined staff. Licking him! Heavens, now she knew what was meant when her mother wrote that a woman could control a man with her lips. She'd thought that her mother had meant conversation.

She'd seen Samuel's penis, all erect and eager. This man's was fatter and bigger. Really, it was quite shockingly large. The man, with his dark wavy hair, was rather handsome. But Sophie found it hard to keep looking at his face.

She couldn't resist looking lower.

The man's erect member disappeared inside the woman's mouth. The woman kept her lips all soft and relaxed around him, holding him tight as her head bobbed and she took him in and out. The woman sucked so hard, her cheeks hollowed.

Oh, the man looked as if he were in heaven. Obviously, men really did delight in this. Could she—?

She thought she could, with the Duke of Caradon. Her rescuer.

Then the man in the room put his hand on the woman's head to hold her in place and pumped aggressively into her mouth. Harder and faster. Saliva dribbled down the woman's chin. She took hold of his buttocks and the ballocks between his legs, and squeezed both.

The man threw his head back. "I'm coming!" he hollered, and surged his hips forward. Grabbing his hips to hold him in place, the woman sucked so hard, she made the man scream. Literally.

"Bloody hell," the Duke of Caradon muttered behind her. He pulled her back from the door. His broad chest rose and fell with his heavier breaths. "I wanted you to see the kinds of things a man would demand of you."

"I would be willing for a man I desire," she said honestly. "For *you*."

The duke rubbed his temple. His teeth were gritted. "That is not what I wanted you to discover."

She moved toward him until her bosom almost brushed his chest. "But it's what I have discovered. I'm not innocent, you know. I certainly know what desire feels like. And I want you." She gripped the duke's solid forearm and surged up on her tiptoes.

Sophie sucked in a scared breath, softened her lips, and pressed her mouth to his.

Her first kiss as a courtesan!

3

It was never my intention to move downward from an earl to a viscount. Practicality dictated I use my wiles and my expanding circle of acquaintances to conquer greater peaks. On the arm of my devoted young earl, I was introduced to marquesses and dukes.

So imagine my great surprise when I was whisked behind a large tree in Hyde Park by an eager and gorgeous viscount, and I found myself unable to put a stop to his ardent seduction.

It was not because he was insistent, but because I was weak at the knees, bubbling with desire, and I had never wanted a gentleman more. He lifted my skirts, and in two clever strokes of his thumb, he brought me to the climax that had eluded me through several love affairs. "You are mine now," declared the viscount. (Alas I cannot even indulge the first letter of his name. He would be identifiable at once.)

"No, I am not."

"I made you come, my dear." His youthful and beautiful face glowed with pride. He was twenty-one, and I was younger by two years, but I felt worldly wise.

"There is more to this business than simply that."

"You are filled with arrogance, are you not?" I added.

"When you see me without my trousers, you will know why."

"Harumph," I said. "A coronet on a carriage is of more importance to me than an endowment in your linens."

"You are a heartless thing."

"A woman cannot be practical and have a heart. The combination is far too volatile."

He merely laughed. "You will come back. I know you will."

I stuck my nose in the air and left him. But in a few stolen moments behind the trunk of a spreading oak, I had fallen in love.

—From an unfinished manuscript entitled *A Courtesan Confesses* by Anonymous

Her soft mouth moved over his in a messy attempt at a kiss. She was all eager enthusiasm, fierce passion, and no finesse. It was like capturing a willing but innocent dairy maid behind a milking shed. Miss Ashley had to be innocent, probably virginal.

Cary stood there, letting her lips rub against his. Until his conscience demanded to know what in hell he thought he was doing.

Stop kissing her and save her, damn it, it said.

I will. In a moment. This is just a kiss. I'm not going to ravish her.

You might, answered his conscience. *When was the last time you kissed a woman? When was the last time you were burning inside? If you unleash the lust boiling in you right now, you'll regret it.*

I have no intention of unleashing anything.

She kissed him harder, mashing her lips to his. She pressed her bosom against his chest. Then she clasped his hand and lifted it to caress the swell of her breast. Full, encased in tight silk, her bosom was a warm temptation.

Apparently, she's ready to unleash.

Shut the hell up, he muttered to his conscience.

He should drag his hand away, but she held him there, his palm cupped around the sweet, full curve swathed in pale blue silk.

God . . . he groaned against her mouth as a surge of desire almost cut him off at the knees. In his confining trousers, his cock straightened.

He hadn't had sex in a long, long time. He couldn't even relieve himself in his own hand anymore. Memories flared up at any kind of sexual contact.

Moans fluttered from her lips. Her fingers clung to his shoulders. She had closed her eyes, and her jet-black lashes curled against her cheek, making her look even more sweet and innocent—though she kept his hand clamped against her soft, lovely tit.

She was trying for a sensual kiss, but she kept pushing her lips around on his with no real skill and no idea how to inflame his desire.

Despite this, his cock was as heavy as an iron bar, pulsing as all his blood rushed to it. His body was on fire.

Damn, what in hell was wrong with him?

He believed her story—he believed she had people to support and she had no other options. He believed it, and it made his heart ache. She was so lovely, and she had no idea what happened to most girls who tried to find a rich protector. He had to make her see the truth. He had to do something to save her—

Wanting to lift up her skirts and bury his aching cock in her lush heat was not going to save her. She was innocent, and if he fucked her, he would be taking that innocence. Only monsters did that. . . .

His memories snapped at him like growling beasts secured by tethered collars. Soon the chains would break, and the dark tormenting images locked in his head would overwhelm him.

His cock swelled and throbbed as if to shout: *I'm here. It's been a long time, so I thought you might have forgotten you've got a cock.*

She moaned into his mouth and shoved harder against him.

Memories exploded in his head, dark and vile. They clawed at him, trying to pull him down.

No. No, hell no . . .

If he didn't stop, what in hell was he? A blasted monster.

Cary jerked his hand free and away from her round breast, and broke away from her mouth. "Stop," he growled.

For a moment, she stared at him as she'd forgotten who he was, where they stood. Then she moved close to him again and touched his forearm. "Why are you stopping? That was dazzling. My heart is pounding, and my skin feels as if it's on fire. I've never felt like this. You wanted me to see what courtesans do to their protectors. Don't you want more?"

"No, I don't want more," he said tersely. "I want to frighten you so much that you run back to the country and find yourself a good, solid dimwitted husband, and you understand how precious and beautiful your innocence is. I want you to know how much you will regret it, every day of your life, if you let your innocence be taken away from you."

Sophie didn't understand. The duke had pulled back from her and shut the door to the room. Now he shoved his hand through his blond hair and scrubbed his jaw. He kept doing all these things that spoke of nerves, of regret, of some intense emotion coiled up inside him.

"Didn't you like it?" she asked again.

"I did." He hesitated. Then continued, in his deep, hoarse voice, "But it was wrong. Wrong of me to plunder your innocence."

"Even if I want you to?"

"I can't," he growled. "Even if you want me to. For me, touching or kissing like that starts out hot and erotic and exciting, and then it changes."

She gaped at him. Pure, raw agony showed on his face. He looked worse than she had when she'd cried herself sick after being thrown out of her house and being told she was actually the daughter of a whore, and her blood was as immoral and rotten as her mother's.

"What's wrong? I don't understand, Your Grace."

"I can't explain it, Sophie. That kiss brought back a memory I don't want to have."

"I did something wrong then."

She'd felt his passion when he'd kissed. She'd felt his erection straining in his trousers. But also in the strong, sensual way his mouth moved over hers. His tongue had slipped into her mouth, and she'd been transfixed, realizing how much that mimicked sex, and she'd been sure he wanted her.

She wanted him. Even though she barely knew him—she *wanted* him.

It was just like with Samuel. She'd known, from the very first moment she saw him, she loved him.

She might be tumbling into love with the duke.

"You did everything right," he said softly. "Except to choose to kiss me. I'm no good, Sophie. Tonight is making me realize that."

"That can't be true!" she said in a fierce whisper.

He was *perfect*. He was everything she'd dreamed of in a protector.

He was watching her face, his handsome face drawn in a frown. "We're leaving," he said abruptly.

Sophie gasped at the inside of the Duke of Caradon's carriage. Velvet seats of dark crimson, a polished wood floor, silk on the walls, and brass lights. The ceiling was painted with all the delicate beauty of an Italian master—she'd been raised in a doctor's house, and he had had a large library filled with books. One of Dr. Tucker's prize possessions had been beautiful plates of famous paintings of the Renaissance. This was every bit as spectacular.

Her heart drummed a song of hope. Caradon claimed he was taking her to a place to show her the error of her decision—to show her what happened to most hopeful courtesans. She had protested at first. She had to become a courtesan, no matter what.

But once the carriage started off, she realized what this meant.

He liked her!

He must care for her; otherwise, surely, he would have given up on her.

She knew he had not whisked her away from the ball because he had some nefarious intent. Why rescue her from Halwell if he had? And he'd stopped kissing her because he thought she was innocent. She would have to make him see she was not.

He had deposited her on the seat, where she faced the way they were traveling. He sat opposite. The carriage lamps made his hair glow like it was gold spun by fairies. His eyes were so unusual. In the light, they were as pale as diamonds—almost silvery.

She smiled at him, glowing with joy.

He looked at her with suspicion. "Why do you look so happy?"

She couldn't announce what she had figured out—that he liked her. She must be careful. In the book, her mother had pointed out that a woman must be able to tell when a man is smitten, and she must use that knowledge carefully. Sophie was not quite sure what was meant by "carefully," but she knew she had to heed the advice.

"I am in a carriage with a handsome duke. It's rather exciting." Joy bubbled into her voice.

"And you are hopelessly naïve. I haven't told you where we are going—though if I did, it would sound no safer. I told you I intended to show you the error of your decision to become a courtesan. You know nothing about me. I could be a damned evil villain, I could be intending to hurt you, and you still came into my carriage with me, trusting as a lamb."

"I don't think I am naïve. People did say I have always been hopeful and always look for the good in things." Well, she had, until she had been thrown out when enceinte. "Anyway, I can tell you don't want to hurt me."

"You can't tell anything of the sort," Caradon said shortly. "Some of the most cruel and vicious people hide their violence and perversions behind kind smiles."

She shivered. "Are you warning me? I have known an evil man. See—I am not completely unknowing. I do know you are nothing like him, for example."

"I won't hurt you, Sophie. But there are so-called gentlemen who will."

"Yes, I do know that. They live in more places than London." And one of them—Lord Devars—would have her in his clutches if she didn't get settled in a role as courtesan, if she didn't get money. "There is a solution. A way I know I won't end up with a terrible, dangerous man. I just have to convince you to take me on truly as your mistress. Isn't that why you were there? To find a mistress? I am more than willing to take on the role. And you would be perfect for me."

He looked worn-out and rather grim. "How would I be perfect?"

"You are rather wonderful," she said bluntly. "You're handsome. You came to my rescue. You are good and kind. And you are a duke. So you see, you are perfect."

"You are the most remarkably ingenuous woman I've ever met." He sighed.

Impulsively, she leaned forward and planted both of her hands on his knees. His legs were long, splayed so they fit in the carriage without bumping her legs. "But don't you see it would be the perfect solution? You get what you want. I get what I want."

"Miss Ashley—"

But she jumped in. "You can't save me. I can't be saved. And I won't be, not at the expense of my family. It's my fault we are in such trouble—" She sank her teeth into her lip. Her words had run away with themselves.

Of course, he caught it at once. "Why is it your fault? What happened that you feel you have to ruin yourself?" His tone was filled with tenderness. He looked truly concerned.

He really did care about her.

And she cared terribly about him. Already.

But she could not tell him of what she'd done and that she had a child—and what she'd been forced to do when they'd needed money. "It's just that I'm the only one who can become a courtesan. And I have my book, so I know what to do and what to expect."

"You have a book?"

"A memoir written by a famous London courtesan." She couldn't help but speak with pride about her mother. She didn't know her mother's name, but from the journal, she knew her mother had been pursued by dukes, earls, and even royal princes. Mrs. Tucker had called her mother sinful. The woman admitted she had only agreed to take in Sophie because Dr. Tucker wanted to do it. Her mother had given them a lot of money to support her upbringing. But to the doctor, Sophie had been an experiment—the doctor believed a good upbringing in a decent household would result in a decent girl.

He had been proven wrong, Mrs. Tucker had declared with venom.

The duke's voice brought her back to the present. "A book is what spurred you to come to London to become a courtesan? My God, Miss Ashley, you are so sweetly unsophisticated, it is a wonder you haven't plunged into trouble before."

She swallowed hard. She *had,* but she couldn't let him know that now.

If she wanted to land him, she must get him lusting after her, desiring her, wanting her.

She had to try to seduce him. In some way.

She quickly stood and moved across to sit on his lap. But he caught her by her bottom before she could land on him. "No, Sophie." He leaned toward the window. "We've arrived."

"Where are we?"

"A brothel."

Panic hit. For a moment, her faith in him wobbled. "Why are we here? Are you going to sell me to them?"

He rolled his eyes heavenward. "Now you understand that you have to be wary. You are far too impulsive. But no, I am not going to sell you to a brothel. I want you to see what can happen to young women in London."

"I'm going to become a Cyprian. I'm not going to work in a brothel."

"What if you do not become a highflyer, one of the elite courtesans? What then?" he asked.

"I *will* become one. I am highly determined to do it—and that means I shall succeed! And I would be perfectly fine, if you would be my protector."

He did not answer. The door to the carriage opened, and without another word, the duke jumped out, ignoring the steps. He held out his hand and clasped hers to help her down.

Awareness rushed through Sophie in a big whoosh. She tingled all over.

Surely, it was plain to him—the magic that happened when their hands touched.

She saw the glow in his eyes as he looked at her. The fire in them. But he quickly shook his head as if to wave out the fire of desire the way you would wave out a match.

He did feel the same intensity!

Yet he was refusing to acknowledge it.

What she would do in that brothel was seduce the reluctant duke. He said he couldn't kiss her because he was haunted by terrible memories. But surely, kissing and sex would make him forget his awful memories.

She wondered what they were. But it didn't matter. She had to pleasure him as it was described in the book. Then, for sure, he would want her to be his.

The duke propelled her toward the door of a narrow house on a dark street. "Come, Sophie. We are going inside. I am going to teach you a lesson tonight and make you see sense—if it kills me."

Sophie let the duke lead her into the brothel. The town house, jammed between others on the rather seedy London street, was neither well kept nor derelict. A burly man at the door greeted them with a grunt, and she was whisked inside. Heat crept through her silk gown and plain brown cloak—she had gathered up her cloak when they had left the ball.

She glanced into a parlor filled with women. Most of them wore thick lip cream and had kohl smeared around their eyes; and they were dressed in nothing but their shifts and loosened stays. They lounged, looking bored and fed up. They looked up hopefully at Caradon, but he shook his head. He had a quiet word with the grunting doorman, who then disappeared. Minutes later—minutes where Sophie took furtive looks at the prostitutes—a tall, thin woman appeared. The woman wore a gown of heavy red velvet festooned with lace.

Caradon and the woman conversed, too quietly for Sophie to hear.

This was not going to be her future.

The tall woman smiled at the duke and pointed upward.

Caradon returned to her. "Upstairs," he said.

She followed him up, and he took her into the first room on the upper floor. A sagging bed with four posts stood along one wall. There were a few glowing coals in the grate, and a lamp sat on a rickety-looking bedside table.

Sophie moved to him. Goodness, he was tall. The top of her head only reached his chest. She gazed up at him—at his strong jaw, wide full lips, pale blue eyes that looked almost like silver in the faint light. Her heart hammered. Her legs felt funny—weak, shaky.

She touched his chest. He pulled her hand away. "This, my dear, could be your future."

Then, inexplicably, he walked to the wall and pressed his face to it as if he could see through. There was paper with a painted pattern of faded flowers plastered to the wall.

The duke motioned her over and clasped her shoulders, positioning her exactly where he had stood. Now she saw a glint of light coming through the wall. There were two tiny holes.

"Shouldn't they repair the wall? Someone could see through."

He looked a bit smug. "That's correct. They are peepholes, intended for you to watch. Men enjoy doing it."

He was trying to shock her. She couldn't let him. She couldn't let him scare her away.

It took a while to focus through the small holes and figure out what she was seeing. The room was decorated in garish colors—dark reds, purple, yellows. A canopied bed sat in the middle of the room. A small fire burned in the grate, and candles burned on the tables.

Squinting, she saw two round, naked, white bottoms.

Women's bottoms.

"That can't be right."

The duke came up behind her. His hands gently touched her arms. A light touch, but how she quivered.

"What can't be right?"

"There are two people in there. Both women."

The woman's gowns were bunched up, and they squirmed around on a bed.

"There are three people in the room," Caradon said.

His breath whispered past her ear. How it tingled!

She strained to see. There wasn't anyone else—

A guttural chuckle sounded over the women's giggles and moans.

There was a man in the room. Heaven only knew where—

Then she knew, because she saw two naked, muscular arms emerge from the tangle of sheets and wrap around the two women's waists. The man was on the bed, under the two prostitutes.

The man pushed one girl onto her back and rose up over her. He had a long body, bulky with muscle, and dark brown hair. His buttocks were as taut as knotted rope.

"Isn't he being greedy? Two women? What does he do, have them take turns?"

"Likely a protector might ask you to do it," the duke responded. "You should learn."

In the room, the man tugged down one of the woman's bodices, and while he couldn't work it down very far, he freed one plump breast. That woman was blond. Her hair was a blousy mess, her lip color smudged. The other woman had bright red hair hanging to her waist in curls. The three of them squirmed on the bed like kittens. Each woman took turns grabbing at the thing hanging between his legs. He had the most enormous . . . prick, as it had been described in the book. She had only ever seen Samuel's. This was monstrous. And it swayed as the women tried to grab it and stroke it and bat at it.

"That is the Marquis of Stonely."

"Rather apt," she muttered.

She heard Caradon surprised laugh behind her.

Then Stonely managed to get the blonde's two breasts freed. And he suckled one while the redhead caressed and licked the other.

"Shocked?"

"I don't know. It was shocking, but . . . look, the blond woman seems to be enjoying it. I'm not that shocked anymore. I feel all warm. And excited."

"You are supposed to be shocked."

"Well, I was . . . for a while."

"You are missing the point of this, Miss Ashley."

"I'm learning about being a courtesan. Isn't that the point?" She half twisted to look back at him. "Is this the sort of thing you want?"

"No," he growled. "Not what I want. But what many men want."

"But I don't want many men. I only want you."

He shook his head. "That won't happen, Miss Ashley. It can't."

She couldn't imagine anything happening *but* that. It was all she wanted.

"So you might end up with a man like Stonely. He doesn't make love with a woman; he pounds into her. He doesn't care about her pleasure. He's too busy trying to prove himself."

"Prove what?" she asked.

Stonely got out of the bed, strutting like a rooster. With his large hands, he pulled the redhead to the edge of the bed. Roughly, he yanked off her unfastened dress. He positioned her on her stomach with her legs over the bed and her naked bottom in the air, facing him.

Then he barked, "Come here" to the blond woman, and she complied. She was plump, her lush bosom spilling out of her dress. She swayed a bit, and Sophie saw many empty wine bottles in the room.

"Get a move on," Stonely said, grumpily.

Perhaps she could see the duke's point. Stonely looked aroused, but not as if he were enjoying himself. He was driven, obviously, by desire.

But where was the breathless excitement he should be sharing with a partner, the thrill of making love together?

"Hurry up, girl," said Stonely, then he picked up the plump girl, who had long, long legs, and positioned her on top of the first girl. She lay on top of the first girl, stomach to the redhead's back. Her bare bottom was on top of the other girl's, also pointing at Stonely.

Then Stonely chucked. A dark, leering laugh.

He sounded just like Devars, and Sophie flinched.

She couldn't retreat—Caradon stood behind her.

The blonde on top twisted to see him. "Put your prong in me now! I'll grip you much tighter than she will. I've got skill, and I can milk your big, thick prick. I can do for you much better than she can."

"No, you can't!" the redhead protested.

"Yes, I can. I'm very, very good."

"Not half as good as I!" shouted the redhead

"Can we stop arguing," groaned the man, "and let me get on with it?"

Then he proceeded to move his jutting erection to point at the redhead, and he thrust into her with one fast punch of his hips. He banged vigorously against her bottom, rocking the two girls on the bed. At a few thrusts, his face was red and sweating. Then he jerked out of the bottom girl and thrust back into the top girl.

"I don't see why I have to be on the bottom," the redhead complained. "She's squashing me."

"And I like the idea of her big tits squashing you. Now silence, while I put my rod up your delicate little arse."

"Good lord," Sophie whispered. She had no idea about that!

Caradon bent close to her. "From this angle, I can see your cheeks are flaming red." His hand slid around her waist, making her gasp.

But the trio on the bed didn't notice the quick, sharp sound, fortunately.

"I—I just didn't know." She had to bluff her way through this.

"Do you think you would want to share your man with someone else?"

"Maybe he wouldn't want to." That hadn't been in her mother's book. Nor that other thing he'd said he was going to do. Maybe the courtesan world had changed since her mother's day. Maybe men did expect more shocking things.

"Remember that men take mistresses because they want the sexual games they cannot expect from their proper wives."

"What do you mean—wives?"

"You must know many men who take mistresses are married."

Sophie swallowed hard. That was true. Her mother's journals mentioned that some of her mother's lovers had been married, but usually to wives they despised.

But could she do that—help to betray another woman?

"You aren't married," she pointed out.

"Give up on me, Miss Ashley," he growled. "I couldn't kiss you. I could not fuck you."

She flinched at the word. "I don't see why we couldn't try. And if you won't have me—there must be, somewhere in England, another man as wonderful as you. It's the only hope for me."

He made a strangled sound. "Damn it, why do you have to be so stubborn?" He grasped hold of her elbow.

"I have to know if you will try," she said. "If not, you will have to return me to the ball, and I will have to find someone else."

She hoped the thought of losing her might spur him to make an offer. She hated to manipulate, but she was desperate, and what else could she do?

"Would you tell me why you can't kiss me? Why you can't—make love to me?"

He hesitated. Then he growled, "No. I can't talk about it. But I will show you one more thing."

What would it be? It had to be more scandalous than a man with two women. "You won't scare me."

"Then you are a fool. But I don't think you are. I know you are intelligent. Certainly intelligent enough to understand this is a dangerous game."

Cary saw what he was looking for as soon as he and Miss Ashley left the brothel.

He drew her along the lane and stopped near the entrance to a small, dark alley. From there they had a view across the street to the front of a small pub.

Faint light eked out of the dirty windows of the corner pub. One street flare burned on a distant corner, and the halo of yellow light faded to gloom where they stood. But the light from the pubs and the doss-houses illuminated a short, broad woman who wore a dark velvet dress and a large dark bonnet.

"There's a woman there, leaning against that brick wall," Miss Ashley whispered. "She looks ill. We must help her."

Impetuously, she launched forward, but Cary grasped her forearm and stopped her.

"Wait," he said.

Laughter spilled out of the pub as the door opened. Voices shouted after the figure who stumbled out. A large man, bent over so he looked as ungainly as a large bear. He stumbled to-and-fro on the sidewalk, and screeching laughter flew out of the pub at his attempt to walk.

"Is that a man? I can't tell, for his face is as dark as the night. Heavens, his skin is black with dirt and soot under his cap."

"I believe so," Cary answered.

Built like an ox, the man lumbered down the street. Then he stopped, lifted his head, and peered in the direction of the woman.

The woman crooked her finger. "Aren't ye a strapping one?" she cooed. "Want a little company this evenin'? This is me price." She named a figure—a few pennies.

Cary glanced at Miss Ashley. Her face had paled, and her eyes were wide.

"Here," the woman coaxed, reaching for the man's beefy hand. "We'll slip around the side of the pub, in that little opening there, where it's quietlike, and I'll lift me skirts for ye."

"She cannot do that! Out on the street!" Miss Ashley's face grimaced with sympathy for the poor woman.

"She probably only wants enough for a glass of gin," Cary said.

"Well, something should be done."

Cary sighed. "I donate to charities that help women like her. But they are often in the grip of an addiction. No amount of help, caring, or kindness can save them then."

"I will not end up this way. Not selling my body for pennies on the sidewalk." She gazed at him. "I will be careful. Just because these other women fell into disaster, doesn't mean I will. For a start, I won't drink gin."

"Gin is an escape, especially when you are doing something you have to do that torments your soul."

"If you want to save me, all you have to do is make me yours." Her eyes met his.

God, she was lovely. Her eyes were the most intriguing color he'd seen. Her irises were a deep green, but rimmed in paler green, which made them look as iridescent and ever-changing as a forest of sun-dappled leaves. Long dark lashes swept over them. She was no demure lady; she was tremendously expressive. And impetuous. And hard to shock.

In bed, she would be amazing. He could tell. She had sexual curiosity—which would make her a superb sexual partner.

But he didn't debauch innocents.

It made him angry with himself that he felt desire for her.

He, of all people, should not behave like a lust-driven animal.

"Why can't you kiss me? I can't understand why a young and healthy gentleman cannot make love. It makes no sense? Or—oh, is it that you prefer other men?"

"No, that isn't it," he said sharply. "I have made love to plenty of women in my life. But then—then something happened to me that changed me."

"You were a prisoner of war. But why would that make you not want to kiss?"

"Stop."

But she gripped the sleeves of his jacket and launched up onto her toes. "I know you desire me. I felt your desire for me when you were pressed against me on the wall, when I was watching through the peephole."

"I don't ravish virgins," he said sharply.

"Then you are in luck because I am not a virgin."

The duke's brows shot up. "I don't believe it. You screamed your innocence in the way you kissed me."

Sophie flinched. Had she been so terrible? "But it's true! I—I was married." It was an awful lie, especially since Samuel was killed before he could marry her.

But she had to go on and make the duke believe her. "So you see, I was married, and I had . . . relations with my husband."

He raked his hand through his hair. "But you are still innocent. Innocence isn't a physical thing. Having a husband gave you some sexual experience, but it didn't dim your starry-eyed sweetness. Angel, this isn't a game of semantics. You had a husband—what happened to him? He didn't desert you, did he? I'll have his head on a platter if he did."

He sounded so angry. "He died. At Waterloo." That was the truth. It made it easier to forget the bald-faced lie she'd just given him.

"I'm sorry."

"So you don't have to worry about ruining me." She went up to him, then squirmed right up against him and put her arms around his neck. He pulled them off.

"I'm not going to have sex with you," he said flatly. "Desecrate the wife of a noble soldier? I could never do that."

She was confused. Somehow she had made everything worse by her revelation that she wasn't a virgin.

"You said you won't do it because of terrible memories. I could heal you."

"God, no, you can't—"

He broke off. Tensed. The duke stood utterly still. He reminded her of an animal scenting prey—she had lived all her life in the country. He had the same expectant stillness, the same coiled tension, of an animal ready to attack. "But I know you are hurting," she went on. "I want to help." She did. It was more than just becoming his mistress. He'd saved her, and he was obviously in pain, like a lion with a thorn in its paw.

She wanted to pull out the thorn.

Caradon hadn't answered. He'd cocked his head as if listening to the breathing of the stews.

"I want to help you—" she began again.

"Quiet. Get back, behind me," Caradon growled quietly. He was staring at the dark alley lane a few feet away from them.

"What is it?" she whispered, but the duke grabbed her and hauled her off her feet, forcing her to stand behind him.

Then Sophie heard a muted, shuffling sound. Footsteps coming from the shadows of the alley.

4

Here I was, a courtesan who had snared a most handsome marquis, yet I was slipping away from my lovely new house to meet an arrogant viscount who had done nothing for me except give me physical pleasure.

He was a most irritating man. I did not even like him.

He would tie my wrists together with a white silken cord, and I would wait on the bed while he undressed before me. I would be utterly nude beneath my cloak (though I did wear stockings, for to don slippers without stockings seemed quite wrong).

The Marquis of N—— was without flaw. My desire to flit away from the charming nest he had provided this pretty bird was without explanation. Goodness, on the first night he came to me, he brought me a necklace of twenty diamonds. I counted each one, doubting his claim. Of course, it was an offering of apology.

But I was like a poor opium eater—the pleasure in bed I received from the viscount was a habit and a need I could not conquer.

And even though I knew he would be the architect of my downfall, I continued to return to him. . . .

Until the night I met the perfect duke. Suddenly, I had a choice—the fulfillment of all my dreams and hopes and plans in the person of the duke, or the fleeting physical satisfaction provided by my glorious auburn-haired viscount. An easy choice to make . . .
Yet I could not do it.

—From an unfinished manuscript entitled *A Courtesan Confesses* by Anonymous

His soldier's instincts knew something was approaching even before Cary heard the footsteps or saw the flicker of movement in the shadows.

Miss—he still thought of her as a "Miss"—Ashley's face went white. She began to gasp. "De—" Then she broke off and whispered low as if reassuring herself. "It's not. It *couldn't* be."

Interesting, but there was no time to pursue.

Bouncing lightly on his feet, Cary wished he had a damned weapon. He'd brought nothing. No pistol. No blade. Not even his walking stick with its secreted sword.

Three men emerged from the dark alley.

The center man was short, fat, potbellied, and bowlegged, with missing teeth and a smug smile. The flanking one on the right was tall and built like a pugilist, with arms that bulged in tight sleeves, and a head that merged into shoulders because his neck was so thick. The last one had a ferrety look, small and lithe. All three stank of smoke and foul sweat.

All were armed with blades. Dangerous, but at least it meant they had to engage in combat and not just shoot him with a pistol.

Cary smiled. He had his fingers on his cravat, working at its knot.

"Ye won't be grinning for long," spat the fat one in the center.

In a split second, Cary pulled his cravat loose, then tore it free of his collar.

The fat footpad lunged, sending his bulk forward with surprising speed. The blade glinted as the footpad swiped. Cary had wound the cravat around his wrists and held it as taut as a leather strap. He caught the footpad's forearm in it, stopped the blow, and used the man's momentum and the strained cravat to throw the man backward.

But the fat assailant was back in a heartbeat, staggering forward. He slashed, but Cary feinted and moved, avoiding the thrusts.

One slice went into his coat. Cary knew the man would stab him eventually if he shoved the knife out long enough. It was just the odds. Maybe three blows in a hundred would be what he needed.

So don't let him get in one hundred blows, he told himself.

Cary's leg swung up as he darted from another thrust, and his momentum sent his boot into the man's jaw. Howling with pain, the man flew backward.

Hulking like a gorilla, the second one came forward. Gorilla Man circled, moving slowly and clumsily. He lunged and slashed, but Cary moved like lightning. He had noticed a pile of discarded barrels in the alley—mostly ripped apart by children in search of wood to burn for their families. There were a few pieces left. Cary jumped around the second villain—Gorilla Man—and grabbed one of the nail-studded slats. Holding it in two hands, he blocked thrust after thrust.

He knew he had let himself get on the side of the alley, away from Miss Ashley.

He had to get to her. But the first bastard—Fat One—was back in the midst. With his feeble weapon, Cary fended off the blows from Gorilla Man and Fat One.

Where was the third? Cary landed a kick to the chest of Gorilla Man, and the bulky footpad went down with a thud.

Then Cary heard it—a sound that paralyzed him. A woman's scream. A cry of pure fear and shock. Miss Ashley. Cary had found the third bastard.

He shoved Fat One back and jumped over Gorilla Man. The blade came up and caught his inner thigh. Pain shot through him. Cary had been to war. He knew damn well how to fight through pain.

The third villain, a small man who looked like a weasel, had grabbed Miss Ashley and dragged her toward the alley.

Miss Ashley was kicking and attempting to punch the man. She cried out in a sound that sounded like frustration, not terror now, and she bit the man's arm.

That bought her freedom, and she hauled up a piece of the same barrel. She rose to strike—

Cary ran toward her, his leg ice-cold but also burning with pain. Miss Ashley suddenly made a strange whimpering sound. She staggered back from the third weasel-like villain and let the wood drop.

She looked horrified. Was it because she was just about to hit him?

As she staggered backward, Fat One went for her. Even with his bulk, he was moving faster than Cary was with his wound.

So Cary ran at the fat bastard and drove his piece of wood hard into the base of the man's spine. The man spasmed, jerking back. Cary grasped him and pulled him a few feet away from Miss Ashley. Her face was white—paler than moonlight. Her eyes were huge.

"Go!" he shouted. "Go for my carriage—"

A huge first slammed into his face, snapping his head back.

Lights exploded in front of his eyes.

He couldn't see. Where was the bloody knife?

Even down in the muck of a battlefield, believing it was hopeless, Cary had fought for his life. And saved himself.

He slashed with his nail-strewn wood and heard a cry, then a clatter. But another blow and another sent him reeling, and he fell to the cobblestones.

Someone kicked him in the side of his body. Another boot slammed into his head.

He was being kicked. To death.

Cary put his arms up to protect his head. Where was his coachman? He hadn't brought outriders with him, as he was going to a Cyprian ball. Like most men, he had his plain carriage and was being circumspect. But he had a coachman. He employed a coachman, and now would be a helpful time for the man to show up.

"Leave him alone! Let him go!"

A woman's shout. Miss Ashley. She mustn't have run for the safety of his carriage or to bring his driver. Damn it—

Heavy, hard, solid as a brick, something slammed into the side of his face.

A scream filled his ears. He was aware dimly of a white face, of a slim body flying toward him, then pain smashed into the side of his head.

It felt as if all of London had exploded like shattering glass.

A second explosion sounded close. A different, louder roar. *Pistol shot!* screamed his brain. One of them did have a blasted weapon. Cary struggled to get to his feet, but before he could, the street seemed to drop away from him, and he was . . .

Hell, falling?

Or bloody well passing out?

Oh God, Caradon was just *lying* there.

Sophie fought to get her breathing under control as she scrambled away from the wall and dropped down by the side of the unconscious duke. The cobblestones bit into her knees. Her heart hammered so fast—

As fast as it had done on the night she'd bludgeoned Lord Devars to escape him—when she'd run off with the wretched diamond bracelet he'd forced onto her wrist.

She could have hit the villain who attacked her.

But just before delivering the blow, she'd remembered Devars and lost all her courage.

She couldn't kill someone. Not even their attackers.

But this man had risked his life to protect *her*.

"Your Grace?" She touched the duke's chest. His eyes were closed, his face turned to the side.

She let her fingers trail over his cheek. "Please, Your Grace, can you hear me?"

The fat villain and the one who was almost big as a gorilla had both set on him. He'd been distracted by coming to her rescue—because she couldn't hit the man who had captured her—and he'd been felled by a horrible punch.

She'd heard bone crunch.

Sophie had grown up in a small village, and she'd seen many a boy launch into a fight with another boy outside the pub. But she'd never seen anything like this. Not three men with knives attacking one man. It was hardly fair. But she supposed criminals didn't care.

But Sophie had never seen any man fight like the Duke of Caradon had. He'd fended off knife blows with his *cravat*, and then with a broken stave from a barrel.

He was the noblest, most remarkable hero she'd ever met.

"Don't know who you are, miss, but you'd best get away from His Grace."

She looked up. Standing over her was a coachman—a wiry, small man with a shock of gray hair sticking out from under his tricorne hat. He held a pistol—the one he'd fired to frighten the three fiends away.

Of course, it couldn't fire again now.

She pushed her hair, which had tumbled down partially, out of the way, and put her ear close to the duke's lips.

She heard faint breathing, and she sat up. She cupped the duke's strong jaw. Stroked his high, sculpted cheekbones with her fingertips. Relief flowed through her, almost making her dizzy.

"What in Hades do ye think ye're doing?"

"Checking to see if he's breathing. And he is!" *Thank God. Thank God.* "But he's knocked out. We must get him to a doctor."

"And just who might be you be? Lying in wait for His Grace, were you? Were those your associates? Don't try to steal anything off His Grace. I'm watching you."

"You think I'm a thief?" She swung around, fiercely glaring at the coachman. "One of those men tried to carry me off to do God knows what! I'd be dead except for your master, so I'd suggest you help him. I'm not a thief, I'm—" She broke off. Summoning pride, she tipped up her chin. "I left the ball with the duke. He was going to take me home."

"Was he now?" The coachman was middle-aged but muscled, and wore a look of suspicion.

"To *my* home!" That wasn't exactly true, of course.

The coachman glanced around the seedy area. "Why was he doing that?"

In truth, she did not live far from here. The small slummy room had been all she could afford. Most of the money she'd gotten from Devars's bracelet was set aside for looking after the children and to pay the rent on the cottage where they and Belle lived.

"It doesn't matter what he was doing," she cried. "He is now lying unconscious on a London street. Could you stop asking me idiotic questions? He was trying to rescue me, and look what's happened to him. We must fetch a doctor. I can take care of him"—she could—"but I can't get him into a carriage. Not on my own."

The coachman made a disgruntled sound. "All right. Best to get him back to Caradon House. I'll put him in the carriage and take him home."

"I'll help."

"Be off with ye, miss. I've no way of knowing if yer tale is true."

"Of course, it's true."

The coachman rubbed his nose. "I don't know. It's not the first time something's happened to His Grace. Thieves and vagabonds everywhere, there are. Though it's a strange coincidence, all these things happening so close together."

"What else happened to His Grace?" she asked sharply.

"A footpad almost got him a fortnight ago. And last week, he was shoved in front of a carriage on St. James's Street."

"All those things . . . within two weeks?"

"Aye. Two attacks and an accident. Not a lucky gentleman, His Grace."

"No. But for now, we must get him home. And I will come too. You have to drive the carriage—someone has to watch the duke."

The coachman looked wary. "All right. I suppose ye should. Her Grace and the others are still in the country."

Her Grace?

No, not his wife, Sophie remembered. He was supposed to be looking for a wife.

It must be his mother. Thank heaven, she wasn't there, Sophie thought. But it did mean the duke needed someone to look after him.

Nurse him. Heal him.

Then she looked at his ashen face and clasped his hand. Her heart pounded.

How badly hurt was he? He couldn't . . . couldn't die, could he?

She couldn't deny the horrible stabbing pain in her heart at that thought.

The sort of pain you felt for someone you love.

5

What woman of beauty and grace would not choose to become a courtesan? My servants are girls who came from the country—like me—but who had not the wit to see what power they could wield. Whereas I had the ear of the most powerful men in the land.

Dukes would bow to me and clamor for my attention. My jewels were as magnificent as those belonging to any duchess. Perhaps more magnificent, for inherited jewels are always ghastly.

I was content. . . . No, I had reached a level of perfect happiness. And to my surprise, my love for my beautiful viscount only enhanced my joy. We were both careful and circumspect. I found I could justify my dalliances, because my marquess—my protector—was continually unfaithful to me. I had wealth, jewels, gowns, carriages, and love. I resided at the top of the world.

So there, all you English subjects who live and die by propriety! I found perfect happiness simply by indulging in some rather athletic carnal pleasures.

—From an unfinished manuscript entitled *A Courtesan Confesses* by Anonymous

Cary knew this jiggling, jarring sensation. Knew it from being carried on a stretcher from a battlefield.

But this was different. That time he had only been bleeding from an arrow wound in his thigh and a saber's slice across his hip. He hadn't felt like every inch of his body had been beaten black-and-blue. His arms felt as if they were being pulled off his body.

An arrow wound and a few cuts had been much nicer, in retrospect, than what he felt now. Right now, he felt as if he'd fallen off a cliff and slammed a dozen rock outcroppings on the way down.

Dimly, he began to remember. He'd been fighting three men on sidewalk of a slummy London street. Two of them had gotten him down on the ground—

Miss Ashley? What had happened to her?

Cary's eyes shot open, and he fought to move, to sit up, but he couldn't. He heard grunting around him, and then a female voice said, "Please don't move, Your Grace," just as he looked into huge, worried green eyes.

Miss Ashley. And safe, thank God.

"We are taking you home, Your Grace," she said in her sweet voice. "Then I'm putting you in bed."

In bed? "Hell, no," he muttered. "There is no way in hell I can do anything right now."

Out of swollen eyes, he was certain he saw her blush.

"I mean, you need to go to your bed, and a doctor must come and examine you and stitch you up if you need it, Your Grace. And give you laudanum to get you through the pain. Then I shall look after you. For there might be fever. And you will be in pain, and looking after you is the least I can do after you saved my life."

Look after him? What in Hades was she talking about?

Slowly, he began to figure out where he was. And why his arms hurt. His coachman and three footmen were carrying him across the drive toward his house by his limbs. How had he gotten here from the stews? Apparently, Miss Ashley had been in charge of that.

Bugger it—his front steps loomed before them. That was going to hurt.

"Put me down," he commanded. But it wasn't much of a command—his voice came out in a husky rasp.

No one listened. Four grunting men lumbered over his gravel drive, panting with exertion, and they stopped at the base of the steps to catch their breaths.

"You are not hauling me up those steps, damn it."

"We've no other choice, Yer Grace," his coachman said with irritating cheer. "Unless we carry ye down the steps to the basement door."

That would be worse. There was no way they could negotiate the narrow tradesmen's steps while carrying him. "I am capable of walking."

"I doubt that, Yer Grace. Ye've been badly beaten. I won't have ye collapse and break yer neck, Yer Grace."

"I've walked after being stabbed and shot, Bryce. This I can do."

The footmen looked relieved, his coachman looked doubtful, but they set him on his feet. Pain shot through his legs, but it was just bruising of his muscles. Not as bad as having to pull out an arrow or stop the stem of blood from a blade.

Ignoring the pain, he got his footing and his balance. Then he took slow, agonizing steps. Having Miss Ashley watch him made him fight for stoicism.

He was, after all, accustomed to hiding pain. Second step— he grit his teeth as lightning shot through his side. In Ceylon, he'd fought while wounded. How in blazes had he done it? Maybe, at thirty, he was getting old.

Though it was only two years ago he was in Ceylon.

As a young man, from fourteen onward, he used to seek out physical abuse and pain. He'd liked to fight. Fighting kept him focused on the moment. A man couldn't go off into memories when he was trying not to get beaten to a pulp.

He'd thought soldiering would have given him the same thing.

But the stretches between battles had given him too much time to think. So did being held as prisoner of war, between the moments when he thought his captors would kill him.

They reached the top of the steps. Bryce pounded on the door, and Miss Ashley touched Cary's arm. "Your Grace, are you feeling better?"

God, she looked afraid for him. She went on, "I'm sorry— that's a useless question, but I am afraid you might be badly hurt."

"I wouldn't be able to stand if so, love."

"But they were hitting you, kicking you. Even in your head. I tried to stop them, but they just pushed me away. Then one of them went for his knife again. I desperately tried to find some kind of weapon—"

She went pale.

Then she said, "Even though I hit him with a board, I couldn't stop him. I thought he'd stabbed you before your coachman came and stopped them."

His body felt like he'd been run over by horses, and his head pounded like cannon fire. Now he realized something else. He felt an icy wetness along his right side.

He put his hand there. With his black gloves, he couldn't see the blood, but he could smell it on the leather. "Damn it."

His coachman swung his arm over the man's broad, stocky shoulders. "We'll help you up the steps, Yer Grace."

Miss Ashley surged forward and put her hand against his wound.

"Don't," he said. "It's bleeding, and you'll be covered in blood."

He saw it now. Red against her white glove. She looked

down and paled. But she lifted her chin. "I am fine," she said stoically.

"You're not." He pushed her hand away, determined to protect her. Witnessing his attack must have shocked her.

She bit her lip, her full, lush lower lip that trembled. Her dark curls, half tumbling out of her pins, wobbled around her face. "I'm so sorry!" she suddenly burst out. "You were attacked and it was my fault—"

"Aha!" barked his coachman. "Thought ye were a viper with a bosom. And I were right."

"The expression is a viper in the bosom," she retorted. "And I meant that I . . . uh, distracted His Grace, which allowed the footpads to attack."

He was distracted because she wanted to "heal" him. That was damned impossible.

Still, he couldn't damn well stand by while she threw herself at one man after another until she found a taker.

What in Hades was he going to do with her?

"It was not your fault," he growled.

Now that he wasn't so groggy from punches and kicks, Cary saw a dark shadow around her pale neck—bruises. Her pretty gown had been torn. So had her plain brown cape. "Are you all right?"

"Thanks to your remarkable bravery, I am. I've never seen any gentleman fight with such skill." She gazed at him, her face almost glowing with hero worship.

That expression on her face made him nervous.

She was a sweet thing, but she wanted him too much.

He really needed to get her sent home. Fast.

Then he remembered something else. The explosion he'd heard before he passed out. "I heard a pistol shot, but neither of us appear to have been hit." He was certain he would be aware if a pistol ball had gone through him, even in his battered, dazed state.

"Your coachman fired at them, but he had to ensure he missed so he did not hit you. But he had a second pistol, and the threat of that frightened them away."

"Good job." He managed to turn his head toward his coachman. "There will be a raise in that, Bryce. For saving our lives." They'd reached the top of the front steps. Sweat beaded his forehead. He wasn't hiding his agony as well as he'd intended. He managed to open his eyes again. "Miss Ashley, I need to get you safely home."

"No!" She was trembling, watching him. "I want to stay with you. To make sure you are all right."

"I'm in the house alone, so that would not be appropriate."

"Alone? But you have servants."

"No chaperons."

She gaped at him in shock, but it was the truth. He had no intention of ruining her, and he refused to be accused of it by rumor. Nor did he want Miss Ashley ruined, much as she was willing to be.

"Where do you live?" he asked.

She blushed fiercely. Then she told him. "It was the only room I could afford in London."

God, for anyone who knew London, the address was known as the worse cesspool of the stews.

"Bloody hell." He could not send her back there.

But what was he going to do with her? It was too late to send her anywhere else. Vaguely, he thought of Grey and his wife, Helena. But it was the middle of the night. Would they take Miss Ashley in?

Christ, he was still too dazed to think properly. Most of his servants would be asleep. Except for the coachman, three footmen, and his majordomo, no one else had to know. It was only one night, after all.

"I'm not sending you back there. That's madness. Stay here tonight. I'll have a room made up for you."

He reached out, winced, and rapped on his door. Then his coachman applied the knocker with a lot more force.

"You want me to stay with you? Watch over you?" she asked.

He imagined that. Miss Ashley in his bedroom. Then his brain, long used to abstinence, started to play an evil game with him. It began to play out detailed images of her removing all her clothes. Touching her full breasts and nipples. Exposing her sweet round bottom while he waited for her in his bed.

How did a man with a knife wound get hard? But he did, damn it.

Except he knew he could do nothing about it.

"No." His voice was strangled. "You will be given a bedroom, and I want you to stay there. My majordomo, Penders, will send for a physician for me. You are to go to sleep."

"And tomorrow you intend to send me home," she said softly.

"I don't know what to do with you," he muttered.

She was trouble. And keeping her near his room tonight would be like sleeping over a room filled with gunpowder. All it would take was one spark for a devastating explosion.

He had to ensure he doused any potential spark immediately.

His door opened, and his majordomo stood there in a robe, a look of shock on his face at the sight before him.

The duke was letting her spend the night!

He cared about her too much to send her back to her room—that must mean something, mustn't it?

The front door was wrenched open, and a man cried, "Good heavens, Your Grace. What has happened?"

The man had dressed hurriedly, Sophie realized. He wore a thick robe, and his thin dark hair stuck out to the sides. What time was it? She got her answer then—a distant clock bonged and did it again and again. It was three o'clock in the morning.

"Penders, good man. Unfortunately, I got into an altercation with footpads. Send for a doctor—I need one to stitch up a wound. And Miss Ashley needs a bedchamber prepared for the night."

For a moment, the butler, or whoever he was, looked stunned, but he swiftly composed his face. "Indeed. Very good, Your Grace."

But Penders looked at her then tipped up his nose. Obviously, he thought she was a ladybird. Well, she—

Well, she was trying to become a ladybird, so she had no right to be offended.

If she were a proper girl, she shouldn't stay in his house. But she must be improper. And she could not waste a whole night with the duke.

The coachman and the livery-clad footman supported the Duke of Caradon as they entered his foyer. For some reason, in his house, he seemed even more determined to act as if he were strong and not wounded.

Thinking of his wounds, of the horrific beating she'd witnessed and then the blood that stained her only pair of white gloves, Sophie felt sick. He could have been killed trying to protect her.

It was like Samuel, who had vowed to look after her, even though his family refused to acknowledge she and Samuel were in love. His family had threatened to cut him off.

Samuel had loved her. Was it possible—?

Her heart pattered hopefully at the thought.

Then she looked around her.

Good lord, this was a duke's home? What could a palace look like then?

Dark, intricately carved woodwork soared around her, disappearing far above her into darkness. The light of Penders's candle glinted on something shiny. The gilt of large picture frames.

The floor beneath her was marble so well polished, she had to watch her step. She slipped once. When they reached the stairs, she almost lost her breath. The newel post was covered in gilt and so were the railings.

Awed, she couldn't find words. And when she reached the duke's bedroom, her legs wobbled. She'd known a duke was wealthy, but this was beyond belief.

It was almost as large as the assembly room ballroom in the village near her home, for heaven's sakes. And this was just his bedroom.

A huge bed almost the size of a carriage stood in the center, swathed in silk hangings of exotic turquoise. The sheets and counterpane were turquoise, the carpet a lush Eastern design and enormous. A pure silver ewer and basin sat on a gilt-decorated vanity table. There was only one mirror, on the vanity.

The men carried Caradon to his bed and eased him onto it so he was sitting on it. Then she saw her red-stained glove again and gasped. "No, no! You must put something underneath him. An old sheet or something."

There was a trunk at the foot of the bed, and being useful, she opened it quickly. It contained blankets, but beautiful, thick wool ones.

The coachman grabbed one from her and threw it across the bed so it covered the embroidered counterpane. The duke was looking at her, a ghost of a smile on his lips, then his men helped him lie back on the blanket.

Sophie hurried forward. She'd been raised in the country by a doctor, so she'd seen some wounds on people—

But almost at once, a brusque voice demanded, "What have we here?"

It was the doctor, a short, barrel-chested man with silver-tinged black hair. The coachman and the majordomo tried to explain, but they hadn't been there. She had. She raised her voice and raised it, the men ignoring her until the duke broke in. "The young lady knows and is determined to talk. Let her explain."

"Who is she?" the doctor asked. "The one who stabbed His Grace?"

"No, of course not! I am"—she didn't know what to say—"umm, a friend. The duke rescued me from footpads."

"Now stand aside, young lady," the doctor ordered. He rolled up his sleeves, demanded a basin of water, and got to work.

Throughout, as the doctor cleaned wounds and stitched those that needed to be closed, she saw the duke grit his teeth. His strong jaw clenched, but he never cried out. He was remarkably strong.

He had rescued her—twice.

And paid for it by being bruised and cut. When she saw, in good candlelight, all the cuts on his face and the blossoming blue-and-black bruises on his body, she wanted to cry.

She wanted to make up for what he'd been through.

She couldn't stop the nagging fear this was her fault—and he would never want to have anything to do with her again because of it.

The doctor sloshed his hands in the basin of cooling water. "All finished, Your Grace. You will live," he said brusquely.

The butler—or majordomo, as he'd introduced himself—Penders asked about infection.

"The wound is well cleaned," said the doctor, sounding a bit affronted. "But there is always a risk a fever can set it."

Sophie swallowed hard.

"I will check frequently on His Grace," Penders promised.

Check frequently? He needed someone to watch him. Impulsively, Sophie decided she was the one who must do it.

To the duke, she whispered, "I'll come back. I'll sit by your bedside and watch you."

Caradon shook his head, groaning. "No. You, my dear, are trouble."

Was that really what he thought?

If she was to have any hope of saving herself and her family, she must prove to him she wasn't trouble.

Sophie slipped out of the bedroom she had been given, far from the duke's room. She was certain she remembered the way back. She still wore her gown—the majordomo had not thought to send anyone to help her unfasten it. Her feet were bare though.

Moonlight spilled in through a huge, arched window at the end of her corridor, guiding her way. Even this corridor was magnificent, with little niches filled with enormous china vases. Paintings hung on the wall, more paintings than she had ever seen in her life.

Was she just crazy to try to have a duke for her protector?

If the Duke of Caradon died because he'd tried to stop her from becoming a courtesan, even though she didn't want to be stopped, she would . . .

She didn't know what she would do.

She couldn't go to another man to try to make him her protector. She wanted no one but Caradon.

Sophie reached a large double door that she was certain was the duke's bedchamber. She clicked the latch and opened one door a few inches. "Your Grace?"

Silly—he wasn't going to hear that whisper from his bed.

At least there was no one else in the room.

"See? You made the right decision," she whispered to herself. "He needs someone to watch him constantly."

A moan, a horrible agonized sound, came from the bed.

The sound raised the hairs on the back of Sophie's neck. She stood, paralyzed.

She rushed to the bed as the duke began to toss under his

covers. His arms moved, thrashing at the sheets, and his legs kicked to-and-fro.

The covers slid off him, revealing his wide, hard muscled torso, his tight waist, and the flat expanse of his belly. She saw his lean hips, his solid strong thighs. His—

She stared as his naked cock. Surprisingly, it was at half-mast. And he made Samuel look . . . like a young lad.

He mumbled. "No, don't touch me, no . . ." His voice was hoarse and panicked. He sounded terribly afraid.

She stopped staring, and put her palm against his forehead. At her touch, he ceased to move, but he moaned again. She felt the lumps of his bruises, but his forehead wasn't hot; it was cool. This wasn't a fever.

Was he dreaming of the attack?

"Untie me . . . God, untie me . . ."

She stroked his head. "Shhh," she murmured. "It's over. You're home and you are safe, Your Grace."

He soothed a bit.

She kept stroking his face, gently running her palm along his cheek. The stubble on his skin and the sharp jut of his cheekbone tickled her hand. But she was soothing him, so she kept doing it.

Even bruised, he was so beautiful. She winced, seeing the blossoming purple-and-green marks on his cheeks, his jaw, his temple.

In the light of the glowing coals in the grate, his hair gleamed like pure gold.

His long, black lashes flickered against his cheeks, and he suddenly jerked and started muttering again. He wasn't thrashing, but he wasn't at peace—

Footsteps sounded outside. Light showed at the base of the door. She had to think quickly.

She slid off the bed and ran around it. The door handle turned.

Sophie dropped to the floor, hidden by both the thick mattress and the skirt of the bed. She wanted to squirm under the bed, but in the wretched corset, she couldn't lie down. Stupid, stupid fashion. All she could do was press tight to the bed and pray she was hidden by shadow.

Footsteps came to the bed. Looking up, not daring to breathe, she saw a glow of light. Smelled the burning wax of a candle. Good beeswax, not tallow. It must be Penders checking on his master.

The duke must have fallen into a calmer sleep. She didn't hear any movement of the mattress.

The servant left, closing the door, satisfied his master was all right.

But Caradon was not all right—he had been experiencing a horrible nightmare.

She had seen how bravely and courageously he had faced the three men in the alley. What had he dreamed about that had frightened him?

Sophie gripped the bed, struggled against the tightness of the wretched corset, and pulled herself up to her feet. She squealed— then cut off the sound partway.

Caradon was awake, his pale blue eyes focused on her.

"Christ, Miss Ashley, what are you doing here?" His voice was a croak. "Did you come to get into my bed?"

There was something in his expression . . . in his eyes. . . .

Was it desire? Lust? He looked as if he desperately needed to be kissed. She tentatively touched him again, letting her hand stroke his cheek. "I came to watch over you." Impulsively, she added, "Please call me Sophie."

"Miss—Sophie, God . . . I had a dream."

"I know."

He tensed. "How?"

"You were thrashing. And you said the words no and 'Don't touch me.' "

"That's all?"

Goodness, the duke looked grim and worried.

"You did also say, 'Untie me,' Your Grace," she said.

"It was just a nightmare. And call me Cary."

A nickname. Her heart leapt. She gazed down at him. "But what were you dreaming about? You faced those men without fear. You defended yourself against a knife with a cravat, for heaven's sake. What tormented you in your dream—was it when you were a prisoner of war?"

He groaned. Then said, "Your touch is so sweet."

He wasn't telling her to stop. To go away. His pale blue eyes gazed into hers. "Let me do this," he growled. "Let me make love to you. Let me prove I can."

Her heart hammered with hope. With desire. He was so beautiful. He had rescued her—he was so wonderful.

His hand came up and cupped her neck, and he drew her into his kiss.

6

I must have you. You obsess over me. Leave the Marquess of N—— and become mine absolutely.

Finally, I had a duke speak those words to me.

"You are too cruel and too callous," my viscount declared when he found out I had not refused the duke's offer. "You've broken my heart long enough. I am finished with you."

Then he was gone. I hugged myself and paced by the fire. Really, what was the loss? I had a duke!

I had a duke to please—

Indeed, I began to wonder if I could be more than a mistress. Perhaps my next conquest should be something of great accomplishment. Something on the matrimonial front. All I had to do was capture the heart of the right gentleman through my rather unique endowment—my mind.

I knew I should be able to become a duchess—if I played my cards with patience, skill, and cunning. For now that I had lost my viscount, to what else could I aspire? Not love, surely. It had proven itself to be the playground of fools.

—From an unfinished manuscript entitled *A Courtesan Confesses* by Anonymous

He needed to do this.

He needed to kiss her, and he needed to blank out that damned dream.

Cary cupped Sophie's slender neck and threaded his fingers in her loose black hair. He drew her down and touched his mouth to hers.

Slowly, he caressed her lips with his, and he knew, from her shivers and shudders, that she felt the magical tingle. It would hit his lips, then rush through him like a jolt of lightning.

He let his tongue caress her lips, and he felt her quiver. Heard her moan softly. Breathlessly.

He wanted her to like this. He needed her to like it.

To prove—

Suddenly, he was in the melee of battle, surrounded by screaming cannon fire and the metallic tang of spilling blood. A horse went down beside him, and the great beast slammed into him, knocking him back. A bullet sliced along his left bicep as he went down, neatly parting his tunic and bringing forth a stream of blood—

The shot had been aimed at his heart. If the horse hadn't hit him, the ball would have passed right through him, ripping his heart to bits.

Hit by the horse, stunned by the shot, he lay on the ground. The falling horse had pinned him.

Then something had slammed hard into his skull.

Next thing he'd known, he was in a in a cave, in a makeshift cell built of bamboo, and chained to the rock.

One by one, the other prisoners had died. They had been more badly wounded. Infection had led to fever. Dehydration had killed them. Two had gone mad, screaming like lunatics before dying in seizures.

He'd been tortured to force him to talk but, he hadn't broken.

Mainly, because he'd found he couldn't talk. Something had

gone wrong in his brain, and no matter what his captors had done to him, he wouldn't talk.

He hadn't spoken until days after he'd been freed—

The memories surged up, swamping him.

Cary broke off the kiss, drawing his mouth back. He rasped for breath. His heart hammered. "I can't," he muttered. "You're too sweet. Too innocent."

He couldn't kiss her, damn it. Sexual pleasure wasn't strong enough anymore. Even intense desire didn't push the memories away now.

This was why he couldn't marry. A woman would guess, wouldn't she, that something was wrong?

Sophie ran her tongue over her lips. The poor sweet looked afraid.

"But I'm not sweet, Your Grace! I'm very naughty. When I'm with you, I feel like I'm on fire. And I want you."

Cary watched her hands move. They went behind her back, an action that thrust her breasts forward. Perfect, round little breasts that bulged over the scooped neckline of her dress. Two voluptuous swells like perfect peaches.

His tongue curled instinctively. It had been a long time, but he remembered the sweet, velvety, rubbery feel of a nipple against the flat of his tongue.

Her neckline loosened. She was undoing the buttons of her gown.

Then she stopped and pouted playfully. "I can't go any further. And I want you so much. But I don't need my gown all the way off to make love to you."

Her knee dipped into his bed, and she pulled her shift up, revealing her sleek legs, her rounded hips—and the dark curls between her legs because she wore no drawers. She bunched the shift at her hips and swung her leg over him.

God, she was climbing on top.

"Don't," he growled.

But it was too late. Sophie straddled him, looking down at him, and she settled her rump down on his thighs.

Her sweet, flowery, warm scent wrapped around him. He picked up another scent too. Her arousal. He smelled it faintly as she wriggled, grinding her warm, sweet crotch against the semi-hard lump of his cock. He gave a ragged groan.

God, this was good. He loved the pressure on his cock, which was fighting to harden while trapped between her warm body and his abdomen.

She'd taken out her pins, and her hair showered around her in wild raven waves. What would it look like flying around her as she rode him?

She lowered, her breasts spilling over the brim of her bodice. Succulent, sweet, and he ached to lift his hands and touch them.

He was ready to do it—

Then his brain flashed to the past again. . . .

Where he was pinned down and he couldn't fight. Couldn't protect himself.

"I can't do this, Sophie," he croaked.

"I told you I am not a virgin. I have experienced . . . rutting."

"I'm sorry you lost your husband." His heart hurt for her. "Poor sweet," he murmured. He knew the hell of battle—she knew the loss of it too.

Her sweet mouth was there. She bent just a little farther. He had a good look down her bodice at the swells of her breasts, the hot, tempting valley between them.

She'd been in love and lost the man she loved. No wonder she was impoverished. She'd married young, and her husband had been snatched from her, leaving her with nothing—

She kissed him—and reached down and wrapped her hand around his cock.

Suddenly, blood shot down so fast, he was light-headed. His cock went rock hard.

She was hurting. He was hurting.

He wanted to lose all his pain in loving her. Take her pain away.

She wriggled on his prick, and he felt like a lion in a menagerie ripping free of its chains.

He lifted his hips and ground his pulsing hard cock against her.

She did it! She had tempted the duke beyond control. And he was going to make her his.

Victory made Sophie heady. She giggled in sheer joy—a sound which got silenced as the duke put his lips over hers again.

He kissed her so hot and masterfully, her lips felt like they were sizzling and about to catch fire. Slowly, his hands moved down. One slipped with skill inside her loosened bodice and cupped her breast.

Her hand was wrapped daringly around his most intimate place.

Against her palm, his staff was rigid and so hot. His skin was like velvet, but beneath—oh, it was hard as iron. She stroked him and sensed him tense.

With each stroke of her hand, his finger brushed lightly over her nipple.

Goodness!

It made her sizzle *everywhere*.

She let her hand slide all the way to the head of his erection, fat and firm and velvety in her hand. She breathed in the ripe smell of him.

Sophie trembled.

This man was a hero to her, just as Samuel had been. And he was so decadently handsome.

And—

He pinched her left nipple, and the tweak made her cunny clench. She *ached* for him. Positively ached.

Gently, he rolled her nipple between his thumb and forefinger, and sensation exploded. She'd never dreamed her nipples would like such rough treatment.

His tongue slipped into her mouth. His other hand slid down and nestled between her legs. Aching so much, she rubbed against his hand.

The duke's fingers tapped a place under her skirts and between her thighs—a place that sent a bolt of lightning streaking through her and made her cry out in shock.

His hands did things. All kinds of things. Wickedly good things.

Then he grasped her hips and held her still as he ground his thick erection against her.

Sophie moaned as need hit her with a jolt that made her weak. She was so wet, it made her blush.

He wasn't saying anything. But then Samuel hadn't either on the night they had made love. He'd kissed her wildly and sloppily and made love to her, but he hadn't said much.

She assumed men were like that.

Caradon's kisses were playful one minute, hard and demanding the next. He would touch his lips to hers so gently, her mouth simply tingled, then his open mouth would take hers, and his tongue would come in and thrust inside in the naughtiest ways. She didn't know there was so much to kisses. Caradon's were . . . complicated.

They made her melt. She was shaking, so aroused she was almost sobbing with need.

He lifted her, moving her so she had to let go of his cock and grip his shoulders. Her quim settled down right on top of the ridge of his erection.

He must be eager. Beneath her—and there was nothing between the slick lips of her private place and his erection—he was as hard as a cricket bat. He felt huge where she pressed on him.

He kissed her hungrily, and she pushed on his shoulders to break away from his mouth.

Breathlessly, she looked into his lust-hazed eyes. "Do you want me to put you inside me now?"

He pulled her down roughly, his mouth coaxing her lips wide. His tongue surged in. It was a luscious kiss.

She wanted him so much.

She couldn't wait any longer.

Now!

She reached down and wrapped her hand around his shaft again. Her heart galloped, and she took him inside.

He was so thick and so long, and she felt so full that she cried out. Her cunny gripped tight around him, and she planted her hands onto his shoulders to ride him—

"No, Sophie." He jerked back from the kiss, his breathing ragged. "I can't do it, love."

"What?"

"We have to stop."

No. Nooooo! "But—but why? What have I done wrong?" She was whimpering.

"Nothing," he said hoarsely. He gripped her thighs and lifted her. She lifted off his erect cock, and it went twanging out of her like a bow.

Then he abruptly pulled her forward.

She had to slap her hands down so she didn't tumble—though her corset was keeping her up. Her palms landed on the pillow beside his head, and her skirts spilled over his face.

He could see up her skirts, see her dark curls and the pink nether lips.

A slow smile touched his lips. "You have no drawers."

It was a strange smile—the smile of a man who was in great pain. But she didn't think that pain came from his wounds. "Of course not. Drawers are fast."

His chest moved with a low, throaty chuckle. "Perfect."

Then he moved her again and lowered her cunny—

Onto his mouth.

Shock speared her, making her sit bolt upright on him. How could he breathe? He was doing what the courtesan had done to her lover.

The wet caress stunned her. His tongue had licked her nether lips, had tickled her nether curls, then played with her, slicking over her, until he hit a spot—

"Good lord, what was that?" She gasped.

Pleasure rushed from her privy place and seemed to shoot all the way through her—to her toes and the very tips of her fingers.

He rhythmically flicked his tongue over that very sensitive spot.

Lightning shot past her eyes. Brilliant lights exploded. Her fingers curled, and she clutched his pillow as if she might fly away. She was weak, paralyzed, a captive on his mouth.

With his hands, he worked her quim against his mouth. She gasped. Too intense! Oh, just perfect! No, wait . . . that was too much. . . .

He found just the perfect place, the perfect rhythm, but the tense, sensation growing inside her was something she didn't understand.

It scared her, but it didn't hurt.

It grew stronger. Her fingers almost tore the pillow to shreds. She didn't just let him drive her cunny against his mouth. She started to rub against him. Her body seemed to know what to do—

Oh, something was happening. Her heart—was it even still beating or had it exploded—?

Goodness, her *body* was exploding.

Pure, glorious light seemed to consume her. Her body jolted and writhed on him, and a blinding, intense pleasure rushed over her. She was its slave, floating with it, dancing with it, and the duke's hands cupped around her bare bottom and held her to his mouth while she gasped and squealed with every single second that passed.

"Oh God," she cried over and over. "Oh. Oooooooooh."

Her heart was bursting while ecstasy seemed to make her wits shatter into an explosion of light. It felt so good. So wonderfully good!

Nothing had ever made her feel this way. But he did. This glorious, gorgeous man who'd saved her and who'd made her feel this. "Oh, I love you," she wailed.

He held her while she thrashed about on his mouth. Then it began to ease, and she panted for air. Her hair was a wild mess. Her heart thundered, and she made rasping sounds. "Good heavens, what was that?"

The duke lifted her off his face and settled her across his chest. He looked bemused. "You don't know?"

"No."

"Even though you were married?"

She knew she was blushing. She quickly explained, "We were wed truly just before he went to war. We had only one night together . . . our wedding night."

"Ah."

"I felt that strange tension, but it faded when we did that thing. When we rutted. It was nothing like what you did. I had no idea—" Bother, she was blushing more.

She was naïve, she knew. From the country. Untutored. Did she try to pretend she wasn't? Or just admit the truth. "I am very willing to learn," she said solemnly. Well, as solemnly and seriously as she could, since she was straddling him with her exposed cunny, which was slick and wet.

"You've never had an orgasm before?"

"A what?"

"An orgasm means the release you achieve with sexual pleasure. You've never touched your pussy, love? To pleasure yourself."

"My pussy?"

" 'Pussy' is cant for your quim, Sophie."

"I'm not supposed to touch myself there. I wasn't even supposed to when bathing. Only quickly and with a washcloth."

"Sophie, love, how can you want to be a courtesan?"

She frowned. "Well, I don't know everything yet, of course. But I do have the book."

"This book again . . ."

"It's a memoir written by a famous London courtesan. Anonymously."

"And a courtesan's memoir is your guide?"

"Yes." She clapped her hand to her mouth. "She wrote about a man eating her. Goodness, now I understand what that meant. I never knew before tonight that people used mouths." Tentatively, she touched her lips. "I could use mine on you. I think."

"No, Sophie."

"But why not? Why don't you want these things? I do wish you would tell me. I wish you would let me help. I think"—she gazed at him helplessly—"I think I'm falling in love with you."

Cary groaned. Sophie looked like a lost puppy.

"The truth is, you are not in love with me, Sophie. You know nothing about me. That was pleasure talking."

"But it—" She broke off.

"You don't want me, Sophie. You do not want to be the lover of a man like me."

She giggled. "Of course, I do. You're a duke."

He shook his head. What did he do with the girl? "I'm damaged, love. And even being a duke doesn't make up for that."

"How are you damaged?"

He clasped her hand. "Climb off me, my dear, then help me sit up. I will explain while I undo your corset. You need to go to your bed and get some sleep."

He lifted her from his chest, supporting her as she clambered off him and the bed.

As he struggled to sit up, he was aware how battered and bruised he was. Every inch of his body ached. Even his cock hurt—it ached from unfulfilled desire.

Cary managed to sit upright and let Sophie stuff the pillows behind his back. "Sit in front of me," he directed.

She did. Then she tipped her head forward, caught her hair with a sweep of her hand, and pulled the whole shimmering mass over her shoulder to reveal the back of her gown.

He began to undo the fastenings.

"You aren't going to tell me, are you? You were tricking me."

"I will tell you." He would give her the usual explanation he used for his strange, almost reclusive behavior. "In 1817, I left England to serve as an officer during the rebellions in Ceylon. I was held as a prisoner of war for several months. The experience proved brutal and grueling. Since then, I've found it . . . impossible to have female companionship."

She half twisted around, her forehead wrinkled with a frown. "I would have thought you'd be more eager after going through something so awful."

She was a clever young woman. She'd gotten at the logic— why would a man who had been through hell not want to fall into the loving arms of a woman? After being deprived of freedom, wouldn't any normal man be eager for passion and pleasure?

"I was chained up, starved, beaten. Tortured. And I cannot put it aside. When you wanted to have sex with me, I felt a swift rush of arousal, but getting that near to pleasure brings forth all my bad memories. I don't know why. Maybe I don't feel worthy."

"How could you feel that?" she asked. "You are wonderful."

"You don't know that."

"I do! You rescued me from three footpads without even a thought for your own safety. But if you can't have sex because of your painful memories, why were you at a Cyprian ball?"

"To see if I could heal myself. If I could change. I'm a duke. Expected to marry. To produce an heir." He sighed. "Now it is time for you to go off to bed, Sophie. It's close to dawn. I will ensure you aren't disturbed until late."

"Then what?" she asked.

"We will discuss that in the morning. I'm too tired to think right now."

"Could I sleep with you?"

"That is not a good idea."

"But I'm worried about you!"

"I don't think I will develop a fever now. I think we've proven I'm still fairly strong."

Yet she looked so heartbroken, he felt his resolve yield. "Sophie, I admit it would be nice to share my bed. It's been a vast, lonely place for years now. But you have to promise you won't try to ravish me in my sleep."

She giggled. "Normally, that is what the woman fears. But you have my solemn promise: I won't be naughty."

It had been years since he had fallen asleep with a woman in his bed—back when his father was alive and Cary had his own bachelor rooms.

Sophie stood, and he caught his breath as she pushed her gown down and stepped out of it.

She sat again so he could unlace her corset. Then she said, "Your majordomo has been checking on you. To ensure you haven't developed a fever. He last looked in on you when I first came in."

"He didn't see you?"

"I hid behind the bed."

"I doubt he will return. Not until morning. But lock the door. I'd rather Penders didn't have the shock of finding us together in my bed. There is no point in savaging your reputation when it's my plan to send you home."

"I've already accepted that my reputation is something that must be sacrificed to protect my family."

"Sleep now. We'll worry about that later."

"All right," she mumbled.

He shifted over, making room for her in his bed. "Go to sleep, love."

Cary got out of bed.

He felt damned guilty. He'd intended to save her, send her home—not try to have sex with her.

He poured himself a tumbler of brandy and walked over to the grouping of chairs by the fireplace. He sat on a stool, grimacing as he settled down, and he watched Sophie. She looked so small and sweet in his huge bed—a bed used by four generations of Dukes of Caradon.

He'd learned a stark damning truth tonight: He couldn't get past the hell of his memories.

It was more than what had happened to him as a prisoner of war in Ceylon. All that had done was release the secrets he'd kept hidden for so long.

When he was five years old, he had been kidnapped for ransom. He had been chained up in a decaying house. And his perverted captor had done things to him. . . .

He had almost prayed for death, since he had been forced to do sinful things. Then the day had come where the man had wanted more, wanted to completely rip apart his innocence and virginity. Cary had been young, but he'd understood that the man had intended to penetrate him.

For that, the man had unchained him, unafraid of a child.

But a child could move with lightning speed. He'd run, desperate to get out. But every door had been locked, the windows nailed shut. Sheer terror had led him to grab a weapon to defend himself.

He had hidden, armed with a fireplace poker, standing on a dresser so he could hit the man's head.

He'd intended to knock the man out. But he was so scared the monster would wake up, he'd kept hitting and hitting. . . .

After he'd been rescued, he'd been . . . different. He had never felt right afterward. He saw other boys growing up, and he envied the fact they had no idea what vile monsters existed in the world.

For a long time, he had been the wildest rake in London, and he'd managed to bury the past. Then he had been taken prisoner, and that had unleashed the memories of his kidnapping— the ones he had buried—

Cary downed his brandy.

What in hell was he going to do?

His mother wanted him to marry—she claimed it would kill her if he didn't.

Sophie wanted to heal him.

Should he keep trying with Sophie? Should he make her his mistress and see if he could actually get over this?

But Sophie was naïvely in love with him. What about when he had to let her go so he could get married? He wasn't the kind of man who could marry and keep a mistress.

She would find another man. Then another. After a while, she would be older and jaded and cynical.

He thought of Angelique and the other hardened, tough Cyprians. He didn't want to see Sophie lose her sweet, innocent optimism.

No, he had to send her home.

Cary got up to pour more brandy.

In the morning, no doubt he was going to have an argument with her about that.

What he didn't expect was the arrival of the magistrate, along with Saxonby, at seven o'clock in the morning—because he was suspected of murder.

7

_____

I had not seen my viscount for many, many months. All other gentlemen bored me! I soon gave up any plans to remain with the Duke of Carlyle. For a start, there was already a Duchess of Carlyle. What dreary nights we shared. The duke only wished to speak of cards and horses and hounds.

He condemned me for any desire to indulge in real pleasure— a ball, a masquerade, the theater, condemning all such activities as foppish and uninteresting. "If I wished to be bored at a tedious ball, I could be doing so tonight—with my wife," said he.

He was the sort of man who was far too dense to be put off by an insult, so I replied, with acerbity, "Perhaps you should reveal qualities that I can find interesting."

"You are a female. Your lack of interest is the result of a naturally smaller intelligence."

Finally, I could bear it no more. The Cyprians of London were holding a magnificent masquerade. What a coup to appear with the duke on my arm—even an aging bore would lend me prestige as long as he were a duke. But we were not to go. And I was forbidden from attending without him.

"Well," said I, "I shall not attend the party, but my costume will not go to waste."

My masquerade costume consisted of a mask and seven gossamer thin veils. I wore nothing beneath them. I took my signature curricle that was the pink of a perfect rose. Excitement bubbled in my blood.

St. James's Street was my target. When I reached its wide expanses, I lifted my whip and drove my team of four into a wild gallop. Out of the corner of my eye, I saw gentlemen rushing out of their clubs to watch me.

Then, as I gave the whip another glorious crack in the air, one of my veils broke free. It fluttered in the wind that my horses had whipped up, then it flew away, leaving my right breast completely bare.

—From an unfinished manuscript entitled *A Courtesan Confesses* by Anonymous

Silken sheets whispered over her skin. She was deliciously warm. Warmer than she'd been in bed for five years.

Sophie sat up in the Duke of Caradon's bed, and she rubbed her eyes. If this was all a dream, she'd best face reality as quickly as she could.

She blinked her eyes twice.

No, the magnificent furnishings, the heavy velvet draperies, and the silk curtains tied to the bed columns were still there. She was still sitting in the warm, comfortable bed.

And the duke—Cary—was still sleeping beside her.

Hope actually left her breathless. It embraced her heart so tightly, it was squeezing her. But it was a wonderful feeling.

She was so close! She could feel it. She could convince Cary to keep her.

She had her book, *A Courtesan Confesses,* and now she would understand some of the things she hadn't before. She would learn how to be the best seductress in England, and she would snare her duke.

Sophie felt a bit guilty, since she was in a delightful, cozy bed while her son, Alexander, and Belle and Belle's children lived in drafty, damp, meager cottage.

But all that would soon to come to an end. She could treat Belle and the children to warm, soft sheets. The children could have a bed each. They could build fires in the grates without having to scrounge for scraps to burn.

Men like the horrible Earl of Devars couldn't touch her. Or Belle. Not *ever*.

The children would have futures. They would never fear workhouses. Belle's daughter would never fear the horrors of a man like Devars preying on her.

Sitting up, Sophie watched the duke. The sheets had fallen down, baring his naked chest with its curls of golden hair, planes of hard muscle.

Just being in the same bed was enough to set her pulse pounding—even though he was on one side of the bed, she on the other, and there was enough room between them to fit three other people. He was so beautiful. Golden hair. Long lashes. Lush lips like on Michelangelo's David.

Sophie hugged her knees.

Last night, he had given her so much pleasure, he had made her see stars.

Her heart wobbled.

She wanted him. Wanted, wanted, *wanted* him.

It was like how she had felt for Samuel. She'd gone bald-headed after Samuel.

Surely, pleasure and happiness and love could help Cary forget his painful memories. He was a wonderful man. He *deserved* to be healed.

Sophie wriggled across the bed to the duke. It took longer than she'd expected—it felt like crossing a vast plain.

She pushed down the counterpane and leaned over him. His cock was half erect, even though he was sleeping.

Taking a deep breath, she bent over and took the tip of it into her mouth.

The head was like soft velvet against her lips. The skin was slightly sweet with perspiration, a little salty, and there was a tang of a bitter taste.

He groaned, murmured something. She held just the head in her mouth. Delicately. Her lips formed a tight, but gentle O around him. Her tongue rested against the head. She coasted her tongue wetly around the smooth head and the firmer crown. Her questing tongue found a taut piece of flesh, rather like a bowstring, and she strummed it lightly.

Against her tongue, his cock seemed to swell. It grew bigger, longer, and much more rigid.

Something dribbled, touching her tongue. From a little opening in the very tip of his cock came a tangy, salty fluid. Curious. She had no idea men grew wet too. She did when she was aroused, so this was a good sign. She sucked a bit, swallowing, hoping to arouse him more.

The head and shaft grew, filling her mouth at a shocking rate. Sophie had to draw back. But once she caught her breath, she slid more of him into her mouth. He was rigid now, hard as a tree trunk, and remarkably thick. Try as she would, she couldn't take more than a third of him into her mouth.

She must please him. Desperately, she tried to remember exactly what he'd done to her. Delicious things with his tongue. Some rough things. Gentle teasing things.

At the ball, she had seen the woman's mouth at the man's groin, and she was sure his entire erection was inside the woman's mouth.

She must have been wrong. That had to be *impossible*.

She flicked her tongue around the head. Was she making him feel pleasure? Or was she doing everything all wrong? All she could do was explore and try and, well . . . pray.

Cary thrust his hips.

Obediently, she opened her mouth wider and took him in, cheeks hollowing.

His hips pumped, lifting off the bed rhythmically to drive his erection into her mouth.

Ah, that was what he wanted. Cushioning her mouth around him, she tried sucking him in deeper. Just a bit. Then a bit more.

She slid up on him, then starting bobbing her head—

"Sophie, what in blazes?"

The duke's raspy voice startled her. So much, she almost forgot what she was doing, and she scraped him.

Now she saw he was awake, his blue eyes wide with surprise. He stared down at her, where his shaft vanished into her mouth.

She kept bobbing.

"No," he said abruptly. He cupped her cheeks, lifted her off him so she had to release his cock. "You were supposed to behave yourself."

She flushed with embarrassment. "Is pleasuring you so very wrong?"

A look of agony shot over his face. "It is when I ask you not to do it."

She hung her head, her cheek pressed against his palm. "You were sleeping. I suppose I did play a dirty trick."

A soft, rough laugh came from him.

She looked up. "I only wanted to help you. How could naughty pleasure not make you feel better? I should think it would take your mind off things."

He shoved back his tangled blond hair. "It's more complicated than that, love."

"How is it—?"

A sharp knock on the duke's door made her choke on her sentence.

Someone was going to come in—the valet or the butler or a maid for the fire?

"Aak!" she squealed. She gripped the counterpane and tried to scramble underneath it.

"The door's locked," Cary reminded her calmly.

"And Penders—or whoever—will wonder why."

Since she was going to become a courtesan, why was she worried?

Protecting her reputation was instinct. One she had to forget.

"Stay calm and quiet," the duke said. He raised his hoarse voice. "What is it?"

"It—it is the Duke of Saxonby, Your Grace." Penders, who had perfect, somewhat snooty butler tones last night, now sounded shaky and afraid. "He has come with a magistrate from Bow Street. They asked to speak with you. They have insisted that it is an urgent matter."

"The *magistrate* is here?" Raw panic hit her.

"Sophie, what is it?"

She realized Cary was looking at her strangely. His eyes narrowed. His mouth became hard and grim. "You look afraid," he said. "Is there any reason a magistrate would want you?"

Oh God, she'd made him suspicious.

But if the magistrate had come for her, she was doomed. Should she tell him exactly what had happened with Lord Devars and beg Cary for any understanding and mercy he could spare?

Her lips moved—

Sound wouldn't come out.

She couldn't do it. She could not tell him. Not what she'd had to do to escape Lord Devars and rent a cottage for Belle and the children, then provide them with food and buy herself a gown so she could get a protector.

He would know she had been a thief.

He would never trust her. She would have absolutely no chance with him then.

The last thing she could do was be honest with him.

She shook her head so hard, it made her dizzy. "No. No, I don't know why he would be here."

He looked at her for endless minutes while she fought fear. Finally, Cary shouted. "I will come." It sounded like such a strain on his voice when he raised it. He winced, touching his bruised jaw. "You stay here," he instructed.

Sophie nodded, but her heart was in her throat.

Could she really just wait there in his bed while the magistrate might be telling him about her crime? While they might be plotting her arrest?

Cary grabbed a robe, intending to throw it on quickly. But his body had stiffened up after last night. Laudanum and protective shock had worn off. It had been easy to forget pain last night, when he was struggling with bigger demons—and when he'd been wrapped up in sexual delights with Sophie.

Now he was aware of how his every muscle ached.

Cary had chosen a heavy brocade banyan—something sturdy enough to cover his huge, throbbing erection. He stood with it draped over his arm, his body locked in a spasm of pain. He rubbed his leg, wincing at the tenderness.

White as a sheet, Sophie came to him. She took the robe and helped him put it on without saying a thing. When she'd heard the word "magistrate," she'd turned pale as the moon. She was afraid. And obviously not giving him the truth.

Last night, he'd gone to a Cyprian Ball to conquer his inability to make love. Since then—since he had encountered Sophie—he had been driven wild with sexual frustration for a woman who seemed innocent but claimed she wasn't. He had been attacked by three men, had been beaten to a pulp, and now had a mysterious visit from the magistrate.

Either Sophie was destined to bring him a hell of a lot of bad luck, or there was more to her than met the eye.

He paused at his door before leaving. "Is there anything you want to tell me?" he asked.

And watched her face go stark white again.

"No," she said slowly. "Why would there be? Everything I told you is the truth."

Hell, he didn't know whether to believe her.

By the time he reached his study, Cary had assessed a dozen reasons why the men might be here.

That was battle training. In minutes—moments—he could invent dozens of scenarios and their possible outcomes. He'd developed the skill in Ceylon, where the army had often been ambushed.

But when he walked into the room, he laid aside all his speculation. In this situation, he had to listen—he couldn't go in with preconceptions.

But he couldn't push aside one nagging question—was Sophie the reason the men were here?

This couldn't be related to the attack last night, as he'd had no time to tell anyone about it. The only people who knew were his servants, Sophie, and the men who had attacked him.

"Good morning, gentlemen. What brings you here at this ungodly morning hour?" Cary drawled, taking in the scene.

A gray-haired gentleman sat in one of the leather club chairs positioned in front of the fire, where a good blaze burned. Saxonby stood at the window, looking out of the rear gardens. Sax's hands were clasped behind his back, his shoulders set stiffly. Cary's house occupied the corner of Park Lane and Upper Brook Street, and possessed reasonable grounds for a London house. But he suspected Sax wasn't looking at the gardens.

Caradon had been friends with Sax since they were both boys. Sax could hide things well, but Cary knew the signs. His friend was deeply worried.

Now Cary noticed a third man who stood in the corner of the room, running his fingers over the books on the shelves. This man was younger than Cary, tall and dark haired, with stubble shadowing a square jaw. He wore a belligerent sneer.

The magistrate stood at once and gave a quick bow. "Your Grace, very good of you to make yourself available—" The man's words stopped abruptly. He blinked in surprise.

It was Saxonby who burst out with the obvious question: "What in hell happened to you last night?"

"I was attacked by footpads," Cary answered. "Three of them. Apparently, I'm getting old, because they disarmed me, got me onto the ground, and swarmed me." He spoke lightly, but he carefully watched each of the men. As he'd surmised, that wasn't the reason they were here.

"That must be the explanation," Sax said, turning to the magistrate. "He was with the woman, and they were both attacked."

"And he left her there," sneered the dark-haired man.

"Look, my head was knocked around by a few boots last night," Cary said. He turned one of the chairs in front of his desk to face the three men. His body ached too much to let him remain standing. "I don't have the foggiest idea what you're talking about. I was with a woman. But she accompanied me home, along with my coachman, when I passed out."

"Passed out?" The magistrate scrubbed his jaw.

"Convenient," muttered the other man.

"I beg your pardon," Cary snapped, irritated. "I didn't catch your name." Nor did he know the name of the magistrate. "Would you mind telling me why you are here?"

"Apologies, Your Grace," the magistrate said hastily. "This is John Rycroft, one of the best Bow Street Runners. I am Sir Henry Clemont." The magistrate made a circular motion with his hand to the Runner, obviously requesting a bow.

Rycroft still looked belligerent. He gave a fast, perfunctory bow.

"The nature of your business?" Cary prompted.

Clemont plucked out a large linen handkerchief and mopped his brow. "The body of a young woman was discovered this morning in the mews directly behind your house, Your Grace."

Cary shoved up from his chair. A familiar feeling hit him—sickening horror, cold shock, sorrow.

"Huddled in a corner at the end of your rear wall, she is," the Runner said, picking up the story. Hatred and accusation burned coldly in his eyes. "Given my experience with dead bodies—with bodies that came to that end violently—I would say she's been dead for a few hours."

"There is a woman dead in my mews?" Had he heard this right, or had the blows last night knocked his brain loose?

He looked to Saxonby, who answered, "Yes, Caradon. There is."

Cary turned back to the magistrate. "You are saying she was killed violently. That she was murdered?"

Rycroft answered. "Aye, she was killed violently. Head caved in."

The Runner was succinct. Cary suspected his earlier, roundabout way of expressing himself had been deliberate—to make people say things that incriminated them. Because one look at the Runner's face told Cary that the man believed he had killed this woman.

"You brought a woman home for some fun," Rycroft went on. "What happened? Did she change her mind? Charge you too much? So you lost your temper with her and smashed her head in."

"Rycroft, His Grace is a hero of war," the magistrate said nervously.

"Nothing stands in the way of justice for me," the Runner

responded quietly. "His Grace admits to bringing the woman here."

"Not the one you are talking about," Cary said. "My woman is still very much alive. And I had nothing to do with the murder of this other woman."

Rycroft sneered. "And I suppose you sent your trollop home safely, Your Grace?"

"She is still here, and she is not a trollop. Speaking of which— the murdered girl's body is still there?"

The Runner watched his face. Intently. "It's not the prettiest of sights, Your Grace."

"I know how horrific and pitiable the sight of a murdered young woman is. I experienced it in Ceylon during the uprising."

Cary had dealt with a girl's murder in Ceylon. There he had known who the killer was—one of his soldiers. The man had raped and strangled a young Ceylonese woman.

"I came to you, Your Grace," Sir Henry said, "in the hopes you might have some knowledge as to how this young woman came to be behind your house last night."

He realized Sir Henry was nervous about accusing a duke of murder.

"I do not know anything about a young woman. I have no idea who she is or why she would be there—" He broke off. "It's possible she was a servant. At my house or at one of the others—the mews serves two streets. All the houses have many maids on staff—"

It could have been a girl who worked in his house. Damnation. His gut ached with shock and horror.

Cary strode to the bellpull and yanked it several times.

Penders arrived within moments. "Your Grace?"

"Are any of the maids or female servants missing?"

"Missing, Your Grace?"

"Yes, missing, damn it. Not accounted for."

"The female staff are generally under the charge of Mrs. Kilpatrick."

The housekeeper. "Send her here. At once."

"Maybe you might be willing to trouble yourself to have a look at her," Rycroft said. "See if you recognize her."

"I do not know every servant in this household. Not the female ones." Those issues used to go to his mother. Up until this winter, when she had gotten so ill.

"Don't you? Would have thought all peers knew which young, pretty girls they had in their houses."

"So she was . . . pretty?" Cary asked.

"Assume she was. Though there's so little left of her face, it's hard to tell," Rycroft said casually.

Mrs. Kilpatrick, a woman with graying hair who had worked for his family since starting as a maid, walked in through the open door. According to her, all the female servants were accounted for. They had shown up for their duties as expected that morning.

"Thank you," he said. "That is all for now."

After the housekeeper left, Cary said, "Let me see the girl. Let me see if I know her."

"Would you admit to it if you do, Your Grace?" the Runner asked, impertinently. "Knowing how much your sort hates any kind of a scandal, you might claim you don't know her. Identifying her is an important thing. Even if just to tell her family what's happened to her."

"I am aware of that," Cary snapped. "You will get the truth from me."

He saw Sax flinch at his angry tone.

"I had nothing to do with this woman's death," he repeated. He didn't expect them to believe him, but he had to at least say it.

"It's known you went through a great deal of torture when you were held as a prisoner by the heathens in Ceylon," Rycroft said. "Might have made you snap—"

"I did not snap. Not even while I was being tortured," Cary said, forcing the hot anger out of his voice. Time to sound icy and autocratic, like his father. "Let us discuss some of the facts," he continued, his voice as cold as a glacier. "You believe the woman has been dead for a few hours. When do you think she was murdered?"

"We do not yet have a definitive idea, Your Grace," Rycroft said. "It's an estimation. Perhaps three o'clock in the morning. Or perhaps earlier."

He had been with Sophie every moment since he had encountered her with the Marquis of Halwell at the Cyprian Ball.

Cary strode to the door. "What are you waiting for? Take me to her."

"In your robe, Your Grace?" Rycroft asked.

"Bugger it. Yes, in my robe. I don't give a damn what I am dressed in."

Rain streamed down. In London, spring rain was cold, bone-chilling, and went right through you to freeze your soul. It was a reminder he was at home in England, and not in Ceylon where the rain would be warm and sultry.

Cary grabbed umbrellas from his footmen. Even with the cover, his banyan quickly soaked up the rain. The bottom six inches of it got coated in mud as he strode down his rear lawn, then headed out through the gate to the lane of mud and horse dung along the mews. A young Runner stood there, guarding the body.

Pale didn't describe the young man of the law. The lad was even whiter than Sophie had been, his pallor tinged with green. "Go up to the house," Cary suggested to the lad. "Go to the kitchen at the back and tell Cook the duke has asked her to make you a cup of tea." In the army, he had dealt with many horrified young men.

The lad looked grateful, then sobered and glanced to the magistrate.

"Do as His Grace says, lad," Sir Henry said.

Cary walked over to the body. Saxonby followed, his expression grim. Cary squatted down, trying to make sense of what he was seeing. Then he knew why he was confused.

She was lying curled up, and he had been trying to locate her head. But Rycroft was right. This girl had been bludgeoned in a vicious way, and what remained of her head made him sick. Even after he'd been on a battlefield and had seen men decapitated by cannon fire.

The young woman had dark hair. Blood and dirt coated her gown, but it was a pink silk. It was hard to judge what she looked like. The gown indicated she was not one of his maids.

The dress looked familiar.

He studied her mashed face while his gut roiled.

Now he knew. She was the girl who had been at the Cyprian ball. Sally, the one who had argued with Angelique and who had run when her skirt was torn.

How had she ended up here?

He looked up at Saxonby, who had also squatted to get a better look. His friend had put his hand over his mouth and looked as if he wanted to hurl the contents of his stomach.

"I've seen worse on the battlefield," Cary said. "Do you recognize her? She was at the Cyprian ball."

"And what—followed you home?" Sax asked.

"The last I saw her, she was leaving in a carriage. She had a protector and had no interest in me."

Cary straightened, and Rycroft stalked over to him. "You thought she was a maid. I didn't disabuse you of that, Your Grace," the Runner said. "But the truth be told, that lass is no maid."

"No, she is not. She is a courtesan."

"You knew her. Is she the woman you left with?"

"No." He related what little he knew about the woman—the fight between her and Angelique at the Cyprian ball. The fact that he had seen the girl leave in a carriage bought for her by Viscount Willington.

When he finished, Rycroft said, "A whore, then."

"Perhaps. But I still want to see justice done."

The Runner bristled. "As do I, Your Grace. Doesn't bother me what class a victim or a killer comes from. I don't pursue justice based on anyone's class or position. Just so we're clear, Your Grace. Just so you don't get your back too far up when I come to ask you more questions."

"What sort of questions do you want me to answer?"

"Nothing that will be too troublesome," Sir Henry put in. He had stayed far back from the body.

Rycroft wore his supercilious expression. "What about this Viscount Willington, Your Grace? Is he the sort of bloke who could do this?"

"I would say not. Willington is—he is a gentleman."

"A toff who likes his fun with the ladies, but maybe, if his back were against the wall, he would attack and kill like an animal," Rycroft said.

"I would not have believed him capable," Cary said.

"Is there a Mrs. Willington?"

"There is a Viscountess Willington," Cary answered sharply. "But she is frail and delicate, and I doubt she did this."

"Women can be right tigresses when they feel they're losing their security, Your Grace. Now, what were you doing last night? After you left the Cyprian ball." The Runner nodded toward Saxonby. "You say a female went with you."

"She did. An innocent young woman who had come to London from the country to become a courtesan as her family faces starvation. I intended to take her back to her rooms, then send her back to her home today, before she ruined herself. When we left the Argyle rooms, we went to the stews. It was my intention to frighten her into returning home, by showing her where courtesans ended up—prostituting themselves in the stews. We were set upon by three ruffians. Unfortunately, they ultimately got the better of me, leaving me unconscious. The young woman brought me home, had my servants fetch a physician, then spent the night watching over me."

"I'm sure she did," the Runner said primly. "So this young . . . woman can vouch for you. That you didn't leave your room."

Cary paced. "Given I did not wake up until shortly before you arrived, I definitely did not leave my room. But yes, the young woman can attest to that fact."

"Assuming she was awake the entire time and can make any such statement with complete honesty. And with the assumption her word can be trusted."

"This is England." Cary's voice was raspy and dangerously low. "Where a man is innocent until proven to be guilty."

"Have a care, Rycroft," the magistrate warned quietly. Cary could now see his presence here, afraid Rycroft's belligerent manner would anger a duke, a duke also considered a hero of war.

"All right then," the Runner said grudgingly. "But ye couldn't say if she left yer room, Your Grace."

"You don't seriously think a woman was capable of this."

"Aye, I do, Your Grace. A woman can surprise you. This young woman of yours may have had it in for a rival."

"And met her in the mews behind my house to strangle her in the muck?" Anger coiled in him. He wasn't surprised the Runner suspected he could be a murderer—with a young woman dead behind his house. But to think Sophie did it, was madness.

"I think the question is"—Cary's voice remained raspy and cold; having to speak so much was wearing on his voice—"why was the girl in the mews? Or was she killed elsewhere and brought here? Again, why?"

"You seem remarkably calm, Your Grace," the Runner observed. "I didn't expect you to be so composed."

"I went through battle in Ceylon. The Uva Rebellion of the Kandyan Wars. I've dealt with death on the battlefield, and I've dealt with investigation of improper things that happen during war." He glanced at the victim. "She can be moved now, can she not? We can at least give the poor young woman some dignity now."

"Yes. Yes, indeed," Sir Henry said. "I will have that taken care of at once."

Cary took one last look at the scene. From battle, when there had been questionable conduct, he had learned to quickly absorb details. In this scene, he saw no clues.

He also realized something else. There was little blood. He walked closer to the poor victim. Walked around her. There was blood on her clothes, matted into her hair, on the ravaged face. But there was very little on the ground. Surely, there should be more—

He sensed Rycroft beside him. "I will get to the truth, Your Grace," the Runner said. "You can be sure of that."

Sophie pulled on her gown without putting on her corset. In vain, she tried to arrange it to fit, but the bodice gaped and the skirt was long. It would have to do.

Crushing the skirts in her hands to hold them up, she crept around on the main floor. She hated to eavesdrop, but she had to know whether the magistrate was here for her.

When she heard footsteps, she would dart into a room, praying it was empty.

Then she heard masculine voices coming up the corridor ahead of her, and she darted into another empty room—this one contained a gleaming black pianoforte and a large, graceful white harp.

Sophie held the paneled white door so it was open an inch. She peeked out.

The men stopped in the hallway—there were four of them. Tall, blond, and dressed in his exquisitely embroidered robe,

Cary had his back to her. Across from him, with an uneasy, troubled expression stood his friend with the unusual silver hair, the Duke of Saxonby. The other two men she didn't recognize. One of them must be the magistrate. But why were there two?

The shorter one must be the magistrate—he wore a silk waistcoat with a lavish pattern, a huge cravat, and he carried a gold-topped walking stick. He kept dabbing at his face with a silk handkerchief. The other man was black haired, taller. He wore much less gentlemanlike clothes. And he watched the duke with dark, angry eyes.

"I want this fiend caught," Cary said shortly. "Don't fixate on me. I'm not your murderer."

Murderer? She sucked in a sharp breath.

"And I do not believe Miss Ashley is your killer either."

Her? They thought she was a *murderer*? But she had left Lord Devars *alive*.

"I want this woman to look at the body," the dark-haired man said curtly. "See if she recognizes the dead girl."

A dead girl? Who? At once, her thoughts went to Belle. That Devars had taken out his rage on Belle . . .

Belle was in the country with the children. She must be safe. She *must* be.

What was the duke saying? Sophie strained to hear.

"Sophie cannot look at the body. It would be horrifying," Cary growled.

"I'm more concerned about finding a killer than protecting a whore's sensibilities," snapped the black-haired man.

"She is not a whore, Mr. Rycroft. She is a decent young woman who has to come to London to support her family. I will speak to her."

Her heart soared as the duke defended her. The tone of his voice brooked no opposition.

But who had been killed? A girl—but what girl? Why on

earth would she or the duke be suspected? They had been to-gether last night.

Mr. Rycroft, whoever he was, glowered. "Not alone if it pleases you, Your Grace. I would like to ask the lass some ques-tions. By your own admission, you were under the influence of laudanum and slept for much of the night. The female could be in this up to her pretty neck."

Sophie froze.

This man—this dark, angry-looking man seemed to want her to be guilty.

Of murder.

She felt sick. Did this have something to do with Devars?

But what?

Then Sophie heard the duke speaking, his voice lethally low. "She is not."

At least. The duke believed her.

"You seem very certain, Your Grace? Do you know this girl well?"

"I made her acquaintance only recently." The duke stalked over to stand in front of Rycroft. They glared at each other, eye to eye.

In the country, Sophie had seen male animals fight, circling each other and posturing before an attack. She expected these two to grapple at any moment.

Over her? She couldn't believe it. Why was the duke so pro-tective of her?

He was defending her, and he really did not know anything about her. What she'd told him had been lies. She had never married, and she had borne a child out of wedlock. And she had committed a crime already, one she'd had to commit to try des-perately to save her family.

He was a good, noble man, standing up for her.

And she'd done nothing but lie to him.

"She could be as guilty as sin," Rycroft sneered.

"I can tell she is innocent. As the commanding officer of thousands of soldiers, I learned to read people."

She swallowed hard. Had he seen behind her stories?

No—if he had seen all her sins, he would never want to rescue her.

The duke cocked his head toward the doorway where she hid. She had pressed tight into the wall beside the door and was peeping out through a mere inch crack between the door and its frame. And she stood in shadow. He couldn't see her. That would be impossible.

Yet he studied the door quietly for a few moments. Then said, in his deep, soft tones, "Sophie, would you please come out here?"

8

It was reported that the Prince of Wales witnessed the display I made on St. James's Street. He leapt up from his seat and waddled to the window, where he became infatuated by the "veil-clad Venus." I received a letter the next day from Prinny himself, requesting that I come for an interview. I told him that I would not bestir myself to see him—that if he wished to make me in love with him, he would have to do much more than merely issue a command for an interview.

To my surprise, a modest diamond necklace arrived with a note signed HRH. I returned it. I had decided I would now eschew achievement and select a gentleman I desired—one as young and delicious as my viscount.

—From an unfinished manuscript entitled *A Courtesan Confesses* by Anonymous

Sophie sat on the very edge of a huge wing chair in Cary's study, staring helplessly up at the four men as she explained again that she had never seen the woman before last night. It was the black-haired man Rycroft who did the questioning. He was a Bow Street Runner—an investigator of crime. The magistrate, Sir Henry Clemont, appeared to be playing the role of master attempting to rope in a snarling dog when it came to Rycroft.

She noticed that the Duke of Saxonby kept taking worried glances at Cary.

"The Duke of Caradon is absolutely innocent," she insisted. "I was in his room because I wanted to watch over him after the doctor left him."

Rycroft paced in front of her. He stopped, then turned on her, looking so suspicious, she cringed in the chair.

"Did you go to sleep at all? Maybe after the two of you made love?"

"We didn't." She was blushing.

What did her reputation matter? She had come to London to surrender any shred of propriety she might still have. "I waited until the duke was sleeping, then I do admit I drifted off. I did sleep for part of the night. But the duke was badly battered. How could he have snuck out of bed, gone down to his mews, and attacked a woman?"

"He could be less injured than he made it appear."

"I assure you he wasn't," she cried. "I know he is innocent!"

"And your word alone is not enough," Rycroft said. "To me, your word is meaningless."

Cary made an angry growl. She looked up at him, and then, swallowing hard, she faced the magistrate. "But the truth should matter!"

It appeared the magistrate knew nothing about her attack on Devars to protect herself. Or about Devars's accusation that she had stolen from him. Thank heaven.

"Indeed, it will, miss," the magistrate said. "Rycroft, rein yourself in. Questions must be asked, but you will be civil in your conduct."

"All right. We will speak about the victim then. Do you know her? You were at the Cyprian ball together."

"There were many women at the Cyprian ball," Cary pointed out.

She wanted to say that she had just arrived in London. She had been here for only three days. But that would lead to questions about where she came from. Questions she didn't want to answer to this man who kept peering in a shrewd, unsettling way into her eyes.

"I snuck in. I had never met any of the Cyprians before."

"The balls are by invitation. The Cyprians do not invite many other women—they do not like to invite their competition," Cary said dryly.

"The first time I saw this woman, she was arguing with another Cyprian whose name was Angelique." She related the fight, then the fact that the girl had run away. "Angelique called the girl Sally."

"And the Duke of Caradon went after her," Rycroft observed.

She gave him a withering glance. "Yes, but he returned very quickly. And this was much earlier in the night. The Duke of Saxonby can attest to that. And so can any other gentleman who witnessed the fight. Several were watching."

"I am sure they were. But His Grace could have arranged to meet the young woman later in the night, when he pursued her."

"But I am certain he did not leave his bed. The duke is innocent," she declared for the umpteenth time.

"You could have left the bedroom," Rycroft said to Sophie. "You could have met this woman in the mews. You could have caved in her head with a weapon."

"But I didn't!"

Rycroft leaned close to her. "If I were you, I would make

certain I told everything I knew. There would be those happier to see a courtesan arrested for a crime than a duke."

Panic gripped her, and she gasped in fear. Would they try to make her appear guilty?

Suddenly, Cary was at her side, tall, towering over her, his face was livid with anger. "No one is going to wrongfully accuse Miss Ashley. If you are looking for a scapegoat, not justice, you can get out of my house."

The magistrate got to his feet, sweating, trying to placate the duke.

"I am looking for justice. I would never put an innocent person in prison, Your Grace. I will pursue the truth. You can rest assured of that."

Saxonby also got to his feet. He murmured something to the magistrate.

Sir Henry, the magistrate, said hurriedly, "That will be enough for this morning."

Then the three men left them.

Alone, in the duke's study, Sophie felt strange. Both cold and hot at the same time. She'd intended to convince the duke to keep her.

Yet a woman was dead. . . .

He couldn't have done it! Not only was it impossible, how could this man be a killer? He'd risked his life to rescue her.

Cary walked slowly over to a tall narrow table that held a carafe and glasses on a silver try. He poured two small glasses of an amber liquid.

He cupped one glass in his hand, then gave it to her. "Brandy. You're pale, Sophie."

"I don't understand what has happened. Who killed the girl? Why was she there, in the mews behind your house?"

Rycroft had insisted she see the body. She had looked for one moment, almost collapsed, and then Cary had brought her back into the house.

"I have no idea as to the answers, but I intend to find out," Cary said grimly.

"But the Bow Street Runners are investigating. Aren't we supposed to let the law take care of such things?"

"That Runner does not like the aristocracy. That may blind him to the truth. But that is not relevant to the task at hand. Today, I have to deal with you, Sophie."

She jerked her head up. "Deal with me?"

"Send you home."

She remembered how he had stopped her this morning when she had tried to pleasure him with her mouth, just before they'd been told of the magistrate's visit. She touched his forearm. Panic made her heart pound at a dizzying speed.

"You want to overcome your past and your nightmares. Couldn't you try with me?" she begged. "Maybe if you told me what these awful memories are, I can help."

"No." His face was like stone. "You cannot help. I have reached that conclusion."

How could he do this—give her hope, then crush it in front of her? She couldn't go back home, impoverished. She either had to let Devars do what he liked, or she would be transported, or even hanged, and the children would starve. "What are you so afraid of? It's as if you are scared to tell me about your memories."

He flinched.

She hadn't meant to say any of that. Her emotions had gotten the better of her.

His eyes narrowed. "I can turn that question back on you, Sophie. What are you afraid of? I saw how you behaved around the magistrate. I don't believe you are a murderess, but you are afraid of something."

Suddenly, she saw he was right.

She had to get away from him. He was suspicious of her.

"What did you do?"

"Nothing." She put the brandy glass down so quickly, it fell over. But it was empty. She surged to her feet. "But I am not going home."

She began to hurry toward the door.

"Where in Hades are you going?" he snapped.

But she didn't answer. She gathered up her skirts, and she ran.

He would have caught her, except a hackney was trundling down the road, having dropped off a passenger at one of the other houses.

She leapt inside. "I'll give you twice the fare if you take me away from here as quickly as you can!"

9

A marquis pursued me, but again I refused. He did not take well to my rejection. At a soiree given by a famous London courtesan, the marquis waited while I visited the retiring room. He grabbed me like a common footpad, and dragged me into an empty bedchamber.

"I will have you," he crowed. And he tore my silk skirts.

"No man takes this from me. It is my gift to bestow." I shoved at his chest to no avail. I tried to lift my knee and slam it into his sensitive parts, but he was too quick. He ripped my bodice at the neckline. He took my nipple into his mouth and scraped it roughly with his teeth.

I had fought too long and too hard in my life to be forced to submit to such a hateful man. I reached out and gripped the lip of a porcelain vase now filled with fading roses. Letting out a scream of exertion, I lifted it, swung it, and slammed it into the head of my arrogant rapist of a marquis.

The fine china shattered against his head, slicing into his temple and cheek. Water sloshed over him.

"You bitch!" he shouted. His fist rose, for like all cowards, he was quite happy to hurt a fragile woman.

But suddenly, he was torn away from me.

*It was my viscount. My rescuer and my beloved marquis.
"Damn it," said the viscount to me, after the marquis had
stalked out. "I love you. You threw me over to pursue men with
better titles. But still I love you, and I cannot see you hurt."*

*I was shaking, but it was with a powerful and potent rush of
desire, stronger and more intoxicating than anything I'd ever
known.*

I had been afraid of love. I was not any longer.

—From an unfinished manuscript entitled *A Courtesan Confesses* by Anonymous

"So did you make love to the lovely Sophie Ashley?" Sax
asked as Cary, Sax, and another Wicked Duke, the Duke of Sinclair, searched the mews behind Cary's house for clues.

The Duke of Sinclair lifted his head from his study of the
mud. He'd traced a path from the nearest cross street at the
mouth of the mews and had walked back to the place where
the victim had laid. "The dark-haired beauty I saw you with at
the Cyprian ball? She is new to the game, isn't she? I would
have noticed her if she'd been at a ball before. Have you
claimed her as your mistress? I tried to find out who she was
from our fair Cyprian hostesses, but they are all too competi-
tive and jealous to tell me."

"I didn't know you'd attended that Cyprian ball." Walking
around the spot where the poor victim had laid, Cary frowned
at his two friends. "Regardless, we're supposed to be hunting
for clues. Not discussing my sexual proclivities."

"I just wondered if the Cyprian ball idea had worked," Sax
said.

"Worked at doing what?" Sinclair—known at Sin to friends—
dropped into a crouch, close to the end of the mews. The wind

blew back his brown hair. "Chocolate" was how women described it.

Cary thought of Sophie again. Her lush dark hair, the raven waves all tangled after she came.

Hell.

"Nothing," Cary muttered in answer to Sin's question.

"Have you made her your mistress?" Sin asked.

"No. She's a young widow from the country. Naïve and sweet. It was my plan to send her back home, but she's run off, and I can't find her."

"So she is available," Sin mused.

Cary straightened, all but spitting fire. "Damnation, I just said I intend to send her home for her own protection. I won't stand by and watch her be corrupted."

"Easy, Cary." Sin stood and gave a short laugh. "You seem surprisingly possessive over a woman you haven't slept with."

"Neither of you is going to sleep with her," he said shortly. "Remember that."

"Would you mind coming over here and looking at something, or do I run the risk of getting your fist in my face?" Sin asked.

Cary left his place. Some blood still stained the mud, though the rain had washed most of it away. He had found lace torn from the woman's dress, also spattered with blood. A dainty silk reticule that must have been dropped by the woman—the color matched her dress. There were a few pound notes and some coins, along with some rouge paint for her lips and cheeks.

He had acquired the woman's name from Angelique—Sally Black. Angelique had only surrendered it to him when he had promised to dance several times with her at the next Cyprian ball. She'd told him his presence at the ball had provoked London's Cyprians. Each one wanted to become the mistress of the handsome war hero, the Duke of Caradon. If he showed her special attention, it would be a feather in her cap.

He had managed to get the information and commit himself to nothing more than dances.

"Did you talk to her protector?" Sin asked.

"I ran into Viscount Willington at White's yesterday afternoon," Cary said as if it had been a chance and casual meeting. He had questioned the viscount carefully, but then his simmering anger had gotten the better of him, and his direct, harsh questions had terrified the viscount. Willington had protested his innocence. And if that were a lie, and Willington were guilty, Cary knew his damn anger would put the man on his guard. The thing was, he didn't see Willington had the sense of daring to hurt the girl and put her behind Cary's house. That would take more presence of mind than Willington possessed.

"She was Willington's paramour? Hell, he's the meekest gentleman I've ever known. Still, if he's her lover, he is the most likely suspect. Given you saw her flee to his carriage."

"Agreed, except he claims he did not see his mistress the night she was killed. The carriage she used was one he'd purchased for her. Instead, he spent the night gaming at a dockyard tavern. Early this afternoon, I confirmed it at the tavern, called "The Anchor." He played cards through the night, and only left when the sun was up, well after six o'clock."

Sinclair held out his hand. In it was a silver watch, coated in mud, the silver visible only where Sinclair had brushed it off.

"It could be anyone's, but I assume your killer must have entered the mews from either this end or the other," Sin said.

"And waited for his victim? He could have taken the watch out to check the time." Cary took the watch, withdrew a handkerchief, and wiped the watch clean. "It bears initials. Y. Y."

"Unusual initials," Sin said. "But unfortunately I don't know anyone who has them. They don't belong to Willington. His family name is Tinsdale."

"What we have to do is find out whether anyone in Miss Sally Black's life has those initials."

Sax came over. "This is all we've found. A watch that may not even be related to this murder. Some torn lace and a reticule. Those last two items don't help us in any way. What we need are links to the man who did this."

"If it was a man," Cary said thoughtfully.

"You think a woman did this? For what motive?"

"Jealousy. Anger. Revenge. To clear the path to Willington as a protector, possibly."

"I can't see Cyprians fighting over Willington. He's no prize." Sax gave a wry grin. "But I've heard rumors they intend to fight over you. All of London's premier Cyprians want you—Nell, Angelique, the one nicknamed the Fiery Rose, and the Swan sisters. And probably a dozen others. Maybe one of them could get you through this . . . uh, problem that occurred after you were held prisoner."

Cary curtly shook his head. If Sophie couldn't, he couldn't see how any woman could.

"We should talk this over with Grey," Sin suggested. "He's had experience in hunting down a killer. And he needs something to take him mind off the impending event."

"Impending—?" Cary broke off as he understood what Sin meant. "You mean the birth of his first child."

"Last week, he said he was warned it could happen any day. He's almost gone bald from tearing his hair out with worry," Sax said. "There should be no danger—Helena has been healthy and happy throughout, but Grey is like all men. They worry. Come on. Let's go and confer with the fourth member of the Wicked Dukes."

The three men rode along Park Lane, turning into the drive of Grey's house. Footmen and grooms sprang forward to take the horses.

Grey's majordomo met them at the front door. "His Grace

is in his study," he intoned. "I believe His Grace will be pleased at the visit."

They found Grey pacing in front of his fireplace, a tumbler of liquor in his hand. "They have thrown me out. I'm not allowed in there. Damn it, I want to be there, holding her hand. Making sure she is safe."

Cary, Sax, and Sin exchanged glances. "What are you talking about?"

"I believe he is telling you that his wife is having her baby." Grey's brother-in-law, the Earl of Winterhaven strode through the study door. "Grey, I've been through this many times. The midwives don't want you in there."

"I need to be there. What if something goes wrong?"

"It won't," Winterhaven said confidently.

"But it happens, damn it. I know that." He took a long swallow.

Cary had never seen his friend look more fearful, and he knew Grey had been through hell during his life.

"You need to sit down." Cary led Grey to a wing chair by the fire. He got Grey to sit, but it was only for seconds before his friend sprang up again.

"I need to be with her, Cary. We belong together, and I can't stay here, being useless."

"Grey, the women will turn you away," Winterhaven said.

"Did you really let the midwives keep you away from Jacinta?" Grey asked.

Cary had loved Jacinta, but Winterhaven had won her heart. He had been too damaged to seriously pursue her, so he had backed off and let Winterhaven sweep her off her feet.

Winterhaven blushed. "I did. They were adamant I would only be in the way and hinder their work. But it was hell to wait, to not know."

"Go and be with her, Grey. Being at her side is the most important thing," Cary insisted. He took the tumbler from Grey's clenched hand and set it down. He realized Grey had barely drunk from it.

Sax picked up the glass and started to drink from it. "I hate this birthing business, and I've never had to do it." He shuddered.

"Obviously," Sin remarked, grinning. "You'll never be birthing anything yourself."

"I mean, I've never been at a woman's side as she went through it," Sax muttered.

Cary put his hand against Grey's shoulder and led him up the stairs. They reached the corridor to the bedchamber. A cry of pure straining agony floated down it.

The feminine wail of pain speared Cary's heart, and he stopped dead. He couldn't voice the words in his heart: Was everything all right? He couldn't do it because he didn't want to frighten Grey.

"God, Cary, do you think I could lose her? I love her so much. I feel I've done this to her—put her in danger for my own selfish needs."

"Doesn't your wife want a child as much as you?" Cary asked. "Whenever I saw Helena while she was enceinte, she glowed with happiness."

Grey hesitated. Cary was astounded by the change in Grey—he was a man deliriously happy with being in love, with being a married man. Now he was haunted with fear over losing his wife. "Jacinta tells me I'm mad for being so afraid. But she also admonished me to be at Helena's side. Yet the dragon-like women in there won't let me in. Even Jacinta, who is in there with Helena, could not convince them to change their minds."

Cary rubbed the back of his neck. "Since I'm not a father, I'm no expert." But he thought of how desperately he had wanted his mother and father when he'd been kidnapped. He knew the pain of loss—even if he was returned to his family eventually.

"Grey, I've heard the business is intense and painful, but that doesn't mean anything is going to go wrong. Helena is strong and courageous. I know she will come through this fine, and the baby will be fine as well. Believe in that. And go and be with her."

"Thank you." Grey squared his shoulders. Then he opened the door to his bedroom—from which he had been barred.

A burly woman, whose hair was damp with perspiration, barked, "Be off with you, Your Grace. With all due respect."

Grey walked inside, looking every inch the powerful duke. "I love my wife, and my place is at her side. Now, do you intend to bar the way again?"

The plump midwife lifted a brow and put her hands on her hips. But then she smiled. "All right then. At least you don't look like you are going to pass out when it gets noisy and messy, which I feared you might do before."

"Madam," Grey said with pride, "I do not pass out."

"So you think. You'd be surprised how many supposedly strong gentlemen sink to the floor when they see a babe appear." But the woman stood aside and let Grey in.

She firmly began to push the door shut. But not before Cary glimpsed Grey's wife, Helena, in a damp shift, her hair in a sweat-soaked tangle. Sitting up in the bed, she clenched the hands of Jacinta and a midwife. Her normally lovely face was bright red with the strain and tense with agony.

The door slammed. Cary couldn't see anything more. And he didn't want to—this should be as private as possible between Grey and Helena.

But then, on the other side of the closed door, Helena let out a cry that made his toes curl in his boots.

And he'd been on battlefields.

* * *

She hurt all over.

Sophie woke in her narrow, simple, and uncomfortable cot in the tiny room she had rented on a narrow lane off Whitechapel Street. Faint morning light filtered in between a gap in the tattered curtains. With all the fires burning, there was always a gray cloud hanging over the streets.

She ate a meager breakfast of tea and gruel. She rubbed her lower back ruefully. After one night on the duke's wonderful bed, her sagging bed felt horrible.

A letter came for her, shoved through the letter box of her door.

Belle's lovely handwriting! Sophie clutched the letter. She closed her eyes and said, "Please let there not have been a disaster. Please. Please. Please!"

She had less than a week to come up with a solution. The Earl of Devars had given her a week to return before he threatened to tell the magistrate she had stolen a piece of jewelry from him—the bracelet he had given her before trying to rape her.

Quickly, she scanned the letter. Thank heaven, there was nothing amiss. Belle had written a cheerful summary of the last few days, recounting how the children had created their own version of cricket with fallen pinecones and thick twigs. There was no mention of Lord Devars. Did that mean he was waiting and leaving her family alone—or just that Belle hadn't written about it so she wouldn't worry?

And here she was, one more day in London, running out of time, and still without a protector. Dazzled by the Duke of Caradon, she hadn't even found out when the next Cyprian Ball was. . . .

How was she going to do that?

Sophie thought of Cary showing her the brothel and the poor woman on the street, waiting for drunken men to emerge from the pub.

She wouldn't have to do that. And it wouldn't help. She wouldn't make enough money to keep away from Lord Devars. And keep her family safe.

No—if she didn't find a protector before her week was done—in five more days—she was going to have to agree to his terms. She was going to have to let him do anything he wanted to her.

Why couldn't Caradon have let her become his mistress? There was no mistaking the passion between them. And the pleasure he'd made her feel . . . Ooh, even now she felt an ache deep inside just remembering it.

It meant something. He'd almost lost himself in sex with her. But he'd been too stubborn to see the obvious.

They were right for each other.

They belonged together—at least as gentleman and mistress.

Five days left!

So she couldn't waste time trying to make Caradon see sense. She must find a rich protector.

Her heart ached when she thought of being in another man's bed. But her heart could *not* ache. She didn't have time for the hope of love anymore.

Her teakettle boiled, startling her. She had scrounged up wood for the fire, so she had a small one to drive away some of the damp cold and to boil water. She poured tea in a cracked cup—she had only the one cup, almost ready to break, a plate, two dented pots, a highly dented teapot, and some misshapen forks, spoons, and one knife.

She poured a weak cup of tea—her leaves had been used for two days.

Goodness, she had the answer!

And she had tea all over the table. Half her precious tea had missed the cup when, in her excitement, she'd jerked the metal pot.

But she didn't care. She had a *solution*.

At the Cyprian ball, Angelique had complained about the courtesan who took bribes. All Sophie had to do was find the woman, bribe her with the money she had left, and get into the next Cyprian ball—hopefully it would be *soon*—then find a protector.

She might be able to save them all—and save herself from the horrible Devars.

All she had to do was forget the glorious, handsome Duke of Caradon.

"Hades, how long does this business take?"

The question came from Sin, who paced by the windows at the west end of the south wall. Cary was wearing a hole through the rug at the east end, walking up and down. A grandfather clock out in the hall began to strike—it was eight o'clock, and the sky was dark.

The business of birthing had gone on through the afternoon and into the night.

Sax stood at the mantel, finishing his third brandy. He had one arm braced on the marble as if he were entrusted with the duty of holding up the wall. His silver hair stuck out at strange angles from his raking fingers. He looked up with worried eyes. "I've heard it can take days," he said. "A friend of my sister's was three days in her labors before the baby came."

"Three days? How in God's name do women endure this?" Sin asked.

"They are incredibly strong," Cary answered softly.

He realized how strong Sophie was. She was taking the responsibility for her family after being tragically widowed. She had faced a murder victim with astounding courage and composure.

She had tried to come to his rescue, insisting on his innocence.

Cary realized one thing—it should be his duty to look after her. She needed help. Maybe he couldn't have sex or marry, but he could do decent things.

He could do good.

He could prove he wasn't a monster.

Except he'd lost Sophie now. She'd run off, and he had no idea where she lived. When he'd talked to the other courtesans to ask what they knew about Sally Black, he had also asked about Sophie. He had tried to find out where Sophie lived, but the other courtesans had no idea. He believed that—he didn't think they were lying out of jealousy. They honestly knew nothing about Sophie.

She came into your life, then you were attacked again, and a woman was murdered. . . .

He was always suspicious now. Yet instinct told him Sophie was innocent.

But there were two times in his life when his instincts had been wrong. Once, when he was a five-year-old captive and believed a girl a little older than he was would help him. He never dreamed she would be as evil as the man who held him.

The second time was in battle, when he hadn't believed a British soldier would try to kill him in revenge.

"Behold—I've got a son."

The almost reverential tone came from the doorway. Pulled out of his thoughts, Cary looked to the entrance to the room and saw his friend Grey. Grey's cravat was undone, and his hair was a tangled mess, but he looked like he was going to burst with joy. White lacy blankets spilled over his arms. Where was the child in all that?

Sax and Sin walked over first. Grey drew back some of the swaddling on the bundle.

Sin had scars from fencing duels, Sax from schoolboy brawls. Both had fought hard in their lives and had broken most of Society's rules. But both tall, broad-shouldered men suddenly said, "Awww," and went soft as melted butter as they looked down on the baby boy.

Moving slowly to the group of men, Cary saw a tiny hand emerge. Grey let his bare finger touch the palm of his son's hand—a perfect hand in miniature with fingers spread wide as if feeling the air.

As Grey's finger touched the baby's hand, the tiny fingers wrapped around Grey's index finger, clutching tight.

It was amazing.

Enough to choke a man up.

So much innocence. So brand-new and untroubled with no idea there was evil in the world.

"Can I hold him?" Sax asked.

Grey carefully transferred the bundle, which squirmed as Sax's hands curved to cradle the tiny body.

"Hold him carefully," Grey admonished. "Cradle him in your arms."

A grin spread across Sax's face. "He's so tiny. I've never seen one who is brand-new before."

Cary stood apart from his three friends and watched as three grown dukes made ridiculous faces at the baby.

"Jacinta says they don't smile for a few weeks, but look at him—he's smiling at us."

A ripe smell filled the air.

"I think that is gas," Cary observed.

The pain around his heart was like nothing he'd never known. It was as brutal as the pain he'd felt when the monster who had taken him when he was five told him his parents weren't going to come for him. That they didn't love him or care about him.

That had been a lie, but he'd been terrified, and the pain had been worse than a blade or an arrow in his body—he knew because he'd suffered both.

"He's a bonny boy, Grey," Sax said. "Congratulations. Look at his legs kick in my arms. He's already strong."

"A beautiful boy. He looks like Helena—fortunate lad."

"Other than the little bit of blond hair, he looks like Grey," Sax argued. "He's got dark eyelashes. And look at the color of his eyes. Like Grey's. What do you think, Cary?"

Cary couldn't speak, for the tightness in his throat. He gave a gruff sound of agreement.

Sax looked at him, surprised.

It was a moment of joy, one both Sax and Sin could anticipate. All they had to do was decide to settle down and take wives. Cary knew he would never have this—

"Why don't you hold the lad?" Sax suggested to Sin. He had gathered up the boy, the blankets loosely bundled around him.

"Keep your hand behind his head to support him," Grey instructed.

Sin did, cradling the tiny head with his black-gloved hand. He cooed like a lovesick dove, then walked over to Cary. "You take the little one now, Cary. Have a turn."

Sin held the baby out to him. He took the child, hoping instinct would kick in.

It didn't.

He had no idea what to do.

He felt a rumbling sound. The baby made a small pained noise. His tummy vibrated against Cary's chest—

A squirting sound filled the room. So did another intense smell. This one was worse than the gas smell.

"I think he has pooped," Sin observed.

Cary glared at Sin. "You knew he was going to do that."

"I felt his stomach rumble, but I had no idea it would lead to that."

"Yes, you did. That's why you gave him to me as fast as you could." He couldn't hold the baby out from his body, since he had to keep the bottom and head cradled. The odor made his eyes water.

But he held his arms toward Grey. "He's your son. You take him."

"I'll have many days of this. One of you should hold him. Feel the stirrings of fatherhood," Grey suggested.

"What on earth are the four of you doing?" Jacinta demanded as she sashayed into the drawing room. "This is a precious baby, not a game of hot potato. You cannot pass him off from one to another of you. Let me take him."

She held out her arms and, sheepishly, Cary surrendered the infant. "Dukes, indeed. You are all felled by a tiny baby." Then she smiled. "Though I suppose all of us are, at first."

"You weren't," Cary said. He had once loved Jacinta and had let her go to a better man, a man without a shadowed past. But as he looked at her, he thought of Sophie—she reminded him of Jacinta. Strong. Sophie felt the same love and concern for others.

"I was," Jacinta said.

"I thought females had innate knowledge about this," Sax said, puzzled.

"No. We have maternal love, but very little clue of what to do. Especially when things go wrong. That is why we turn to other females for help."

"What have you named the boy?" Cary asked.

"I don't have a name yet," Grey said. "I don't want to use family names. Helena and I will have to decide."

Jacinta took the baby away. Grey poured them all a celebratory drink. Then said solemnly, "Is it true a murdered woman was found behind your home, Cary?"

"Yes. But this isn't the time to discuss murder and mayhem. This should be a happy moment," Cary said.

"True. But that woman was cheated of happy moments. And that should concern us," Grey said.

"It does." Cary outlined what they had found—the woman's name and a pocket watch. He could tell Grey was fighting to focus, obviously thinking of his son.

As Sin and Sax traded theories, Grey came to him. "This is what your mother wants for you," Grey pointed out gently. "The happiness of marriage and children."

But Cary knew the truth now. "This is not going to be my future."

"If you want it enough, I don't see why you can't make it your future. Marry a lovely girl, have babies."

"It's not that easy. I can't force memories away."

"I don't believe that," Sax put in. He and Sin were listening to the conversation.

Grey looked up. "It is true. I know it's true. You can't forget. It's impossible. But what happens is that the memories lose their power to hurt you. That's how you get healed."

"That will never happen," Cary said.

Grey opened his mouth, likely to argue, but was interrupted when Jacinta returned, carrying the baby. She handed the baby to her brother, effectively silencing him.

"I should go back to Helena," he said.

"Let her rest for a while," Jacinta said quietly. "Heavens knows she will have little rest for the next few weeks, since she wants to feed the baby herself."

Cary saw Grey's gaze fix on him. Damn, he hadn't forgotten their conversation. He was going to be pushing Cary to try to accept happiness.

He couldn't do it. He'd been wounded forever when he was five. If all this time hadn't healed him, nothing would.

Then the baby, with perfect timing, made an *eep, eep* sound, and Grey, Sax, and Sin riveted their attention on Grey's tiny son. Cary joined them to admire the tiny miracle. He felt joy for his friend—and it was the closest he would come to his own joy.

10

My viscount arranged me on my knees, my bare derrière facing him. He mounted me like a stallion and, after stirring my honeypot to the point where I was sobbing in delight, he then took his slick staff and entered me in a most surprising way.

How slow and gentle he was. How tightly I gripped him. At first, I was uncertain, but he eased my worries. Such intense pleasure! When I reached the epic peak, my entire body sang with explosive force.

Then he surrendered with a cry that speared my heart and captured it for him.

I have been most circumspect about my dear viscount, but after this passage, you must be consumed with curiosity as to his identity.

I shall reveal only this: his title is one of courtesy, and he is heir to a grand dukedom. His initials are most unique. Once I set them to paper, my secret is out. So cheekily I give you this— the initials of the most delicious lover in London are X. Q.

—From an unfinished manuscript entitled *A Courtesan Confesses* by Anonymous

Armed with the Cyprian's name—Nell—Sophie asked all around the stews. Her hope was that they'd heard of the Cyprian because she would be scandalous. Gossiping was as popular in sprawling London as it was in tiny villages.

She learned Nell had been an actress once, so she went to Drury Lane. There she heard wild stories. That Nell had juggled both a duke and an earl as lovers at the same time—Nell had even had them both in her bed at the same time. Then Nell had thrown both rich men over for the younger son of a viscount because he was so handsome.

It was said that Nell had turned down the Prince Regent seven times.

Allegedly, Nell had broken apart a diamond necklace she'd been given by the Prince Regent, and she had put all the money in accounts for all the children in a foundling home.

But Sophie couldn't find anyone who knew Nell's exact address. It was always described as "somewhere near Mayfair."

Finally, in Spitalfields Market, Sophie found an elderly man whose son worked as Nell's coachman. The older man had a flower stall that he operated with a buxom woman of about forty, who called him "Da," which was an endearment for "Father," and told him not to say a word. At least, not until Sophie produced a few shillings.

She surrendered them with a gulp. It was hard to give up money when she had so little. But if it got her a protector, it was a wise investment.

The elderly man thought his son worked for a gentleman's widow. His daughter snorted, rolled her eyes, but didn't correct her father.

The man gave her Nell's address, and Sophie bought a flower for her bonnet. The man tried to give it to her for free, claiming it was because she was so pretty. But upon seeing the daughter's sour look, Sophie paid. Then she hurried off to Nell's.

She had no idea how to appeal to Nell's good nature. But she knew Nell took bribes, and she prayed she had enough money to do so.

So to save a few more pennies, she walked from Spitalfields. She was used to walking. Mrs. Tucker, her adoptive mother, had treated her as a servant—she had worked hard, had walked everywhere. She had cleaned the house, fetched food from the village, delivered things for Dr. Tucker.

Sophie knew, from her mother's journal, that she hoped her daughter would be raised as a gentleman's child.

But Sophie hadn't been. The doctor's wife took advantage of her, threatening to send her away or to a workhouse if she didn't work harder at her chores. And the doctor was too caught up in his practice and his medical experiments to notice.

Sophie didn't know life could be any different. She had worked hard, and she grew to like working hard. She'd liked walking in the country and talking to people when she delivered medicine to them. Most of the countrywomen had liked her and invited her in for tea or a treat. She'd loved to get a taste of fresh pie or a sip of milk, and she had loved to visit the farms at lambing time.

She knew she was illegitimate, and she'd known she could have been abandoned and left to die. That happened to poor, innocent babies.

So she'd never resented Mrs. Tucker. She'd thought she should be grateful, and that had made her happy.

Belle said she always looked for the best in things. She supposed that was true.

It had been only when she'd gotten pregnant and she'd been afraid for the future of her child that she had finally seen Mrs. Tucker for the cruel, grasping woman she was. The doctor's wife had always hated her because of who her mother was. The woman had taken the money left for Sophie's care and spent it on herself and her own children. And she'd been waiting for Sophie to make a mistake—for "her blood to show"—so she could hurt Sophie.

And when Sophie had been turned out of the house, after she'd had her baby, she and Belle had walked for miles with the children to try to find work and a place to live.

Walking to Nell's street barely left her breathing hard.

When she saw Nell's home, a brand-new town house in a block of gleaming new white houses on the outskirts of Mayfair, Sophie stopped in her tracks.

It stood four stories tall with so many windows that sparkled in the sun. Freshly painted railings enclosed planters filled tidily with pretty crocuses and other spring flowers. The door had a gleaming brass knocker and handle. Delicate curtains were tied back in the windows.

The house spoke of taste, comfort, and money.

Her heart lifted with hope.

This was what she could achieve as a courtesan. What she must achieve!

If she found a protector, she could raise her son in a lovely house with clean beds and lots of food.

She walked up and boldly rapped on the door.

After a while, it swung open. Sophie expected a footman, but a young, slender girl in a brown dress gaped at her, then said, "No, you mustn't come here. Deliveries and the like go downstairs. At the tradesman's door. If you're applying for a kitchen maid's position, that's where you go."

Sophie's heart plunged. In her old wool cloak over her ordinary dress, she supposed she looked like a servant. "I am here to speak with Mrs. De Lyon. It is in regard to a ball and to a—a payment she is expecting," Sophie bluffed. Surely, Nell's servants must have been told to admit certain young women, the ones who had come to give bribes.

The girl opened the door. "Follow me, then, miss."

Sophie was lead into a small foyer with black-and-white tile. Nothing as ostentatious as the duke's house, but still lovely. Ornate Queen Anne tables stood in niches, topped by vases filled with an explosion of white orchids. Those must have come from hothouses—there was a fortune in flowers surrounding her.

For all Nell sounded so wild, she had good taste.

She obviously loved beautiful things.

This was the life Sophie could have. And Cary thought she should run back home, where she would end up in a workhouse when she ran out of money, and leave herself prey to Devars, who just wasn't going to leave her alone. The only way she could save them all was with money.

Cary meant well.

But he was wrong.

Sophie never used to think about money. She believed in love and happiness. But now, with a child to support and Belle's family to help, it was all she could think about.

The maid, who was young, stopped in the doorway to a parlor and pointed to a chair. "Wait there, miss, and I'll see if the mistress will see you."

Left alone, Sophie was too nervous to sit.

Did she have enough money to tempt Nell to help her?

She walked to a window. It overlooked the small, neat rear yard. There were roses, and plots of earth obviously laid out for a kitchen garden.

It seemed so strange to think a woman who had stood naked in a fountain of front of hundreds of people (mostly men) thought of mundane things such as kitchen gardens. But Cyprians were people too of course.

Someone cleared her throat behind Sophie, and Sophie jumped

and whirled around. The double doors of the drawing room had been opened, and a tall and graceful woman stood framed between them.

A dark crimson sheath of a dress clung to Nell's slender form. Her black hair was lifted in a smooth, elegant knot. One long streak of white ran through her hair. Her lips were obviously painted, but that only enhanced their wide beauty. Nell was not young, but she was strikingly lovely.

Sophie had been called beautiful, but she felt like a plain brown wren beside a spectacular black swan.

"I am very intrigued," the Cyprian said. "I take it you lied your way into my house. So who are you and what do you want? Or should I just have you thrown out now?"

"No, no, please don't throw me out! Please. I'll pay you for your help. I'll pay you anything!"

Nell lifted a suspicious brow. Then she pointed at the silk-covered settee. "Sit down, girl. You look terrified."

"You want me to sit? You aren't going to throw me out?"

"Should I? Do you intend to hit me over the head and steal my silver? I wouldn't try it. I learned how to fend off strong, big men when I was younger than you."

"You did? I should like to know how to do that!"

Nell laughed. "Whoever you are, I do not think you are a threat to me. You wear every expression on your face. I take it you are a girl from the country who desperately wants to get into a Cyprian ball so she can live a glamourous life as a pampered courtesan?"

Her reasons to become a Cyprian had nothing to do with glamour and everything to do with survival and protecting the children, but she said, "Yes. But how did you know?"

"It is rather obvious."

Sophie surged up from the settee. "I know I am asking a lot. And I'm sorry I told a lie to get in. I was afraid you wouldn't see me. I have to go to the next Cyprian ball. I have to find a protector. The children will starve if I don't, or I'll have to let—no, I must become a Cyprian and you are my only hope. My only hope!"

Nell had not sat down. Her vehement speech had made Nell step back, startled.

Had she gone too far? But she had to go on. Nell must have been young and struggling once too. "You see, I was married"—she hated to lie, but it made her sound far more sympathetic—"but I lost my husband at Waterloo. He was only nineteen!" That was true, and it made her chest construct. It made her shudder in pain.

Nell sighed.

"It is now my responsibility to look after—well, my family."

"You have children?"

Did she admit to it? "Yes. I have a son. And my very best friend—my only friend—lost her husband to war. She has children too. But she couldn't do this. She would never be a courtesan. So it is up to me."

Nell was not ringing any bell or summoning a servant to toss her out.

So she rushed on. "I desperately need to become a courtesan. All my life I've been told I was pretty. I know I am not beautiful, but I thought there might be some gentleman who would want me. My mother—my mother was a courtesan. I never knew her. But I knew she survived. She survived well. And I thought I could too."

"Who was your mother—what is your name, child?"

"I am almost one-and-twenty, so I am no longer a child."

"That is true. I am sure you have not been a child for a long time. Since you learned of your husband's death, I should imagine."

That *was* true, and Sophie nodded. "But I don't know who my mother was. She gave me to a family in the country, paid them to raise me. I never even knew that until—until my husband had died. They would not even give me my mother's name. I wish I did know who she was."

"It is probably best that you do not know. You should go home."

Nell was as bad as the duke. What was it about her that screamed she should not become a courtesan? With a courtesan mother and no money, what else was she to do?

"There are so many reasons I can't. I do have some money. I heard"—she had to say this politely—"that you help young women, in return for a . . . gift."

"Sit, and we shall have tea." Nell swept to a tasseled bell pull and gave it a yank. She moved as though she floated above the ground.

Gentlemen would be transfixed just watching her walk. "How does a woman become as bewitching?"

The words came out of her mouth before she could stop them.

But Nell looked pleased. Returning, the woman smiled. "She becomes the protégé of an experienced and successful woman."

"How would she do that? Would it cost money?"

"Not in this case. I have been careful, and I have sufficient money for my needs. The bribes do help though. They pay for little luxuries." Her eyes twinkled. A rattling sound came from the hall. "Tea," she said.

Minutes later, Sophie held a cup of tea in a fragile, gilt-rimmed cup.

She realized Nell was a truly independent woman. She had her own house, her own income, and she apparently did as she pleased.

Few women in England could make such a claim.

All Sophie had to do was forget the Duke of Caradon, and this could be her future.

But as she was looking at all of this, her heart *ached*.

She remembered what it had been like when she'd fallen in love with Samuel. Logic told her it was hopeless. She was an adopted daughter with uncertain parentage, and he was an earl's son. But that didn't stop her heart from relentlessly loving him.

In one night, she had fallen headlong into love with Cary, and it hurt terribly now.

But she had to think of her son. She had to forget love.

"Would you help me?" Sophie asked. "Do you think I could get a protector as I am? Do I need . . . work?"

Nell tapped her chin thoughtfully.

"I think I have potential," she continued awkwardly. "I thought I might become the Duke of Caradon's mistress—"

"Caradon?" Nell cried. "You do aim high. After he returned a war hero, he was an utterly reformed rake. Many women want him; none have tempted him."

"I thought I had. He took me to his home. At the last minute, he pleasured me, but then he decided he had to send me home."

A biscuit dropped from Nell's fingers. "He took you to his home? To his bed?"

"Well . . . well, yes." There were so many other details, but she didn't want to explain them all. And the things he'd told her, they were private.

They sipped tea. Nell studied her. "It is unfortunate the Duke of Caradon did not succumb to your charms, my dear. He is a wealthy man."

And gorgeous. And he had done the most wonderful thing to her with his mouth. He had given her the very first climax she'd ever had.

Unfortunate was hardly the word. Devastating. Disastrous. Heartbreaking.

"It was," she said in a small voice.

"But there are more fish in the sea," Nell said cheerfully. "I cannot see how you could not be successful. Your story has touched me, and I am willing to help. At the next Cyprian ball, which will be three days from now—"

"Three days!" Sophie cried. "I can't wait that long. He'll have come back by then. He'll—" She broke off.

"Who will have come back? Not Caradon."

"No, not him. I can't talk about it. It doesn't matter."

"I think it matters very much. You are terrified of this man, aren't you? He's threatened you, has he? With what? Hurting your child, perhaps."

Sophie's heart almost stopped. "No. No, not that." He's threatened to see her hang, and she knew that would mean disaster for her son, left alone in the world. But Devars had never threatened her boy directly. No, he wasn't capable of hurting an innocent child, she was sure of it.

"No, he hasn't done that. Because he knows he can hurt me." She knew Nell was waiting for her. Waiting for a name. "I can't tell you who he is."

"I won't help you unless you tell me everything."

"Then I have to go." She couldn't reveal what she'd done. It was too powerful and dangerous—she couldn't let anyone know she had hit Devars and that she had taken his bracelet.

Sophie stood. Blinking back tears, she hurried for the door.

"My dear, whoever you are, wait," Nell called.

Sophie stopped. And she turned back.

This was it.

Tonight she would find a man—other than the Duke of Caradon—and she would convince him to make her his mistress.

Sophie licked her lips nervously. She sat beside Nell in the woman's carriage. They were traveling to a notorious private party in the country.

Nell had warned it was more scandalous than any Cyprian

ball—and would be stocked to the rafters with gentlemen seeking mistresses.

Sophie shivered.

She *had* given up on Caradon. She had.

"Cold, my dear?" Nell asked.

"No." Sophie pulled her cloak tighter around her. It was Nell's old cloak, made of dark green velvet. It was lovely and warm. She felt like an empress wearing it, though Nell had dismissed her gratitude. "It's not that kind, my dear. It's getting rather worn."

She wore the same gown as she had at the other ball, of course. She owned no other dress. Would gentlemen remember that? Would it matter?

"I'm not cold," she said slowly. *I'm heartbroken and fighting not to show it. Or even feel it.*

"You are pining for the Duke of Caradon, aren't you?"

Sophie stared. "How could you tell? I'm trying not to show it."

Nell smiled mysteriously. Nell was truly beautiful. Her face possessed fabulous bone structure. Her figure was trim. Lines bracketed her mouth and radiated from her eyes, but Sophie thought that made her look even more elegant and rather patrician. When Nell gave that enigmatic smile that barely curved her lips, Sophie could understand why Nell had been successful—she was still a mistress to a duke, Sophie had discovered—for she looked sensual and intriguing.

Sophie was no woman of mystery. She wore everything on her sleeve.

Nell watched her curiously. "You never did tell me what he did to you to make you besotted with him after just one night."

He rescued her. He cared about her. He pleasured her. Nell had coached her, taught her how to walk and how to look sultry. And had asked her a lot of questions about Caradon and what he was like as a lover. Sophie had been too shy to answer.

And the things he'd revealed to her were private. She knew he would want them to stay secret.

"He was just perfect." She sighed. "But it doesn't matter because I am over him."

"You had best be. You won't find a protector if you are mooning over the duke."

"I am not," she insisted.

"Good. And you must be ready to be naughty. Are you afraid of being naughty?"

"Well . . . well, no. No, I don't think so." She had wanted to try to suck on Cary's cock, and it had been surprisingly, wickedly fun. Until he had stopped her.

Nell put her gloved hand on Sophie's knee. "What you must understand is that many gentlemen want a mistress because it is only with them that they can get the strange, wicked, and sometimes perverse things they desire."

"Perverse?"

"You will see. What you must remember is that wives are not supposed to do such rude things. They are ladies. You are supposed to look ladylike but provide a harlot's skills in the bedroom. That is why men come to you."

Sophie nodded. "I can do that."

"Even with a man who is not the Duke of Caradon?"

She so wanted it to be with the duke. "I need to find a protector within five days so I no longer care about the duke."

"Your lover will expect you to take his cock in your mouth."

"I know."

"And some men enjoy putting their staff in a woman's derrière."

Sophie blushed. That was what had been meant in that passage in the book. "Oh goodness!"

"Men are highly inventive when it comes to sex, dear. They will do the most remarkable things when driven by lust. Some like to tie a woman up, or spank her. Some enjoy inflicting pain. Some like to dress in a woman's clothes. Some like to be ridden like a horse. And for everything a man wishes to do to a woman, no matter how odd, there are always men who want it done to them. Do you feel you are up to that task?"

Was she? Sophie swallowed hard. But she must be. And she said, "I *will* be."

"We will start you with someone easy, my dear," Nell continued. "Someone who is not too demanding. I have a few gentlemen in mind."

Sophie nodded. She should ask who. But she didn't care.

She couldn't help it. All she could think of was Caradon. She would try *anything* he wanted. But with another man—

"Have you ever fallen in love with one of your protectors?" she asked Nell.

Instead Nell said, "I have just realized that the night you spent with Caradon was the night that girl was murdered behind his mews. You must know all about it."

Nell was watching her carefully, and Sophie realized Nell was not going to answer her question about falling in love.

"I don't really know all about it," Sophie said. "The magistrate came and asked us questions, but we had been in bed . . . um, asleep for most of the night. I did recognize the girl though." She realized she could maybe learn things from Nell. In the days since, she had seen stories in the newssheets about the murdered girl found in the mews behind the "Hero-Duke's" house. Gossip was already going through London that maybe the duke was not such a hero after all. Maybe he was a murderer.

But it was the insidious kind of gossip that couldn't be traced. Or stopped. Sophie kept protesting he was innocent to the few people she saw near her rooms. But no one believed her.

Maybe Nell knew something about the girl. "She was Sally

Black, and she was at the Cyprian ball that night. She had an argument with Angelique. She must have been going to meet someone near the duke's house."

"Or maybe she went to see the duke. You told me about that night. I am sure he didn't plan to be attacked. He might have made an arrangement to see her."

"You think he killed her, just like all the other people who like sordid gossip. He didn't."

"No, dear, I know the Duke of Caradon had no hand in her death—I knew his father well, and know that the current duke is a very noble man. A bit wild in his youth, but then he went to battle. Distinguished himself as a complete hero. He is not the sort of man to hurt an innocent. But I wonder why she was there."

"I don't know. But at least you think he's innocent." Sophie thought of how the village where she'd lived had reacted to her. Once she had been thrown out of her home, even before it had been widely known she'd been pregnant, everyone had judged her. "Why does everyone leap to the conclusion that he is guilty?"

"A duke and a war hero who has fallen from his pedestal? Unfortunately, that bit of speculation will be too delicious to resist. Some would be very delighted to see him hang."

"But he's innocent."

"Innocent men have hanged before, my dear."

The carriage stopped. Nell's stunning white carriage looked like something Sophie would picture Marie Antoinette riding in—pure white, with light blue trim and curlicues everywhere. With blue ribbons and ribbons on the white horses.

Nell's footman, in powder-blue livery, rushed around from the back of the carriage, opened the door, and helped them down. They stood in an enormous drive in front of a house so large, Sophie gasped. Dozens of carriages stood in the drive. A crush of people made their way up the steps. Women held up velvet cloaks and silk skirts. The men wore immaculate evening dress. Everyone wore cloaks and masks—it was a masquerade.

"Here is a mask for you, my dear." Nell held out a white mask and helped Sophie tie it in place. "Tonight you cannot think about Caradon. Remember."

But he was all she could think about now! She was terrified for him. "But haven't you ever fallen in love with a protector?"

"I enticed aging earls and dukes for money. I seduced young titled men because it was fun. But love is a dangerous thing. If you want to survive, Sophie, do not fall in love."

"My mother wrote about love. It was in the book she was writing about her experiences. She was always falling in love. That was why she had me. Because she was in love."

"Then you must not make her mistakes, Sophie. And take this advice—do not ever be the first one to speak of love when you are with a protector."

With that, Nell propelled her inside.

Sophie gaped in shock. In the foyer of the huge house, a woman stood on a low pedestal of marble. But she was shackled at her wrists and ankles. Her arms were lifted above her head, suspended from a gold chain that hung from a chandelier. Two women in only corsets and stockings were on their knees in front of the woman and behind her. Their bottoms were bare. Their breasts spilled over the corset cups.

Not only that, the kneeling women held the gauzy fabric of the suspended woman's skirt aside and thrust two long, dark phallus-shaped wands inside the woman.

Nell had been right. About bottoms.

Sophie's face was on fire.

The woman moaned. A strip of heavy white lace over her eyes, tied at the back of her head. The woman had red hair, henna red, and it hung to her waist.

Then the woman's moans came faster. The woman thrashed against the shackles, writhing wildly. Being suspended allowed her to move like a houri in a mad dance.

The crowd moving in pushed Sophie along.

But she couldn't stop staring.

As Sophie walked past the woman, she had to look behind to see what happened. The slit skirt was pushed aside to reveal a plump, pink bottom. And a wand of dark jade protruded from between the lush cheeks, with the other courtesan's hand wrapped around it.

A strange twitchy feeling struck Sophie all over. It seemed to shoot through her and throb between her legs.

The woman screamed, and Sophie knew she was having her climax. In front of all these people. This might be just a bit too scandalous.

"Nell—" she began.

But Nell did not stop. "Come this way, my dear. There is usually a rather thrilling display in one of the side rooms."

A door stood open, but a curtain had been affixed in the entrance. Nell drew it aside. "Ooh, I do love games where handsome young men play together."

Billiards? Cards?

No, it certainly wasn't that kind of a sport.

On a large mound of pillows, a man was on his hands and knees. A young man, beautiful as a Greek god with pale blond hair tied in a queue. Sophie's eyes could not go any larger. The young man on all fours took the cock of another young beautiful man into his mouth. Then a third man joined in, his breeches pushed down low on his hips. He took his long, jutting staff and worked it against the derrière of the blond.

Sophie retreated, face aflame.

"He pays for these tableaux to arouse his guests," Nell said. "And of course, they are all supposed to service him afterward."

They left that area. Nell grasped two champagne flutes from a passing footman.

Sophie gulped hers. "Service who? Whose party is this?" She realized she didn't actually know. Then she thought—surely, it was just the women he engaged for himself.

"One of the Wicked Dukes."

Cary was a Wicked Duke. But this couldn't be his house—

"The Duke of Sinclair. He is the wickedest of the four of them. Greybrooke is tamed now that he is married. And your favorite, Caradon, has become reclusive and noble. The only ones left who are fun are Sinclair, known as Sin, and Saxonby, known as Sax."

Sophie felt very relieved.

Nell glanced around the room. Then she smiled. "It is time to take you into the ballroom. I believe you will be surrounded by gentlemen in no time."

And she was. Soon she was in the center of a group of eight gentlemen, all gathered by Nell.

A gruff voice growled, "This is my mistress, gentlemen. Do not poach on my preserve." Suddenly, two of the men were shoved out of the way.

Caradon! He lifted her hand and kissed it. Quivers went through her. His eyes captured hers. In a low, dangerous voice, he growled, "What in Hades are you doing here? Are you completely mad? Of all the daft things to do—you come to a damned orgy?"

She registered his furious gaze, his narrowed blue eyes. He wrapped his long fingers around her wrist and dragged her across the ballroom.

144 / Sharon Page

She was too stunned to resist.

Then Sophie gathered her wits. She couldn't dig in her heels on a parquet ballroom floor. But when he reached a door to the outside, which must have led to a terrace, she gripped the doorframe. Obviously, he could have pulled her free, forced her to go, but when he felt resistance, he stopped.

Goodness, here by the wall, in the shadows behind potted plants, couples were making love.

There were groups of three as well.

"I can't leave," she cried, though he was right—she was not ready for this. But she wouldn't admit it to the man who wanted to send her back to the country. "I have come to find a protector. And why are *you* here? If you are looking for a woman to make love to, why couldn't she be me?"

"I came," he said, between gritted teeth, "because I received a note telling me that you would be here. What was your game? To get me here to rescue you? Well, I'm here."

"Note? What note?"

"The anonymous note you sent, Sophie."

"I didn't send any notes to you. Anonymous or not. Why did you think I did?"

"Who else?"

"I don't know—" Nell knew she would be here. Why would Nell—? Oh, heavens, had Nell hoped Caradon would come to her rescue?

But why, when Nell had told her that love was dangerous?

"Why in God's name have you come here to find a protector? Sinclair is my friend, but his entertainments attract some of the most perverse and dangerous of London's rakes," he said curtly.

"They just look like gentlemen to me."

He lifted his brow. "In name only," he said. "And you are

far too intelligent for me to believe you saw those displays in the entry and you still believe that."

"Well, you refused me," she pointed out, "so I had to come to another ball. I found Nell, for she gives out invitations for money. And you are just scaring men away! You told those men I am your mistress when I am not! It's hardly fair."

And it was agony on her heart. Why was he so possessive of her when he didn't want her?

"I need to think," he growled. "I am not going to stand by and let you turn yourself into a whore."

That word pricked her pride like a burning hot fireplace poker. "One protector, if I'm devoted to him, does *not* make me sinful. I believe that. Even if I haven't said vows, it's not wrong if I'm faithful." That was what her mother had written in the anonymous manuscript. That she was more faithful to her protectors than most *ton* wives were to their husbands. "If I'd had my way, my night with you would have been the first of many nights with you."

When he didn't answer, just watched her, she grew furious. "It is easy for you to judge. You are a rich duke. Do you know what it's like to have nothing and starve?"

"I know what it is like to face death and to be starving and held prisoner. I know the last thing I would surrender would be honor."

"What if it was the choice between your honor and watching three innocent children starve? What would you do then?"

"There has to be another way," he barked. "Look at the women here—pretty enough, but they are hard, ruthless survivors at the core. You are so sweet."

"I have to learn to be ruthless. I want to survive."

"Goddamn it," he said, his voice low and hoarse. "I will give you an offer. I will give you all the things you dream of having as a courtesan. You'll be mine. But you will not make love with me. You'll have your house, your allowance, and food and safety for your family."

She gaped at him. All around them, people were having sex in all sorts of tortuous positions, but she was blind and deaf to it all. "You're making me an offer for—"

Another man stepped right up to them, so close she had to see him. He was shirtless, wearing only trousers and boots. Wicked intent glittered in his dark eyes, and his coal-black hair hung over his brow. He was breathtakingly handsome, with a broad chest and huge arms.

"I am the Earl of Stratham." He bowed over her hand, in the middle of an orgy, like a knight of old. "I overheard that Caradon made you an offer. Ungentlemanly of me to eavesdrop, but when such a beauty is about to be claimed, a man can be excused for some desperation. I promise you three times whatever he offers you." His voice lowered, and he bent to her ear. "As well as jewels, gowns, carriages, and a town house, I am prepared to offer an allowance of five thousand. I believe Caradon won't top that."

Five thousand! It was a fortune. If a gentleman came with that, debutantes would club him over the head to drag him to the altar. A year of that and Sophie could keep her family for a lifetime. The children's futures would be secured. With a fortune like that, it wouldn't even matter that her son was illegitimate. Well, it almost wouldn't matter.

And she could tell Devars to take a long walk on a short pier.

She knew what she must do—she must say yes.

But when she met Cary's shocked gaze, her heart flip-flopped in her chest. What should she do?

Would he really give her a house and an allowance to not sleep with her? And he said he needed to marry—he wouldn't keep her then.

She suspected Stratham would.

Oh God, then she would be kept by a man who had a wife. The Earl of Stratham might already have a wife. She hadn't thought of that.

But she had only days—then Devars would destroy them all.

"What's your name?" Stratham demanded.

"Sophie," she managed.

"All right, Sophie," Stratham said heartily. "What's your choice?"

She parted her lips. She couldn't look at either of the men. She knew what she must choose—

11

How naïve was I! I believed X. Q. was now mine, and we would look forward to a future of happiness. After all, he could not resist me. We played such delightful bedroom games— naughty, delicious games with the judicious use of ropes.

Yet his father disapproved. In face of losing his allowance, X. Q. cooled our relationship once more. By this point, I was so deliriously in love, I would have taken him without a penny to his name. But losing his allowance mattered far more to him than to me. But I had been a fool!

So from love—and its bitter lessons—I toiled onward and upward.

—From an unfinished manuscript entitled *A Courtesan Confesses* by Anonymous

Couples—and threesomes—actually stopped making love to watch the competition between the Duke of Caradon and the Earl of Stratham.

Before Sophie could speak, Stratham grabbed her wrist and yanked her closer to him, forcing her to stumble. Her back stiffened. The brandy on his breath almost made her eyes water. A lecherous grin twisted his handsome mouth into something horrid.

"I know, my dear, what your answer will be." Stratham lowered his voice and he gripped both her wrist and her bottom. His squeezing fingers almost crushed her wrist. He pinched her derrière. Hard.

"When you are mine, you will belong to me. Completely. Do not ever cross me; do not ever stray. If you even look at another gentleman, you will know the force of my wrath and you will not forget."

It was more than possessiveness in his eyes. Sophie read belligerence there—as if she had already done something wrong. It scared her.

This "gentleman" was just like Devars. He felt he owned her, when she had done nothing to encourage him. He'd decided he wanted her, so she was his, and she had no choice and no say.

She struggled to push Stratham's hand away.

"I am afraid you are mistaken, sirrah. Your offer is most generous, but I must decline. His Grace did make his offer first, and I fear it would not be fair to accept."

"Fair? Dear lady, in matters of the bedroom, I never play fair."

Suddenly, a look of pain shot across the man's angry face.

His hand was yanked away from her, and his entire body jerked and straightened. Cary had grasped his forearm and twisted it, pinning Stratham's arm behind his back.

She marveled at Cary's strength as he carelessly captured the earl. Stratham cried out in agony—though he bit it short.

"Keep the hell away from her, Stratham, before I call you out," the duke growled. "And I would not plan to shoot wide. I've killed a lot of men in battle. I don't miss."

The Earl of Stratham was pale with pain, shaking. "All right."

Cary released him. But before Stratham went, he said in a low deadly tone, "I accept your choice, harlot. But I have not been dealt fairly in this matter. Until we next meet."

Oh, they were never going to meet again.

"There will not be another meeting. If you even see her enter a room you are in, you will leave it immediately. You will keep far away from her. Or I'll damn well shoot you." Cary's chest moved with angry breaths. He looked like he could breathe fire.

Stratham straightened, then tried to salvage his pride by grasping a courtesan who was standing nearby, wearing a harem girl costume. "Come with me," he snapped. "Let me fuck you."

"Of course, my lord," the woman simpered.

Then they were gone.

Sophie's pulse thundered. She looked up at Cary, up at his pale blue eyes. "You rescued me again."

His long fingers gently stroked her wrist. Lightning sizzled through her at even the soft, delicate touch he gave. "Does it hurt? He bruised you. I should have called him out."

"No! Not a duel. I won't have you shooting at someone. Or getting shot."

Cary shook his head. "You are trouble, aren't you, Sophie?"

"I'm not. These gentlemen are," she declared, indignant. This was hardly her fault. She glanced toward the earl, who was pushing his way through the crowd. A sense of cold washed over her. She shivered. "I fear I've made a dangerous enemy."

Cary studied the earl's retreating back. "Don't worry. I'm your protector now."

"Yes, you are. But how can I let you be my protector if I'm not giving you anything in return?"

"You are," he said curtly. "And it's time I take you home, before you get into more trouble."

"I should tell Nell I am leaving."

But then she spotted Nell strolling through the crowd, her arm linked with the arm of a tall, extraordinarily handsome gray-haired gentleman. Nell saw her.

And winked.

Soft gray tinged the sky, promising dawn, and Sophie hurried along the carriageway to the door of her room, located at the end, where the gravel drive opened out into a small courtyard. A man passed her, lifting both his cap and his brow as he said, "Good *evening*, Miss Ashley. Out a bit late, aren't ye?"

She saw a hint of a teasing smile on the man's face—he was handsome, had a wife and five young children, but he watched out for her. "Good *morning*, Ben. You're right, it is beyond late, and now it's early."

She was coming home while many people were leaving their rooms to go to work—bakers, butchers, coopers, laborers.

"As long as ye're home safe and sound."

"I am. Not to worry," she said cheerfully. She was all but bursting with joy. And it was kind of him to be concerned about her.

Strange smells touched her nose as she opened the door to her small room. The building was a rabbit warren of corridors and rooms. Hers was accessed from the outside—from a small carriageway that ran underneath the building. She also had a tiny, dirty window.

Sophie took a deep breath. A mistake—no matter what time of day it was, the stews smelled of coal smoke, chamber pots, smelly fish, cabbage . . . and damp.

She turned the key in the lock, pushed open the door, and stepped inside—into pitch dark, of course, for there wasn't much light in the sky yet. Even if there were, it wouldn't penetrate the grime and grease on the miniscule window.

But after several days here, she could make her way in the dark to her table—and her candle—without bumping into things. She shut the door. Then she spun around. This was to be one of her last days here. Caradon had promised to have a house for her quickly. She might not be a courtesan for real, but she was about to get all the advantages.

And everything was solved!

Sophie closed her eyes, tipped back her head, and squealed with joy. A restrained squeal—so she didn't wake any sleeping children in the building.

She would bring Belle and the children to London. They would have warm beds. She could thumb her nose at Devars, for she would be under a duke's protection. She would have money to replace the dratted bracelet, and he would never dare offend a duke by having her arrested.

Even though Cary wasn't going to be her lover, he was going to protect her.

It just showed what a wonderful and perfect man he was.

But she wanted him. *Really* wanted him.

She would find a way to heal him. She would turn him into her lover for real.

Spinning around again, she got dizzy. She stumbled and knocked the teapot to the floor. She bumped her one rickety chair with her hip, and the leg finally parted from the seat. It toppled over with a *thud*. She sank to the bed—rather, the cot—in the dark, and she laughed.

Her son would be safe now. He would have a future—!

A floorboard creaked. The sound didn't come from under her feet.

Sophie froze. Her heart pounded fast, but that was the only part of her willing to move. Her entire body seemed to have turned to stone in an instant.

It was only a creaking board. It could be coming from the

room beside hers. It could be anything—the house groaned at the slightest provocation.

She strained her ears, listening for more. But sound filled the stews. Dogs howled. Carts rattled. So much sound now, with people waking and leaving in the weak dawn light to go to work.

Suddenly, her tiny room felt vast and dangerous. She couldn't even speak—why ask if anyone was there? There shouldn't be. Oh heaven, there shouldn't be.

There *couldn't* be.

She thought of the girl huddled on the mucky ground in Cary's mews, and she wanted to shriek.

Get hold of yourself!

Sophie launched off the cot and stalked with determination toward the table and her candle—and her flint—

She was suddenly thrown to the side and slammed up against her closed door. Her chest hit hard, and all her breath flew out. Then she was shoved harder by ruthless hands and banged repeatedly against the unyielding door. Pain shot through her breasts and her ribs. The weight pressing on her, pushing her against the wooden surface, was crushing.

A gloved hand clamped hard against her mouth. She bit— sank her teeth in desperately—but all that got her was an evil chuckle. Leather was crammed into her mouth. The side of a hand was jammed in there so she couldn't scream.

That courtesan, Sally, had been killed. The same was going to happen to her.

She bit at his glove, lashed out at him with her feet, her hands. It was useless.

Then his hand moved away. For a moment, she was stunned by her good luck.

Scream, you fool!

She screamed. Screamed and screamed. And fought to push

back against him enough to open the door. She managed an inch, then his huge hand slammed it shut again.

Wrapping her hair in his fist, he yanked her head back, and she cried out. Tears blinded her. She should have gone for a weapon, not the stupid candle. The frying pan. The fireplace poker. Anything.

That had been what had saved her with Devars. Why had she been so stupid?

She was propelled back across the room so fast, she almost didn't touch the ground. She still couldn't see the man who was going to kill her.

He threw her onto the table, and all she saw was shadow. A feeble shaft of daylight touched the white of his eye and sliced along the ridge of his sharp cheekbone, but there was something black over his face. A mask.

Then she saw a bit of gold. It was blond hair peeking out from under his hat and touched by the light.

"Don't do this," she begged. "I'll give you money. I'll—"

"I've been given more to kill you. But a little fun first wouldn't go amiss."

He grasped her skirts, and she fought. She kicked at his hands, but he grabbed her flailing legs and shoved them apart. His bulk pressed on top of her.

His body was all hard muscle, not fat, and weighed a ton. She fought to breathe. He smelled of cologne—an exotic, expensive one.

He backed off and flung her over. The table plowed into the small of her back. She could barely see through the tears of pain.

You have to fight!

His eyes. Go for his eyes.

She desperately poked with her fingers.

The flat of his hand cracked across her face, pounding her

head to the side. Pain exploded. Lights burst before her eyes. Like being hit by a board!

He hit her again.

Leaving her dazed. But she must fight against the pain and confusion; she had to fight for her life.

She couldn't—

Her door flew open, slamming into the wall. Plaster dust puffed out, and another large shape filled her doorway. She screamed, "Help me, please!"

At least that was what she thought she'd said.

Her head swam from the blows, she could barely see, but meager fingers of daylight touched the second man as he strode in. Her attacker backed off her to confront this new intruder.

Silvery light illuminated golden hair on this man. Then light shone on his face, and her heart leapt with hope.

"Bloody hell," Cary spat, and his fist arced through the air and sent her attacker's head on an arc of its own.

The man reeled and stumbled to the side; he was off her. Her whole body ached. She slithered off the table and struggled against her binding corset to stand. She stumbled toward the fireplace, trying to find a weapon in the gloom.

Cary fell back, having been hit.

Then the bulky shape of her attacker went back.

Each time they staggered at each other, swinging, then grappling.

Cold metal touched her hand. She hefted the poker and went for the huge bastard who'd planned to kill her. But the iron bar was so heavy and she was so hurting and weak, she stumbled as she lifted it.

Cary hit her attacker in the stomach, then the jaw. The man teetered back, but suddenly laughed, grabbed Cary, and pushed him at her as he ran out of her room.

The poker was on a deadly arc.

"Cary!" she shrieked.

"Bloody hell again!" the duke yelled, and he jumped to the side as the poker came crashing down. The weight pulled her forward, and he caught her.

"Are you all right? Wait here. I'm going after the bastard."

Wait here? She could barely move. She stood, swaying. She still gripped the end of the poker, but its tip was stuck in the wood floor.

Cary was going after a killer.

Brandishing the poker, she went after the duke. She stopped in the doorway. The carriageway was empty except for Cary, who had reached the main street and stopped. He looked up and down the street. Even from where she was, she knew he was cursing. He turned and sprinted back. He passed her and reached the courtyard beyond the carriageway.

Tentatively, she stepped out and went to him. Dawn was lightening the sky, turning the buildings into planes of slate-gray and giving some form to the things around them.

If Cary hadn't come, she would have been dead.

The buildings around suddenly took flight around her, twisting and writhing like fanciful things. She reached out to fight them off, and suddenly felt as if she'd fallen off the edge of a precipice—

"I wish I could take this away from you. Make this so it never happened."

Cary spoke so softly to her, his voice ravaged and raw, but Sophie found she couldn't stop shaking. In his carriage, he had wrapped a fur throw around her, surrounding her in the warmth of black sable. And in the strength of his powerful arms.

But nothing seemed to stop this awful trembling.

"It is all right," she whispered. *You are safe with him,* she told herself. *With Cary, you will be safe.*

If she could be with him forever, she would always feel safe.

"It's not all right," he said softly. "An attack . . . it changes you. It makes you never feel quite safe again."

She snuggled harder against his chest and felt his heartbeat against her cheek. His heart was pounding terribly fast. "I do with you," she told him.

"I will keep you safe. That I promise. I know what it is like to be hurt."

His time as a prisoner of war had hurt him deeply, and that touched her heart. "I want to make you forget about those horrible days when you were captured." She wriggled up from his chest and cupped his jawline with both of her hands. "Let me do that."

He hesitated.

She moved in to kiss him.

"No." He stopped her. "You are vulnerable and you are scared. You're turning to me out of fear—it's instinct to want someone to protect you."

"It's because—" She stopped. Nell had advised her never to talk about love to a protector. She had already broken that rule. She shouldn't make it worse by doing it again.

"I know what happens," he went on. "You start to believe no one can take care of you, and that fear hardens you and makes you cold. But because I know what it is like, I know how to really take care of you."

She gazed into his eyes. He seemed so strong. "What did you suffer in Ceylon? It must have been horrible to have hurt you so deeply."

He just shook his head. "It doesn't matter."

But it did. If she wanted to heal him, she had to understand what had happened to him, didn't she?

The carriage stopped.

Cary conferred with his majordomo for only moments, then

he led her to his study. She still shivered even though a good fire blazed in the hearth and she was still wrapped in the fur throw.

"I'm going to undress you," he said softly. He walked behind her, but he kept his hand resting gently on her arm. It was soothing to have him touch her.

Quickly, he worked to undo the fastenings of her gown. Sophie looked down and saw all the tears in the bodice and skirts from where she'd been thrown to the table, shoved against the wall. Even with the heat of the fire filling the room, she felt cold.

She never wanted to wear this dress again.

"I will have this destroyed," Cary said. "I'll get you other clothes."

It was so exactly the answer to her question—if she destroyed the dress, what would she do?—that she whispered, "You do know what this is like." She met his gaze. "What happened to you in Ceylon? What did they do to you?"

He hesitated. His long lashes shrouded his eyes. "It doesn't matter. It was a long time ago."

"Not that long," she declared. "It was only three years past."

"Yes, that's right. It feels like longer."

Her bodice sagged, and the duke eased it down. She shoved it. She wanted the wretched thing off as fast as possible. When she looked down at her skirts, she remembered the man pushing them up. His laughter. His mockery.

A little bit of fun before he killed her!

Cary helped, pulling the bodice off quickly. He took her hand to help her step out. "Where did he hurt you?" he asked. "What did he do to you?"

"He just pushed me around. You came before he did anything more. I was only bruised."

Cary unlaced her corset and took it off, over her head. Her shift was thin from many washings, and through it she saw her bruises. Green and purple ones bloomed on her arms, her chest, and her stomach where she had been slammed against the table edge.

"I'm going to find the bastard and kill him."

She looked up, into Cary's eyes. So unusually pale, they glittered in the firelight. She saw anger there. The same anger that pulsed when he'd looked at Stratham. Cary's jaw twitched.

She remembered how much rage he'd shown the four times he'd rescued her—from Halwell, Stratham, her mystery attacker, and from the footpads. But when he had been fighting, he hadn't been facing those foes, she realized. He was fighting the foes of his past.

"But they hurt you, didn't they?" she asked.

"Sophie, that was not important. What matters is what happened to you."

"But—"

"Sophie, stop talking about it." Impatience vibrated in his husky voice.

She knew she had to stop. She couldn't make him angry.

He was right—she needed to feel safe, and she only did so with him.

He bade her to sit down, and he took off her dainty shoes and her stockings. They were ravaged beyond repair. Tears sprang to her eyes.

"Are you all right? Damn, I didn't mean to be so curt with you, Sophie—"

"It's not that. It's"—she gulped on tears—"it's so silly, but it's my stockings. And not because they were the first nice pair I had. I did so much for the money I used for them, and it was all a waste—"

She broke off. Oh no.

"What did you do?"

"Oh, it was all the labor I had to do to get them," she murmured. "I managed to get several menial jobs for pennies." Not entirely a lie. She had tried that at first—she had tried honest work—before Devars went after her, forcing her to need so much more money to keep them all safe. But where she got the money for the stockings was Devars's bracelet, and she couldn't tell Cary that.

"Not such a disaster," he said softly. "You have me now."

"I do. Then it is all wonderful." And she meant it.

"Now your shift." His tone turned matter-of-fact. He stood and looked ahead, not down at her. "Do you need help?"

"I—" She needed him close to her. How else was she to start to heal him? And . . . and she just needed him close.

"I do," she said.

He crouched down, and together they grasped the hem of her chemise. Their hands brushed. For her, it was like sparks and electricity. For him—his teeth were gritted.

Slowly, she drew up the shift, his hands following. This was the last piece of clothing she wore. She revealed the tops of her legs, the dark curls between her legs—he had seen those. Then her belly, and her breasts bounced as she lifted the shift.

He took the shift away from her. Walked over and tossed it into the fire. Flames flared and ate it.

For the first time, she was completely naked in front of him. And he wasn't reacting. He didn't even look.

"There is a robe and nightdress. You need rest, but there are things I should do first. I'll return in a moment."

"Where did you get a woman's robe and a nightgown?" She knew his majordomo had sent a footman with a bundle of things.

"They belong to my sister Claudia. My majordomo had them brought here as I brought you to this room."

"I can't—"

"Yes, you will. Now get dressed, love, before you catch cold." With that, he walked out.

That wasn't what she'd hoped for.

But she did feel shaky. Could she really work on seducing him, caressing him, trying to heal him?

A bit of fun before I kill you . . .

Sophie shuddered. She felt sick. A chill went through her, but from the inside out. She hurried to the clothes. The silk nightdress slithered over her fingers, soft as heaven.

She shouldn't wear his sister's nightclothes. He was a kind man, but he'd gotten a steely eyed look of determination, and he'd ordered her to do it.

She couldn't displease him. He was going to be her protector.

The silk nightdress skimmed over her skin, gliding on. Her bosom was a little large for it, as were her hips, so it tugged oddly. But it fit.

And the robe. It was voluminous—an acre of thick, warm velvet.

She'd just gotten the belt tied, snuggling into the warmth that touched her bare toes, when the door opened. Cary came in and shut it.

He set a basin of water on a table near a small sofa. Steam rose.

Someone must have heated the water. She swallowed hard. "Aren't your servants shocked?" Gentlemen might have mistresses, but there was a reason they provided their ladybirds with houses.

"Probably, though not the servants who were here in my father's day." He dipped in a facecloth—a neat, elegant square, not the worn-out things she had used on the farm. She'd always had worn-out things. Lifting it, he wrung it out.

She had a fleeting thought—that the money her mother had given for her upbringing had supported the doctor's house, had funded her adoptive mother's dreams to elevate her own children. Sophie had always got the worst. The scraps. The hand-me-downs. The roughest fabrics, the chewiest morsels of food.

She hadn't really cared. It was only when her son's fate mattered, that she suddenly cared.

Had her mother deliberately left her to that fate? But if so, why leave so much money for her care? Why give her to a doctor's family anyway? Did her mother have no other choice? Maybe no one else would take in a courtesan's bastard?

"Come here and sit on the sofa," Cary instructed. His voice was gentle, but it held a quiet, irresistible command. Probably a skill he had developed in the army, when he had led men.

She, for example, would follow him anywhere.

Sophie sat, and Cary got on one knee before her. Samuel had done that, to propose marriage—well, at least to promise her they were engaged.

But Cary's blue eyes were full of concern, and they crackled with anger as he gently cleaned her face. She had no idea she was dirty. Or she was actually cut, until she felt a sharp sting.

"Ow." She lifted her hand.

"It's all right. A cut on your cheek. I want to ensure it's clean. Nor large enough to require stitches." His eyes darkened. "It will likely mar your cheek though." He looked furious at the idea.

"You look so angry. But I'm alive! He was going to kill me. A scar on my cheek is nothing—" Or was it? Courtesans were supposed to be beautiful. The more lovely, the better. Maybe the scar ruined things. If he hated it . . .

Suddenly, she remembered something she hadn't told him. "That man—he said he was paid to kill me. This wasn't just rape or robbery!" Her voice rose. "Who would do that?"

"Shh." Cary gently bathed her cheek. With care. Watching her carefully. Sometimes his gaze was so intense, it took her breath. "You need care first. Then we'll talk about what happened."

Someone knocked on the door. She jumped, but his hand cupped her cheek for a moment. He gentled her like a horse, took his hand away. "Enter," he commanded.

His majordomo, in a robe and a nightcap, came in, carrying a tray. On the tray sat a bowl of cut ice. Strips of cloth. A silver pot and a teacup on a saucer. The pot gleamed. The cup was edged in gold.

A fleeting look of disapproval was emitted by the servant as he set the tray down. That was directed at her from behind the duke's back.

"That will be all," Cary said. He wrapped the small pieces of ice in cloth and held the wrap against her face. The cool soothed. "This will take down some of the swelling. It's late, but it will help. Hold it while I pour your chocolate."

Chocolate?

It was. Dark and thick and so piping hot that coils of steam rose. Placing his hand over hers, he said, "I'll hold this against your bruises. You take the chocolate."

"Th-thank you."

"I thought this would be better than brandy. Hot and soothing, and a bit of a stimulant also."

She sipped. It was like silken heaven in a cup. Now her insides were as warm as her outsides, which were wrapped in a thick, perfect robe. Well, her outsides were all hot except where Cary gently held the ice.

Wrapping her hands around the cup, Sophie sipped and sipped until she finished the drink. She'd been hungry, and the drink was thick, creamy, delicious.

When she finished, he got her to hold the ice while he refilled her cup.

"What did you see of the man who attacked you?" he asked. And she felt full of warmth and so much calmer. It felt more difficult to grasp on to fear and panic again. She felt . . . sleepy. He was a very smart man. He had known exactly what to do for her.

"Almost nothing. My room was in the dark. He was in there, when I went in—" And danced like an idiot! "And I didn't even see him."

"You didn't hear anything?"

"Oh yes. I heard footsteps in the other rooms and carts rattling and dogs barking at the dawn. I didn't hear him until he moved out of the shadows. Then he made a board creak behind me. It was too late to run then. If you hadn't—how did you know?"

"I had waited to ensure you were safely inside, then I heard something crash in your rooms."

"That was just me at that point, I think."

He stared at her, confused.

"I was twirling around the room—dancing around it—and I knocked over the teapot and fell on the bed."

"In the dark, you were dancing around the room?"

"I was happy." She looked up at his face. "Because of you."

He didn't react to that. "You said he told you he had been paid to kill you."

"That's what he said," she explained. "I offered him money to spare me, and he said he'd been given more to kill me."

"Poor love." He looked at her so tenderly, she almost melted. Then he asked, "By whom?"

"He didn't bother to tell me."

"Sophie, you are remarkable. Any other woman would be sobbing and in a mess."

"But I'm safe now."

His gaze lingered on her eyes. "You are."

"I didn't see hardly anything of his face. I think he wore a cloth over part of it. In the light—there's barely any light in that room, even on the middle of the sunniest day—I saw his eye, his cheekbone. Oh, and hair. He had golden hair. Rather like yours."

"No, he did not."

"He did. That much I am certain of, because I saw it."

"You saw this, Sophie." Cary picked up something from behind him, on a table. At first, she thought he'd picked up a cat. No, it was a handful of blond curls.

"A wig," he said.

"But why? Why wear a blond wig?" She stared at Cary's beautiful sculpted face and his golden hair, which was a mess, drifting over his brow.

"A woman was killed—a woman I had been seen pursuing at a Cyprian ball. Last night I was seen with you, and subsequently, you were attacked."

"But you had nothing to—" Then she understood. "You mean, someone is trying to make you look guilty of this? But why?"

"I don't know. But you are not going to return to that room. You can spend the night here. Tomorrow, I will have a house rented for you."

But he said it with a sigh. He did not look particularly happy.

Why would he be happy? He was not going to have any of the pleasure of having a mistress. She felt suddenly nervous. He was rescuing her, but at a huge cost.

She really must become his lover. She must give him something back. "I wish you would . . . come to my bed. I don't understand you. Why would you buy me a house and give me so much?"

"Apparently, now, my dear, I owe it to you. You were attacked because of me. I don't why, but that's what happened."

"But you will have a mistress and no—no fun. That can't be enough for you?"

"Yes, love. It is enough for me."

But she didn't believe it. "Nell said you used to be wild. She said you were the most wicked of the Wicked Dukes."

"I had a lot of sex to make me forget. That no longer works. Now, come on. We will get you to your bed."

He took her to the bedchamber she had used before—just a few nights ago—and she slipped into the bed. The bed was cool, but a fire burned in the grate.

"Try to sleep and remember, you'll always be safe now."

"I—Thank you." It was so sweet, so good of him that she wanted to cry.

As he closed the door, and Sophie closed her eyes, she knew the truth—she was unstoppably in love with the duke.

This was not a love she could forget, or force herself to ignore.

She shut her eyes. Coals in the grate lent a soft red glow that faintly lit up the room. Sophie heard the faint tick of a clock.

Then suddenly she was in a great house, in one of the corridors, and there was no light but eerie silver-blue moonlight. A young boy cried out. Her son, Alex! She began to run down the corridor, but the cries got farther away. Terrified, she turned, but in any direction she ran, she was only going away from her son—

"Alexander!" She gasped, launching up in the bed.

Sitting there, with the covers at her waist, her body drenched in cooling sweat, she knew what had happened.

A dream. Just a dream. "Oh, thank God. Thank God." She almost sobbed in relief.

Cary was haunted by fear, and so was she. His fears were memories. Hers were for a horrible future that could come true—she could lose her son, maybe even her life.

Would Devars really leave her alone?

She couldn't think about that now. She must go forward. Cary's protection had to be the answer; otherwise, what could she do? He would save her, and maybe she could save him. . . .

Sophie frowned.

Cary had said he used sex to forget. She assumed he must mean the awful memories that haunted him. But Nell said he had been a wicked rogue *before* he was kept as a prisoner of war. It was *after* that he had changed.

The memories that bothered him couldn't have been from Ceylon.

They had to be from something that had happened before.

12

Cary heard the creak of his bedroom door behind him, and he turned away from the window. He met Sophie's startled gaze.

"Oh!" she said. "I thought you would be asleep."

He quirked a golden eyebrow. "And you intended to get into bed with me. Or get on top of me?"

Her cheeks went scarlet. "Well ... er, I wanted to be with you. Of course I had no intention of doing anything you didn't want—"

"Sophie, no."

"But you're unhappy, and I wanted to heal you."

He'd had women desire him, but never quite like Sophie. He almost felt like a blackguard for not taking her to bed, as if he were personally wounding her. Once he made Sophie his mistress and got her a house, he couldn't visit her. She would probably leap on him as soon as he got in the door.

"I realized something tonight," she said. "I realized that if you used sex to blank out your memories, then your terrible memories had to be from long before you were taken prisoner in Ceylon."

Framed by her loose black hair, she looked at him so earn-
estly.

Christ, how astute she was. She had figured that out. She
was waiting for him to explain. To tell her what had happened
to him.

He couldn't. "Go back to bed now. But why don't you join
me for breakfast, Sophie?"

"You are trying to change the subject," she accused. "Please
tell me what happened."

"No," he growled. "That is my condition for you to be my
mistress. You can't ask me questions. I won't talk about it."

"All right," she said.

He looked at her with suspicion. She had agreed too easily.

"But I would like breakfast with you. Your breakfasts are
smashing."

She was so adorable. And he was so damned destroyed.
How had she figured this out so quickly? She was going to have
to give up.

He got up, led her to his door. "Now, go back to bed and
sleep. You have nothing to worry about."

She nodded, again arousing his suspicions. But he closed the
door behind her as she went back to her bedchamber.

He would set her up in a house, give her an allowance, and
then he would not see her again. He would know she was safe.

It was enough.

And what about his promise to wed? That meant being able
to put his past behind him and perform in bed. He could keep
quiet about his past, not tell a wife anything. But he couldn't
seem to put it behind him to have sex, damn it.

Cary had no idea what in hell he was going to do.

Cary had to smile as Sophie mounded food on her plate
from the hot breakfast dishes laid out on the sideboard. She
took ham and sausages and potatoes.

She blushed as she sat opposite him. "I suppose you fear I will end up fat. Now that I'm your mistress—"

"I'm not condemning you, Sophie. I suspect you haven't had much to eat."

"What are we to do today?" she asked. Her ham had already vanished from her plate, and half her potatoes were gone—all in the blink of an eye. The poor thing was starving. She sipped tea and gave a blissful sigh as if she were savoring heaven on a breakfast plate. "Are we to stay here? Perhaps in your bedroom? Or we would simply talk, if you prefer. There is so much I would love you to tell me about . . . well, you."

Two dangerous things—bed and the temptation of sex, and talking. "Neither today," he said. "I have to get a house for you. And I want to return to your room in the stews and look for clues. That will take me a while."

She set down her tea. While he'd been thinking about what she probably wanted to talk about, she'd consumed a sausage.

"And me too," she said. "I am going with you to investigate."

"No, you are not."

"Why not? It is my room, and I was the one who was attacked. Besides, I know the people who live there, and they know me. They will talk to me."

"I can bribe them," he pointed out.

She folded her arms over her chest. She was wearing a dress that had belonged to his sister. A pretty ivory-and-yellow muslin that looked lovely and spring-like. It was an innocent-looking dress, but strangely, that made Sophie look even more seductive and alluring.

"I am still going," she declared.

"No, you are not. Protectors issue commands. Mistresses obey."

"Yes, but you have told me I am not really your mistress.

And when I believe I can help you, you cannot expect me just to wait for you and do nothing!"

She could be so sweet and innocent, yet Sophie had a backbone of steel.

Damnation, she was trouble.

Guilt followed the thought—Sophie was in trouble now because, apparently, someone was murdering young women and trying to make it look as if he were the killer. One woman had been murdered. There had been an attempt on Sophie's life by a man paid to kill her.

That had to mean the bastard would try again.

Cary wanted to keep her safe—that was why he had wanted her to stay here. He didn't have a house for her yet, so if he went, he would be leaving his "mistress" in his family home. All he needed was his mother and sisters to show up. That would be awkward, to say the least.

And given his mother had threatened to intervene if he didn't get engaged . . .

He had no idea when his mother would decide he was not progressing and would show up at the house.

It would be best to take Sophie with him.

Sophie peered out the window of the duke's carriage. She wore a gown borrowed from the wardrobe of one of his sisters—a beautiful dress that a London lady would wear for shopping, topped by a smart dark blue velvet pelisse. She wore a bonnet too. At first she'd protested, but he insisted the clothes were no longer those worn by Claudia, his sister. And since Sophie had been determined to go with him, she needed to wear something.

Now, as she got closer to her old room, the place where she'd been attacked, she began to feel cold with fear, stiff with tension.

But she had nothing to fear. Not now.

Cary's hand rested gently on hers on the velvet seat. "Are you all right, love?" he asked.

Love. That made her heart wobble. But she knew it was just a careless endearment.

If she were to say it, she'd mean it.

She looked at his handsome but troubled face. "Do you really think someone is trying to make you look guilty of—of murder?"

"I admit it's just an assumption. But the man who attacked you wore a blond wig, and that likely made him look like me to anyone who saw him."

"But why would someone do that?"

"I don't know. I spent last night trying to fathom a motive. If it is to attack me, it's a sick and sadistic way to do it—harming innocent people. It could be that this person wanted to hurt both you and Sally Black, and thought the best way to get away with it was to throw suspicion on me."

"What reason would he have to attack me?"

"There are men who like to hurt women for pleasure—" The duke broke off and shook his head. "But you said he told you he was paid to hurt you. So it wasn't because he's a bastard who gets pleasure from hurting women. You were chosen by someone else."

"And that leads back to you, doesn't it? Someone trying to destroy you."

"But not kill me," he said softly.

Sophie shivered. "I guess we need to know who your enemies are. Who would want to hurt you?"

He hesitated. Then shook his head. "I have no idea."

The carriage stopped. It couldn't fit in the narrow lane that led to her door. Cary jumped down before his servant lowered the steps, then he took her hand. He helped her down just as if she were a lady. He'd done that last night too—

She looked down the lane. The sun shone, but the narrowness of the lane cast it in cool shadow.

"I realized that if I hadn't done my impetuous, silly dance and knocked things over, you would have gone before I was attacked. If you hadn't heard the crash, you wouldn't have come back. My adoptive mother had always scolded me for being impetuous. Sometimes she scolded me just for being happy. But this time, my foolishness had actually saved my life."

"Sophie, you really are—" Suddenly, Cary pulled her into his arms.

"I am what?" She gasped.

But he didn't answer. He kissed her.

In the narrow, impoverished lane in front of her former home, the duke wrapped his arms around her and held her tight. His mouth took hers in a slow kiss. A slow, firm, caressing kiss. Her lips sizzled hotter and hotter. His mouth coaxed hers to open, and his tongue came in to play.

She loved his kisses and the parry and thrust of his tongue. It was so intimate. It was like having sex standing up—it made her heart pound, her private place get achy and wet.

She wriggled against him.

But he eased back.

She looked at him, dazed and half drugged with pleasure and desire. "You are adorable," he said.

Then he asked her for her key.

"Couldn't we kiss again first?"

"Not now. Serious work now," he said softly. He turned her key in the lock, then thoughtfully studied the door. "He was waiting for you, which means he got into the room before you unlocked it."

"Could he have gotten through the window?"

"Too small for a man of his size. He must have picked the lock, then used a similar device to relock the door from the inside. He is intelligent."

"He smelled like a gentleman," she said suddenly. She hadn't thought to say it before. "I mean, he smelled of some kind of cologne. Something exotic and astern. His leather gloves—" She shuddered. "They were as fine as yours almost."

"So not a ruffian from the stews?"

She shook her head. "But why would a gentleman be . . . attacking women for money?" She couldn't say the word "kill."

Cary stroked his jaw. Watching his fingers skim himself left her rather breathless. "Debts?" he pondered. "Or he's a man from a lower class who has earned enough to emulate gentlemanly behavior—I mean, in method of dress."

Cary unlocked and opened her door. He stepped inside, then turned to her. "It's all right for you to come in, love."

She stepped into her room. She wrapped her arms around herself. "Do you think he will try to hurt me again?"

She wanted Cary to put his arms around her. Ever since she'd been thrown out of her house, she'd had to be strong. She'd had to be so positive and hopeful, it hurt. Now she was crumbling.

As if he knew, he suddenly looked up. In two strides, he'd crossed over in front of her. His arms went around her. "No one will hurt you now. You are under my protection." Then softer. "You are mine."

Those words made her shiver. In a good way.

She watched as he looked around her room. What did he think of what he saw? He grimaced. She felt ashamed, then defiant. It had been the best she could do.

"Where were you on the bed when you heard him behind you?"

She sat as she thought she had done. Cary walked behind her. "The fiend must have stood here, in the corner."

"I got off the bed and went to light the candle—" She stopped. Next thing she knew Cary held her hand. He lifted her to her feet. His fingers stroked her palm in her borrowed white gloves. Firm, soothing strokes. Strokes that gave her courage.

"That was when he grabbed me and shoved me against the door. He stuffed his hand into my mouth to smother my scream."

Cary cradled her close to his tall, strong body. He was such a good man.

"But then he moved his hand, and I could scream. Then he dragged me across the room and slammed me into the table so hard, I lost all my breath. That was when I offered him money to leave me alone, and he told me about being paid to kill me. . . ." She sucked in a shaky breath. "Then you came in and you saved me."

His lips brushed the top of her head, on the brim of her bonnet, for he couldn't get any closer. Then she gasped. "Look there. That isn't mine." She pointed at a fragment of paper.

Cary picked it up. It was torn from a larger sheet, a diagonal tear along one edge. All it had on it was her address.

"Someone gave the villain this so he knew where to find me," she said softly.

"That's the curious thing."

She gazed at him, not understanding. "What do you mean?"

"When was the fiend given this? Sally Black was attacked on the night I encountered her at the Cyprian ball. I'd never met her before. So if it was the same scenario—he was paid to kill her—when was he contacted? Was he given this after the orgy, when I was seen with you?"

"Which means it was someone at the orgy?" she asked.

"It could. Or this could have been arranged days ago, after the Cyprian ball. But to start, we will assume someone at the orgy contacted this man—maybe sent a messenger with your address. And he came immediately to your room, broke in, and waited for you."

There was something in his tone. He didn't sound as if he

believed what he was saying. "You don't think that was what happened?"

"I don't know, Sophie. But regardless, it doesn't give us the important answer. Who contacted the assassin?"

The word made her legs wobble.

Suddenly, Cary's arms were around her again. She smelled his gentlemanly smells—good smells on him. Sandalwood, clean skin, something sharp and bracing that he must have used after shaving.

"It must have been someone at the orgy."

"Not must, but it's a theory we have to explore. This person was also at the Cyprian ball. It gives us a large field." The duke looked around the room. "I don't think this room has anything more to tell us."

"What can we do?"

"Talk to people. Ask around. If anyone saw this tall, blond gentleman, I doubt they would forget him." A wry look touched his face.

"They wouldn't." And that was the idea. Her body would have been found. And people would have remembered seeing a man who looked like Cary. "People must have seen him because he wanted to be seen."

"So you've thought of that too." He looked at her with admiration.

"But how can you question anyone? People might fear you are that man. See, you do need me—they know me. They will tell me."

Sophie might be impetuous. She was stubborn when it came to seducing him. But Cary admired how she was also quick-witted and clever.

He stood back and allowed her to rap on the door of the room next to hers, farther down the narrow carriage lane—more of a cart lane. An elderly woman opened the door. Her gray hair was unkempt and stuck out around her head. She held a tattered shawl over a dirt-streaked brown dress.

"Goodness, Sophie, child. You look like a right lady."

Sophie blushed. She was beautiful when she did. It heightened the green of her eyes, made her hair look even more raven-black. "Thank you, Mrs. Mill. Now, there is something—"

But before Sophie could finish, the elderly woman stepped forward and peered at Sophie's face, squinting. "Who hit ye, dearie? Don't put up with any man who raises 'is 'and to ye! That's what I always said. And I kicked my man to the curb for doin' that. I'm right better off, I tell ye."

If this was better off, Cary hated to think of what life had been like with the man around.

"It's nothing like that." Quickly, Sophie told the story of a man breaking into her room, waiting, and attacking her.

Mrs. Mill clutched her heart. "Are we all to be murdered in our beds then? Oh dear!" The woman flapped her elbows and began to heave about like a demented chicken.

But Sophie soothed the woman. She spoke kindly. "I don't think he will be back. But I wanted to know if you had seen him. I want to put the law on him—"

"Don't want naught to do with the law." Mrs. Mill backed up and closed the door until she was just peeping out at Sophie.

"You won't have to. I just need to know if you saw a gentleman with blond hair. A tall, broad-shouldered man."

"I did."

"Where did you see him?"

"On High Street. 'e stepped out of a black, shiny carriage drawn by four horses. 'e came down the steps as I was 'urrying by, and 'e all but shoved me to the ground. Pushed me out of the way and stalked off toward our lane."

"Did you see him when you reached our lane?"

"No. 'e'd disappeared by then."

Sophie asked questions about the carriage. She tried to hand Mrs. Mill a few coins, but the woman refused. "I don't take charity, dearie. Just don't go telling the law to ask me questions. And ye'd best be careful."

Sophie told the woman she was leaving the room.

"And where might ye be going?"

"I—I have befriended a duke, and he is renting a house for me." She blushed again.

Mrs. Mill's eyes narrowed. "Oh, dearie, I always thought you a decent lass." She stepped back in and shut the door firmly.

Cary felt a spurt of damned guilt. But hell, Sophie was right— there were few ways for a woman to support herself. He wasn't going to hurt her. And he was going to ensure she was quite well off at the end of their relationship.

Why, then, did he feel like the villain?

After knocking on two more doors, where Sophie spoke to an elderly man, then a youngish, tired-looking woman who seemed to have children crawling over her, Sophie ventured into the upper floors of the ancient building. He followed—he didn't want to let her out of his sight, but he could not be close enough to frighten people.

Finally, she returned to him. "Three people saw the blond man. Truly, from the description they gave, it would sound as if it were you. One person also saw a woman he didn't recognize. A ladylike woman."

Could a woman be involved? Cary doubted it. This seemed more of a man's business—violence against defenseless young women. But a strange woman on the night of Sophie's attack might be more than a coincidence. He had to find out who this woman was.

He handed Sophie up to his carriage. She turned to him. "Have we learned anything at all?"

"I don't know," he admitted. "One thing I would like to do—determine if Stratham could be responsible."

"You think Lord Stratham murdered that other poor girl? And attacked me?"

"I don't know about the other girl, but I know he wanted you. He was humiliated when you refused him. He's an abusive man who does not take rejection well."

Sophie was about to speak, but Cary lifted her hand to his lips. At the touch of his lips to her fingers, she made a squeaking sound and she couldn't say a word. She just gazed at him as if he were the sun.

He hadn't expected her to look quite so enthralled.

"Now we go to the races," he said. "Stratham is a notorious fan of horse racing."

Quite a few gentlemen took their mistresses to the races, Sophie discovered. She knew this because the women wore brightly colored, scandalous dresses with flounces of lace, and snug, low-cut bodices. In her modest clothing, she actually looked out of place.

The gentlemen drank copiously. Many had ladybirds sitting on their laps. With each race, some men cheered and drank more. Others moaned in despair, swore—then drank more.

"How are we going to find Lord Stratham?" Sophie stared wide-eyed at the crowd.

Men greeted Cary with reverence, begging to join them. At once, Sophie realized he was truly a war hero and was worshipped for it.

Was that why someone was trying to make him look guilty of the awful crimes? To destroy him? Was one of these men so jealous?

No, that didn't make sense. Would anyone hurt innocent women just to destroy a duke?

But sometimes, when she looked at Cary and he didn't know she was looking, she saw how haunted and haggard he looked. Was it his memories? The ones that had to have come from long before the war when he was held a prisoner?

Cary offered her the crook of his arm, and she laid her hand on his forearm and walked with him. They went to the private boxes. "This one is Stratham's," he said.

But although the box was filled with gentlemen and females who shrieked with laughter and guzzled champagne, there was no Stratham.

"He's here," declared a young, portly gentleman who was groping two giggling, chubby women. "Took his tart down by the paddocks, I believe. For a ride."

The drunken crowd laughed uproariously at that.

Was this a Cyprian's life? Sophie wanted to run as far and as fast as possible. Cary wasn't like these men. . . .

But what happened after her relationship with Cary? Would she have to go to another protector? Would she have to cling to some drunken fool to survive? She hoped not. She prayed not.

Cary rested his hand on the small of her back. She felt utterly aware of him. After seeing those men, she thought: *I may never want any other man but the gorgeous, wonderful Duke of Caradon? What am I going to do?*

A whinnying sound came from one of the stalls. But it hadn't come from a horse. A man had made that sound.

"What was that?" she asked.

Cary put his finger to his lips. He led her to the stall. He could stand on his toes and see over the door. She saw him bite back a laugh.

"What is it?" she whispered.

He lifted her by her waist, and she grasped the top of the stall door to steady herself.

Stratham was naked and moved around the hay-strewn paddock on all fours. She saw his black, gray-touched hair, his muscular body, his naked, hard, tight buttocks. She would have seen even more of him, except her view was mercifully blocked by a woman in a snug muslin gown who rode on top of him. He had on a leather bridle of sorts, and the woman tugged on the reins. She smartly slapped his bare bottom with a riding crop.

"Oh goodness," Sophie said.

13

His Grace of Garlandshire was my next admirer. But when I accompanied him to a Drury Lane play, I could not help but turn my gaze to X. Q. My former lover was in his box, cuddling a young woman of dubious repute. She could not hold a candle to me, and I knew he could see it.

The next night at the theater, X. Q. was without female companionship. And he watched with thunder in his eyes as I flirted with Garlandshire.

Garlandshire attempted to introduce me to foolish games. Ropes and floggers indeed.

I disposed of him in the morning at the same time the kitchen maid disposed of the scraps and leavings. And in much the same manner—tossed out the door.

—From an unfinished manuscript entitled *A Courtesan Confesses* by Anonymous

Sophie stared at the sweeping row of white-stuccoed town houses that arched around a crescent in a well-do street. The carriage stopped at the last house, which had a dark red door and a tiny garden framed by a wrought-iron fence.

"This is your new house, love. Come, let's go inside." With that, Cary stood, then went down the steps of his carriage. As he always did, he held out his hand to help her.

She just sat there. Stunned. Everything she'd dreamed of was right in front of her.

A gorgeous man—a wonderful, unimaginably powerful seductive man was waiting for her, his hand outstretched to take hers.

"Sophie, what's wrong?"

"Everything is perfect. Have you ever had everything you'd ever imagined in your heart come true?"

His mouth twisted in a jaded smile. "Not for a long time, love."

He opened the door with a key, then handed the key to her. He took her through the house, introducing the small staff to her. There was an elderly butler, a housekeeper, maids, and a cook.

Sophie was dazzled. "How were you able to do this all in one short day?"

"I'm a duke."

He had used his amazing power and importance as a duke to do this. It was the kindest, most generous thing anyone had ever done for her.

She couldn't wait to write to Belle—but she needed money to send to Belle so she and the children could all take a stage to London. She needed money at once.

But it would be wrong to ask Cary for money. She couldn't do that—but she had to get her family here as quickly as she could.

He walked ahead of her, through the foyer with its tiles of black-and-white marble, through a double door of paned glass, and into a lovely sitting room. Large arched windows gave out onto a small garden.

He turned, looking pleased with himself. But his smile disappeared. "Is there something wrong? You continue to frown."

She was going to be honest. "My friend Belle and . . . her children. Can I bring them here to live?"

When he didn't answer, her heart started to pound.

He ran his hand along the back of his neck. To her surprise, he was actually blushing. "Would that be appropriate? Young children here?"

"They would stay upstairs. You would never even know they were here." Her son would be here—wouldn't that be strange? And she didn't want him to know she had a child. If he thought it awkward now, wouldn't it be worse if he thought she had a young child here? "I can't leave them in the country. I have to know they are safe."

"Sophie, it was my intention to install you in this house and not visit. The problem is, I don't know if I can stick by that."

"I don't want you to!" she cried. "I want you to come here."

"Then your friend and her children must live elsewhere. I can arrange to have them move to another place, where I can have servants to look out for them. I assure you that they will be safe. Country life would be more pleasant for children."

He didn't want them in the house. But it was true—it would feel strange to go to bed with him, which is what she wanted to do, with her little boy upstairs.

He was right. She could not have her son and the other children here. Even Belle—Belle hated the whole idea of her being a courtesan.

And she had to convince the duke to go to bed with her. After seeing what those courtesans at the racing stables had to do, she didn't want to lose Cary.

Shyly, she asked, "Do you wish to . . . take a look at the bedroom with me?"

"Not today, angel. I have things I must do. First, I will send a note back with the carriage, instructing my secretary to secure a country house for your family." He strode over to a writing desk—a rather feminine one situated by one large window. He looked huge and muscular when he sat on the delicate stool. "Tell me where they are located now."

"Please find a place quickly. An obsessive man wanted me as his mistress, but I evaded him."

"I can have them moved tomorrow. That I promise you, to set your heart at ease." He dipped a quill in ink—someone had filled the inkwell in readiness—wrote swiftly. Paused and looked up at her. "You will have a carriage, love. You will be able to visit them."

He was so noble. Somehow he took her every problem and made it vanish. Without questioning her.

Sophie wished she could do the same for him. She had to make him let her try.

He folded the letter. He used a candle to melt wax and seal the note with a blob. He pressed his signet ring into the wax. "Write a letter to your friend as well," he said. "She will not recognize my man of affairs. Instruct her to trust him, to do as he says."

"Of course." He thought of everything.

When she finished and sealed her letter, the duke yanked on the bellpull, summoned the footman who had answered the door, and gave the man instructions to send the message via his carriage.

There. All her problems whisked away.

The next morning, after a night spent in a lavish and comfortable bed, Sophie made her very first visit to a fashionable London modiste, where she had carte blanche. The bell over the door gave a delicate tinkle and, holding her breath, Sophie walked into the smart Bond Street dressmaker's, Madame Bouvier.

Madame quickly came to her. "Ah, you are lovely. It shall be a delight to dress you. You need almost nothing to make you stunning."

"Yes, if I went out in nothing, I would stun people."

Madame, who Sophie suspected was not French, looked confused. Then she clapped her hands, and Sophie was led to a dressing room. Assistants quickly removed her gown, leaving her in her shift. Thank heaven, Cary had let her keep his sister's day gown. If she had come in her old country dress . . .

Of course, Madame must know why the Duke of Caradon was paying for her clothes. Her mother had written in her book about crushing modistes and keeping them in their places. Not allowing them to be haughty. But Sophie couldn't quite adopt a bold stance.

Standing in her shift, waiting, she got on the low, fabric-covered dais. Her heart was bursting with relief. She knew her son was safe. Belle and her children were safe.

It was a miracle.

She was so happy she barely noticed the measuring, the pinning, the chatter of Madame. She didn't really care what she wore.

As she was leaving the shop, she spotted a flash of color out of the corner of her eye. Something about it made her stop in her tracks. Made unease rush over her—

It was a color of light green. A putrid color. And she'd seen it before.

Lord Devars's silk waistcoat was that color on the last night she had seen him—when he had brought her the bracelet and gloated because he thought she would soon be in his clutches.

Sophie shoved through the crowd, ducking into the doorway of a store that was set back from the street. Pressing her back to the side of a paned glass bow window, she peeked out.

And saw him.

A towering beaver hat. A long greatcoat in the first stare of fashion. And his hair—it was actually a tawny brown, with many streaks of silver-gray, but in the sunlight it looked almost blond.

It was Lord Devars.

Could he have been the man in her room?

No, that man was wearing a wig. And he wouldn't say he was paid to kill her. She had the feeling if he wanted to rape and kill her, he would want her to know it was him and be terrified of him every moment.

He'd enjoyed her fear that time he had brought her the bracelet and made his offer. That was why she had picked up a vase and hit him. Because she thought—

She thought he was going to force himself on her. Then kill her.

His gold-handled walking stick flashed in the light. She shuddered and drew back. He had hit her with that. Struck her across her face. He'd thought that one blow would terrify her so much that she would be frozen in fear. But she hadn't been. She'd fought back.

She could not let him see her. Blindly, she turned and yanked open the door to the shop and rushed inside.

And crashed into a tall, masculine body. She gazed up into pale blue eyes.

Cary frowned at her. "Sophie?"

Heavens, he was here, of all places? She didn't want him to know about Devars. She had to bluff. Quickly. "Your Grace. I saw you and—"

"You wanted to see what I am buying for you?" He smiled the beautiful smile that made her knees weak.

"You were buying something for me?" She stared blankly at the glass display cases in front of them. Dimly aware of the sparkle.

They were in a jeweler's.

She looked at the door. Through the thick glass, she saw that sickly green color. It looked like slimy algae in a pond. But it did reflect the man Devars was.

Devars stood at the door. Facing the door.

Oh God. Devars was going to come in here. She was with Caradon. He would protect her. . . .

Would he, when Devars accused her of stealing the bracelet? And it was true! She had been desperate. Terrified. It had been either steal food or take that wretched bracelet to get money to feed the children. So she had run, the bracelet hidden in her clenched fist—

"Take a look at this, my dear," Cary said softly. He looked at her strangely.

Numbly, she walked to the counter. If her back were to the door, maybe she would survive this. She looked nothing like she had when Devars had cornered her in his drawing room.

She leaned over as if looking closely at the glass. But if there were jewels in there, she had no idea. She couldn't focus on anything but fear.

"Do you like that one? Rather simple, but I think elegant pieces would suit you better."

He wanted her opinion. She made herself look at what was in the case—

"Oh God," she whispered. Not a ladylike thing to say, but she thought he was pointing at a necklace that was made up of a kind of collar of dozens of small diamonds. In the center dangled a pink pear-shaped diamond.

"Not that one." She could barely form words. Those three seemed to drain her wits.

"You don't like it?"

The bell above the door tinkled. It must be Devars. She muted her voice. "It's the most precious thing I have ever seen. I—I can't—"

"I would like to see you wearing it." As she lowered her voice, he did too. He leaned close to her to speak. Her earlobe tingled as his warm breath teased it.

Her whole body tingled.

Devars! *Be on your guard.*

She took a quick peek over her shoulder.

Devars had indeed come in, and he was speaking heartily to the jeweler.

"Was the bracelet satisfactory, my lord?" The jeweler asked.

"Unfortunately, that bracelet was stolen." Devars spoke curtly. He always bit off his words and threw them at you, as if what he really wanted to do was hit you instead.

Her knees were turning to jelly. She thought she could become a courtesan and solve everything. But if Devars took one look at her and recognized her, she'd probably hang. He was a marquis.

Sophie kept her head down, her eyes downcast. The deep brim of the bonnet hid her face.

She realized Cary was purchasing the necklace. It was placed in a box, and Cary slipped it into the pocket of his greatcoat. He offered his elbow and led her outside.

As the door closed behind them with that tinkle, her legs sagged. She had to put her hand to the glass window so she did not fall down.

She had done it. Escaped.

"Sophie, are you all right?"

She didn't know why—she happened to glance into the store. Just to make sure—just to know—Devars wasn't looking at her now.

But he was.

He was going to catch her. Expose her. Watch her hang. Or maybe he was planning to take out his rage by killing her himself—

Sophie's heart almost exploded. Though the window she could see Devars heading toward the door. Coming for her!

He was in London. She had been attacked. But none of that mattered now. All that did matter was *escape*.

"Your carriage!" She met Cary's eyes, knowing hers must be stark with terror. "Would you take me home now? Right now?"

"What is wrong?"

She could tell him she was desperate to make love to him, but that would put his back up. Make him refuse to go. He was the most impossible man—he acted in the opposite way of all other men when it came to sex.

She was desperately seeking an answer, when she spied a tall figure with unusual silver-frosted hair. "The Duke of Saxonby! Shouldn't we talk to him? Now? Perhaps we could take him to your house and ask him questions about the Cyprian ball."

"In the middle of Bond Street? No, angel—"

But she didn't obey. She was sure, through the fashionable people strolling, she saw Devars now on the sidewalk. She hurried toward Saxonby, which took her deeper into a larger crowd. Cary followed.

She realized it was getting harder to move through the people.

They were all slowing down to look at Cary.

"Cary!" Saxonby had seen him and called out to him. The friends greeted each other, then two other tall men joined them. One had dark hair and brilliant green eyes and was introduced as the Duke of Greybrooke. The older had dark coffee-brown hair and flashing dark eyes, along with the longest, blackest eyelashes she'd ever seen. That was Sinclair. The man who had hosted the orgy.

They began to discuss the murder, and Cary described the attack on her. She was so afraid of Devars, she didn't even react to the horrible details.

Sophie moved around so she stood in the center of the group of men. She was surrounded by all four of the Wicked Dukes. Each duke was tall and broad-shouldered with a sculpted, handsome face and enough solid, beautiful muscles to make any woman swoon. With his golden hair and blue eyes and his almost boyish features, Cary was the most gorgeous of the four handsome men. Her savior. But would he be if Devars revealed she was a thief?

She peeked between Cary, who she stood close to, and Saxonby.

Oh God. Devars. He had stopped on Bond Street and was large enough to force others to walk around him. He stood near a store, and he appeared to be lighting a cheroot.

But with a sick feeling, she saw he was furtively watching the group of them. He took a step toward them. Her heart skipped so many beats, she got dizzy.

Then he stopped. Shook his head at her. Her eyes widened with shock—he was communicating with her. His lips mouthed something.

She believed it was, *Later.*

She realized he was not willing to approach her when she was with four powerful dukes. They were discussing things about the murder of Sally Black. She heard only the end of their conversation. Saxonby was stating that he had investigated where Sally had lived and had spoken to her family, who lived in Hertfordshire, and had found no motive for her death.

Cary then introduced her. Both Saxonby and Greybrooke bowed to her, and she curtsied.

The Duke of Sinclair bowed over her hand and lifted her fingertips to his lips. The look in his eyes—it burned bright as an inferno. "It was a delight to make your acquaintance."

She took a step closer to Cary.

Sinclair grinned. "Not to worry, my dear. You are remarkably lovely. But Cary is a good friend. And he is a better man than I. True, he was once as wicked as I am, but he's turned over a new leaf. You will find he is a most devoted protector."

Cary was speaking to Greybrooke. The green-eyed duke glowed with joy, and she overheard a bit of their conversation

192 / *Sharon Page*

and learned why. He was a brand-new father, delighted with his son.

Her heart panged. Samuel would have been just as happy to see his son, but he was killed before he could.

Did she wish she could be married to Samuel now? Did she wish things had been different? She couldn't imagine that now. Cary was busy talking with Greybrooke, who they called Grey. He wouldn't overhear what she asked Sinclair.

Impetuously, she asked the Duke of Sinclair, "But why did he change?"

"He was held as a prisoner of war."

"But he was wicked before that, and he told me he had love affairs so he wouldn't be haunted by memories. But now he won't make love." She knew she was blushing foolishly. As if Sinclair, the orgy host would be shocked. "He says his memories haunt him too much."

"I don't know."

"Or do you mean you won't tell me?"

"The truth is that I don't know. Grey and Sax were his closest friends. They might know."

"Thank you, Your Grace."

Sinclair bowed again. "Call me Sin," he said. Then he left, alighting into a carriage that displayed a coronet on the door. Grey and Sax had gone as well, so she couldn't ask them questions.

Caradon smiled at her. "Should I take you home?"

Sophie nodded. She knew what she must do.

14

"Would you pull down your trousers?"

Sophie knew she'd startled Cary—he had been lost in thought. Now his head jerked back, and he stared at her in surprise. "Sophie, what?"

"Would you open your trousers?"

"Sophie, I am not going to make love to you in the carriage."

"That is fine. Because I want to make love to you."

She was sitting beside him, which worked perfectly. Sophie leaned over and kissed the slight bulge in his trousers. He felt warm there. Against her lips, she felt the ridge in his trousers grow bigger.

She ran her lips along the ridge with soft, quick, teasing kisses. "You did this for me. Please let me do this to you. I very much want to try."

Cary took a long, harsh breath. "Sophie, this is something that will give only me pleasure, not you."

She shook her head. "That's not true. Because pleasing you and watching you feel arousal and delight is actually very pleasurable for me." She stroked her fingers along the now large bulge. "Please?"

He laughed gruffly. "Any man would think me insane if I turned you down."

"Then don't."

"But having you do that will likely bring forth memories I would rather forget."

"Why? Can't you forget those things and just think of me? Please try."

"All right," he said huskily. With his gloved fingers, he undid the buttons of his trouser falls. He reached into his linens, and she saw the head push against the fabric, full and adorable. Then out it popped.

She pressed her lips to the dusky head. Heard him moan. How she loved that sound. She loved knowing he must feel the same thrill she did when he had touched his mouth to her private place.

She licked, running her tongue around the head and the firm ring that almost completely encircled it. He was so warm against her tongue. And his scent was rich and spicy.

She opened her mouth and took him deep inside.

She wanted to take him in to the hilt, but she couldn't. He was much too long. And too thick.

Now that she had him in her mouth, she didn't know quite what to do. He had licked her to ecstasy, but she could barely get her tongue to move around his enormous cock when it was filling her mouth.

His hand stroked her hair. Cupped her cheek. Then his hips moved, thrusting slightly into her mouth as he groaned.

He went too deep! She scrambled back, letting him all the way out.

He stopped. "Sorry, love. You're too new for that."

But she understood. This must be much the same for him as making love. He needed to have the sensation of sliding in and out. "You mustn't move," she said.

And she took him into her mouth again. She planted her hands on his hips to keep him steady. She sucked him deep into her mouth, then slid back. Over and over, she made the same motion. Her cheeks hollowed with the sucking sensation. Saliva coated him and dribbled from her lips.

But he watched her with his glowing blue eyes, and she could see lust and desire and pleasure in them.

He liked this.

But she'd thought that liking it meant he'd climax quickly.

It seemed he could last forever. And she couldn't.

Already her jaws were tired. And he was still rigid and big in her mouth. Bigger than when she'd started.

She had to stimulate him more. But how?

She stroked down in his linens, finding his ballocks. Those were sensitive. She cradled him, rubbing them with her thumb. She sucked on his cock—at least the top half of it—and gripped the hilt with her hand. She squeezed, suckled, toyed.

"Sophie, it's so good."

Her fingers strayed beyond his balls, and she touched the bridge of skin there. She rubbed him, fascinated by the seam and the firm heat of his skin that she felt. Then her finger slid back farther, and she realized it was caught between his hard, hot cheeks.

"Not there," he said roughly.

So she grasped his cock with both hands and bobbed fast and hard. She felt a terrible failure. He was moaning again, but how did she take him to—

"Sophie, stop. I'm going to come."

If she stopped, he might stop. She wanted to give him an orgasm. She *had* to.

She sucked and sucked. All at once, his cock grew, and she felt a whooshing within it, under his skin, and his juices shot into her mouth. All of his seed. She swallowed in surprise. Then sucked more from him.

That made him howl, and his hips jerked up.

She kept sucking.

Then he gently drew her back off him.

He pulled her to him and kissed her. Heavens, she could still taste him on her lips, ripe and sensuous. He must be able to taste himself too.

When he let her go, after kissing her with wild ferocity, she felt rather dizzy. "Did you like it?" she asked breathlessly.

"You were spectacular." He smiled, but it was a troubled one. What had happened?

He shook his head. "There can't be more than that, Sophie. It's not possible for me. But I don't want to leave you unsatisfied."

"I'm just happy you liked it." Thank heaven, he did.

He did up his falls, then he held out his arms. "You are so amazing, Sophie. You won't take no for an answer. And I almost believe you could heal me."

"I can," she murmured. But she said nothing more. She must do this slowly. She let him cradle her in his embrace and savored the kisses he brushed to her forehead. And then the carriage stopped, and she knew they'd arrived at her new home.

Cary and the other dukes had been her protection—Devars had not been willing to approach her when she was with them. Maybe Devars would leave her alone if he thought she belonged to Cary.

She had to make sure Cary wanted to keep her. And she was sure that if she could give him pleasure, he wouldn't want to let her go.

But then he said something that made her heart plummet.

"Sophie, love, don't get your hopes up too much." Then he exited the carriage.

"Now to pleasure you."

Sophie sat on her new bed, legs curled beneath her, naked.

She was sitting there as Cary had instructed, and at his words, she quivered with anticipation.

"I brought these for you, love." Cary wore his trousers and shirt, and he moved to the bedside table. She suddenly noticed that a box, which was closed with a gold lock, sat there.

Cary took a key from a small pocket in his trousers. He opened the lock. She had walked over on her knees to see. "What are they?"

He took one out, and she giggled in surprise. "It's shaped like your—"

"It's a toy you can use to pleasure yourself, Sophie."

"You mean, I put that in me instead of having you inside?"

"Yes."

"Is it safe?"

"Of course, angel." He withdrew something else. A small glass vial that contained a golden fluid. He poured a little on the head of the wand and smoothed it on. "To lubricate," he explained.

He held it up and put it in her hands. She studied it. "It's quite like yours, isn't it? Heavens, did you model for it?"

His brows shot up. "No, angel. I assume the sculptor wanted to model an ideal cock."

"Then yours is ideal." She knew she was blushing fiercely. She held it in her hands. "See, my fingers barely meet around it, just like with you." Her thumb stroked over cool, glittering green stones in the ivory base. "These are not emeralds, are they?"

"They are. They remind me of your lovely eyes. Now, let me show you what to do."

At his command, she lay on the bed and opened her legs.

He teased the head of the ivory cock over her cunny lips and the sensitive nub. "Your clit enjoys caresses," he said. "Play with it, and you can give yourself a climax whenever you want."

Slick with the oil, the wand slid easily into her cunny an inch.

She gasped at the sensation. Slowly, he thrust it deeper. She moved in rhythm with him. Until the wand was all the way inside her.

Then he stroked her clit as he thrust it in her. He watched her as he pleasured her—

Oh God, she reached her peak swiftly. Intently. Her hands clutched at her sheets. She had to scream, as the orgasm sent her soaring.

She floated back to earth. He withdrew the toy. Then he cleaned her gently with his handkerchief.

"See, love, you don't even need me."

That made her panic. "But you are going to be my protector, aren't you?"

"Of course. And I like to watch you come."

After he left her to go to his home, Sophie went to her bed. She wore her nightdress and her robe. She undid the belt of her robe, preparing to go to sleep.

But she was worried. Learning how to pleasure herself was not what she wanted. She needed to work on healing Cary. She must find out what tormented him.

She had met all of his friends. They had been together since they were boys at Eton. Surely, they must know what had happened to Cary.

She just had to find the Wicked Dukes. And make one of them give her the truth—and reveal Caradon's secret.

The next morning, she did something very daring. She looked up the address of the Duke of Saxonby in the London street directory. Then she went to his grand house on South Audley Street.

To her surprise, when she was escorted to the duke's study, she found herself face-to-face with all the Wicked Dukes.

Including Cary.

15

The Prince Regent pressed his suit once more. He commanded that I visit him.

I had invested cleverly over the last years. Not for me was the foolishness of other women. I bought no baubles of my own. I did not gamble. Drink was an evil I knew to avoid. I had enough of my own fortune to refuse Prinny.

And no longer did I need to endure a duke for a duke's sake. My next lover was a young earl. A mere twenty-two. Randy, vigorous, enthusiastic, gorgeous. He thought my pleasure more important than his. Fancy!

—From an unfinished manuscript entitled *A Courtesan Confesses* by Anonymous

She stood surrounded by dark wood paneling, paintings of horses, books, and the scent of cigar smoke while Cary stared at her, dumbfounded. "Sophie, what are you doing here?" He looked swiftly at Saxonby, frowning. "Have you been pursuing Miss Ashley, Sax?"

"No, no," she cried. "I came here on my own. He's never

even spoken to me—well, other than when we were introduced."
She blushed. She would have to tell the truth. "I wanted to
learn more about your past, and I thought your friends could
help me."

"Did you indeed?" Cary asked.

He must be furious. But then he shook his head. "You are
a sweetheart, Sophie. But alas, even my friends know little
about me."

"Oh." Her heart fell.

"Would you care for a drink, Miss Ashley?" Saxonby offered. "A glass of sherry? We are all about to have brandies and
discuss what Cary has learned."

She agreed, amazed they intended to include her.

Minutes later, she was seated in a comfortable wing chair, a
delicate glass containing sherry in her hand. The men were
seated with balloon-shaped glasses of brandy.

Cary sat in the wing chair beside hers. He gave her a smile,
then continued with his explanation. "Both Halwell and Stratham
were interested in Sophie and thwarted by me. From talking to
the other Cyprians, I learned both men had also tried to acquire
Sally Black but were rebuffed when she chose Viscount Willington. They are brutal men who like to mete out pain and
punishment to their sex partners. There is a veritable stable of
other suspects—a quarter of the gentlemen of the peerage were
at both events. Those are the two who appear to have an ax to
grind. And therefore a motive."

The three other men considered. Then Sin said, "The attack
on Sophie was well planned. Sorry, love, for bringing it up, but
we want to catch this bastard. You're implying that Stratham
arranged for it after you and he argued over Miss Ashley at my
event."

"It's possible."

"But why attach the murder of pretty Sally Black to you?

Stratham had no reason to resent you and want revenge at that point. Halwell did."

"Stratham and I were both in love with Grey's sister, Jacinta," Cary said.

Sophie stiffened. She hadn't known about that. Was he still in love with Greybrooke's sister? Was the duke's sister someone Cary had wanted to marry but couldn't because of his memories?

"And you both lost out to Winterhaven. I would have thought Stratham would have lashed out at Winterhaven if that were his motive."

"True," Cary admitted. "It does not sound likely."

Greybrooke's sister had married someone else. Had that broken Cary's heart? He could still be in love with her, even if she belonged to someone else.

Sophie's heart gave a foolish jolt of pain as if it had cracked. She was only ever going to be his mistress. She *knew* that.

She wanted him to heal—and that meant he would marry. But if he were pining for Lady Winterhaven, would he ever marry?

Was it a way she could keep him for a long time, if she could find the secret to helping him? Even if she didn't ever have his heart, she could have him.

"I need to corner both rats in one of their filthy holes," Cary said. "I intend to do it tonight. Down near the docks. A house on Horton Street."

"Number four?" Sin asked.

"Figures you would know it." Cary grinned. He turned to her. "I'm taking you home, angel. Then I have to go out."

Sophie set down her sherry. "I wish to go with you."

"I am not bringing you to this place. It makes an orgy look tame."

* * *

Cary took her home and put her up to bed even though it was morning. Sophie hadn't learned his secret, but she did know she was right. Something had happened to him when he had been a child.

"Don't go yet," she whispered. "I want to make you climax."

"Sophie"—he raked his hand through his hair—"you want to come, love, and I'm happy to oblige. But I've got too much on my mind to find ecstasy."

He opened the bedside table drawer and drew out one of the wands. Then he tossed it onto the bed, along with the vial of oil for moistening it.

With his elegant hands, he stripped off his clothing. All his clothing. He bore scars on his body from the war, but he was so muscular and beautiful.

She watched, breathless, as he rubbed oil along the ivory wand. Then he lay back on the bed and said, "Come over here."

She did. She had already undressed. Now she moved in front of him, naked with confidence.

They were getting closer to his being able to make love. She was sure of it.

He had let her pleasure him with her mouth. He had then shown her ecstasy when he'd used the wand on her. He'd told her he was teaching her how to pleasure herself, but she was sure she could coax him into more.

She climbed onto the bed.

He cupped her bottom and moved her so she straddled his chest.

"What are you going to do?" she asked.

He didn't answer. He just showed her. He slid the slick wand inside her, moving it with long, slow thrusts. Sophie moaned. She felt her clit swell and tighten with arousal.

Cary began moving the wand quickly. Then he pulled her

forward and lifted his head, and he flicked his tongue over her clit.

Goodness!

She climaxed almost instantly. But he kept pleasuring her. She rode the wand and each movement brought her clit against his tongue. *Oh! Oh!*

She burst again, seeing stars.

Gently, he drew the wand out of her. Then she sat down on him and took his mouth in a passionate kiss.

He broke the kiss and rolled over so she landed on the bed.

He got up and went over to where his clothes were strewn on the floor. Firelight gleamed along his lean, muscled body.

"I have to go now, angel."

"Well, I'm going too. We are in this together."

He bent and retrieved his drawers. She had a magnificent view of his tight buttocks. The small dimples at the small of his back. And the hollow way his haunches indented. He half turned. The sharp lines of his hipbones were undeniably sensual.

She slid out of the bed too and padded over to him. Naked.

She liked to be naked, bathed in the warmth of the fire. Naked with him.

He shook his head. "You are not coming to this damned place."

Lightly, she touched his bare back. "You act like you are going to face something terrible. What happens at this place?"

"You don't need to know."

"How can it make an orgy look tame?"

His eyes searched hers. Pale blue and beautiful but filled with some distant pain. He was trying to hold something in—and failing. "Some people like pain with their sex."

She remembered Stratham's threats—or promises?—of what he would do to her. "How can anyone do that?"

"People are strange animals when it comes to sex. There is nothing more perverse and twisted than the human mind."

"You are not like that."

He straightened, pulling up his linen drawers, then his trousers. He looked down to fasten them. Under his breath he muttered, "You would be surprised."

Then she heard his last words to himself as he walked out of the bedroom and left her.

Low, so it was barely a murmur, he muttered, "At this place, I will likely remember all the hellish memories I want to forget."

She looked out her window and watched him go to his carriage.

She didn't care what he said—after what she'd overheard him say, she had to go too.

All she had was the address, No. 4 Horton Street. Sophie had no idea where it would lead. . . .

Her carriage arrived at an old, dark building on the shore of the Thames. Fetid smells made her nose curl. Tall masts were silhouetted against the silver of moonlight.

She looked at the stone building. Really, any woman would be foolish to walk in there. But it was the address she had—she must do it.

There was only one lit window.

Another carriage arrived. Sophie hung back and watched.

A couple stepped out.

They wore dark cloaks, their hoods up, covering their heads. The door opened, and another cloaked man—in the dark rough brown of a monk's cloak, with a rope around the waist—urged them in through the door. As soon as they passed within, the door shut with a clang.

Whatever this place was, people wanted not to be seen going inside.

Sophie had worn her cloak, for the spring nights were cold. She pulled up her hood to look like the others.

She walked up toward the door.

"What are you doing here?"

It was Cary. He wore a cloak and had pulled up the hood, but moonlight glinted on his eyes. "I told you to keep away," he growled.

"I was attacked by someone in my own room. I've already faced grave danger."

"This place will carve a hole in your soul. One you will never fix."

"You're afraid for my innocence? Your Grace, don't you see that doesn't matter anymore?"

"Don't you see that it does?" He pushed back his hood so she could fully see his irate expression. "If I send you away, it won't work, will it? You will come back."

"You can't tell me this place will ruin me and not expect me to want to see it."

"For any other woman, I might think she would listen. And have a sense of self-preservation. But not you. You are the most stubborn, impetuous woman I've met."

Those were not good attributes. "If I hadn't been stubborn, my family would have starved."

Sophie turned to the door. She let out a small scream. A dark figure stood there—

It was the door monk.

Cary's deep voice played against her ear. "You can't think of a good thing caused by being impetuous."

"I met you. So don't be so certain you are right. I met you, and that has been the most wonderful thing that has ever happened to me."

He let out a ragged breath. "At first I thought you were trouble. Now I see the same is true for me. I am trouble for you. But you are my chance at redemption, Sophie."

206 / Sharon Page

"From what? What happened to you?" This was the first time he had put it that way. As if he had done something for which he needed redemption. That was why he was rescuing her? He didn't answer, just propelled her toward the entrance.

The monk put his hands together in a gesture of prayer. He bowed to both her and Cary, and pointed a long, bony finger toward the now open door.

"Good lord, we *are* walking into hell," she whispered as they stepped inside. They were in a cavernous space lit by six torches on the walls. The light danced and writhed on the water. Magnified and echoing, the lap of water against stone filled her ears.

They stood on a stone walkway. It ran around three sides of the building. The middle was only water. The end of the building had large doors, and windows in the roof let in light from the moonlit sky.

"We go to the doors on the end." The space echoed Cary's deep, soft voice. "Follow the walkway."

She balked. "I'll fall off that."

"You won't. I promise." Cary put his hand firmly on her hip. Just having him touch her gave her the courage she needed. Carefully, she made her way along.

A slippery bit. Her foot skidded—

Cary caught her and set her down on her feet.

"You're strong."

"That's battle. If you don't have the strength to fight, you don't survive."

They'd reached the end, and Cary rapped on the door.

"This is like a Minerva Press novel." Sophie gasped. "I expect to find a deformed monk waiting around the next bend to kidnap me."

Then she realized he knew to rap three times sharply on the door. How had he known that? It could mean he knew this place, that he had been here before.

The door opened, and a second monk admitted them. So-phie laughed out loud. She didn't mean to; it was just exactly what she'd pictured. And she was so nervous, she giggled.

On and on they walked, then a figure stepped out—a woman, naked but for leather draped around her hips. Her large breasts hung and swayed heavily. And they were utterly bare, though the nipples were a scarlet that couldn't be natural.

The woman cracked a whip against the ground. "Halt. To pass you must answer my questions. What is your darkest fantasy, my lord?"

"My fantasies aren't dark, my dear. They are as pure as fresh snow. Innocent and sweet." A kind of wryness dripped from his tones. "And I am a duke."

"My apologies, Your Grace." The raven-haired woman assessed Sophie. "Would you enjoy watching me whip your darling companion?"

"No!" Sophie said—then she tried to swallow the word as the woman's very dark brows lifted in surprise.

"Not now," Cary said coolly. "Perhaps later."

They were walking in a space that looked like a tunnel built of stone.

Out of earshot of the woman, farther up the tunnel, Sophie squeaked, "Later?"

"I have to make it look like we are here for fun, Sophie, love."

"But would you . . . want her to hurt me?"

"Of course not." He grasped her hands. He stopped and pulled her to him. "Have I ever done anything that would make you think I would hurt you?"

"No. You have rescued me."

"Remember that. I will never hurt you. I promise you. I care about you."

Cared about her? Her breath flew out. Was he saying . . . Could he possibly . . . be falling in love with her?

He let her go. "We're almost at the house," he said.

* * *

Sophie gasped.

The house proved to have long corridors running front to back, with many rooms that led off the main hall. Like the other brothel, the sweaty, heavy tang of people having sex filled the air. She heard grunts. Cries. Even screams! Muted and from behind closed doors.

There were all sorts of strange contraptions. Long, slender benches made of leather and iron. Along one wide bench, four women kneeled, their bottoms bared. A tall man with huge muscles spanked each woman with a riding crop. One spank in turn, moving along the line, making all the voluptuous cheeks jiggle. The man wore no shirt, only breeches. His skin was coppery brown and slick with sweat. He wore a black mask, and dark stubble shaded his cheeks. He was handsome, if one liked big men. There was a huge bulge in the front of his breeches.

Sophie looked away, blushing.

She realized Cary was watching her. Only her. Not the naked women, the scenes of pain. All around them gentlemen watched, and while they did, they fondled half-naked women. The women fondled them. All sorts of members were exposed and being touched.

The Duke of Caradon was looking only at her.

At another contraption, a standing one, a woman was tied hand and foot. She was half naked, her shift pulled down to her waist. Her red hair hung loose, falling in a flood of bright ringlets down her back. Behind her, a handsome black-haired young man applied a whip with frightening force. The woman took each stroke. Her back was marked but not broken, which meant the whip's lash could not be very strong.

Sophie recognized the woman by her red hair. She was one of the five courtesans who had sponsored the Cyprian ball. The Fiery Rose, she was called. Obviously, because of her hair.

Women were not the only ones taking punishment. A man

lay naked between a woman's spread legs while another woman whipped his derrière.

The whipping at the large frame ended. The dark-haired man gently untied the woman. Sophie was struck by the tenderness he showed after the whipping. A robe was brought by a man without a shirt—a servant, or man who worked here. The dark-haired gentleman wrapped it around the woman and led her away.

"You next." The hooded, barrel-chested man pointed at Sophie with his riding crop.

"Not her," Cary said.

"If she won't play, you have to leave," grunted the dungeon master. "You are to do the honors of punishing her, my lord."

"I'm a damned duke."

"Your Grace," the man corrected.

In a soft voice that only Cary could hear, she said to him, "We have to find out about Halwell and Stratham, and we can't be thrown out. I'll do it. If you are the one holding the whip, you won't hit me hard."

"Sophie, God no. I can't do this."

But she knew they must. They were drawing attention. And they had to find out who had attacked her. That had been far worse.

And she remembered what the man had said—he'd been paid to kill her.

He had not finished his job. Did that mean he would try again?

She stepped forward. "Do you wish to have your dress removed?" the man with the whip asked.

She hadn't thought about that part! Though he asked as if she had a choice.

"She will remain clothed," Cary said.

"As you wish, Your Grace."

The man smelled of sweat as he got close to Sophie. She held her breath.

"Hold out your arms. Press your wrists and ankles against the pads," he instructed.

Coarse rope slid around her wrists, then her stocking-clad ankles. He pulled them tight and knotted them. She couldn't move.

She twisted to see Cary approach, holding the whip.

It hadn't really hurt the other woman. She had nothing to fear. Except she probably looked afraid.

Cary gazed at her. There was such pain on his face. Suddenly, he shook his head abruptly as if a bee were buzzing around him.

He straightened, his face revealing absolute anguish. He threw down the whip. "I won't bloody well do it."

The large man stepped right in front of Cary in a menacing way—

Suddenly, the man was on the floor, and Cary's boot was on his back, pinning him against the floorboards. The leather-clad man's right arm was twisted behind him, and Cary held it. The man couldn't move, and his face was pale with pain.

Sophie had barely seen Cary move. But in seconds, he'd overwhelmed the huge man.

"You won't throw us out. You will take us to the madam of this godforsaken place," Cary said.

He'd been stunned when Sophie had agreed to be whipped. More so when she revealed how much she trusted him.

Cary rubbed his temples. The memories had brought on a throbbing in his head. She had trusted him, and he had been afraid to apply the whip.

He remembered the last time he had been here and how damnably wrong everything had gone. . . .

The next morning, he'd decided to get the hell out of England and become a soldier. But that night, he had been here, playing sex games. He'd come with the other Wicked Dukes.

While playfully whipping a nude courtesan, he'd lost control.

He'd hurt the poor woman. Fortunately, Sin had stepped in and stopped him. Cary had blamed it on his drunken state. But in his soul, something had snapped. An uncontrollable rage had gripped him. It had been illogical, but he'd wanted to hurt the woman. He'd been enraged with her; he'd reacted with her that way, believing her to be one of the people who had hurt him.

After he had been touched by his sick, perverse kidnapper, he could never lose the feeling that sex was wrong. Bad. Every time he tried to enjoy it, all he could remember was the man's sick, lustful glee. It warped everything for him. Made any desire he felt seem repugnant.

That had snapped when he was whipping the courtesan. He was furious at his desire. He wanted to punish her and himself, even though she was entirely innocent.

Despite his confused and mixed-up feelings toward sex, he'd fought to be normal. He had made love to many, many courtesans to prove to himself he was normal. But that night, he realized how much of a mess he actually was. . . .

With Sophie at his side, he was being taken to the brothel's madam.

"There is something wrong," Sophie said. "You looked so haunted when you held the whip."

"I will not discuss it," he said as they reached the madam's rooms.

The woman who ran the brothel was plump, with black hair piled in a mountain of curls, and an enormous bosom. She greeted them, then said, with glittering excitement in her eyes, "Are you a murderer, Your Grace? If so, how utterly intriguing. You must tell me all—what drove you to do it. And how it felt."

"For Christ's sakes, I am not a killer. I came to ask about two of your patrons." He pulled out a wad of notes and handed them to her. "The first is Lord Stratham. Was he here—?" He gave the date of Sophie's attack.

"Yes, he was here that night."

"When did he arrive?" Sophie had been attacked close to dawn.

"It was after midnight, and he remained here until long after the sun had come up."

"What of Lord Halwell? He is one of your regular clients."

"Lord Halwell has not been here for several weeks, Your Grace."

"Then where does he go to satisfy his need for the perverse?"

The madam shrugged. "I have no idea. His tastes no longer profit me, so I no longer care." She snapped her fingers. "I dismiss him. Like so."

"I believe you do know. He was a wealthy client. You would want to know who poached him away."

"Why do you ask me all these questions?" Her face lit up with understanding. "You suspect Stratham or Halwell of the murder of that strumpet because they like to tie up women and whip them."

"They are just two of a large pool of suspects," he said casually. "Thank you for your help, Madame. My partner and I will now leave."

"Your partner is very sweet. Very lovely. She exudes innocence." The woman leaned toward Sophie. "When His Grace tires of you, come to me. I could make you a fortune, my dear."

"That will not happen," Cary said.

"I would never want to work in a brothel," Sophie said quickly. "Never."

"Of course. And with your beauty, if you are clever, you will never have to."

As they left the madam, Cary said, "Before we go, I want to question some of the women here. I want to make sure the madam told us the truth."

"But you paid her."

"And another might have paid her more to lie for him."

It was hard, at first, to watch while he spoke to the beautiful bevy of courtesans. But Caradon kept looking away from them. Watching Sophie. And when gentlemen approached her, Cary leveled a predatory stare at them. A warning.

He watched over her like a wild, possessive lion.

After speaking to many women, he returned to her. "Several women saw Stratham here that night. And also on the night of Sally Black's death. Other men I suspected were also here at the times of Sally's murder—when we speculate it was committed—or at the time of your attack. But as your attacker claimed to have been paid, unfortunately, we are at square one." He groaned.

As they traveled home, she said, "I am so confused. I keep trying to sort out my thoughts. There seem to be three possibilities. It is someone who wanted to kill Sally and me, and needed someone to make a scapegoat for the crime. It is someone who wants you to look guilty because they want you to be arrested, or at least shunned. Or it's a coincidence—Oh!"

"What, love?"

"Your coachman told me you had suffered two accidents and a previous attack by footpads. What if those were also done by the murderer?"

"For what purpose? If I had been killed, I wouldn't be alive to be a scapegoat."

"That's true," she admitted.

"There is another solution," Cary said.

"What's that?"

"You said there was a man you feared. A man who tried to force you to become his mistress. The attack could have been motivated by his lust for you. He likely hates me for taking you from his clutches."

And she knew Devars was in London.

"Who is he, Sophie?"

She couldn't say. If Cary confronted him, the theft would come out and she would be arrested.

"His name, Sophie."

There was more than she in danger. If it was Devars who had done this, he intended to hurt or destroy Cary.

But if she told him, and Cary went after Devars, she would go to prison.

"I can't tell you." Tears came then, spilling down her cheeks.

"Damn, don't cry. All right. But I will find out," he said.

Breakfast in bed. It was so decadent. Sophie supposed courtesans did that. Her lady's maid had worked before for an actress who had many male admirers who gave her gifts and "visited." Her maid claimed the actress always took her breakfast in bed.

She would enjoy it much more if she weren't terrified Cary would find out about Devars.

Her maid set down the tray. "There is a message on there for you, Miss. From the Duke of Caradon. It arrived this morning."

Ignoring the food, Sophie tore open the letter.

Dearest Sophie,
Something of an unexpected nature has happened.

Oh no.

My mother and my sisters have arrived in London. This was a shock to me—my mother is ill, and I never thought she would attempt an arduous journey without asking me to help her. Or at least warning me. Fortunately, she has not heard the gossip falsely accusing me of murder. That could devastate her health completely.

It is my mother's intention that I marry quickly. For the next few days, I will be unable to see you. This will drive me mad.

Please keep yourself safe. Do not venture outdoors. You will be safe in the house. The instant I am able, I will come to see you. Even if only for a few moments. To reassure myself you are well. And you are obeying me.

Cary

She looked at the note. Cary's mother wanted him to marry. Then what would happen to her? And how could he? He wasn't yet able to . . . to be properly married.

Her gaze went back to what he'd said. That he wouldn't be able to see her, and it would drive him mad.

He must care about her to say that.

But he was supposed to find a bride. Marriages of the aristocracy did not always involve love. Her mother had written that in her book. For many, marriage was about power, wealth, land.

She wanted Cary to have a good marriage. She wanted him and his wife to love each other. Which meant he had to be healed and able to make love.

It also meant that once he could make love, he *couldn't* be with her. She would want him to be faithful to his wife.

So once he was healed, she must give him up.

Sophie wrote a letter to Belle that afternoon, and enclosed almost all of the allowance Cary had given her as his mistress. This was her first payment, and she would receive it monthly. She'd kept enough to pay her bills, which was very little, as she planned to live frugally. In the letter, she asked about the children, and her heart fluttered as she thought of her son. She did tell Belle that Devars was in London, but she lied and wrote that she saw him but he did not see her. She did not want Belle to worry. At least it seemed her theft was still secret.

Her heart ached as she sealed the letter.

She must go and see her son, Alexander. She missed him so much. She'd never been apart from him before. Cary was going to buy a carriage for her. As soon as she had it, she could go. She would make it a quick journey. She had to try to keep seducing Cary.

But after they had been to the brothel near the docks yesterday night, he had not even touched her.

Her maid came into the parlor where she was writing. "Miss, there is a woman come to see you. She wouldn't give her name, but she said you would very much want to talk to her."

A woman, so not Devars. She told her maid to send the woman in.

Sophie jolted in shock as soon as she saw the woman. It was the Cyprian who had been tied to the strange metal rack at the brothel. The one who had been whipped.

The woman plopped down onto the settee. Her red hair was caught in a chignon. She wore paint on her cheeks and lips and something to darken her lashes. Sophie realized this was the courtesan who was known as the Fiery Rose.

"I came here to tell you that I know who killed Sally Black and who attacked you," the Fiery Rose stated. "I wanted to go to the Duke of Caradon, but when I went to his house, he was there with his mother and some girls I thought must be his sisters. I knew he'd come to see his mistress soon enough. If I tell him the name of the killer, I'll be in danger of getting killed myself. I need money. Money to get away. To make a new life for myself."

"I will give you money." Though Sophie would have to rip open the letter to take it out—

"I don't want it from you." The woman sneered. "I want it from His Grace. He must have piles of money. Enough to let me buy a lovely house in a warm, sunny country. Enough that I can have gowns in the first stare of fashion. And jewels."

"I have no idea what the duke would give you. Or even if he will give you anything. If you know about the murder, it is your duty to tell the truth."

The redhead laughed. "Duty? That's rich. As for His Grace— I think he'll pay a great deal to save his own neck." She sobered and gave Sophie a cold, hard look. "Let me tell you, Miss Ashley. Being a mistress is a short-lived career. Right now, I have an adorable viscount wrapped around my finger. But I know it won't last forever. That's what happened to me mum—she died in poverty. This is my chance to build my future."

"But you've been a courtesan—haven't you saved money for your future?"

The woman laughed mockingly. "All mistresses have some kind of vice. Some way to escape."

"Escape?"

"Escape the sin of having sex with men you don't love. Half of them I didn't even like." Her laugh was cold. "So courtesans turn to drink. Opium. Gambling. My escape was opium. I was introduced to it by one of my protectors. Now I can't fight it. That's where all my money has gone. So here is a note for your precious duke. He is to meet me in Hyde Park in the morning. At seven o'clock. He must bring me a bank draft for ten thousand pounds."

"Ten thousand? Good heavens—"

"Once he can hand over the real killer, he'll be safe. So if he wants to save his hide, he will pay it." The woman swept to her feet. "Seven o'clock. With ten thousand pounds. He is to send me a note to confirm he will be there."

The woman hurried out of the room.

Sophie followed but reached the door as the woman jumped up into a hackney.

She would have to send him the note. She just prayed his mother and sisters didn't see it.

She would take the letter and give it to one of Cary's servants. At the tradesmen's door. Since a mistress shouldn't run into her protector's mother.

Only gentlemen went to the park at seven o'clock in the morning. Out for morning rides, they trotted huge, beautiful horses along the Rotten Row.

Sophie had come by hackney, had been dropped off at the gate at a quarter to seven. She chose deliberately to come early. She suspected Cary wouldn't want her to be here—but she wanted to know who had attacked her, so she was going to hide and take up a spot where she could overhear.

Cary didn't come to her last night. In his letter, he'd said he would come to her as soon as he were able. She'd hoped he might have slipped out and seen her to talk about the demand from the Fiery Rose. But he hadn't.

So she hadn't been able to try to seduce him.

The thing was, she had hoped all night he could come—even when it was obviously a hopeless business. Even though he'd warned her that he wouldn't come, it had hurt when she had not seen him.

How in heaven's name was she going to let him go eventually?

It would be like tearing out her own heart. But she had to do it.

Sophie hiked over the grass, damp with early morning dew. Water rippled on the Serpentine, the lake within Hyde Park. It shimmered and glittered. Sophie tried to stay screened by trees. She didn't see anyone yet.

A dark shape was stretched out by the water.

Sophie's heart flip-flopped. It looked like—

She ran across the grass, heart pounding, her lungs heaving

for breath. She saw boots with a heel. The white froth of petticoats beneath skirts. A cloak that had fallen open. Vibrant red
hair spilling across the new grass.

Sophie reached the body and sank to her knees.

It was the Fiery Rose, the Cyprian who had come to see her
yesterday. The one who said she would tell the duke everything
she knew—for a price.

She lay on her stomach on the grass, her face turned to the
side. From where Sophie was on her knees, she could see one of
the woman's large brown eyes, open and horribly blank. The
woman's arms were outstretched and limp, her white gloves
soiled.

Sophie saw bruises around the woman's throat.

The woman had been strangled.

Something was clutched in the woman's hand.

Sophie leaned close. Carefully, she pried it out. A small,
crumpled note. It was from the duke and it read:

I will meet you at seven. By the Serpentine. Caradon.

It was the confirmation he was supposed to send.

It wasn't yet seven o'clock. Someone had come here, had
found the woman before Cary got here, and had killed her.

Sophie knew she should go and fetch the magistrate. But
what should she do about the note? The magistrate would see it
and think Cary had done this.

She could take the note with her. What harm would there be
in that? The duke hadn't done this. She knew that. Someone
had gotten here and found the woman first.

Cary would be here any moment. He was innocent—but
would anyone believe him? They wouldn't arrest a duke based
on this.

Or would they?

She should put the note back where she'd found it.

But she could protect Cary just by taking it.

Morality won. Sophie put the note back into the girl's hand. What she would do was find Cary. He must be on his way here. If he wanted to take the note away, he could. As long as no one found the poor girl before she brought him back.

But she knew, in her heart, Caradon would not take away the note, even though it was a false clue against him.

She knew he would be too honorable.

16

Sophie ran headlong through the Park Lane gate. She careened into the road—someone shouted. Horses whinnied, and she whirled to see flying hooves and a huge carriage bearing down at her. Crying out, she jumped back, and the carriage passed by her so close, she could feel the suction of the air.

Her lungs heaved. She used to be able to outrun any boy in the village, and now look at her. Her throat was burning from frantic breathing as she stumbled through the gateposts of the house.

"Sophie?" It was Cary. He was walking down his drive, and now he ran toward her. He must be going toward the park to meet the Fiery Rose at seven o'clock.

He was innocent. He had to be. But what if—what if he were hanged for this? Panic and shock and horror all exploded in her. She ran at him and grasped his arms.

In front of his house, he folded her into his embrace. "Sophie, what's wrong?"

"The woman you were going to meet is dead. She's by the Serpentine. She's lying in the grass. And she's holding a note from you. She was strangled. Oh, it's so—"

He drew her tight to his chest. "Shh, love. You've had a bad shock, but we can't speak about this out here. Let me take you to my house. You need brandy. Then I will go and see."

She shook her head, but that made her dizzy and sick. "You need to come with me. Now, Cary. Please. I—I was going to take the note she was holding. It is your note to her. The one telling her you would meet her. But then I thought I shouldn't. But maybe I should have. Someone might have already found it. I didn't know what to do—"

"Calm down, Sophie," he said.

"Caradon, what is happening?"

The soft, cultured feminine voice came from the steps of his house. Sophie choked on her voice. Cary turned around, Sophie in his arms.

She saw pale hair—white hair—and an ivy-green dress with beautiful trimming. Clutching the railing, the woman limped down the steps. Soft lines surrounded the woman's mouth. Concern etched more lines in the woman's high forehead. She looked like an older, female version of Caradon.

His mother.

Sophie recoiled in shock. Numbly, she thought: *What did I just say? No wonder he tried to stop me from speaking.*

"Caradon, this child in obviously in shock, and you are now as white as she is. What woman has been killed? What has this to do with you? I must know what is going on. Take me inside, please, and bring this girl in. You will tell me everything. I know there is something going on—all the people I have encountered today look at me as if there is something I should be told, but everyone is too afraid to give it voice."

Sophie looked helplessly at Cary.

"She can't know the truth," he murmured into Sophie's ear. "She's ill and not strong. Having me suspected of . . . This could kill her. If I'd known she planned to come to London, I would have stopped her. She wanted to catch me by surprise, so she can push me into marrying."

Sophie looked at up him. She kept her voice low. "But she will know you are innocent. She is your mother."

"She may not believe completely in my innocence."

She was about to ask why—why his mother wouldn't have complete faith in him, when his mother commanded, "Stop whispering, the two of you. Caradon, we will go inside now. And I wish to know everything that is happening."

Cary sighed. "Mother, this is Sophie. A dear friend of mine."

"A dear friend?" his mother echoed.

"Yes," he said. He turned to Sophie. "Sophie, this is my mother, the Duchess of Caradon. Please go inside with her—instruct one of the footmen to tell my man of affairs to have the magistrate fetched. I will examine the body. Tell Sir Henry to meet me in the park."

Sophie lowered her voice to the softest whisper. "Are you going to take the letter?"

In a soft voice he answered, "I'm going to give it to the magistrate, Sophie. I have to."

"She must have been followed. Or the killer knew she was going to meet you—"

"I know. I will track down those leads. Go with my mother—now."

"I shouldn't be with your mother. I'm your mistress."

"Well, love, maybe don't tell her that."

"I don't want to be dishonest with your mother."

"All right, damn it." Cary walked over to his mother. "Mother, I have to give you fair warning. Sophie has newly become my mistress. I will take her to her home rather than bring her into the house—"

"No, do send her into the house here. I would like to speak with her."

That Sophie had not expected.

* * *

Sophie sat in the duchess's morning room, across from Cary's mother. The duchess sat with her spine stiff, her posture utterly perfect—she was like a swan transformed into human form. Her every movement was elegant, and even when she sat completely still, she looked unearthly, like an unreal and perfect creature who would disappear if Sophie tried to touch her.

Sophie stood. "I am so sorry, Your Grace, but I should go to Cary—to Caradon."

"You will sit down . . . Sophie, I believe. My son instructed you to stay here. You must listen to him. Tea will arrive in a moment. And you must tell me what is happening."

The duchess spoke imperiously, if quietly. But Sophie shook her head. "I am sorry, but I need to be with him. I found the poor woman, and I might be able to help."

Tea came then, brought by a maid in a crisp apron and white cap, and they had to stop speaking. Sophie saw the girl's gaze slide to the side and drink in every detail of Sophie. Had they already been talking of her downstairs? She had been here three times, and one time she had been bruised after the attack.

The duchess poured the tea.

Sophie was rather stunned when the woman handed her a gilt-rimmed cup. "I shouldn't be here," Sophie said suddenly. "You—you wouldn't have me in here if you knew what I am."

"Someone had best tell me what is going on. Since you seem to know much more than I do, I thought I would speak to you."

The thing was, she was a courtesan, but she hadn't actually slept with Cary. And the duchess was pouring her tea, while her adoptive mother threw her out of her home for something less scandalous—because she and Samuel had been planning to marry.

Sophie set the tea on her lap, untouched. "It's rather gruesome. I don't know how to explain it without horrifying you."

"My dear, I had to endure it when I learned my son had been

taken prisoner of war. And before that—that other time so many years ago. I have faced terrible things. I doubt very much whatever you say will make me swoon."

The duchess was very strong. Sophie wanted to ask her about the "other time." Did it have something to do with Cary? Was "that time" the thing in his past that haunted him? But the duchess went on, "Why has my son gone rushing off to look at a dead woman? Does he know this woman?"

Sophie tried to explain as best as she could. Beginning with the woman murdered and left in his mews. Then the attack on her. "This woman claimed she knew who had attacked me and killed Miss Black. Your son was supposed to meet her so she could tell him."

"And now she is dead. I am so sorry for what happened to you, my dear. That must have been frightening. And that area you spoke of, where you lived, it is a rather violent place, is it not?"

"The people there are poor. So there is some violence. But there is also violence amongst the upper levels of society." Sophie was speaking rather defensively.

"But why was this other young woman in the mews in the middle of the night?

"She was a courtesan."

His mother paled. "And she had come here to see him?"

"No. Cary—the duke, I mean, has no idea why she would have been here. He hadn't arranged to meet her when he went after her at the Cyprian ball."

His mother sipped her tea. The she set it on a table with a rattle. "My son was at a Cyprian ball? He promised he would look for a bride."

"That was why he went. He knew he couldn't marry until he healed himself, and he needed a mistress to do that—" Sophie broke off. Her impetuous words had gotten her in trouble.

How could she say to Cary's mother that he couldn't make love?

"I do not understand."

"I—I can't really explain it," Sophie said helplessly.

The duchess had gone pale, frightening Sophie. Then the woman said, "But why is my son involved in this? This is the job of the magistrate."

"Because the woman's body was found behind the duke's house, and there is a Bow Street Runner who suspects he is responsible, so Caradon is trying to find the truth."

"A Runner suspects him?" The duchess picked up a biscuit and nibbled at it. Then she put it down. "I cannot eat. This is terrible. How could such a thing have happened?"

"He is innocent," Sophie assured her.

The duchess had been gazing out the window toward the park. She jerked back to Sophie. "Of course he is." But she looked frightened. The terror on her face spoke of a woman who feared it could be true. Then the duchess said, "You do understand that my son must marry."

"Oh yes. And I want him to. I want him to marry happily."

"I saw the way he embraced you. He seems to be . . . rather taken with you."

"Your son did not want to become my protector," Sophie blurted.

Oh bother. Her tongue had run away with her. She went on, "He did it to save me, you know. He did it for the noblest motives."

"I beg your pardon?"

"I married a young man who went to fight at Waterloo, Your Grace. He did not come back, and I was left with no place to go." She wanted the duchess to know Cary was a good, wonderful man. Since there was some reason she feared he might not be—if she could think him capable of murder. And since the duchess was sick, Sophie wanted her words to comfort.

"My son became your protector. . . . But did you have no family? Did this young man not have family?"

Sophie flushed again. "His family did not accept the marriage. He was a viscount's younger son. I was—I was adopted and raised by a doctor and his wife, but my . . . husband's family considered me beneath him. And my best friend also lost her husband, leaving Belle and two—rather, three—children without anyone to look after them. I wanted to help her too."

There was something in the quiet way the duchess scrutinized her. . . .

But even a duchess couldn't see through the lies, could she?

"And you had no family. What of the doctor and his wife?"

Should she say they were dead? It would be the easiest. "They didn't approve either." She said it softly. She probably screamed guilt. Then realized her words made no sense. Why would they not approve of a viscount's son? Heavens, they would have been delighted at such a match! Had she given herself away?

His mother sipped tea, then gracefully set it down. She was very thin. Her hands trembled slightly, as if it were a strain to lift a cup. "You seem a sweet and dutiful girl, Sophie. You are most certainly responsible and kindhearted. Surely, *this* is not the right path for you."

"But there isn't another one. My friend has young children, and they will starve unless something is done—and done quickly."

"Could you not become a companion? A governess, perhaps?"

"If it were even possible, that would rescue me alone. I would never have enough to keep the rest of them. I prayed I would find a kind and generous man to—to look after me."

"My dear, as a woman who was once a wife, I cannot help but balk at your hopes."

"But I would not want to be—be with a man who had a

wife," Sophie assured her. "That would be heartbreaking for a wife, and I would not do that. When the duke wants to marry, I would not interfere with that in any way. I promise," she said breathlessly.

"Oh, my dear, you already have."

"I don't understand."

Color rose on the duchess's cheeks. "I saw the look he gave you. I do fear that you have engaged my son's heart. You are very beautiful and very sweet, and I fear it is going to be very difficult for any other young woman to compete with you."

"Of course not. I'm not—not of his class at all. I do know what I am. I aspire only to protect my family."

"Now I understand my son's concern about you. He is correct—you do not belong in the world you have chosen."

"I have to learn to belong," Sophie said. "I have no other choice. There is no other way I can feed five mouths. No other way I could hope to give the children any kind of future." She faced the duchess. "About the duke getting married . . . I don't believe he can. Not yet. You see, I am not really his mistress in that way. Because of his terrible memories, he can't—" Her cheeks were flaming hot.

"What on earth do you mean?" The duchess's voice became sharp.

How could she explain it? "He is tormented by something that happened to him. For some reason, it interferes with his ability to . . . I mean . . ." She tried again. "He told me he won't marry because he is haunted by these memories. I want to make him better. I want to make them go away. I have tried, but it isn't working yet, and I don't know what to do."

The duchess was scarlet.

"It was from before he went to war, Your Grace. I'm sure of it. It must have been something that happened when he was young. Before he was old enough to—"

"I do not know what you are talking about," the duchess interrupted. "There is nothing in his past. Being a prisoner of war almost destroyed him. He never told me what happened to him in Ceylon—he said he could not speak of any of it. But he was in a terrible state when he returned home. So thin, he was almost skeletal. I feared he would be like that forever. I was not well. I had fallen ill. I have never had a great deal of strength. But my son believed he had to look after me. Caradon fought to recuperate so he could take care of me. But whatever haunts him must be related to the time he was a prisoner. That is what it must be!" Her voice had risen in a panic.

The maid came in then. "Your Grace, the magistrate is here, and Mr. Rycroft, a Bow Street Runner, with His Grace, the duke. They must speak with you."

Before the duchess could agree or refuse, a tall dark man slid past the maid and stepped into the room.

It was that suspicious Bow Street Runner, Rycroft, accompanied by Sir Henry, the magistrate. And Cary came in after them.

To Sophie's surprise Rycroft was gentle with the duchess. Rycroft poured her tea and handed it to her. Then he took a seat opposite her.

"If you find this in any way upsetting, Your Grace, please advise me. I want to spare you the details—and spare your sensibilities—but I have to tell you that your son, the Duke of Caradon, had arranged to meet a woman in Hyde Park to acquire some information. That woman was murdered, ostensibly before His Grace arrived."

Rycroft consulted a notebook on which he had written with a pencil. He asked the duchess several questions. Had she seen her son that morning? Had she seen him leave the house?

The duchess claimed she took an early breakfast with her son rather than have it in bed. She had felt the desire to go downstairs. Cary had then told her he intended to ride in the Park, which so many gentlemen did early in the morning.

"You were with His Grace from what time to what time,

Your Grace?" Rycroft asked it bluntly, but with tones filled with respect.

Sophie was quite startled. It appeared there was more to the Runner than just belligerence. He had been harsh and suspicious when questioning her and Cary about Sally Black, but he was quite gentle with the duchess.

"I believe it was from half past six until just before seven o'clock," the duchess answered.

Then Rycroft turned to Sophie. "I must ask you questions, Miss Ashley, as you found the body in the park. Do you want me to question you here?"

She shook her head, afraid upsetting details might come out. She went with the men to Cary's study, though Sir Henry spent much time fussing over the duchess before they went, and he left the duchess in the morning room.

She told them about the visit of the Fiery Rose and her demand. "I don't think the duke would have killed her, since she was going to reveal the identity of the real murderer."

"Perhaps not. If the duke were the killer, she might have been demanding money to keep quiet. But she didn't want you to know that, Miss Ashley."

"This is ridiculous. Instead of bothering the duke, why don't you investigate? Why aren't you questioning the men riding in the park? Perhaps they saw someone! You saw the note the woman was holding, didn't you?"

"We did. The one that confirmed the duke would be there— at about the time of the murder."

"If he had done this, why would he let you find the letter? Wouldn't he have taken it? Of course he is innocent. He was only just leaving his house when I went running to find him and summon the magistrate."

"And why were you there, Miss?"

"I was attacked by this person, as His Grace told you. I wanted to find out who the killer is."

They asked more questions—asking her to go over every detail she saw.

She learned that two gentlemen riding saw a woman in a cloak near the Serpentine, but they claimed they saw her later, leaving the park.

Once the Runner had left, Cary said thoughtfully, "I assume the person they saw was the killer leaving. A person in the cloak."

"They thought it was the woman in the cloak." Sophie frowned. "Do you think it could be a woman? Or they just saw a figure?"

"It was a man who attacked you."

"Yes, but witnesses also mentioned seeing a strange woman." Her heart pounded with fear. "Rycroft thinks you did it. He was kind with the duchess, but he is so determined not to show favoritism to a duke that I fear he would like to see *you* convicted just because you are a duke."

"That won't happen," Cary said softly. "We are going to solve this. And I think Rycroft does want justice."

We. He spoke of them together.

"The Fiery Rose was a Cyprian, and she said she knew who the killer was. If that was true, maybe one of the other Cyprians knows too. She was at the Cyprian ball the night Sally Black was killed. I think we should question the other Cyprians. Maybe she confided in one of them—oh! Maybe one of them is the mysterious woman seen near my room. Or this woman in the park."

"You have a remarkable, clever mind, Sophie. That makes sense. I will question the Cyprians."

"We could do it together?"

"They want to seduce me, love. I think it's best if I do it alone. Now, I'm going to take you home. I want to ensure my mother is all right."

Sophie went with him, but stayed outside the morning

room, near the door. He crouched down beside his mother. He touched her hand, but she moved it away.

He straightened. "I am going to take Miss Ashley to her home, Mother. She should have some breakfast. And rest after this ordeal."

His mother's eyes stayed on him as he took Sophie's hand and lifted her to her feet. He tucked her hand in the crook of his arm.

"Is there anyone to look after her?" the duchess asked.

Sophie was startled that the duchess would be concerned.

"There are servants—maids, a cook, a butler," Cary said. "They will be able to take care of her on my instructions."

"Yes," his mother said softly so he didn't hear, but Sophie did. "You seem to have thought of everything. You seem very concerned about this young woman. And that will have to stop."

Cary took Sophie up to her bedroom in her town house, intending to tuck her back into bed and send her maid upstairs with a breakfast tray.

But the moment he saw her draw up the covers in her new shift, her black hair loose, he realized—he could have lost her.

"You shouldn't have gone there this morning."

She lifted her chin, looking stubborn, but he growled. "If you had been there a little earlier, you might have witnessed the murderer, and he might have attacked you. He'd failed in his mission to take your life, Sophie. You might have handed him a second chance."

She went very white. "But I had to go—"

"Don't ever take such a chance again."

How easy it would have been for the fiend to have killed Sophie by the lake with no one there to protect her. He wouldn't have known until he found her.

"I want to savor you," he said softly.

He needed to touch her. It was as if he had to do it to convince himself she was really safe.

With his fingertip, he traced her lower lip. When the sensation made Sophie tremble, he drew her forward, kissing her slowly.

"That was so beautiful," she whispered. "I'm sorry. I never thought there would be any risk. I was going to hide."

"Don't talk about that. Don't think about that."

She was so pale and shaky. He had used sexual pleasure to make himself forget hellish memories and events. Sophie needed that.

He nuzzled her neck, making her moan. Her skin tasted so sweet. He skimmed his tongue along the length of her throat. He could have applauded when her fingers clutched his shoulder and she clung to him.

He broke away from her. His body felt so hot. The way it did with her—only Sophie. She was the only woman to make him feel on the brink of control. To make him get steamy with desire. He had always been too distant before Sophie.

He yanked open his cravat, tore off his coat, and tossed them aside. Damn all the clothing, but he finally got to his bare chest. He had to sit on the edge of the bed to haul off his boots.

Sophie ran her hands over his back.

He let his head drop back, let himself enjoy her touch. It set his skin on fire.

She pressed to him. In the past, he could only endure intimacy if it was leading right to sex. Tonight, he realized how beautiful it was to have her warm body pressed against him. She moved, and her hair spilled over his skin. That silky mass was like being caressed all over at once.

She kissed his neck, which tickled but felt good. Sank her teeth lightly into his shoulders. Nibbled his ears.

Her hands ran all over him. Just her panting alone had him rock hard, aroused beyond belief.

Then she whispered, "I love being able to touch your warm body all over. I love tasting your skin. Won't you let me kiss you down there?"

Her voice was so throaty, so sensual. He wanted to howl with need.

His hard cock strained against the placket of his trousers. It was so hard, pushing so eagerly.

"Give me a moment, love." He stood to push down his trousers and linens. She watched. On her knees in just her shift, her lovely legs folded beneath her. Her hair a gleaming, raven river. The shift clung to her full breasts, hinting at them.

He couldn't make love to her, but he could make her come until she screamed.

"You are so beautiful," she said.

"I'm not. I'm a man—hairy, smelly in places, scarred up. You're the lovely one, Sophie. Soft, sweet-smelling, beautifully curved."

"I think every inch of you is gorgeous, Cary," Sophie said, and she whisked off her shift.

Cary eased her back, both of them falling onto her large soft bed. He had it all decorated in white—embroidered white counterpane, silky sheets, white bedposts, white bed-curtains, tied with white tassels.

He had her down, naked on the bed. Her arms over her head, her breasts jiggling. He lay between her legs, his weeping erection pressed to her. Silken skin. Heat.

To make her giggle, he nuzzled her neck again. To make her squeal, he stroked between her long, slender legs.

He breathed in the smell of her. So rich and sweetly juicy.

Gently parted her dewy nether lips. He wet his fingers, then rubbed her clit, massaging her own creaminess into her soft, satin skin.

"Where are your toys, love?"

She wrapped her arms around his neck. "I want you. Not toys, as fun as they are. I want you."

Delicately, her fingers wrapped around his prick. She squeezed and ran her hand up and down. He caught his breath at the tug on his skin. She caressed his ballocks with her left hand. She was so good. So innocently wanting to please him.

This was what sex should be about. Joy. Pleasure.

Love.

That realization hit him—

Then Sophie kissed him hard on the mouth, sighing against him as she did. She lifted and pressed her hot cunny against his shaft. It trapped his hand against her pussy, and he played with her.

She broke the kiss to moan. He teased and rubbed her, making her moan harder, louder.

He pressed his cock against her lips. Closed his eyes—

Damn, that was a mistake. He lost touch with her lovely, blissful face.

It started to happen again. He wanted to make love to her, but all he could see around him were gloating, leering faces. Like monsters.

He wanted to run. To scream. To flail out at them, until he could get free—

Cary backed off, drawing away. "I'm sorry. I am so damn sorry, Sophie. I can't do this."

She was panting. "It's all right."

"I need to make you come. To make you forget. Let me do that."

17

After my randy and youthful lover of twenty-two, I found I craved having a gentleman of greater sophistication. Charming though it was to play tutor to an enthusiastic student, I felt I needed a man of greater . . . cynicism. Youthful joy can grow wearing.

I chose the Earl of Easton, a grizzled man of thirty. What a wild and vigorous lover he was—though he enjoyed one position only. He wanted me to lean over an object like a chair, my dining table, my vanity table, a fence near the stables on his country estate—and he took me from behind with the ferocity of a stallion. And with remarkable endurance. The position was the only one that provided him with satisfaction. Alas, it gave me none.

Was there only one man in the world for me—X. Q.?

Surely not. I would find another gentleman.

After all, there were far more peers in the sea known as London Society.

—From an unfinished manuscript entitled *A Courtesan Confesses* by Anonymous

"Spread your legs, angel."

Lying on her bed, Sophie did as Cary commanded. She spread her legs wide. His hand was wrapped around one of the large phallus-shaped gewgaws. He had brought out the vial of oil, had warmed it over a candle, and now he made the phallus slick and shiny and slippery.

She could barely draw breath, watching his hand stroke along the thick shaft.

It was so erotic.

She wanted him inside her. His thick, heavy cock buried deep in her.

She couldn't have that—yet. But he was with her. And she needed him. She wanted to be with him, to think only of this—of sex and pleasure—and not of fear and death and killers.

He touched the tip of the thick fake cock to her nether lips. Looked deeply into her eyes, his fiery with lust, as he worked the cock inside her.

So full!

He thrust it in and out, and she moved with him. She moaned. Licked her lips. Touched her nipples. Tried everything she could to entice him.

He smiled. He pushed the phallus deeply in her, and Sophie let out a long, fierce cry of sexual agony. The emeralds in its base sparkled in the morning light. She began to rock on the phallus. As he'd shown her, she reached down and caressed her clit.

His eyes glowed. Then he shook his head and stopped her. "Not yet, angel. Roll onto your tummy."

He helped her. Sophie lay on her silky sheets.

"I'll do this slowly. But I want to introduce you to the pleasures of double penetration."

She twisted, met his gaze.

"Do you trust me?" he asked.

"You've done nothing but protect me. Of course I do."

He held up the vial of oil, and she watched the warm golden

fluid spill onto his fingers. Then his long, elegant finger stroked between the cheeks of her bottom.

"What are you doing?"

"You can feel the most incredible pleasure through your derrière, Sophie."

She remembered that from the display at Sinclair's party. She held her breath. And nodded to say: *Yes, she wanted it.*

"I'll be gentle," he promised

She felt a tug on her anus. Felt his finger push against her. It was slick with oil, and he was massaging her. Slowly.

"It feels good." Stunningly good. She'd had no idea.

She felt pressure, and she gasped.

The movement stopped. "Relax, Sophie. I'll let you get used to the feel of my finger. You can take this, and it will feel good. I promise you."

"I like it," she whispered. "Do more."

She rocked with the slow thrusts of his finger. Being filled back there made her cunny feel more full.

"My finger is all the way inside you." His deep voice sounded almost reverent.

"Would you like to make love to me back there?" she asked breathlessly.

"I would, but I can't, darling. But I can fill you with one of the dildos."

"All right."

She held her breath, watched as he oiled the shaft of a more slender phallus. She kept her head half turned so she could watch him introduce the long, slender thing between her cheeks.

He gripped the hilt with his hand, thrusting with long, slow motions.

"Play with yourself," he urged. "I want to make you come, angel."

Her fingers went down, and she touched her clit, stroking it.

She wriggled on the phallus filling her cunny, and he thrust the other deeper and deeper into her derrière.

"Oh yes," she cried.

She was working harder and faster. Begging for him. Gasping his name—

Her fingers pressed hard and fast, and pleasure simply crashed into her.

She was coming. So hard, she had to scream with the sheer intensity. She squealed. And cried his name.

Then she opened her eyes. He was roughly jerking his cock, watching as she writhed and spasmed with her pleasure. "Oh yes," she cried. "Jerk yourself hard."

He let out a growl like a bear, then his hand clenched tight, his hips rocked forward, and his come jetted out. It shot to the bed. It shot over her belly. It dripped over his hand.

Then he let go of his cock and fell on his back beside her.

"Someday, I'm going to make love to you," he growled. "I want to so badly. It has to happen."

This was the first time he'd spoken as if he would fight to make it possible!

"It will," she said.

Then he got up, slid the toys from her, and put them in a basin. He cleaned her with his handkerchief. Then he lay beside her on the bed, but he frowned and cocked his head.

He had remarkable senses—he'd explained he had honed them during battle. Though he said he was surprised the cannon fire hadn't deafened him.

There seemed to be some kind of commotion outside. Sophie got out of her bed, curious, and went to her window. People had walked out of their houses. They stood on the sidewalk, looking up the street.

Four white horses pranced down the lane, pulling a carriage painted a deep blue. The blue of precious sapphires, or of a deep, clear lake. The coachman wore elegant attire, along with a tricorne and a wig.

The carriage stopped in front of her house.

"For some reason, I think royalty is visiting us. Or your mother." It looked like a carriage fit for a duchess. Sophie clapped her hand to her mouth. "Why would your—"

"My mother? What the—?" Cary had jumped out of bed, and he moved her to the side so he could look out the window too. Then he grinned. "That's not my mother's carriage. That's yours. Finally, they are delivering it."

"Today of all days," she whispered. On a day where a desperate courtesan had lost her life.

"You're safe and sound. And I plan to keep you that way. Do you like the carriage?"

"It's lovely beyond compare. A fairy-tale carriage."

Cary put his arms around her. His hands cupped her naked breasts.

This was an intimacy he would have refused mere days ago. "Why don't you take the carriage and visit your friend and her children? I'm going to question the Cyprians. I'll do it this afternoon—none of them will have stirred from bed before noon. Now that you have the carriage, why not travel and reassure them all they will now be safe?"

"But I was going to question the courtesans with you."

"No, you are not. This morning, it was sheer good luck that kept you safe. I need you to stay out of this. I can't think straight when I'm worrying about you. Sophie, I couldn't bear losing you. I feel like I want to hold you forever. So I know you're safe."

"I will be safe. I promise."

He kissed her then. Cupping her cheek, he bent down to her from behind her and gave her a long, deep kiss. But when he drew back, his mouth was bracketed with harsh lines. "I know what it's like to be too late."

* * *

"What do you mean?" Sophie asked, her eyes wide and surprised. "You weren't too late for me. You saved me!"

Cary closed his eyes. He had to make her understand how afraid he was—so she did not disobey him again.

"I haven't told anyone about this." His voice was a hoarse rasp. With his eyes shut, he remembered every detail of the way the Fiery Rose had looked, lying on the ground by the Serpentine.

And that reminded him of the uprising . . . of what happened in Ceylon. . . .

"No one. You can't speak of it either, but you need to understand."

"I will keep it secret," she said softly. "Please tell me."

In his mind, Cary could hear the rushing stream beside their camp in the jungle. "It was in Ceylon. We had been ambushed by the rebels the day before, but we had fought off the attack. However, many of our men were injured. I was helping our doctor with the wounded. When I was done, I needed to take a walk. I needed time to think and strategize. Some of the men wanted a violent retaliation. I didn't want to lose more lives for some rabid, blind desire for revenge. But when I was walking, I heard a woman scream. . . ."

He opened his eyes and looked at Sophie's lovely green ones. "I heard a man shout at her. He called her filthy. Told her to 'shut it' or he'd make her shut her mouth. The man was obviously English, and I ran toward the sounds. When I reached a clearing in the jungle, I saw one of my soldiers bent over a young, slim Ceylonese girl. The girl's garment was torn off. The soldier had his hands wrapped around her throat, cutting off the air so she couldn't scream."

Sophie's hand rested on his biceps. Stroking him. Giving him comfort.

"I barked at him to stop, but he wouldn't. I hauled him off

the poor girl. But her limp body fell to the ground. Her eyes were wide open and blank. I checked in vain for a pulse, but I knew I was too late. She was dead. I took out my pistol and put the soldier under arrest. He had been a disciplinary problem from the beginning, and he always fought my orders. Corporal Yew was his name. He had to be court-martialed, and I was speaking about that with my superior officer, when we were ambushed again. That was when I was taken prisoner. Months later, when I was rescued and released, the corporal had been killed and buried. But to this day, I still hate the fact that I was too late."

"It wasn't your fault," Sophie cried.

"Sophie, this is why I need you to stay safe. I couldn't bear it if anything happened to you."

"I will stay here. Just as you asked."

She kissed him. A sweet and tender kiss. Then he moved to his clothing and began to get dressed. "I have to go and put an end to this."

As soon as Cary had gone, Sophie dressed and summoned her brand-new carriage. He had told her she couldn't question courtesans, but she was going to see Nell.

She should tell Nell that she had the duke as a protector, shouldn't she? She hadn't spoken to Nell since the night of the orgy.

And with her new carriage and her coachman, there would be no danger in going to Nell's.

With Sophie settled safe and sound at her town house, Cary took his carriage home. His mother knew about the murders, but his sisters didn't. Would he have to explain it to them? They were younger than him by ten and fifteen years. Now he saw that it must have taken a long time for his parents to recover from his abduction and to try for more children.

His mother had been weakened by his kidnapping for a very long time. She had him watched incessantly. His father had retreated from him.

Still, how in hell did he explain this to girls who were not yet twenty? His sisters should not even know what a Cyprian was; surely they had no idea women traded sex for money. He wanted to keep them far away from this.

While he had just taken Sophie to bed. He was a damned hypocrite, he realized.

But Sophie had been glowing after he'd pleasured her. She had no longer looked pale and afraid.

He'd done a good thing.

At home, he went straight to his study, avoiding his family.

In his drawer were two lists. The guest list for the Cyprian ball he had obtained from Nell. She was willing to do anything for money—give tickets to balls or sell private guest lists.

The other, for the orgy, he had gotten from Sin.

There were twenty gentlemen who had attended both events.

Sophie was correct. Questioning the Cyprians was the best way to start. At the top of his list were the two sisters—the Black Swan and the White Swan. They were close in age to the Fiery Rose, whose real name was Gwendolyn Longbottom. He could see why she'd taken a nickname.

But there was something that bothered him.

Both Sax and Sin had been at the Cyprian Ball and the orgy. He believed his friends couldn't be involved. Sax was wild—but not wild enough to hurt a woman. Sin's sexual appetites were notoriously inventive, and he reputedly never had sex in a scenario that involved less than four people.

They weren't guilty. The four dukes had all grown up together—he, Greybrooke, Saxonby, and Sinclair. First at Eton, then at Oxford. He knew Sin and Sax had secrets in their pasts. But they were men. They didn't talk about that, didn't ask questions. So he did not know what those secrets were.

Still, he could not see Sax or Sin capable of murder. Not of the cowardly murders of defenseless women.

And there was the watch with the initials "Y.Y." His story about Corporal Yew had made him wonder . . . Yew had reason to hate him, but the man had died in Ceylon.

His best line of action was to question the Cyprians.

He had been just in time to save Sophie when she was attacked. This morning . . . God, he could have lost her.

He was realizing how much he knew he wanted to be with her.

He was supposed to marry. He couldn't make love to Sophie today, but pleasuring her had fought off his demons, had made him forget everything but her.

But when he married, he wanted to have a loving relationship with his wife. He couldn't keep a mistress.

When he could marry, he would have to let Sophie go.

On her way, Sophie reviewed what she knew of the Cyprians. Angelique had fought with Sally Black. The girl had insulted Angelique, and Sophie knew that had angered Angelique. But bold Sally might have argued with other Cyprians.

Angelique hadn't been at the orgy, but Sophie had recognized four other Cyprians—Nell had given her their names. The Fiery Rose, but she was now dead. The Venus Callipgye, known for her beautiful, full, round bottom (the nickname actually meant "Venus of the beautiful buttocks"). The Black Swan and her sister, the White Swan.

And Nell—Nell had been at both events.

She rapped on the door at Nell's town house, and the door whipped open. The young maid peered at her.

This time, Sophie wore a pelisse of dark green velvet and an elegant day gown.

"Cor, I thought you'd be the doctor, mum."

"The doctor?" Sophie pushed in. "What's wrong?" Another murder? Was she too late, too late for Nell?

"She took laudanum last night. She does sometimes, when she can't sleep. She must have taken too much. I can't wake her up."

"Let me see her. Where is her bedroom?" Sophie demanded.

The girl never questioned Sophie; she just pointed up the stairs and said, "The first room on the left, past the glass doors. At the back, with the best view of the garden and the roses. There's no early sun on those windows. That's what my mistress liked best." The girl was babbling and was almost pure white with shock.

Sophie pushed the girl toward the drawing room door. "Have a sherry for your shock. Wait for the doctor to come, and then send him up at once."

She raced up the stairs. Was it murder?

Another maid was in the hall, wringing her hands. "I don't know what to do," she cried.

Sophie rushed past her. Nell's bedroom was fit for a duchess. The bed was oval, with a tall silk canopy. Nell's form looked tiny amidst the large bed, with sheets and a counterpane of pink pulled up to her chin.

This woman had helped her. Had saved her life—and her son's life, and those of Belle and the children—by intervening with Cary. She couldn't be dead just because Sophie was too late.

Sophie reached the bed. "Nell? Can you hear me?"

Desperately, she searched for a pulse. She couldn't tell if it was actually a pulse she was feeling. She bent close to Nell's lips. Felt the lightest flutter of air. Heard the soft sound of air going inside Nell's mouth.

Nell was still breathing. Faintly, but she was still drawing breath, and that was all that mattered. But Sophie felt like the maid—what should she do?

"She is in here, Dr. Grace!"

Sophie stood as a tall, thin man strode in. "She is still breathing. She's still alive."

He didn't ask who she was. The doctor curtly told her to "stand aside." Sophie did, retreating to the mantel by the fire. "If you need anything, doctor, ask, and I will fetch it at once."

All her life, she had been much like a servant. Here, that was all she wanted to be. A servant to help the doctor save Nell.

She put her hand on the mantel because she was shaking—

Something fell. It was a gold locket, and it had fallen open. It contained a miniature picture of a man. Obviously, a gentleman. Sophie picked it up. The tiny painting depicted a dark-haired man with green eyes. On the other side, a paper had been tucked in. It read:

My beloved X. Q. The Viscount Mowbray.

The journal—in her mother's journal, she had used the initials X. Q. to describe the man she had been deeply in love with.

Perhaps Nell had been in love with him too. Or—

It was hard to tell on such a small picture, but X. Q. had Sophie's color of eyes, and his chin looked like hers. So did his nose. This man was her father.

And Nell, with her dark hair, could be her mother.

But her mother was dead. Mrs. Tucker, her adoptive mother, had told her that. Or had that been a lie? Maybe to hurt her, or maybe Mrs. Tucker did believe her mother was dead.

But she wasn't.

Sophie took a hesitant step forward, but the doctor was hunched over Nell. He was using a brusque voice on Nell as if he could bully her awake.

"Is there anything I can do?" she asked impetuously. "I must help her."

"You can keep out of my way, miss," the doctor said curtly.

Sophie retreated. She was quite sure Nell was her mother—

but it could still be that the Viscount Mowbray was Sophie's father and her mother could be dead.

She wanted Nell to be her mother.

She walked around the room, pacing, praying Nell would live. Had this been an accident, and she had just taken too much laudanum? Had someone tried to silence Nell, the same way the Fiery Rose had been killed before she could talk?

There was another possibility. Nell could have done this deliberately.

Sophie walked over to a small writing desk. Then she knew the truth. A small book sat on the desk blotter—a book with a red leather binding, just like the journals Sophie had. The ones that contained her mother's manuscript.

The book was in her hand and open before she realized what she was doing.

It wasn't right to read it, but she had to know.

The handwriting was the same. It had been so small on the miniature, and it had not been a flowing script, so she hadn't noticed that fact. But here she did.

She began at the last entries. They were all about a handsome viscount. Nell used a code for the names, but there was a folded piece of paper tucked in the book. Sophie unfolded it. It was a charcoal sketch of a handsome, dark-haired man.

Sophie had seen him before.

He was the same man Sophie had seen whipping the Fiery Rose at the brothel on Horton Street. In Nell's journal, there were catty remarks about all the famous Cyprians. And Nell wrote about being furious because a young upstart stole the Viscount Willington out from under her nose. He was the peer who was Sally Black's protector.

Nell was furious with both Sally and the Fiery Rose.

Nell wrote about her desire to win the Duke of Caradon. To prove she was still the superior courtesan.

Sophie looked at the date where she had come to see Nell.

There was no mention of her, beyond a small note about acquiring a new protégé. Nell didn't mention her as her daughter. But Nell had written several paragraphs about how much she desired Caradon.

Three women who were involved with men Nell wanted had been murdered, or almost murdered.

But Nell must have recognized Sophie's story. She must have *known* Sophie was her daughter. Nell had, Sophie assumed, invited Caradon to the orgy. She thought it was because Nell had been kind and was giving her the chance for a good match—well, a good match with a protector.

If Nell wanted Cary for herself, why do that?

From the bed, she heard a soft groan. Some babbling. Sophie turned around.

"Have some black coffee sent up. We must keep her awake now," the doctor ordered.

Sophie looked back at the bed. Did Nell know who she was? Was her mother—who she had dreamed of meeting—responsible for two murders and the attack on her?

Who was the man who had been paid to kill her?

When the coffee arrived, she held out a cup for Nell. Carefully put it in the woman's hands. After Nell had drunk some, she looked weakly at Sophie.

The doctor was packing his bag.

Sophie said, "I need to know if you are innocent, Nell."

"Innocent? Hardly that," she said weakly.

"I mean of the deaths of Sally Black. And the Fiery Rose. Someone killed her. And then you—you took too much laudanum."

"I did that . . . in the night. I knew you were safe now. How beautiful you turned out. I saw what I'd lost. I'd lost you. . . ."

"You took too much laudanum because of me?"

"I gave you up. I am so sorry."

"I know you are my mother. And I must know if you hired someone to kill me so you could have Caradon."

Nell struggled to sit up, but Sophie touched her shoulder. Weakly, Nell put her hand on Sophie's. "No. No, I would never hurt you."

"Do you know who did? Someone broke into my room to murder me."

"I don't know. Oh my dear, I don't know. But you are all right—?"

"The Duke of Caradon rescued me."

Nell smiled. She settled back against the pillows that Sophie had arranged to prop her up to drink coffee. "Thank heavens," she said.

18

"Caradon, please. It is time you began to seriously search for a bride."

Cary looked up. His mother stood in the doorway of his study. He had been reviewing what he had learned from the Cyprians—mainly that each and every one despised other females. They were all ruthless. They had clawed their way to their positions over other women. When it came to claiming a rich protector, they would fight any other woman to the death.

All of them had been at both events, except for Angelique. She had not attended the orgy.

He had offered each woman a generous bribe. Either they knew nothing about the murders, or they weren't willing to sell their secrets.

What it came down to was that all this was directed at him. He was the common thread between the three women—between Sally and Gwen Longbottom who were dead, and Sophie who had been attacked. If Corporal Yew had still been alive, he would have been Cary's main suspect, since the man had strangled a woman and blamed Cary for court-martialing him. But Yew had been killed and buried in Ceylon.

"Caradon, are you listening? I am very tired, and you are not even answering me!"

He got to his feet, hastened over to his mother, and led her to a seat by the fire. "I'm sorry, Mother. I can't search for a bride until I solve these murders."

"Why on earth is it your job to do that? You are a duke."

"One of the victims was found close to my house. I was supposed to meet the other. Sophie was attacked. I am innocent, but someone seems to be trying to make me look guilty."

His mother paled. He quickly poured her brandy. "I don't want to worry you with any of this. Let me deal with it—let me find the blackguard and put an end to this."

"And after that, you promise you will marry? I want to know there is an heir. I fear—I don't understand why you won't marry. Sophie told me that you have terrible memories, that you are unable to do your duty in the bedroom."

It was his turn to be stunned. "You discussed that."

"She told me that you made her your mistress to rescue her, not sleep with her."

"She is better than that world." But he was using her for pleasure. He was bringing her into that world, damn it.

"Tell me what's wrong."

"What she said is true. I can't—I can't do my husbandly duty." Christ, he never dreamed he would have this conversation with his mother.

"But you were a thorough rake as a young man. Before you went to Ceylon—"

"You know what happened to me when I was a boy. You and Father forbid me from speaking of it, but you know what I experienced. I had to prove myself. That was why I was a rake. But after Ceylon—after I was held prisoner, all the memories came back. When I even kiss a woman, that's what floods my mind. The memories. So I can't marry."

"But all you have to do is your duty, Caradon."

"A hell of a sorry life for the bride, don't you think?" he asked bitterly. "Sophie believes I can be healed somehow. That I can forget. It's not possible."

"It must be," his mother said. "I think—I think I must rest, Caradon."

Sophie hurried through her dining room. Was everything in readiness? Flowers graced the table. The silverware shone. The dinner service and elegant crystal glasses provide by Cary sparkled under the glow of the hundred candles in the chandelier.

Cary had sent her a note. He intended to visit her that evening, but not for the reason she would have thought. It was not to be a night of pleasure and seduction.

It was a council of war.

She straightened some forks and adjusted a few plates. She was fussing, she knew, but she had never entertained before.

When she'd lived with the Tuckers and they had had guests, she'd helped in the kitchen, doing a kitchen maid's work. This time, she had been in charge. She had created the menu, had instructed her cook, had ordered sherry and brandy put out.

She had spent the morning with Nell, fetching Nell coffee while she was recovering. And talking.

"I wish I hadn't had to give you up," Nell had said. "Your father, who I called X. Q. in my memoirs as his name was Xavier Quentin, was a viscount, and I was madly in love with him. But he had to marry—and certainly not me. Some men marry their courtesans—even Prinny tried, making an unrecognized marriage to Catholic Mrs. Fitzherbert. But Quentin needed his allowance. He was heir to a dukedom, and of course his father threatened to cut him off. He could have waited, but I learned that Quentin was not willing to live solely on love. He ended our relationship that very night. Ironically, after his father died, he was the duke for all of two years. His father lived to a ripe old age, and Quentin died quite young, killed in a du-

eling accident. He came back to me once, before he became the
duke. It was two weeks after he had married a duke's daughter
who had a huge dowry, a long nose, and bulging eyes. He was
drunk and insisted he could not live without me. When he
sobered up, he threw me over again. I swore I would never,
ever, be fooled by him again, but it was already too late. The
last night we had together left me enceinte. I knew I had to give
you away. You would be a reminder of my folly. Selfish, wasn't
it? But back then I believed I couldn't bear to look at you.
What an absolute fool I was."

Then Nell had asked Sophie whether her life had been good
with her adoptive family. Nell had looked so hopeful. "You
turned out so well. So lovely, and you look like a lady," she
said.

Sophie realized her mother had meant well. Nell had hoped
that being raised by a doctor would give Sophie more re-
spectability. Sophie hadn't the heart to tell her the truth. Besides, she had grown up with a roof over her head and she had
never been really abused. Being treated like a servant had
taught her how lovely it was to be treated well.

Nell had expected her to be resentful and unforgiving. But
Sophie understood. Sophie worried about her son. Maybe she
would be willing to give him up so he could have a good future,
if she couldn't provide one for him. . . .

Now, everything in the dining room was in readiness. She
knew no one truly cared what they were eating and drinking.
They were here to solve the mystery. But she wanted her first
attempt at playing hostess to be successful.

The guests began to arrive, and Sophie greeted them as they
were announced and filed into the drawing room. First, the
Duke of Greybrooke. To Sophie's surprise, Greybrooke approached her. "My wife wished to be here, to help Cary, but
she decided she must stay at home with our newborn son. She
did ask me to tell you that she will be happy to receive you

when our son is a little older, and she is less tied to feeding the wee mite."

"Receiving me? But—"

"My lovely wife was a governess before I saw sense and married her," Grey said softly. "I would like Cary to do the same. See sense."

Before she could think of an answer, the silver-haired Duke of Saxonby was announced. A few minutes later, the Duke of Sinclair arrived

"I have all the Wicked Dukes in my drawing room," she whispered to Cary, awed. "I think there are women who would give anything to be me right now."

"Many would aspire to be as good and loyal and noble as you, Sophie."

Her footman stepped in. "Mrs. Carlyle," he announced.

Who could this be? Sophie looked to Caradon, and he grinned. "A special guest. A very special woman."

Sophie had no idea who this special woman was. The softest fragrance filled the room, mixing with the scent of the orchids that had appeared this morning (apparently, Caradon had arranged for fresh flowers to be delivered for her each morning). It was a subtle, sinful kind of fragrance. Sophie even thought of a tumbled bed when she smelled it.

Mrs. Carlyle wore white—all white. A column of a satin gown clung lovingly to her generous bosom, then fell in an endless sweep of gleaming fabric. For the gown to fall like that, the woman's figure had to be very slim, her legs incredibly long. Her hair was raven-black, braided and curled and decorated with diamonds that winked like stars. She wore paint, but in a way that made her eyes large and slanted and seductive. Her lips were two plump, red curves.

She was the most beautiful woman Sophie had ever seen.

"Good evening, Miss Ashley," she said to Sophie. "So, you are the woman who has wrapped the Duke of Caradon around her finger."

"Oh! Hardly."

Cary said, "Mrs. Carlyle worked as a British spy during the war."

"A spy? Really? That must have been thrilling. And dangerous."

"We need a woman for this who can use a pistol and take care of herself."

"Well, that certainly describes me." Mrs. Carlyle's laugh was enchanting.

Sophie noticed Greybrooke was looking at the beautiful spy but without the look of avid interest and desire she saw on the faces of Saxonby and Sinclair. As for Cary—

He was looking at her, Sophie.

"You got nothing from the Cyprians. So, what is the plan, Cary?" Sin asked.

"There is another Cyprian ball tonight. It's my plan to lure the killer out. To give him bait by showing special attention to a particular woman, even have her offer to sell me the name of the killer, like the Fiery Rose did. Then we catch him when he makes his move."

"I could do that," Sophie said.

Cary turned to her, frowning. "Absolutely not. There is a villain out there who attacked you, Sophie. I am not going to hand you over to him on a silver platter."

"You could watch me every minute—"

"In that crowd I could lose sight of you. It's a risk I'm not willing to take. The woman will be armed, and she will be a woman who knows how to look after herself."

"But she will be in danger. I should do this," Sophie said.

"Sophie, I need a woman willing to kill her attacker if she must. Are you willing to take a man's life?"

"I—" She wanted to say that of course she would if he were a villain. But—"I don't know. I think I could. I think I would have the courage."

"Killing a man doesn't take courage. It takes a hefty streak of self-preservation. The willingness to do anything to anyone else to save your own life."

She remembered hitting Devars, and she flinched. She had been sick at first, fearing she'd killed him. Even though he was willing to hurt her, she didn't have the heart to take his life. She realized he must be speaking of his time in the war. "You are right," she said softly. "I couldn't do it."

"I want you to stay out of this completely."

"But I want to at least be there—"

"I want to make sure this madman does not have any opportunity to go after you. You will stay here."

She sighed. "All right. But please, please, please, be careful."

In Sophie's drawing room, after the men and Mrs. Carlyle had left, Sophie paced in front of the fireplace. "Ma'am." Sophie's footman entered and stood with perfect correctness. "The Duchess of Caradon, ma'am."

The duchess? Here? Sophie whirled around, stunned. Slender, swathed in a fur-trimmed cloak, the duchess walked in. Stammering, Sophie offered tea or sherry, but the duchess quickly said, "I must speak to you about my son, Miss Ashley. This is unconventional, but I do not know where to turn. You were correct, dear, with what you said. There is something I must tell you—"

Sophie approached the duchess. "You are terribly pale. Let me pour you sherry."

She gave Cary's mother a small crystal glass, led her to the settee, and sat beside her.

The duchess sipped and sipped, then found her courage. "I fear what troubles my son is more than what happened in Ceylon. I've never spoken of this to anyone else. Almost no one knows about it—with the greatest care, we were able to cover it up. Only certain members of the law and our most loyal servants know."

The duchess hesitated. Curiosity consumed Sophie, but she knew she must wait for the duchess to find the courage to talk. Then the older woman gently touched Sophie's hand. "There has been no one else, outside of our immediate family, who is as close to him as you. He has not allowed anyone to be so close to him."

Was that really true? How could she be the only other very close person to him? But then, in her mother's book, sometimes mistresses were. A man might live a separate life from his wife, but he needed someone to confide in, someone to believe in him, flatter him, care about him. So he did it with his mistress.

"When he was only five years of age," the duchess said, "he was kidnapped for ransom."

Sophie's blood went ice cold. Five years old! The same age as her son. Pain at that thought twisted inside her. "But—but what happened?"

The duchess eyed her warily. "I trust you not to tell Caradon that I told you of this. Or anyone."

"Of course. I would never tell anyone. I can keep secrets." She'd kept so many of her own. "What happened to him? He was freed, obviously." Thank God. Thank God! "But was he hurt?"

"In terrible ways. Unspeakable things happened to him."

"Unspeakable? I don't understand."

The duchess put a lacy handkerchief to her mouth. "He was chained up so he could not escape. And hit. But he was also . . ." The woman was white as a ghost and shaking.

"You needn't go on," Sophie said.

"I must. He has said he won't marry. And I fear it must be because of what happened to him. This man—this monster who took him—touched him. In ways that should only be between a husband and a wife. A man and a woman. And he was but a child."

The duchess hurried on. "He had to kill the man to escape.

He created a trap and sent a brick hurtling down onto the man's head. That only enraged this monster, and he grabbed up a kitchen knife. Fitzwilliam—he was not the duke then, of course—ran and took up a fireplace poker. The man tried to stab him, but fell, and my son hit him in the head with the poker."

"Poor—the poor child. How awful." There weren't words to express the horror. It was so much like what had happened to her with Devars. But Cary had been a child!

"He was afraid he would be hanged. For killing the monster who had kidnapped him."

"But he wasn't."

"No. It was covered up. Hushed up. He had already been through hell. There was a girl there too. The daughter of this monstrous man. She was sixteen years of age. Caradon had hoped she would help him. But she—she beat him terribly. Burned him on his legs with hot sticks. And she would make tiny cuts on his arms. Nothing to badly wound him, but it was awful torture to a child. He endured hell. And when he came back, my husband learned what happened to him. . . . The duke was terrified his son had been made into something monstrous too. He was so cold and fearful, because he believed he must straighten Fitzwilliam out. We were all so afraid, and instead of embracing our son and showing him great love, we retreated." Tears spilled onto the duchess's cheeks. "We ruined him as much as that monster. That's what I fear. Can he ever be made right?"

The woman shuddered with tears. She was so thin and fragile.

Impulsively, Sophie hugged her. "I do believe he can. I am going to fight to try." Then she blushed. "I mean . . . oh . . . er . . ."

"I never dreamed I would be saying this, but I need your help, my dear," the duchess said. "If anyone can heal his heart, I believe it is you."

* * *

Sophie helped the duchess outside, both women wearing cloaks with their hoods up. Sophie realized she had never felt accepted or respectable in her life, yet Cary had tried to make her that way by rescuing her and protecting her. Her heart was filled with sorrow for him as she helped his mother into the duchess's carriage. Sophie climbed up the carriage steps. The duchess had fallen into several coughing fits after she had told the story, and Sophie wanted to watch over the duchess until she reached her home.

"I will have the carriage return you home," the duchess said.

They sat in silence as the carriage started off. Then the duchess gave her a look—the sort of look her son would give her when he'd done something naughty.

"I do have a terrible admission to make," Cary's mother said. "I sent Caradon to London to find a bride. He was visiting me in the country, and I told him he had to come back for the Season and get married and produce a grandchild. I told him I was dying."

"Oh goodness, I am so sorry."

"You see, it wasn't true. I felt very sick after the winter, and I feared it could happen. But I was feeling better. Yet I lied, and I used that lie to blackmail my son. For that, I feel awful. But I was so desperate."

"You must tell him the truth, because he will be very worried about you," Sophie said passionately. "I think he will forgive you. He loves you and his family very much." Of course he did. He knew what it was like to be torn away from them. Was that why he had come to her rescue and offered to give her the house and allowance of a mistress while demanding nothing in return?

"I want to see him be happy," Sophie said. "And I know he will understand why you told him what you did."

"It was wrong. I, who knew what he suffered, had no right to manipulate him."

Sophie patted the duchess's hand. "You want him to have a partner in his life, and the joy of children." But what had Cary suffered? It sounded as if . . . as if he had been abused in perverse ways. No wonder he had said he indulged in lots of sex with courtesans to prove himself.

How did one erase memories like that?

All along she had been confident.

Now, she realized she didn't know what to do.

She also thought of the terror of a five-year-old boy, afraid he would be punished for defending himself. "The man who took him was killed. Who was he?"

"He had been a footman. He had been dismissed, as my husband believed he had stolen some valuable snuffboxes. It turned out he had gotten a village girl into trouble, and after she had the baby, he had turned to theft. However, he used very little of his ill-gotten gains to support the young woman and his daughter. That was the female who was so horrible and so vicious to Fitzwilliam. The villain's daughter. After Cary was saved, the magistrate looked for her, but she had vanished. She left a note though, threatening revenge for her father. In the letter, she said he'd been falsely condemned for the theft. Of course that was not true. He was quite guilty."

"She threatened revenge?" Sophie repeated. "All these terrible things have happened. Accidents to the duke. And these murders—"

"It was years and years ago. Why would she have waited until now? She would be more than forty years old."

"I don't know why she would have waited," Sophie admitted. "Maybe she wasn't able to exact her revenge until now." Cary had never mentioned this, but then, he had not told her about the kidnapping. He had wanted to keep that ordeal a secret. So of course he could not have told her about this girl.

There were two courtesans who would be the right age.

Nell. And the haughty one, Angelique, who had fought with Sally Black on the night she had died.

She must go to Cary and tell him. As soon as the duchess's carriage took her home, she would rush to the Cyprian ball. At least Sophie knew where it was—from their discussion during the council of war.

Sophie knew they had reached the Cyprian ball by the large number of discreet black carriages on the street, and the enormous number of well-dressed men streaming through the open doors. Street flares illuminated them, and the moon was out.

Once the duchess's carriage had brought her home, she had hastily commanded her carriage take her to the ball.

Suddenly, her carriage stopped. She leaned out and saw they could get no closer. "Let me out here."

She wished she could bring her coachman in, but someone must stay with the horses and the carriage. She had raced there hastily, and of course had not thought to bring a footman to take in with her. All she had thought of was Cary—warning him.

And she supposed she had been embarrassed to drag a footman into a courtesan's ball with her.

She would just watch at all times. Stay with the crowd. She flipped up the hood of her cloak and accepted her coachman's help down from the carriage.

Pushing her way through the gentlemen, she reached the doors and was stopped by a young servant, resplendent in red-and-gold livery and a powdered wig. But she wasn't going to be thwarted now.

"Your invitation, madam?"

She needed a distraction. "My God, that gentleman has collapsed! Someone fetch help!" she shrieked. Several men, including the servant, turned. She raced past, only to collide with men who were coming *back* to see what the commotion was.

Useless men!

"No, you don't." The servant grabbed her cloak.

She ripped open the ties and ran right out of it, elbowing her way through. The man at the door was left with a look of shock and her empty cloak.

She was inside. Now where was Cary?

Desperately, she looked around.

In the center of the crowd, at the end of the ballroom, stood a bevy of women in brilliant dresses. The Cyprian hostesses.

Sophie spotted the two sisters. The Black Swan was dressed entirely in black silk decorated with glittering jet, and her pale blond hair was decorated with a black comb tipped with diamonds. Her sister, the White Swan, wore white and pink with many flounces.

And there was the courtesan famed for her voluptuous bottom. She wore a clinging gown that revealed its large curvature.

Angelique stood there, dressed in bronze silk with a gold overlay.

Of course, there was no Fiery Rose in brilliant scarlet. And she didn't see Nell, as Nell must still be recuperating.

She was praying the culprit was not Nell. That it was Angelique. Though why kill innocent women if it was Cary she hated? Why not attack him? There had been attempts on his life. Why had she turned away from that and started to have women attacked instead? Who was the man who had helped her?

And how could she blame a five-year-old child for having to do whatever he could to save himself? Angelique should blame her horrible father!

Of course it might be neither of them. The man's daughter may not have become a courtesan at all. But it was a possibility, and she had to tell Cary.

Again, Sophie searched the crowd. She strained up on her tiptoes. Cary and the rest of the Wicked Dukes were tall. Surely, she would see Cary's beautiful pale gold hair—

Stratham passed by her field of view. At once she sank down, praying he didn't see her. He was heading toward the Cyprians, fortunately.

Blond hair! In a small gap in the crowd, she glimpsed a shock of light blond hair. That had to be Cary.

Something hard jammed into her back. She half turned, ready to protest.

She didn't recognize the man leering at her. Sandy brown hair was pulled back in a queue, and pockmarks made a mess of his cheeks. His eyes were cold and hard. From behind her, he reached out and grabbed her hip. The hard thing pushed more painfully against her back.

"Where do ye think ye're going, my dear?" He sneered. "I've got unfinished business with you."

That voice.

It was the man who had attacked her.

"Don't scream or do anything stupid. I've got a pistol against your back."

"You wouldn't sh-shoot me here. In front of all these people."

"Because I'd hang? But you'd still be dead, sweetheart." His arrogant smirk froze her blood. "I've been following you. First you were riding with the Duchess of Caradon, then on to here. Busy, interfering little whore, aren't you?"

So that was how he'd known who she was. He must have been watching her house, waiting for her.

She didn't know what to do. What if he did shoot her? She should shout or warn Cary or do something. Roughly, the man pushed her toward the side of the room. She saw a dark entrance.

No. No. She opened her mouth to scream, when a cloth was pushed over her face and half of it was shoved into her mouth, almost choking her.

She struggled.

A hand came through the air in a ferocious arc. She couldn't move, and the palm slapped her hard on the face. The force sent her head snapping to the side.

"You will do what you are told. Stop moving, you stupid little bitch."

Sophie blinked against the pain as Angelique stepped forward. Angelique also held a pistol. Sophie had no chance—not against two weapons.

"You will come with me," Angelique snapped.

She would die for sure! "No, I won't." She could be shot here, but they might hesitate to do it right beside a crowded ballroom.

"Yes, you will. With Caradon here, his mother and his sisters are unprotected in his house. I've paid two ruffians to watch his house. If they do not get word from me in another half an hour, telling them to abort, they will sneak into the house and slit the throats of Caradon's mother and sisters."

Sophie gasped, ice-cold with horror. "How could you?"

"He took my family from me. But if you come with me without a fight, I will call off those men."

"How can I trust you?"

Another slap. Sophie gritted her teeth to keep from screaming or crying.

"You have no choice but to trust me," Angelique snapped. "If you do not move now, they will definitely die. Wait long enough, and I won't have time to stop the men."

"All right," Sophie said. "I will go with you."

19

I have made a dreadful mistake. X. Q., my viscount, has married. A dull girl with a long nose, she came with a staggering dowry. It was the final blow, and I swore I would have nothing to do with him again.

But he came to me one night in a frenzy of passion and angst. He had been a fool to listen to his father, he declared. To marry for duty and not to possess me as he wished. He could not live without me, he swore.

He pulled out a blade and put it to his breast.

I pulled it away. I declared my love, my true and undying love.

That night—oh, it was a precious night. Like an ornament spun of delicate glass. How it glittered at first, how lovely and perfect it was.

But it had to shatter, of course.

In the morning, he was gone.

But I had not taken the care that I should have, and in two months, my folly could no longer be ignored. I was with child.

I had to look forward to many months of being reminded of how dangerous it was to fall in love. And then, could I spend each day in the presence of a reminder of my most foolish mistake? Would not resentment follow?

Surely, the best I could do for both the child and for myself was to give the wee thing away.

To be a successful courtesan, a woman must be prepared to be a survivor. She must fight and struggle and never let herself be foolish with regard to love.

Indeed, that is the making of a successful courtesan.

It may not be the making of a happy woman.

—From an unfinished manuscript entitled *A Courtesan Confesses* by Anonymous

"I need to see you stop the attack with my own eyes," Sophie insisted. Angelique had hauled her to a black carriage. The hard muzzle of the pistol pressed into Sophie's back.

She couldn't give in to fear. Fear that the pistol would go off by accident. She stopped, lifted her chin, and spun to face Angelique. She wasn't going to cry. Or give in to vapors. She was going to have courage—as Cary had when he had been a prisoner of war, when he had confronted a kidnapper. "Do you have to shove that thing into my back? I fear it will go off."

Angelique, swathed in a rich black cloak, looked startled. She must have expected sobbing. Then a twisted, mad smile curved the courtesan's painted lips. "That hardly matters, my dear. You will soon be dead. But I did want the pleasure of torturing Caradon. I do think it would destroy him to watch you die."

But the horrid witch moved the pistol away from her back, still smirking.

There, Sophie thought, she had won a small victory. But she wished she could understand. Surely, even a madwoman could be made to see sense, to have empathy, to care, if only Sophie could understand why she was doing this. But first, she must ensure Cary's family was safe.

Angelique motioned with the pistol for her to mount into the carriage, but Sophie went on. "Please," she begged. "I want to know they will not be harmed. You can make haste with the carriage and call off your men. These are innocents. Please do this."

"You think you will be able to escape. You won't. You will not escape your death this time."

Don't believe that. Don't. Don't. "I just don't want anyone else to be hurt."

"By the end of tonight, my dear, many people will be hurt. But if you obey me, the victims may not include the duchess and her daughters. Perhaps." Angelique laughed.

How she obviously loved having this power.

"Get into the carriage, you stupid girl."

Sophie scrambled in. The man who had attacked her was acting as the coachman, and he had jumped up into the driving box.

Angelique had killed two innocent women—and had tried to kill her. The woman wanted to destroy Cary—and she was willing to do any ruthless thing to do it.

Two defenseless young women were gone, all because the woman sitting beside her in the carriage was obviously mad.

All her life, people had told Sophie she had a remarkably optimistic disposition. She had not hated her adoptive mother for treating her badly—she'd been happy to have a home. Even when she'd lost Samuel and had been thrown out, she'd been grateful for her son. She had looked at the bright side of becoming a courtesan—and she had found a wonderful man who she could love passionately.

She wasn't going to die. She had too much to live for. Somehow she would escape. She would survive. And she would make certain Cary's family wasn't hurt.

Was there any way she could get a message to him?

The carriage stopped. Sophie looked out and saw the top of Cary's beautiful house above the wall surrounding it. Angelique opened the window, leaned out, and made a strange whistling noise.

Two shadows, tall and lean, slunk out of the dark. Their caps were pulled low, so the street flare barely illuminated their faces. Sophie glimpsed stubble-covered cheeks. One had a scar that slashed through his upper and lower lips.

"Your business is done for the night," Angelique said. "You are not to attack."

"Why not?" one whined. "Would have been right fun."

"Aye," said the other. "I was hoping to fondle a noble tit."

"Be off with you," Angelique snapped. "Disobey me, and you will both die." She threw down some coins to them. "For your trouble tonight."

"Enough for a few rounds and a few tarts," the first one said as they both scrambled to pick up the coins, bumping each other.

"And if you do not hear from me again tomorrow morning, you are to carry out the original plan and kill the duchess and her daughters. That will be insurance for all of us."

Then they tipped their caps to Angelique and ran off down the road, away from Cary's house.

At least Cary's family was safe for now.

"Now we have the long part of our journey," Angelique said. "And soon Caradon will receive a note at the ball, telling him where you are. I have no doubt he will come to rescue you."

"Why are you doing this? How could you hurt so many innocents? How can you hate Caradon so much?"

"He took something from me. Something very, very dear to me."

"Do you mean your father?"

The inside lights of the carriage were off. They passed another street flare on the lane. The light painted Angelique with harsh precision. Her face had changed. Raw anger and gloating triumph had transformed it. Every line and wrinkle showed. Her age was apparent. "Your father kidnapped Caradon when he was just a child, and you were there."

Angelique did not answer Sophie's accusation, but Sophie saw the flash of surprise. "Where are we going?" Sophie demanded.

"To the house he was kept in as a child. I do not see how you knew this."

"I figured it out," Sophie answered. "But I still don't see why!"

"We were poor, terribly poor. A footman's wages could not support a family. The Duke of Caradon was fabulously wealthy, and my father saw a way to get his hands on some of that money. All we had to do was keep the child until the ransom was paid. But that was not to be. The horrible young brat escaped. After bludgeoning my father to death with a poker."

"And you blame him for that?" Sophie cried. "A terrified five-year-old? He was fighting for his very life, and your father did terrible things to him. What did you think would happen? You committed a crime!"

Would Angelique shoot her now? Her heart thundered, but Sophie squared her shoulders. If she was going to be shot, she would face it bravely.

"Shut up, you wretched tart!" Angelique snapped. "Think you are so high and mighty? You are naught but a jade yourself. I had to scrape and fight for everything I had. I had to survive. And I learned early that the way for a female to survive is to allow a man to have sex with her. It's the only way to guarantee a roof over your head. Then I realized I could get much more than just a roof! What was I to do? I knew I'd be thrown out of my house by my father if I didn't do what he asked—" She stopped. Her hand stroked the muzzle of the pistol.

"Goodness." Sophie had grown up in a doctor's home. She had overheard tales of the worst kinds of abuse. "You are saying your father forced you"—she could not actually say it—"into his bed?"

"He came to my bed. Or cornered me in various places of our grotty little cottage."

Pity and horror blended in her. "That is awful! Oh my goodness, what horror you lived through."

"Oh, shut up. I don't want your pity."

"Well, you have it. I cannot imagine how horrible that must have been." She remembered having been punished at times, though being locked in her room had seemed severe for simple, childish mistakes. Now she knew her adoptive mother had been punishing her for what she was, not what she'd done. She remembered how sad she had felt. How she had wanted to please. What about when love and the hope to please parents was all warped in a perverse way?

Then she thought. "But surely you would empathize with the duke! You should feel sorry for him. How could you hurt him this way? And those two women were innocent. You must have understood them too. You must have understood the need to survive."

"They were hardly innocent. Sally Black, who thought she was so young and lovely, so arrogant. And you—you snuck in, defying the ruling queens of the Cyprian world. What loyalty should I have shown to the Fiery Rose? She was going to give my name to Caradon. You were all young and pretty. It is hardly any tragedy for me if a few lovely, young courtesans are no longer competing with me."

"Well, that was not justification to take their lives," Sophie said. "And this cannot be Caradon's fault."

"You argue with me? I'm holding a pistol."

"Well, you are in the wrong. I must make you see that."

"For what purpose, you stupid chit? You are going to die.

You want to know why this is Caradon's fault? I knew what my father did to him was wrong. I would have simply continued on, keeping the secret. But then Caradon did something to me. . . . He took the last thing I had in the whole world. He had my son court-martialed and shot in Ceylon."

"Your *son?*" Never had she seen such pain on a woman's fact. Raw, agonized longing. "Your son was a soldier in Ceylon? But he—he attacked and strangled a woman."

"He was a young man, barely more than a boy. Caradon should have understood why he snapped after the terrifying battles. And the girl was only a filthy member of the enemy. One of the wretched, horrid native people who were attacking British soldiers. She tried to sneak up and kill my son. Of course he had to defend himself! His friend returned from Ceylon in 1819, and he told me the truth about my son's death. I knew I wanted to make Caradon pay. He'd stolen everything from me. My entire family. My son was my world!" Angelique cried with passion. "At first I thought I just wanted to kill him. But those attempts failed. Then I knew I wanted him to *suffer*. I wanted to do more than kill him. I wanted to destroy his name. I wanted it to be spoken with disgust for all time!"

Angelique was insane, but she was a woman who had lost her child. "I know you loved him, but he did something terribly wrong and bad. As his mother, you must still love him. Your loss was terrible, but you can't hurt Cary."

"Caradon cares about you so deeply, it is sickening," Angelique spat. "But he is also getting too close. I wanted to tighten a noose around his neck little by little. I wanted to make him suffer, and I shall. For he is going to watch you die. Then I shall shoot him in the head and put the pistol in his hand. The poor, mad Duke of Caradon finally takes his own life, because he has been warped by the horrors of war and has become a monster. He will leave a note, explaining everything he has done. Not only will he die, but his name will be infamous!"

Angelique had not even listened to her. Spittle formed on the woman's lips in her excitement. She was too far gone in her plan to be reasoned with.

Sophie's hope wavered. But she knew, to survive, she could not give up. She had to cling to hope. Hope had landed her Cary, after all.

Hope—and keeping her wits and fighting to survive—might get her through this.

Then she understood what Angelique was doing. "You are luring Caradon to the place he was imprisoned, where he suffered hell."

"That should hurt him deeply. Destroy his mind. Then I will kill him. I will kill both of you."

Sophie stood at one of the two small front windows that looked out onto the lane leading from the highway to the cottage. The lane wound around shrubs and bushes, so the building was well hidden from the road. Her hands were bound in front of her, tied at the wrists with rough rope.

Cary had set a trap—but he would be the one walking into one.

She must warn him. She must protect him. Angelique thought it would be hell for him to watch Sophie die, but Sophie was already in hell—knowing Cary, who had done nothing wrong, was going to walk into Angelique's clutches.

To save her.

Unless . . . perhaps he wouldn't come.

Sophie remembered how he had so brutally beaten up the man who had attacked her—Angelique's man who was acting as her coachman now. The man had been armed with a knife and was huge, and Cary had beaten him to save her without any thought to his own safety.

He would come. Because he was noble.

In her mind's eye, she could see a small child being carried in here in the arms of his evil, horrible captor. Had Cary been blindfolded, perhaps even drugged? Did he see the cottage, a low structure with a rotting roof and walls of piled stones?

The floor was flagstone and cold beneath her feet as she paced in front of the window. Angelique trained the pistol on her.

The cottage consisted of two rooms—one big main room with chairs circled around the fireplace, and beds at the other end, and a separate kitchen room with a large hearth and a big wooden table for cooking. A low doorway led between the two.

It could have been a quaint, sweet little home once, but she looked around it and imagined a five-year-old boy held inside it as a prisoner. It made the house seem to breathe evil.

What nightmares would come back to Cary when he walked into this place?

She acted as though she were watching anxiously for Cary, but Sophie kept glancing around. Cary had escaped this hell, using the fireplace poker as a weapon. Her captors were armed: Angelique had a pistol. Her coachman—Angelique had called him O'Malley—was in the kitchen, drinking ale, and he also had a pistol.

There was no fireplace poker to hand—Angelique had sent it into the kitchen with O'Malley. Angelique had taken off her cloak and hung it by the door. O'Malley had pulled off his greatcoat. The fire was burning, but the cottage felt cold as a tomb. Sophie could not see anything in the cottage she could use to defend herself.

She looked out the window once more. Moonlight spilled onto the fields around the house. In the silver-blue light, Sophie saw movement. A horse galloped down the lane, emerging out of the shadows cast by trees. A large black gelding with hooves thundering. The rider leaned along the animal's neck, urging it to great speed. Dust flew up.

Then the rider straightened and reined in his beast as they neared the cottage.

She saw his face in the pale light. Cary.

He jumped off, then tied the reins of the horse to a wooden post. He slowed as he walked toward the cottage, as if he were afraid to come to it.

He must be reliving all the nightmarish things that happened here.

He must be in hell.

She wanted to scream at him to go back. Angelique growled, "Do not move or make a sound, or I will shoot you now."

Outside the door, Cary ran his hand over his face. Then he shook his head as if shaking off memories. He stalked to the door and hammered on it.

There was fire in the cottage fire grate and a lamp burning in the corner, but she wasn't sure what Cary could see through the small dirty panes of glass.

Angelique shouted to her man in the kitchen. "O'Malley, come and answer the door to his Grace, the Duke of Caradon!"

The large man lumbered out, wiping his mouth with the back of his hand. He turned the iron key in the lock and flung open the thick wooden door. "Welcome, Yer Grace. Why don't ye step inside?"

Cary walked in, his face tense and expressionless. Then he saw her. "Thank God, you are all right, Sophie. Thank God."

He came toward her, but Angelique leveled the pistol at him. "You are not to touch her, Caradon."

He stopped. "So it was you. You were the daughter of the monster who kidnapped me. I used to beg you to help me, and you refused. You tortured me instead. I can't believe I didn't recognize you." He peered at O'Malley. Frowned. "I recognize you also. You were in my regiment in Ceylon."

"Ye'll forgive me if I don't put me weapon down to salute, Yer Grace," O'Malley sneered.

Angelique pointed to the end of the room, to the corner beside the beds. "You were chained there. Do you remember how piteously you cried? Do you remember how my father tried to soothe you—?"

"Yes, I remember that," he spat.

"Stop it," Sophie cried.

"Shut up," Angelique snapped. She stood in the center of the room. Cary stood with his back to the door. O'Malley had moved close to the kitchen door. Sophie was still near the window, and O'Malley had her in his line of fire.

"You did everything he asked willingly, Caradon," Angelique said. "You were more willing than I ever was. Did you enjoy it? Is that why you've never married? Did you discover your true tastes? Perhaps you now hunger for young boys."

"God no," Cary muttered. His face looked like stone, but he'd gone pale.

"Why do you think my father touched you? He knew he'd found someone like him. Didn't you try to please him?"

"No." Cary's voice was ragged. "I was afraid. Too damned afraid to fight."

"That's what you say, but we both know the truth."

Cary was not believing any of this, surely?

"I was there, after all," Angelique said. "I saw everything."

Sophie wanted to scream that he was a child. But she was afraid she would be helping Angelique by reminding Cary he had been powerless. "You can't hurt him, Angelique," she cried. She hadn't thought this through entirely, but she must go on. "Time has healed his wounds. He is a good, strong, noble gentleman. The reason he has not married is because he did his duty for his country and did it honorably, but now he *is* ready to find love and marry. Whatever you took from him no longer matters, because you only made him stronger."

Cary was watching her, looking startled. Their gazes met. His softened. It was so intense, so bright, she lost her breath.

Cary spoke. "Sophie is right. It was a long time ago. It's over. In the past. That is where it should remain. Stop this now, Angelique."

"It's too late for that," she spat. "You really have no idea why I hate you so much, Caradon?"

He stepped closer to her. Her hand trembled a bit, and she waved the pistol at him. "I will shoot you," she said. "You will die tonight in this place where you were once a sniveling, terrified little boy." She shrugged carelessly. "It would be disappointing to do it earlier, but I will do it."

He gazed at her. "I see it now. Corporal Yew was related to you. Your brother?"

"My son." Her voice broke. "He was my son. You murdered my only child."

"He committed a heinous crime. He knew the punishment."

"He killed one of the enemy's women. He was a good Englishman, and you wanted to see him give his life because he killed a woman. A woman who belonged to the people massacring our soldiers."

"Let me tell you what really happened." He spoke with calm. Slowly.

Sophie shivered. The pistol pointed at his heart.

"Stop," Angelique snapped. "Why don't we talk of what happened to you here when you were a little boy?"

"I was kidnapped and forced to do unspeakable things by your father. I killed him. This is just a cottage, Angelique. That is in the past."

He looked to Sophie. "I won't let memories master me, Angelique. But I will tell you what happened to your son. It was the day after a long, hard battle. Indeed, we had lost a lot of men. Despair and anger were both whipping us. I tried to keep the men calm—I was afraid tempers would explode and something rash would happen. Your son was the worst powder keg of the lot—he seethed in rage at all times, and he had found the mutilated body of the youngest lad of our regiment and had vowed revenge. I understood how he felt, but I tried to make him see sense. To be honest, I was afraid he would get himself—or someone else—killed because he was being driven by blind fury."

"He would never listen to you. He knew who you were."

"Let me finish, Angelique. Your son stalked away, and I let him go—to give him time to clear his head. On the outskirts of our camp, he apparently encountered a Ceylonese woman. Perhaps she was acting as a spy or an assassin, or she had just innocently come upon us. I went in search of him. I found the girl sobbing, her clothing torn. His breeches were unfastened, and he was strangling her. I shouted out to him to stop, but by the time I reached him and pulled him off the girl, it was too late. He threw her body away. I was appalled. It is one thing to kill on the battlefield—another to destroy a defenseless woman. I intended to speak to my superior officers, but at that moment we were attacked from two sides. Most—hell, all of the other soldiers were killed. I thought I was the only survivor. I was taken prisoner, chained up in a cave."

"Oh, you poor thing," Angelique said sardonically. But she was listening. "So, you are telling me my son was killed in the attack."

"No, he wasn't. He deserted and hid. Then he found me. What he did to me—he attempted to kill me. I was chained up, fighting for my life. He thought if I were dead, there would be no one to condemn him for the murder of that woman. It was he or I, Angelique. I'm sorry."

"And when you were found, did you tell the truth? Did you admit to killing him?"

"I told the whole story. It was decided there was no need to reveal it all. He was dead and had paid the price for what he did. His name was protected—it was said he died in battle. What more would you want, Angelique?"

"Justice! What was wrong with what he did? He merely killed an enemy spy. And you—you act as though what he did was wrong! You murdered an Englishman. You will not get away with it!"

Cary took a step away from Angelique, toward the door. Sophie met his gaze, and he motioned with his head. She edged toward the door to the kitchen. She was against the wall by the doorway, and O'Malley was watching her.

Cary looked at Angelique. "Of course I will," he said. "And so will Sophie."

Oh dear God, what was he doing?

"No, you won't!" Angelique screamed. In one furious motion, she pulled the trigger. A flash of flame. A roar that shook the room. Smoke spewed out of the pistol.

Cary jumped to his feet. He had thrown himself at the ground. As he got up, he shouted, "O'Malley!" to keep the lackey's attention on him. He threw a knife, and it arced through the air, but with the warning, O'Malley was able to duck. Sophie was near the door. The key was still in the lock—

No. She turned to see O'Malley straightening, preparing to shoot Cary. "O'Malley!" she shrieked. "I've got a pistol, and you are going to die."

He whirled to face her, and Cary lunged, shouting the man's name to draw his attention again. O'Malley's pistol exploded.

"Cary!" Sophie cried.

Cary slammed his fist into O'Malley's face with such force, he knocked the man out cold.

Angelique. What was she doing? Then Sophie saw the courtesan wrench at her bodice. Silver glinted in her hand.

"She has a blade!" she cried, and she looked for some kind of weapon. Her hands were tied, but that wasn't going to stop her.

Cary was struggling with Angelique, trying to get the knife out of her hand. Angelique seemed to have the strength of a madwoman. She'd cut Cary's face and his throat. Lines of dark blood welled.

Then Sophie saw it—the one thing she could use as a weapon. With her bound hands, she grabbed it. She lunged forward, just as she'd done to save herself with Lord Devars. Struggling against the ropes binding her wrists, she swung as best as she could and threw the thing—

Angelique's cloak fluttered though the air. It fell short, missing Angelique. But it distracted her, and Cary grabbed the woman. With two swift moves, he had Angelique disarmed.

He held the woman with her arms pinned behind her.

Sophie's heart still thundered faster than speeding horses. "Cary, are you all right? Were you not shot?"

"No, love," Cary said. He breathed hard. "O'Malley shot the wall instead."

Cary shoved Angelique away from him and pulled a pistol from his pocket. "Sit on the chairs." He growled at Angelique. He motioned for Sophie to come to him. She knew he couldn't look at her; he was watching the villains. But he sliced through the ropes securing her hands, holding Angelique's knife in his left hand. He murmured, "Thank the Lord, you are safe. I was afraid—afraid I would be too late."

"You weren't."

"I can't believe you threw Angelique's cloak. It was brilliant."

She glowed at the praise. "It was all I could think of."

"Brilliant," he said again. And added, "The other dukes were traveling behind me in a carriage."

Sure enough, she heard thundering hooves, rattling traces. Sophie ran to the door and opened it as the other Wicked Dukes leapt out of the carriage.

They would be able to tie up Angelique and O'Malley and give them to the law.

Sophie almost sobbed. They had survived, and they were safe.

"Sophie, are you all right?"

She found herself turned around and pulled into Cary's strong embrace. But she drew back and faced him. "This place is just a house. A terrible thing happened to you here, but it does not have magical powers. Everything Angelique told you is rubbish. You were never willing; you must have been terrified. I know—why do you think I let Angelique put me in a carriage? She threatened your family. I was trying to protect them, and I was playing for time. I didn't fight her every step of the way because, to save myself and you and your family, I had to wait for the right moment. Of course, it didn't come. I needed you to save me. Here, when you were a child, you did the most amazing thing. You saved yourself, Cary. Angelique is going to pay for her crimes. You committed no crime, Cary. You don't need to pay for the rest of your life."

Sophie almost held her breath. What would he say?

"This place is the setting of my most hellish nightmares," Cary said hoarsely. "Even being held prisoner in Ceylon, where I was certain they would kill me, was not as bad. But you are right—this place is just a building of stone. It has no special power over me."

"Those memories don't either. You don't have to let them. You are not to blame."

"I could have run away. I didn't understand what was going on. I let the man approach me, and I should have run. My mother would have been spared hell too."

"Stop blaming yourself. Stop tormenting yourself with nightmares. I have—I know what children are like. My friend Belle has children, and through them I've seen that children are innocent and trusting, especially at such a young age. They don't yet understand that people can be monsters. Let us walk out of here and, at the same time, please walk away from your memories. You deserve some happiness."

"So do you. Sophie"—his raspy voice cracked with emotion—"you are so precious to me."

At that moment, the other Wicked Dukes entered. As they took over watching Angelique, Cary cupped Sophie's face and drew her to him. Her hair was in tangles. With the palm of his hand, he pushed it back. He gently ran his thumb along her lower lip.

"I know what I want to do to you tonight," he murmured.

"What?" she whispered.

But he wouldn't tell her.

It was almost dawn when she rode with Cary to a nearby inn. With the Wicked Dukes, they had taken their prisoners to the nearest jail. Sophie discovered Cary had left his horse at the inn and had taken a strong, fresh gelding to gallop to the cottage. He engaged a carriage to take them home while Saxonby would ride his horse back. The other two dukes would use the carriage they had traveled in to the cottage. Grey was anxious to return to his wife.

In the carriage, Cary drew her close.

And he kissed her.

Such a kiss! It could have melted rock and turned it into boiling lava. A long, lush, heated kiss. She wanted more kisses, but the warmth and the pleasure relaxed her.

They were safe. It was all over—

The next thing Sophie knew, she was in her bed in her town house, naked and under warm covers. She sat up, confused. A roaring fire had been built, and Cary was prodding it with the poker. "Oh, what happened?"

He turned, and she lost her breath. He wore a white linen shirt, open at the throat, the tails hanging out, cuffs undone.

Black trousers clung to his long legs, his taut buttocks. His blond hair was mussed, falling over his eyes.

He was *en déshabillé*, and she wriggled under the cover. She grew wet and achy just looking at him. "I remember you kissed me. It was a volcanic eruption of a kiss."

His slow grin stole her breath again. "I'd intended to kiss you the entire way home, but you fell asleep on me."

She flushed. "I'm so sorry. That's not what mistresses are supposed to do."

"You deserved it. You must be exhausted."

"I'm not anymore." Taking a deep breath, she pushed the covers off her body. Slowly. Suggestively, she hoped.

"What do you want to do?" She shifted so her arms squished her bare breasts together, making them look more full and round. "Would you like me to suck you?" she asked. "Or would you like to do that to me? Or something with toys again." She knew she was blushing. "That was rather fun."

"You ask that so cheerfully and sweetly, as if you're asking what I want in my tea. You made me understand a lot about myself. Tonight, I realized something. You are utterly irresistible, Sophie."

"I am?"

"You helped me face my demons, love. You never judged me. You never condemned me. Even when you were dragged into danger, because of me, you only wanted to help me."

"Of course I did."

He walked toward the bed. Propped his knee on the end of it. She couldn't tell what he wanted. He'd kissed her passionately. Right now, in the glow of the fire, he looked so handsome. But also younger than usual. Vulnerable.

"I want to make love to you, Sophie. I still don't know if I can. But I want to try."

She held out her hand. "I want that very much."

It was like dealing with an animal that had been abused. She knew that from life in the country, from living near farms. She couldn't do anything too quickly. Push too hard.

She slipped out of the bed and walked around to him.

The fire crackled, and the light of it danced. It was warm in her beautiful room. He watched her come to him. This moment was charged, special.

She was almost afraid to speak, as if she might break a spell. She stroked his broad shoulders. "Let me help you undress."

Together, they lifted the hem of his shirt, whisking it up over his flat abdomen. She could count each muscle if she wished. She could only lift his shirt so high. He took over, pulling it over his head.

More wetness rushed between her legs as he threw the shirt, his chest, arm, and back muscles flexing and moving as he did. Underneath, he was naked, the golden hair on his chest flattened in whirls. His skin was so smooth and the color of milky tea—just kissed with a bit of sun browning.

Sophie pressed her hands to his taut, flat belly. She ran her fingertips on his hot, silken skin, to his jutting hipbones, which flared up above the waist of his trousers. She ran her hand saucily along his hip. "This is going to be so much fun," she said lightly. Tracing them made her shiver inside. Made her cunny ache for him.

They were going to try to make love. She was thrilled. And a little bit scared.

She had to make this perfect for him.

Cary caught her hands, lifted them from his hips. "I have to sit down and fight to get the boots off, angel."

"I could help."

Cary set his rump on the edge of their bed. That was how she wanted to think of the bed—their bed, not her bed.

"Hmmm. I have a bootboy. He puts his arse facing me, lets me brace against his backside to pull them off."

"You are joking."

"I'm not."

"And gentlemen claim that women's clothing is idiotic." She turned, then pointed her naked bottom at him. She bent over and took hold of his right boot. "You brace and I'll tug." She turned to look at him. His eyes gleamed at her, and with a swift motion of his hands, he undid his trousers. He stood, shoving them down. His erect cock was caught in his trousers for a moment, then sprang upward.

"I can't wait, angel," he said hoarsely.

He helped her up, drew her back to the bed. He fell back onto the mattress, pulling her with him. She squealed with surprise as she landed on his broad, bare chest. His hand cupped the back of her head, drawing her into a kiss.

Sophie wanted to play. She threaded her fingers in Cary's silky hair. She parried her tongue with his. She knew how to kiss now. The beauty of kissing was it wasn't just about kissing him with skill, but about sharing something exciting and sensual together.

She let her mouth caress his. Gently. Teasingly. Then she kissed hard and passionate and thrust her tongue into his mouth. When she backed off, he was breathing hard. His blue eyes were hazy with lust.

He pursued her, kissing her, holding her so tight to him that there was no air between them. They were both essentially naked. Two now warm bodies pressed together. She felt steam rising between them.

She almost wanted to sob. With happiness.

She loved Cary. She knew she did.

Cary rolled her gently onto her back, then he got on top of her. She sank a little into the soft mattress. She wanted to be so close to him. As he kissed her, she hooked her leg around his legs. Wrapped her arms around him.

He kissed her mouth. Her cheek. Even her chin, which made her giggle.

His head rested in the crook of her neck, and he kissed a spot under her jaw. Oh God! That one made her shiver and gasp.

She touched his back. Felt his warmth. She pressed her hand against his chest to feel the beat of his heart. Ooh, fast.

His lips closed over her right nipple. He knew just what to do. Lick. Suck. Tug. Flick with his tongue. He would tease her like this until she was ready to explode—

He stopped. His mouth skimmed lower. Down to her navel, and each kiss along the way made her wind up more, grow more aroused. Lower and lower he was going—

Then he suckled her clit. She was so ready. She felt her juices flow. Smelled them and blushed.

Something bumped her inner thigh. Heavens, it was his cock, so rigid that it felt like being prodded with a cricket bat.

She wrapped her hand around it. So thick. So hard. Pulsing in her grip. But he unwrapped her fingers. He took his cock in his own hand.

Once, they had pleasured themselves in front of each other. That had been shocking . . . and deliciously fun.

Did this mean he wanted to do that instead of making love? Had he realized he couldn't do it? She would share this with him no matter what.

She let her fingers slide down through her nether curls—

Cary got between her legs, and he pressed his erect cock against her pussy lips. She moaned at the wonderful tug as his cock tried to push between her lips. Her hand was trapped between their bodies, pressing on her clit.

Slowly, he parted her wet, sticky lips. She was almost holding her breath! His hips thrust, and his cock slid in a few inches. She gripped his shoulders. He was big, stretching her, but it felt so good. He shifted his hips and hit that magical place inside her. She clutched tighter to hard muscle, quivering.

"Oh!" She gasped.

Deeper and deeper he went. His eyes were half shut, and she

didn't want to look into his eyes in case she spoiled this moment.

His groin bumped hers. He was all the way inside her. Filling her.

Her eyes were wide. Every sensation—she wanted to know every sensation.

His mouth caressed her nipples, his finger stroked her sensitive, aching clit, his cock thrust deep. So deep. Sometimes so deep, the agony was both pleasure and pain, and her nails gouged his skin.

He thrust faster, and she moved with him. His hips flowed like silk over her. She closed her eyes. Heard his rasping breaths.

Yes. Oh yes.

She moved faster. His fingers played with her, he kissed the sensitive place on her neck, and she cried out, "I'm going to come. Just do this. Keep doing this."

A rough laugh against her neck. But he did. Bliss built in her, bubbling and boiling, and then her orgasm welled up and rushed through her.

She clung to him. Sobbed as she curled to put her head against his.

"Sophie."

When he said her name like that, he was going to—

He bucked against her. A rush of heat filled her. Heat and wetness, and he rode out his orgasm with a look of intense agony and low, soft groans. Then he slumped on her. Half on his side so he wasn't crushing her.

"That was beautiful," he said. He brushed back his golden hair, darkened to amber with sweat.

"You did it." She gazed at him. "It means you are healed. You did it!"

"Did I do it well?"

"Of course. But what does that matter?" she asked ingenuously. "All that matters is that you now can! Which means you can be married—" She broke off abruptly.

He rolled up onto his side. Kissed her forehead, then the top of her nose. Gently. Sweetly. Cary lifted from her, then got out of bed. "Yes," he said. "I can."

20

The next morning, Cary went out and bought a newspaper from a lad on the corner. Then he returned to Sophie's house before she awoke. The newssheet contained the story of Angelique's arrest for two murders and the attack on Sophie.

The story of his kidnapping had been included. Angelique had been identified as the daughter of the man who had abducted him. The sordid details of what had happened to him were not there. He had wanted to spare his mother and sisters the scandal of it. So he had arranged for Angelique to escape the noose in return for her silence on the details of his kidnapping.

The hell of his past was behind him. He'd spent a wild night making love to Sophie.

First in the bed.

Then, from behind, with Sophie leaning on her vanity table so they could both watch his thrusts and her delightfully bouncing breasts in the mirror.

Then they had tumbled onto the carpet in front of the fire. To be gentlemanly, he had her ride him so she didn't get sore from rug burns.

After, they had some dinner in the dining room. There he'd

locked the door, sank to his knees, and licked her sweet pussy until she'd exploded in another orgasm.

Exhausted, they'd fallen asleep together in her bed. Laughing. He had continually kissed her until he'd drifted off to sleep.

He hadn't dreamed a thing. All Cary remembered was having a long, blissful sleep. And the joy of waking up with his arm around Sophie.

He had the cook give him breakfast on a tray, which flustered the older woman. "Here you are, Your Grace," she said. "I've made coffee as well as chocolate."

He took it upstairs and then poured a cup of steaming chocolate.

Sophie stretched, wriggled under the sheets, and opened her eyes, blinking. "Something smells delicious."

He handed her the cup of chocolate. Fed her delectable morsels of food.

She blushed. "I'm the mistress. Aren't I supposed to serve you?"

"I'm enjoying this."

When breakfast was done, she went to her bedside table and drew something out. A series of leather-bound journals. "This is my courtesan book," she said shyly. "My mother's memoirs that she never finished and never published." She had told him in the night that Nell was her mother. "Now that I've found my mother, I find I can't really read it anymore. But there was one thing that it says a courtesan must do. Something all men enjoy."

She fished around in the drawer and drew out lengths of white silk rope.

Now he really understood what it meant that Sophie had a book detailing how to be a courtesan.

"Apparently, men like to do things with rope. I wanted to surprise you. But I wasn't sure. . . ."

He had been tied up when he was five, and tied up again when he was held prisoner. But that was part of his past. And what Sophie had in mind was erotic fun.

"By all means," he said. "Why don't we start with you tying me up?"

Sophie approached him with the ropes, her legs almost trembling with desire. Cary lay back on the bed, his arms pillowed under his head. Utterly naked. The ropes were piled in her arms, and she was staring at him. Savoring him. Long, long legs. Lean hips, with a sensual ridge of hipbone that was so very sexy, it made her pussy clench.

His chest was broad, his arms forged of pure muscle. She loved the way the veins were prominent on his powerful biceps.

Tentatively, she trailed the rope there.

Cary grinned. "Is this what you would like?" He spread his legs so his ankles were closer to the bedposts. He stretched his arms above his head.

"You are so beautiful." The words slipped right out of her mouth.

"Sophie, you are the one who is beautiful."

His cock stood upright along his belly, thick and long and rigid. Threads of silver fluid led from the weeping eye to his stomach, glistening like they were made of spun diamonds, if such a thing were possible.

Holding the rope, she leaned over and planted a kiss to the head of his cock.

Then suckled it in—just the head—and sucked hard. He moaned, and his hips bucked up to her.

She wanted to take him to the same place he'd taken her. That heavenly place of extreme pleasure. Where it built so much, you just knew that one little touch would make ecstasy explode for you.

So she toyed with his balls, stroking the seam up and down

as she backed off his cock and only lightly strummed the head—and sensitive opening—with her tongue. She loved how he tasted. So earthy. Tasting him made this feel so special and intimate.

She took the ropes in her hands. She licked the head of his cock and rubbed the ropes back and forth along his hard shaft.

She watched Cary through her tangled hair and her half-lowered lashes. His hands clenched into fists, his expression was a thrilling blend of agony and pleasure.

Now to tie him up.

Following the jaunty instructions in the book, she moved up and wrapped a rope around one of his wrists. She was on her knees on the bed beside him to do it.

Cary closed his eyes. His mouth tightened. His breathing became more harsh.

She hesitated. "Should I stop?"

"No, don't." Intense and blue, his gaze met hers. "I trust you. I know you won't hurt me."

"Of course not. I never would."

"Then tie me up, angel, and make love to me."

Cary said he trusted her, but his instincts still screamed to fight as she wrapped a rope around his wrist. *That was the past,* he reminded himself. *This is just play.*

She tied a knot, and he felt the rope lightly biting into his skin. Very lightly. It was more of a caress.

Biting her lip and concentrating, Sophie wrapped the other end of the rope around the bed column. His cock bucked as she pulled the rope around the post, slowly, gently stretching his arm. She tied a bow, but he gave a tug and it undid.

"I'll pull against the ropes while I'm coming. You should make them tight," he advised.

She did, pulling again, then knotting it. She did his other arm the same way.

His heart pounded. Once his hands were bound, Cary felt panic rise.

Sophie moved down and kissed him on the lips. A hot, slow, arousing kiss.

He caught her lips and answered her kiss with a hungry one of his own. Fear faded away. He wanted to cup her breasts, but he couldn't, so he broke from the kiss and arched up against the ropes to capture her nipples with his lips, one after the other.

She squealed in delight. "I should tie your legs."

"Just make love to me now, angel. I can't wait."

She got on top of him, naked, her breasts swaying.

With his hands bound, he couldn't tease her clit with his hands as she bounced on him. So he tried to shift his cock as she moved.

Suddenly, she gave a cry of shock and pleasure.

There, that was the place his shaft needed to stroke.

He lifted his hips, supporting her in midair. She gasped, planted her hands on his chest to hold her body steady. "You're so strong!"

He laughed. This was the best sex he'd ever known. This joy, this connection. She was so sweet.

So perfect.

He jerked his hips, making her breasts bob.

Then he lowered and used his stomach muscles to thrust up into her. Sophie worked down on him. She gripped his shoulders and met his thrusts with such vigor that sweat damped her hair and beaded on her chest.

Yes.

With Sophie, he could find ecstasy. It was there, waiting for him.

As long as he took her there first—

She cried out. "Cary!" Rocked on him. Her face went very pink. Her head fell forward as the orgasm claimed her.

He thrust into her, wanting to take her there again—

He couldn't hold on.

Like a blinding streak of heavenly light, his climax shot through him, searing him.

He felt reborn. He felt new.

She sank down on him, gasping for breath. He laughed lightly as strands of her long black hair tickled his face.

Sophie had healed him. She had made him whole. She had let him see and enjoy sex as a healthy, fun, normal pleasure.

"You don't need a book, love," he murmured. "You are a goddess."

The next morning, his mother found him at the breakfast table. Cary hurried to help her sit down, but she said in a heavy voice, "I do not need your help, Caradon. I am quite able to pull out my own chair. You see, I was not honest with you."

She sat, and Cary poured coffee for her. "I don't understand, Mother."

"I have an admission to make." She gazed at him, eyes filled with guilt. "I have exaggerated how ill I really am. I wanted to push you into marriage, so I lied to you. I am not on death's door. What I did was wrong, terribly wrong."

"You are not ill?"

"No. I have been very worried about you, and that left me tired, but I am not going to leave this mortal coil anytime soon. I am so sorry. Miss Ashley told me to admit the truth, and I do indeed feel better. She said you would forgive me. I do not expect your forgiveness, but I wanted to ease your mind."

Sophie had told her to give him the truth. "Mother, I understand why you did it. It's a shock to know you lied, but I am so happy you are not dying. And I do intend to propose to a woman."

He got up and left the breakfast table. His heart hammered and his wits were spinning. If his mother was not ill, was it possible that he could have what he hoped for . . . ?

Leaving his mother because he needed to think, needed to clear his head, Cary went to his stables, then guided his horse across Park Lane into Hyde Park and to the Rotten Row. He'd spent two glorious days making love to Sophie. He'd never had so much fun during sex. They had been partners in their pleasure, coming up with playful and inventive places and positions. He showed her some exotic ways they could entwine and embrace while he thrust deeply into her, taking it slowly to make their pleasure last.

Late last night, he'd taken his leave and returned to his house on Park Lane, knowing what he had to do. He was a duke. He was now able to put his past behind him and make love.

He had to marry.

But things had changed if he did not have to worry how his choice would affect his mother's health. . . .

As he'd hoped, he saw Grey riding his large gelding along the Row. He galloped over and explained what he had to do. Propose to a woman. He posed his other problem to Grey first, knowing Grey would have the answer. Satisfied with what Grey said to him, Cary admitted, "I'm nervous about proposing. I had no idea I would be so nervous."

Grey grinned. "No need for nerves. There's no doubt she is going to say yes."

"What do you put in a proposal? I've never done this before, and I want to get it right. What do you say to a woman to convince her to marry you?"

"You don't have to convince her, my friend. Just ask her. You say you believe she cares about you? Tell her what's in your heart."

"How exactly do I tell her? I am not good at poetic words."

"Tell her you love her and you want to marry her. That's all you have to do."

Cary had intended to spend some time riding, then returning home to have breakfast. His mother had given him a list of eligible names when she'd first arrived. For all he was fairly reclusive, he knew most of the young women. He knew which ones seemed sweet of disposition, and which of those had clever brains and would make good duchesses.

Now he felt a pressing need to get on with the business. "I was going to ride, but I've changed my mind. What I need to do now . . . is talk to Sophie."

But when he arrived at her town house, he was told she was gone.

"What do you mean gone?" Cary stared in confusion at the maid.

"To the country, Your Grace."

Ah, now he understood. "To see her friend?"

"I believe so, Your Grace."

He knew where that was. He would go there and speak to her. It would be good that she would be with her friend when he spoke to her.

Then he could get on with this business of marriage. His mother wondered which woman he intended to choose to be his duchess—an earl's daughter, a marquis's daughter, or a duke's daughter.

He had already made his choice.

Cary saw Sophie the moment his curricle pulled into the drive in front of Ivy Cottage, the small, stone manor house he had acquired for her friend and her children. He had driven his curricle himself, driven at neck-or-nothing speed on the Great North Road. Had turned off with such haste, he'd thrown up a spray of mud and had almost gotten stuck in the mire left by rain. It must have rained yesterday, but he had been in bed with Sophie all day and hadn't noticed.

He had trotted his tired horses up the small drive. Apple trees hid the house from view for seconds, then the gravel drive opened to a clearing beyond the rows of trees, showing the two-story house with mullioned windows and doors, a neat stretch of tended lawn, and dark green ivy embracing the stone. The April air was sweet, filled with spring scents.

And then he saw Sophie.

She stood away from the house, beside a wooden stile that separated the meadow from the tended lawn and gardens of the cottage.

"What are you doing, young man?" she called.

Instinctively, Cary started and was about to explain himself, but then she wagged her finger at someone on the other side of the stile.

"You haven't been playing at the pond in your new jacket, Alex."

Morning sunlight bathed over her. Her dark hair was pulled into a sleek bun. She wore a simple dress and a shawl.

Even in the simplest clothes, she was so beautiful, it made his heart ache.

Cary brought his horses to a halt. Sophie hadn't noticed him, and he got down, hand resting on the flank of one of his lathered horses. While he soothed them with words, promising them rest and hay, he just watched Sophie.

He was going to ask her to marry him.

He'd realized he wanted a marriage filled with love. He couldn't spend a life doing his duty, nor could he trap an innocent woman into a loveless marriage.

He wanted Sophie. Somehow he was going to have her.

First, he wanted to know if she would say yes. Grey believed she would. Sophie always looked for the best in things—she wouldn't hesitate to marry for love, regardless of social position. Anyway, Grey had pointed out, before Cary had left the park this morning, Helena had said no to Grey at first. Now they were the happiest of married couples. Grey and Helena had feared scandal, but they had overcome it.

Cary knew he could too.

Now he could see the young man she was speaking to. A young boy of about five emerged from a path between the tall meadow flowers. His hair was gold. His clothes were dirty and disheveled.

"Had to," the boy declared. "I wanted to catch a salamander. And I got one!" He held up two small hands, a tiny green lizard clutched between them.

Cary was taken back in time—transported—to when he was a child and he'd run up to the kitchens of Carvenleigh, their favorite estate for summer, with a frog or a lizard in his hands, and the wicked plan in his five-year-old head to tease Cook.

Once, Cook had just threatened to cook his "little nuisances," and that had been the end of his plan.

And after he'd been kidnapped, he had never trapped anything again—

"Don't make me let him go!" The strident cry of the little boy brought Cary out of his memories. Quick as a wink, the memories were gone. So was their power to hurt him.

Because of Sophie.

A smile touched his lips. She argued feistily with the boy, who she called Alex. Obviously, short for Alexander.

Alex ran a few steps away from her, his back half turned and his precious find held to his chest. "But I want him to be my pet, Mummy!"

Mummy? Cary stared at the two people—at raven-haired Sophie and the blond stubborn little boy. Had he heard wrong?

He looked around. There was no other woman there but Sophie.

Sophie held out her hand to the boy, but the lad mulishly shook his head. "No, Mummy!"

He hadn't been wrong.

Sophie had a son. A child. This must be the son of the young man she'd married, the soldier who had died at Waterloo.

Two other children ran up, a boy and a girl, both dark-haired. The girl carried a tin bucket from which frogs jumped out. They called her Aunt Sophie, obviously a term for the best friend of their mother.

Why had she never told him? Did she think he wouldn't want her if he knew she had a child? It didn't matter. She'd been married. God, this was why she had been so desperate. She had been desperate to protect her son.

Her son was all she had left of her husband.

They had been married for one night, and Sophie had been blessed with a son.

What had she gone through when her husband had died and they had faced poverty?

He remembered how sunny and determined she'd been. He'd had no idea.

She was so incredibly courageous.

As he watched, Sophie and her son debated. Then her son reluctantly nodded. "All right, Mummy. I will put him back where he belongs."

Sophie marched them all back to the pond. Cary followed, stopping a few yards back as Sophie's boy got down on his haunches, opened his hands, and let his pet go. The salamander moved like a streak of light, scurrying under the turnstile and disappearing. The other two children carefully took their frogs out of the bucket.

Cary grinned. Sophie had won.

"Bravo," he said softly. It was hard to speak when his heart ached so much.

Farther ahead of him on the narrow path, framed by waving cattails, Sophie spun around. Her face was white, her hand clenched in a fist. Then she saw him. "Oh! Your Grace! I didn't know you were there."

She smiled, but she flashed a look toward her son.

"I know he's your son," he said softly. "I heard him call you 'Mummy.'"

"Oh. Yes, I did keep him a secret from you, didn't I?" She gave a nervous laugh. "Are you very angry?"

"Of course not. But you looked really afraid before you knew it was me. Have you been bothered by the man who tried to force you to become his mistress?"

"No. He hasn't come near me. I suppose I was just taken by surprise. I never expected you to come here. I thought, when you went home, it would be to prepare for a wedding."

"Wedding?"

"I mean, after you have proposed marriage." Then she clapped her hand to her mouth. "Oh! Now I understand. You've come to say good-bye? I vowed to be very stoic. I shall take this very well. You will be impressed."

"Sophie . . ." He shook his head. She *was* trying to look stoic, and it made him want to chuckle. "I haven't come to say good-bye. I haven't done any proposing yet."

"Oh. Oh, I see!"

"What do you see?"

"You wanted to make love again. To be sure, I suppose? Though you must be quite certain by now."

He wanted to say that wasn't why he was here. But Sophie had already come up to him. She looked to make sure no one was looking, then she leaned against him to whisper in his ear. At the push of her full breasts, the softness of her skirts and tummy against his growing erection, he was lost.

Her breath was a sensuous caress by his ear. "I'll send the children up to the house."

She walked away from him, to the children. "It's time for your lunch," she told them. "And we have a very prestigious visitor. This gentleman is the Duke of Caradon." She made a curtsy.

The young girl did the same, and then Sophie whispered, "You must bow" to the two boys. They made fast bows. Then they ran off, excited for their food.

Cary laughed. Then he saw Sophie brush away a tear. She turned to him, glowing. "Thanks to you, they have a roof over their heads and food on the table, and I know they are safe. You are the most wonderful, wonderful man."

Impulsively, she came to him, grasped the waistband of his trousers, and lifted to kiss him.

He wanted to give her intense pleasure. He wished he had toys or ropes to help him. But all he had was him.

He undid his cravat and pulled it off. "Do you trust me, love?"

Her large green eyes glowed. "Of course. With my life. Which you have saved many times."

Tenderly, he touched her lower lip. "I adore you, Sophie."

He showed her how much fun a cravat could be. Draping it over his shoulder, he took off her pelisse, then undid her gown. He loosened her corset to draw it down. It took a while, but he got her breasts exposed. The shelf of the corset lifted them, and he stroked the cravat across them.

They went plump and hard. And Sophie gasped and moaned.

Once he had her squirming, he lifted her skirts. He slid his fingers between her legs. Already wet, the sweetheart. Gently, he parted the plump, slick lips. He trailed the cravat over her sweet clit. Then held the cravat taut and sawed it across her.

Her hips moved rhythmically. Her cheeks went pink. Her eyes shut, and she panted with pleasure.

He dropped to his knees, pulled her pussy to his face, and suckled and licked her.

"Cary!" She climaxed against him.

Then he lifted to his feet, lifted her in his arms, and lowered her sweet, wet cunny onto his rigid cock.

Supporting her, he made love to her. She jiggled up and down, holding his shoulders. His buttocks were taut, his legs shaking with the exertion.

"I'm going to come," she wailed.

"Let it come, love, because I want to come too."

She squealed. Her nails drove into his shoulders. He let go. His climax roared through him. His cock felt like it had swelled to double the size. His come shot through him so fast and hard, he almost fell over.

He buried his face in her neck and rode out his orgasm. Then they sank down together. Laughing, he held her close.

He'd had sex in all kinds of positions—on top, on the bottom, once upside down.

But making love with Sophie had been more precious than all of that. He smiled down at her. Her eyes were closed, dark lashes feathered over her cheeks. Her face was pink with exertion.

But he'd never had sex as an expression of love. True love. A deep love that warmed his heart and his soul, made him smile when she did, made his body tense with anger when she cried.

She was precious to him. More precious than his own existence.

She was sitting at his side, so he shifted his position. "Can you stand up?"

"I'm still too weak." She giggled. "But I must, to fix my clothing."

He helped her up and got behind her to retie her corset, then fasten her dress. The instant he finished, he turned her. He dropped to one knee before her.

Grey was right. He did not need to say anything fancy. "Sophie, I love you with all my heart and soul. Will you become my wife?"

"Oh!" she cried.

He waited for her to say yes. It was going to be the happiest word he'd ever heard.

"Cary, I wish—Oh heaven, how I wish I could. I never dreamed of this. But I can't. I cannot marry you."

* * *

The children had found them then. They had rushed between the apple trees, yelling and squealing like demons. All hungry, because Belle had said they must wait until Sophie and the duke came for lunch. Thanks heavens, Cary had helped her tidy and smooth her clothing and repin her hair before proposing marriage.

She would have been too shocked to even think.

She had been too stunned to even chastise the children about shouting for their food. Cary had done that. He ushered them toward the house, promising to come so they could have their lunch.

Then she'd looked at his eyes and seen such pain, it had speared her heart. "I'm so sorry."

She felt just as wretched. Her heart felt as if it had burst in her chest. She'd never known such pain. So much pure, sheer agony when she'd had to refuse him.

It was like the pain of losing Samuel. It almost drove her to her knees.

"Why, Sophie?"

"I just can't marry you, Your Grace. I can't explain why." The children's whoops and hollers were disappearing as they plunged through the meadow toward the house.

She'd never dreamed he would propose to her! She was a courtesan.

How confused he looked. "I think I deserve some reason. I thought—apparently mistakenly—that you cared about me."

He spoke calmly, but she heard the raw hurt in his voice. He did deserve the truth.

He had done so much for her. For her son and for Belle and her children too.

"Is it because of my past?" he asked softly. Grimly. "I've heard it said that a woman loses respect for a man who cannot protect himself. She fears he will not be able to protect her."

Sophie gaped. Then she realized Cary was utterly serious. "You cannot believe that."

"Isn't it true?" he asked, his voice low and quiet.

"Of course not! For a start, I know you are perfectly capable of coming to my rescue. You have proven it more than once. I know you are strong, courageous, and beyond brave. Anyway, you were kidnapped as a child. The fact you survived is a testament to your strength. How could you have been expected to defend yourself against a full-grown man—and yet you did."

"Then why won't you marry me?"

She wished she could touch him. They were walking toward the house, side by side, but she felt as if there were one thousand miles between them.

She couldn't marry him because of the theft. She could be transported for that. She doubted Devars would keep quiet if she married Cary. She had prayed he had just gotten tired of her and that was why he hadn't pursued her in London. Or maybe he was waiting until he felt she had money—and then he would demand she repay him.

But she doubted Devars would stand back and let her be happy. He would talk, and she would be arrested. And the worst of it—it was true! She had taken that horrid bracelet because he had made her even more afraid and desperate. She'd taken it to escape him and ensure she and Belle and the children were far from him.

If she married Cary, she would be a duchess convicted for theft—it would be a horrible scandal. She would lose everything.

But she owed Cary an explanation.

"I haven't told you everything about me," she said. "You know almost all of it. I am a courtesan's daughter. I told you I was married, but that wasn't true. He was my fiancé and wanted to wait until after the war to marry. But I loved him so much. I couldn't let him go without . . . without making love to him. So we did, even though we were not married. I could have hidden that sin, except I became pregnant. Then Samuel was killed, and I bore a son. I was so happy to have Alexander. He is all I have of Samuel. But my family—the family who raised me because my mother gave me up—threw me out. Belle lost her husband in battle too. So we were homeless and impoverished together."

"Sophie, you've had such a hard time of it." He stopped and touched her hand.

She squeezed his hand. "I am so sorry, but can you not see why I can't marry you? A duchess cannot have an illegitimate child! I could not hope to surmount such an obstacle. I can't pretend I am not his mother. And I feel so terrible for having been apart from him when I went to London. I could not send him away forever like my mother did. I love him, and I can't hurt him that way."

"You pretended to be a widow before. We can continue with that story."

"But people will be curious about where a duchess came from. What if Society learned the truth? There would be a scandal. Besides, people know I was your mistress."

"Other men have married their mistresses. Greybrooke, for example. Helena was a governess and became his mistress before he married her. I believe a scandal can be weathered. It is not as if you have had any other lover but me."

The theft. She could not agree to marriage. "I just cannot marry you. I can be your mistress—and be one happily. But I can never be your wife."

Cary rode back to London with a broken heart.

Grey found him at White's in the afternoon and settled in the leather chair across from him. "I thought you would look happier."

He rubbed his temple. Duty to find a bride still weighed on his shoulders. What in hell was he going to do now?

To Grey, he said, "I am in love with Sophie, I asked her to marry me, and she turned me down. I found my perfect bride, and I lost her. And I don't have the taste for a wife I don't love," he growled. "Damnation, love is an insidious thing. I can't contemplate life without it."

"She said no." Grey leaned back. A servant appeared at once with a glass of brandy, which Grey took. He sipped it, then said, "So did my wife when I first asked her. I convinced her to change her mind."

"I won't convince Sophie. She's refused me for the noblest reason."

"Helena refused me for noble reasons."

Groaning, Cary said, "Grey, Sophie refused me because she has a child." Quietly, he laid out the problem before his friend. "I thought we could continue to pretend she had been married and widowed, but she fears people will find out the truth, driven to seek it because she is a duchess. I would never ask her to give him up; I couldn't deprive him of his mother." God no. Not when he knew what it was like to be taken from his family. When he had been taken, he'd feared he would be forever parted from the people he loved.

He could not do that to a child.

"She will consent to be my mistress. But I have to marry. I'm obligated to do that to protect my own family. If I don't produce a son, the estate goes to a ne'er-do-well second cousin. He would bankrupt the estate in no time. My mother might not be gravely ill, but I could see her becoming that way if my cousin inherits and runs through all the money." A fresh drink was delivered for Cary. He took a long swallow. "The truth is, I want to marry and have children of my own. Thanks to Sophie, I am no longer afraid I might lapse in protecting them."

"That was what you feared?"

"I feared something could happen, and I would be too late. I would lose someone I loved. But I faced that, and I proved I could prevail and keep safe someone I loved."

"Is there any way you can find a compromise?"

"I want to believe there is some way, but she flat out refused to marry me. . . . So do I savor love with Sophie for as long as I can . . . or do I let her go free now, in the hopes she can find love herself?"

He went to her house that night with every intention of letting her go. Sending her home, just as he'd vowed to do at the very beginning. He wanted her to find love, not go to another protector.

But he failed at being noble. Even now, when he knew he loved her and the decent thing was to end this, he walked into Sophie's parlor, took one look at her, and took her directly upstairs to her bedroom.

She faced him with a happy, welcoming smile as he pulled off his coat. The fire flickered in the bedchamber grate, warming the room. She looked happy—he was going mad with frustration and self-recrimination.

She walked up to him, slim and lovely in her gown of pale ivory silk. Her fingers curled around the lapels of his waistcoat, and she reached up on tiptoe. He stayed motionless, letting her lips touch his throat.

"I want you," he growled, flicking open the fastenings down her back. "I need you now." He worked at the laces of her stays. Then he couldn't resist, and he kissed the exposed skin in the crook of her neck. Warm and sweet and sinfully beautiful.

He wanted her for a lifetime, damn it.

But she loved her son—

Now he saw. She loved the child she had borne to the man she'd loved, intended to marry, and lost. She must love him still. He had been a good, honorable, decent young man. But for war, she would be a happy wife now.

Cary was a man who appeared to be honorable and decent but who hid dark anger behind a shield. He'd been afraid to let it out.

She deserved a good man, who could find happiness with her.

Sophie let her loosened stays fall to the rug. She pulled her shift off and stood before him completely naked. He had a glimpse of her full, heart-shaped bottom before she turned. Her nipples, rosy with desire and peaked, pointed at him.

She stepped forward and ran her hand over the front of his trousers. "I want you. I want every minute I can have you."

She kissed his waistcoat while her hand fondled him, stroked him to rigid attention. Her lips trailed down, and she sank to her knees in front of him.

"Sophie—"

"I like doing this." She gave him a bright smile. Not a saucy one or a bold one but one that should be shared by two delighted people pleasuring each other. Then she undid his falls and pulled down his linens, and he was lost.

Her lips parted, and he couldn't resist arching his hips slightly forward and offering his cock to her. As her plump lower lip cradled the head, he felt like lightning shot through him.

He was so aroused, he climaxed after a few sucks of her lush lips. She swallowed, amazing him.

Then he carried her to bed. He was so aroused for lovely Sophie, he got hard again quickly. They made love side by side in bed so he could tease her nipples.

They came together—at the exact same instant.

But after, he realized something. "Your son is in the country, and you are staying in London for me. I'm keeping you apart from him."

"I can see him sometimes—if it is all right if I travel frequently."

"Of course it is all right, Sophie. I feel damned guilty about keeping you from him. Especially during these precious times when he is so young."

Her lip wobbled. She covered it up quickly with a smile, but he had seen it. He knew her happy disposition hid pain.

"I would support you to live in the country with your son," he said softly. "I have other jewels on order for you. They are yours to sell. Your allowance would continue for a year. You don't need another protector—you don't need to stay in London. Let me do at least that for you."

His mother found him in his study.

"Caradon, I know you are in love with Sophie. Is that why you have not proposed to a prospective bride?"

Cary looked at his mother and said, "I proposed marriage to Sophie, but she refused me."

"There would be a scandal if you married her."

"I know, and I'm sorry I was prepared to plunge our family into scandal, but I love her so much."

His mother sighed. She had told him she had exaggerated her ill health, but he could see how thin and tired she was. "I do want to see you marry."

"I will marry soon. I accept that I have to."

"I am not trying to manipulate you, Caradon. I wish you could find love in your marriage. I suspect you will have no trouble finding a woman who loves you. Please choose a wife, my dear boy. I need to know you are happy, finally. . . ."

"I am happy. All the sorrow and pain in my past has been put to rest."

"Thanks to Sophie Ashley," his mother said softly.

"Yes." Damn, he knew he had to do this. He had to for his mother, who had suffered so much. "What if I were to marry the earl's daughter? What's her name—Lady Penelope Bryant?"

His mother walked to the window and looked out over the

gardens. "She would be an excellent choice. Breeding, beauty, wit—and a fortune. An eagerness for children. But do not just choose a name off the list. Meet these young women. You will find one who you like. I know you won't be madly in love, but you can grow to love someone."

Cary's heart felt like stone, but he had to do this. His next logical step would be to choose one of the girls from his mother's list and propose again.

He was fairly sure that this time his intended would say yes. Whether he wanted her to or not.

Then his mother said, "You deserve to have love, Cary. You deserve that more than anything. Scandals fade. I would rather you find joy than do your duty. I will accept your choice. If you marry Sophie, I will do everything I can to help her enter Society."

He stared at his mother, astounded. Before he could say a word, someone cleared his throat and said, respectfully, "Your Grace?"

Cary looked up. His majordomo stood in the doorway of his study. "Yes, Penders?"

"There is a young lady to see you, Your Grace. She is waiting in the red drawing room." The aged man paused. "It is not my place to say, Your Grace, but this is an unusual hour for a caller. But then, there have been young ladies about this place doing the most unusual things."

"It isn't your place to say, Penders. However, I assume it is a matter of importance for that reason." But Cary didn't care. It had to be Sophie. "I have to go to her," he said to his mother.

Penders cleared his throat. "The young lady fought to disguise her emotion, but I believe she is extremely upset and frightened, Your Grace," Penders said.

Cary jumped to his feet. His blood went ice-cold. "Upset?"

"She was laboring to appear composed. But she had obviously been crying. And her hands were clenched."

"Why didn't you tell me immediately?" Cary fumed.

"I apologize, Your Grace."

His majordomo stepped back, allowing him to stride by. Leaving Penders and his mother behind in his study, Cary ran down the corridor. But when he reached the drawing room, he stopped in surprise.

21

The woman in the drawing room was not Sophie. The slender figure in the black cloak who faced him with huge, frightened eyes was Belle, Sophie's friend. He had met her at the manor house in the country. Belle was a lovely young woman with brown curls and large brown eyes.

"Belle, what is wrong?" he asked as he strode into the room.

Had something happened to Sophie? Cary felt as he had in the jungle in Ceylon on the many times he and his men had been ambushed.

"Sophie is in danger! He took her child, and she went running off to him. I told her to come to you or to go to the magistrates. What he is doing is a crime! And I fear he won't simply let Alex go because she's gone to him. He wants to hurt Sophie. I know the kind of man he is."

"Who is, Belle? Who are you talking about?"

"Lord Devars. He wanted Sophie to become his mistress after her fiancé died, especially when she had the baby and was ruined. He offered to keep her. But she refused him. She wanted to find love, you see. And he took it badly. He tried to force himself on her, and she hit him. She didn't kill him, but she—" Belle broke off and put her hand to her mouth.

"What did she do, Belle?"

"I mean, she was forced to flee to London as quickly as she could. She was worried about us, but I never dreamed he would really hurt us. But now he has taken Sophie's son to force her to do whatever he wants."

"And she has gone to him." Damn—why hadn't she come to him? "Where did she go? Do you know, Belle?"

She nodded and held out a folded paper. "He sent her this— his demand that she come to him. In it, he says he would have Alex returned to me if she went. But he never did. He lied."

Cary read the note, and his blood went cold.

Belle said weakly, "He demands that she not tell anyone. I was afraid to come to you because of that, but I knew I must."

"You did the right thing."

"Will you help Sophie? She said she feared you didn't love her anymore—because she had to say no to you."

"I'd help her no matter what," he said gruffly.

He'd been through battles in Ceylon, and he had never felt so sick with fear in his life. He felt even more afraid than he had when he confronted Angelique. He had been terrified she had hurt Sophie. But this time, both Sophie and her son were in danger. Devars was known to be a brute. Arrogant, sadistic, ruthless. He had been barred from some of London's brothels, for God's sake, which proved what a vicious monster he could be. And he had Sophie and her child. If anything happened to Sophie, Cary couldn't bear it. If anything happened to Sophie's son—he knew they both wouldn't be able to live with it.

He knew the truth—he did still love her. He always would.

"You promised me he would go free if I came to you. You swore in your note that you would send him back to Belle!"

Sophie struggled in vain. Her hands were bound together again, but this time they were positioned behind her back. The long end of the rope had been tied around a tree. A second rope was around Alexander's waist. Tears streamed down his cheeks.

Her baby. Her poor, innocent child. She couldn't go to him or comfort him. Or protect him. How could she be so helpless, so useless? She despised herself. She hated Devars. Hatred was like a serpent writhing inside her. "What are you going to do to him?" she cried.

Devars glared at her—though his top hat shadowed his face and she could not see his eyes. She could see his mouth, drawn in a hard, cruel slash of a smile. His greatcoat swirled around him like large wings on a menacing, monstrous dragon. He came close to her, bending, and she instinctively drew back. "I am ensuring that you cooperate. That you do as I say, you stupid bitch."

She flinched. Devars spoke in a voice of ice. Utterly calm. Her son sobbed. Then Devars lifted her son's tiny body and held him over the gaping hole of an old well.

"Dear God, what are you doing?" She gasped.

"I am going to lower him in there, Sophie. He will be perfectly safe—as long as we return to take him out."

"Mummy, no!"

The back of Devars's hand cracked across Alex's small face. His head whipped to the side.

Sophie screamed, "No, stop! Please, stop!"

Devars did, his hand poised for a second blow. His huge body moved with heavy breaths.

"Alex," she said, her voice breaking. "You must do as he says. We will come back for you. It won't be long. Close your eyes and sing a little song. Don't be afraid."

Would they be back soon?

She knew what Devars wanted. To have sex with her while her son was in danger. This was his ultimate punishment for her defiance. He was sick. Unfathomably evil.

Holding the rope with one hand, with it wrapped around his forearm, Devars let go of her son. Alex fell—

Only a few inches before Devars caught the rope with his other hand. Carefully, he fed Alex down into the dark hole.

Sophie was going to be sick. She had to fight for strength.

"Please don't do this," she begged. "It's so cold tonight. He will be frozen and hungry. And he will be terrified down there. Please, do not do this. Please, bring him up. If you do, I will give you anything you want. I will do anything you want."

"You will be more obedient when you fear for his life, my dear. And I like the idea of fucking you while you are terrified."

He drew out a blade from his boot. Hulking and huge, he advanced on her. She wanted to scream.

But Alex would hear, and that would frighten him. "Wh-what are you going to do?"

Devars was like Angelique—too mad to see reason. He believed he had the right to hurt her as punishment. She had tried to thwart him, and she'd lost.

He slapped her. Hard. Then slammed her back against the tree.

Her hands were crushed against the bark.

Tied up, she was utterly helpless. She had to think—

"Won't you untie my hands? Then I can touch you, pleasure you."

"You mean, try to escape from me. I know you're thinking it, bitch. I'm going to take you to a house I've rented. If you pleasure me enough, then we will return for your son. But you will have to work very hard to save his life."

"I'll replace the bracelet." Her throat was so tight, her voice was a croak.

"That trifle? I don't care about it. This had nothing to do with your stealing, whore. You thought you could beat me. I always win. Always."

"No. You don't."

She heard the low, deep, commanding voice and almost collapsed in joy. How was it possible? How could Cary be here? Then she realized he'd heard what she said about the bracelet.

Devars whipped around, partially blocking her view, but she could see enough.

Cary stood there, holding a pistol on Devars. "You know," Cary said coolly, "I am growing tired of people trying to hurt Sophie."

Devars brandished the blade. "I'll kill her unless you put the pistol down, Caradon."

Sophie knew he was standing close enough to plunge the blade into her or slit her throat. She had to do something.

He might try to kill her, but she had to do something useful. Her hands were tied, but Devars's attention was fixed on Cary and he was grinning, certain he had the upper hand—

Hard as she could, Sophie kicked upward, slamming her boot right into his crotch.

He howled and staggered, but he wasn't completely crippled with pain—

Cary fired the pistol at Devars's leg.

The man screamed and squealed, but she realized he was not hit at the exactly instant he did. But by then, Cary had a long blade pulled from his walking stick, and he held the point of it against Devars's throat.

"Step away from her," he snarled.

Devars was white with fear. Or with pain. But he blustered, "You won't kill me in cold blood. You are a war hero."

"Then we'll duel. It is one way or the other. We will duel right here and now. Or I'll let you go—but with a wound to remind you of this night. To remind you to keep away from Sophie, my duchess, for the rest of your sorry life. If you don't shut up and get out of here, I may cut something vital and leave you with a maimed leg."

"Your duchess? This ta—"

"Say it, and the blade goes through your throat. You threatened Sophie, you terrified an innocent child. The world would be a better place without a sick, revolting bully like you."

"No. No, I will go. You're welcome to the—"

"Again, I suggest you hold your tongue, or I'll cut it out while you lie dying."

She'd never seen this side of Cary. The ruthless, tough soldier. He hadn't even been like this with Angelique. She was almost afraid of him.

Devars certainly was.

Cary took one step back, his blade poised. "I am going to the magistrate with a full accounting of what you have done to Sophie. I would suggest you flee London immediately. Go and hide on the Continent. If you return, I will call you out and kill you. I swear to God, I will. Now get the hell out of here."

At that, hulking Devars scrambled away, panting. He sounded a bit like a yipping dog.

Cary used the razor-sharp blade to slice the rope from the tree, then cut through her bonds. "Quickly, my dear. We must get to your boy."

She hurried with him. She couldn't believe it was over. Within minutes, Cary had lifted Alex to safety and placed her son in her arms.

She had to put her face into Alex's sweet neck and sob.

"Mummy, what's wrong? Are you hurt?"

"No. I am happy. You are safe now. You will always be safe."

"He isn't going to get away with this. I've taken steps. He owes money at the gaming hells. On top of that, we will give our testimonies to the magistrate. Lord Devars is about to be destroyed. He will definitely have no choice but to leave England. He will never bother you again."

"Thank you. Oh my goodness, thank you."

"Sophie, do you still care for me?"

"I love you."

"Then marry me. I believe there is a way to make it possible, Sophie. For now, you and your son should both return to London with me."

Before she could explain or protest, he took Alex from her arms and carried the boy back to the curricle. "Mummy! Mummy!" the boy cried desperately.

"It is all right. Your mummy is with us. See?"

Sophie had to hasten to get to his side. She clasped the boy's hand, and they both took Alex to the curricle.

Cary handed her up, then settled the child onto her lap.

He was happy he had been able to save this child. The poor lad clung to his mother now. Cary wrapped a fur throw around Sophie and the child. Young Alex closed his eyes, his long dark lashes lying against his round cheeks.

He was a sweet, handsome child.

Then Cary got up and slowly walked his horses around so they could follow the track back to the main road. He told her how Belle had come to him. The note had brought him to this area, then he had found witnesses who saw Devars's carriage and managed to track it.

"Thank heaven, you did. Now, how can I thank you?"

By marrying me, he thought.

Then she said, "But where is Belle? Is she in London? I must let her know I am safe."

"I had my coachman return her to the cottage so she could be with her children."

"That was very good of you. But I must go to her. I think she would be frightened to be on her own tonight."

That was Sophie—she had been through hell, yet she worried about taking care of others.

Cary inclined his head. "You're correct. I will see you safely home, for your friend will want company. I will send word to tell her you are safe now, but I suspect she will want to see for herself. And then we can tell her that we are to be married. I need practice announcing this."

She flashed a panicked look at her son. The boy had fallen asleep. "I can't marry you, Cary. I—I love you deeply. I love you so very much. It is so wonderful of you to ask me, but—"

"I won't ask you to abandon Alex. He is a sweet, clever child. I love you with all my heart, Sophie, and I will ensure he is well-looked after. I intend to settle an income on him, from money not entailed to my estate. And I believe he can live with us as your son. There is no reason we cannot say you were married to your fiancé before he went to war."

"But it isn't true. As your duchess, I would be under much greater scrutiny. If someone finds out it is a lie—" She broke off. "No, I will tell you the real reason I cannot marry you. It is about Lord Devars."

"Belle told me what he wanted from you, and that you had to escape him."

"I brained him over the head with a vase, then I ran for my life. But he had given me a diamond bracelet, to try to convince me to become his mistress. I didn't want it. I should have thrown it on his unconscious body. But I was so afraid that Belle and the children would starve that I took it. I stole it—"

"He gave it to you. I do not consider that stealing."

"But—but he gave it to me so I would be his mistress."

"He presented it as a gift in the hopes it would convince you. A gift should have no obligation attached."

She managed a smile. "But it did."

"And he said he didn't care about the bracelet. However, to make things right, I will replace it and send it to him. This time he can sell it to support himself when he flees England."

"But you know I was a thief—"

"I know you were forced into a hellish situation. I admire you for helping Belle and the children. Sophie, it doesn't change the fact that I love you. And I am going to find a way to make it possible for us to marry. I promise."

Then he kissed her. A sweet, swift kiss because she was holding her son. "I wish it could be so," she whispered. "I wish it so much."

Two weeks later, Sophie was walking outside with the children when she saw Cary riding up the road on his enormous horse.

She swallowed hard. There was something of great import she must tell him.

Then she saw his glowing smile as he rode up to the cottage. He was grinning at her, and he jumped off his horse and ran to her.

The Duke of Caradon was swinging her around out in the yard in front of the cottage. He cupped her face, and his mouth closed over hers.

She pulled back. Blushed. "Not in front of the children," she whispered.

He clasped her hand and walked her to a small bench between an apple tree in front of the cottage. "You did not tell me your fiancé had acquired a license. It was his intent to marry you—and you exchanged vows."

"I know, but we did it without permission. The rector indulged us, with no idea that we would consummate our pretend wedding. He was very old, and Samuel convinced him to let us do this. Since Samuel was an earl's son, he tended to get his way. But I was too young—I was not quite sixteen, and I needed my adoptive parents' permission to marry."

"And if it could be claimed that you had their permission, you would be legally wed. That way, your son is legitimate and you are a war widow, my dear."

"But I was going to be a courtesan."

"And you have been my private mistress. There have been

other men who have married their mistresses, my dear. As I've said, Grey is one. And the world has not imploded."

"When did you see the rector?" she asked, filled with curiosity.

"These last two weeks I went to see the rector. And I went to visit your adoptive family and your fiancé's family."

She gaped in shock. "You went to see them? And during this time you were supposed to be finding a wife."

"Deep in my heart, I knew I'd already found her. I have convinced your adoptive parents and the family of your fiancé to support the story that you both had permission and were legally married. The rector, who is eighty, has prepared the registry appropriately. No one will doubt you were legitimately a widow, and your son is the child of a hero who died in battle. With your position as a duchess—and wealth and power, not to mention your strength and good character—you will be a success. No one will dare cut you, I assure you."

"But how did you convince our families to agree to this?"

"Your adoptive family can bask in the prestige. I can't forgive them for turning you out, but if it buys us a future, I am willing to help them advance socially. Because that will put them on our side, and they will support the story that you were married. I have made the same promises to your fiancé's family. They lost a son and are starry-eyed at the idea of preference from a duke."

"All this—for me?"

"For you and your son. And some of my motivation is selfish. I want you, Sophie. I want to spend my life with you. And that is worth any cost. If you will have me."

"If I'll have you? Of course. I love you. I've loved you all along. I just—feared I would have my heart broken again, so I was being careful. But I love you so deeply! And there is something I must tell you, Cary. It is possible that you are going to be a father."

He stared at her, stunned. Then let out a joyous whoop. He hugged her, lifting her right off her feet. Then quickly set her down. "I'm sorry. I shouldn't do that to you in your condition. Thank God, we can marry hastily then."

She gazed at him hesitantly. "It's very early. I've only just missed my courses. It might be—well, just a false alarm."

"Either way, I have you. And together we have Alex," he said. "And someday, more children, if we're fortunate. I couldn't be more blessed."

Bells rang out from St. George's church. The sun shone down upon the guests arriving by carriage. Theirs was an intimate wedding—just family and friends. Sophie arrived with Belle and the children. She had decided to invite her adoptive family, but she also invited Nell. She saw Nell as soon as she alighted from the carriage. Sophie held on to her veil with one hand and clutched her bouquet with the other. Nell hugged her.

Dressed in a beautiful, subdued satin gown and pelisse, with a feather-trimmed hat, Nell glowed with delight and looked remarkably elegant.

Of course, Cary's friends, the Wicked Dukes, were in attendance, along with Helena and her and Grey's brand-new baby boy.

Outside the church, the Duke of Sinclair bowed over her hand. "You look truly like an angel, Miss Ashley."

"Thank you." Her wedding dress was a gown of pale ivory silk. Beneath, her tummy was still flat as she was just over a month into her pregnancy. On the bodice and skirt, roses and leaves were embroidered with silver thread and dotted here and there with pearls. Her veil tumbled down her back, a river of handmade lace held in place by a band decorated by pearls and tiny diamonds. She felt like a fairy princess—that was what Alex had called her.

"I have to thank you, Miss Ashley, for making Cary so

happy," Sinclair said. "He's changed so much thanks to you. You helped him clear his name and solve the mystery. And you helped him heal finally from the trauma of the kidnapping, which none of the Wicked Dukes knew about. Grey, Sax, and I are forever in your debt for what you have done to help Cary."

"Sophie. Please call me Sophie."

"You must call me Sin." He winked. "No one uses my first name, least of all me."

She saw him glance at Cary, and she said, "You all truly have been very worried about him, haven't you?"

"Yes. Again, you have our eternal gratitude."

"Thank you, but I also did it for me." She felt her cheeks go red. "I love him so much, I couldn't bear him to be unhappy."

"He is right. You are so ingenuous, you are irresistible."

She was startled.

"I don't mean in that way. I mean—you have my heart, but in a platonic way." A grin revealed the Duke of Sinclair's dimples.

Nell bustled over then. "Two of the Wicked Dukes are wed. You two are going to be chased by girls who are pursuing you with a vengeance."

The Duke of Sinclair looked around nervously, and she and Nell laughed. Nell pointed at two young ladies who were whispering behind their hands and who began giggling. "They will pounce soon enough."

"And miss," the duke said. "I'm quick enough to evade matrimony."

"But why would you want to?" Sophie asked. She couldn't imagine anything more wonderful than being in love and being married.

"Ah, but not everyone is as lucky as Cary, to find you." With that, Sin left to join Grey and Saxonby.

"Nell, I do have something to give you." Sophie had carried it with her, wrapped in white paper, tied with a white bow. "It is your book, Nell, that you wrote about your life. You left it for me, but I never saw it until I found it by accident. My adoptive mother hid it away."

"Did she?" Nell sighed. "I told her not to read it. That was one of the stipulations for the money I gave to her. That the book was for you, when you were older. I wanted you to know I had been desired by the most famous and handsome peers in England. Of course, I suppose I put in a bit too much naughty information for a young woman to read."

Sophie colored but said, "Perhaps. But it is a very compelling story. It's really a tale of love."

"Many loves," Nell said, lifting a wry brow. "And you read it while you were pursuing the duke, didn't you? Perhaps I should finish it and fill it with more advice. Perhaps I should include some of your delicious story and title it: *How to Catch a Wicked Duke*."

"Nell, you mustn't."

"I won't." She smiled. "I won't cause scandal for you. I won't tell anyone I am your mother either. It would be much better if Society thinks your parents are the doctor and his wife."

Sophie bit her lip. "I would rather be honest."

"We had both best be wise. We know the truth. It hardly matters if others know our business." Nell held the book, stroking the ribbon gently. "I hid this away with you because I was afraid one of my gentlemen might find it and destroy it. I was rather dramatic then. But if it has helped you find true love, then it was a worthwhile labor."

"It did," Sophie said, and hugged Nell.

As Nell left, Cary's mother came to her. In front of the waiting guests, the duchess—who would soon be the dowager duchess—embraced her. "Welcome to our family, my dear."

"Thank you," Sophie whispered, "I know this was a shock for you."

"My son is happy. I have learned, over the years, that I want him to be happy and to have love. I almost lost him twice—when he was young and was taken from me, and then in Ceylon when he was at war. I was the one who pushed him to be married. I finally realized he deserves love more than anything. He loves you deeply, Sophie. And there is no one more deserving for my good and wonderful son than *you*. For you are a good and wonderful young woman."

"Thank you." Sophie brushed away tears.

The dowager handed her a delicate lace-trimmed handkerchief. Cary's sisters ran up. They both hugged her too. Claudia, the eldest, who was now twenty, whispered, "Thank you for making my brother so happy. And Mama is so happy too. I have decided I am going to marry too. We were so often in the country. Mama was so protective of Lydia and me—"

"She never let us do anything," Lydia agreed in a whisper.

Both girls looked like Cary with their blue eyes and blond hair.

Sophie understood. "She just wanted to keep you safe. You will both have more freedom now. Cary and I intend to ensure you attend every Society event you can."

"We should go inside, dears," Cary's mother said to her daughters.

Then, as Sophie watched most of the guests enter the church, Dr. and Mrs. Tucker came to her. Her adoptive mother wore a fussy gown festooned with lace and ribbons, and an elaborate turban with a large feather. "Oh, my dear, you look so lovely," she gushed. "My adoptive daughter, a duchess! What a feather in all our caps."

The doctor rolled his eyes. "Sophie, I am so sorry for what we did. It was wrong to turn you out. Wrong and unforgiveable."

"But it's all worked out for the best," said his wife. Then after meeting Sophie's gaze, she changed her tune and gave several effusive apologies.

All her life, Sophie had been kindhearted. But she faced the woman who had sent her away, knowing she must be blunt, honest, and harsh, for this was important. "I know you feel I committed a sin. Perhaps I did. But I gave birth to Alex, and every time I look at my son, I see Samuel in him. Samuel has left a lasting legacy to the world through his son. I cannot feel that is wrong. If you wish never to see me again, I am content with that. I don't care what you did to me—but you turned your back on an innocent baby, and that I cannot forgive."

"Please, Sophie. My dear child—"

"I never was your dear child." Then, she could not help it. "Perhaps I can forgive you. If you are very, very good and respectful to Alex. You must treat him no differently than any other children I hope to have with the duke. At first, Caradon wanted to punish you for your treatment of me. I convinced him to not do so. He has now asked for your help."

Mrs. Tucker said, "I just feared you could end up bad, like your mother—"

"That is the problem. My mother wasn't bad. She had to survive too. And she tried to give me a respectable future. But I *will* try to forgive," Sophie said. "The duke has said you have promised not to reveal the truth. If there were scandal, or Alex were hurt in any way, I know the duke would be very angry."

"Our lips are sealed," the doctor said. "All I feel is tremendous guilt for what you have been through. We were foolish and proud. And so very wrong. We shall do our best to make amends, and we will begin by vowing to never speak of anything hurtful to you or your child."

"Thank you." She touched her adoptive father's hand. "Now you may take me down the aisle to my soon-to-be husband."

To my wonderful, perfect Wicked Duke, she thought as she entered the church with her father. She gazed around her. She was used to country churches. St. George's was enormous. So many elegantly dressed people sat on the pews—they could not all be friends and family. Flowers decorated the end of each pew and sat upon the altar.

She gazed down to Cary, who was standing in front of the reverend and waiting for her.

It was all she could do not to run to him. But here, she had to be sedate and ladylike.

It felt like an eternity. She knew people were watching her, but she only had eyes for Cary.

She reached him, dimly aware of her adoptive father agreeing to give her away—or something like that.

The reverend cleared his throat. He read rather a lot of poetic-sounding things, but Sophie was too nervous and excited to hear. Then he got to the best part.

"Do you, Sophia Elizabeth Ashley, take this man, Fitzwilliam Augustus Flavius Montcleif, to be your husband?"

She was deliriously happy, but her eyes widened at his names. A faint blush touched his cheeks, and she couldn't help it. She giggled. It was just her joy trying to burst out. The reverend looked rather shocked. She choked down her giggle and said, "I do."

Then it was Cary's turn. Under his breath, just for her, he whispered, "God, how I do. How very much I do take you, Sophie." Then out loud, he said, "I do," and her heart took flight.

And continued to soar as Cary bent to her and she lifted on tiptoe to him and their lips touched. Sophie felt a shower of sparks rush through her.

Their first kiss as husband and wife—

His lips parted hers, and his tongue slipped gently inside her mouth, teasing hers.

Goodness, he was doing this to her in church.

Cary was, at heart, a Wicked Duke. She knew that now.

Slowly, he broke the kiss. The reverend was blushing as he led them to sign the book while the guests filed outside.

Sophie watched Cary quickly move the pen, signing his name with a flourish. "I cannot believe your given names are Fitzwilliam Augustus Flavius."

"My father loved Roman history, and I bore the brunt." He handed her the pen, and she wrote her name.

He clasped her hand, and they walked back up the aisle together toward the doors of the church. Sophie hesitated at the closed door. Soon, they would walk out in front of all their guests.

"Our wedding is the talk of London. Everyone must be gossiping about us—and I am not sure if I can go through with this."

"We can weather the gossip together," he assured her. "I invited several important and open-minded members of the aristocracy. Their presence here assures your acceptance."

"That's why there were so many guests—"

Cary's mouth closed over hers again. He gave her a slow, luscious kiss. In the church, again. She pulled back, face aflame. "You must stop," she squeaked. "We're in church."

"But we're married now. Nothing is forbidden."

"Nothing? Heavens, what do you have in mind? Remember, we are supposed to be going to the wedding breakfast. There is a reason it is called a wedding night."

"I can't wait that long," he admitted. "Race you to the carriage."

Then the doors opened and cheers rose up. Rice showered over them. Laughing, Cary ran with her to the carriage and quickly handed her up. She leaned out the window to wave, then turned to discover Cary was unfastening his trousers.

She laughed, joyously. "You are eager."

"I'm in love."

Their carriage rumbled on toward their wedding breakfast. But inside, she settled on Cary's lap, taking his beautiful hard cock inside.

His arms went around her, and he kissed the nape of her neck as he drove inside her. Under her skirts he teased her nether lips, found her sensitive clit, and lightly caressed it.

Sophie moaned softly and sucked in frantic breaths.

All the joy and excitement of the day blended with the sheer frantic eroticism of their hurried lovemaking, becoming something explosive.

"Oh! Oh! Oh!" she cried.

She was coming, then he was too. Together, they found their peak. Moaning together. Laughing in unison afterward.

"I always hoped I would find love. But I never dreamed I would find you, Cary. That you would marry me, and we could have a family together. And that Alex would have a wonderful home and a future. It is like a dream come true."

"It is more happiness than I ever let myself dream about," he admitted.

She gasped, realizing he growing hard again. "Can you? Already?"

"I can because I desire you so much. Because I love you so much. You are my dream come true, Sophie." Then he said, "My mother intends to hold a ball. She admitted to me that she lied about being gravely ill to convince me to marry."

"Do you forgive her? She didn't mean harm by it."

"I did forgive her, Sophie."

"That was very good of you—" She broke off and gasped as he wriggled his hips, teasing her with his cock.

"I know all her worry over me had weakened her, but she is genuinely happy about the marriage. And the anticipation of a grandchild is doing wonders for her—"

"You didn't tell her yet, did you?"

"I'm afraid I did. I warned her it was early yet." He thrust deeply into her. "But I did want to tell you about the ball."

"I do like balls," Sophie said.

Cary laughed, knowing he'd never felt happier. "Sophie, that has another meaning, you know."

"Well, I mean both of them when you are involved," Sophie said, looking a bit indignant at his laughter. "I am looking forward to waltzing with you again."

How adorable she was, he thought. "You'll only get one dance with me."

"Only one! Why?"

"After that, I'll want to steal you away and make love to you all night."

"Hmmm, perhaps that would be better than dancing."

He laughed again. Then he held her hips to spear her on his rock-hard, throbbing cock as he thrust into her tight, hot pussy.

He was so deeply in love with her. And had never felt more deeply ensconced in pure joy and delight. Little by little, he and Sophie had fallen deeper in sin.

Only to find heaven at the end of it.

He kissed her just as she climaxed, loving the way she bounced on him and scratched his shoulders and moaned frantically against his mouth.

Happiness was going to be theirs. Forever after.